THE RISE OF VARDYA

THE RISE OF VARDYA
BOOK ONE

E WHELLY

CSG PUBLISHING HOUSE

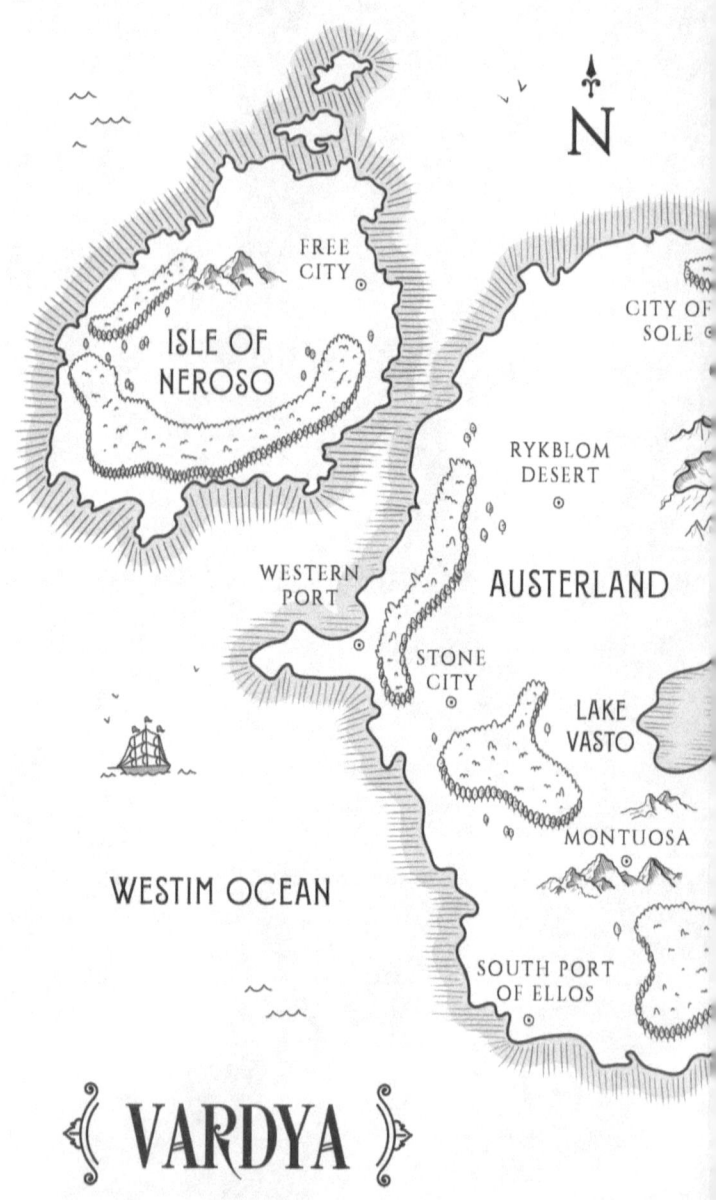

N

FREE
CITY

ISLE OF
NEROSO

CITY OF
SOLE

RYKBLOM
DESERT

WESTERN
PORT

AUSTERLAND

STONE
CITY

LAKE
VASTO

MONTUOSA

WESTIM OCEAN

SOUTH PORT
OF ELLOS

{ VARDYA }

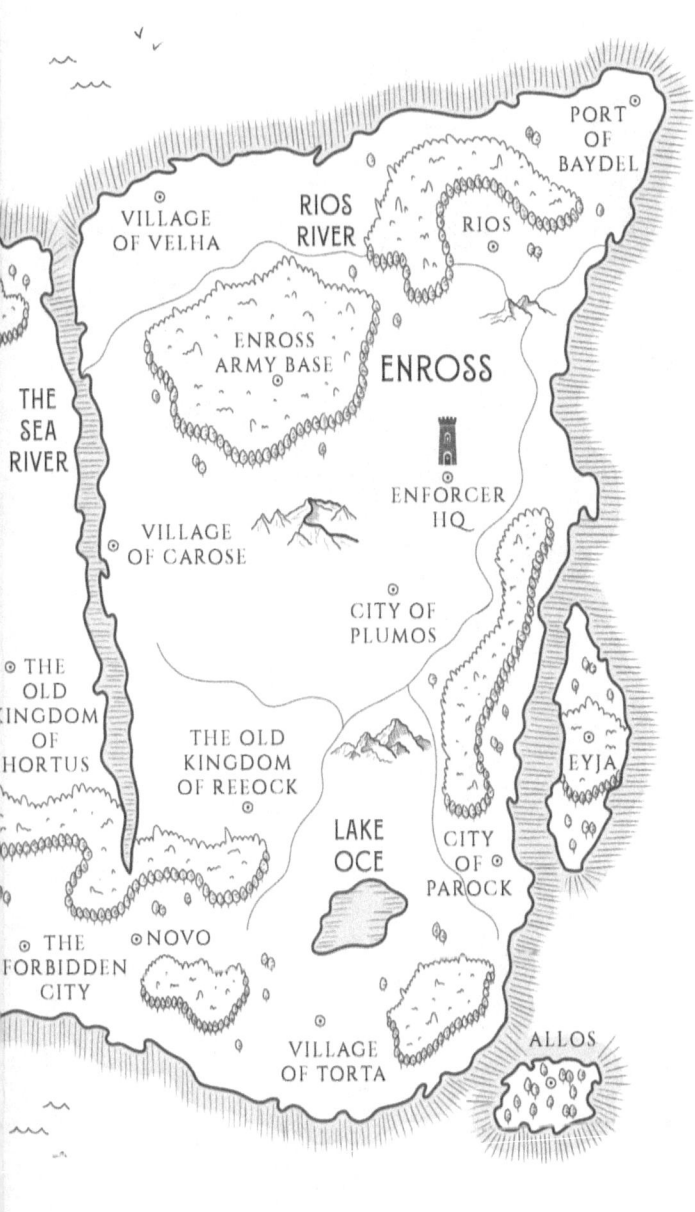

CHAPTER 1

GIDEON

Gideon stood outside his castle of crystal, glistening high upon Mount Ursid, watching the sun set over the harbor where great black ships rocked against the ebb and flow of the ocean. His ships. His power. All used for the advancement of his people who had never known hunger or poverty thanks to his family. Pride filled him as he leaned against the glass railing. His line spanned the history of Neroso as far back as records were kept. All men of great accomplishment and strength. That is, until his father. The name Ulrich Ursid was held in shame. A shame that weighed over him despite all his efforts and triumphs.

Gideon stuffed his clenched hands in his pants pockets as he turned his attention from his ships in the harbor to his beautiful city. The Free City. Great towers of glass and steel covered as far as the eye could see. While his city expanded, the forests receded with the ever-growing population of his people. All that remained of the natural wilderness was the sanctuary reserved for preservation of his family's sigil. The Sun Bears; great beasts with thick yellow coats of fur, bright as the sun. A glow radiated from their pelts signifying they were no common creature. Only that of greatness, like the line of the Ursid family.

Despite being an avid scholar and admirer of his family's history, he couldn't help but be mortified by the long-banished role of the Sun Bears—when his ancestors would train them for battle. He shuddered at the thought; not his precious house sigil and certainly not his Rovoss, the bear he'd raised from a cub. Out of respect for the bears and his house, he did honor those heroic beasts by keeping a display of their armor for his own personal viewing, but never would he send the magnificent beasts into battle.

A fire rumbled deep within him, recalling his shame, or rather what should've been his *father's* shame. On his father's watch, their people thrived more than ever, but at the cost of the Sun Bear population. Gideon wouldn't have it, not on his watch. Had he not intervened and plotted his father's demise, he feared the Sun Bears would've been long lost. He put forth new laws. Anyone caught harming a Sun Bear would be sentenced to death without question. Not that anyone ever dared, the Sun Bears were far too vicious for anyone but an Ursid to be near.

To help control their numbers, he placed restrictions to control the population of the Nerosians. Anyone looking to parent a child must gain permission and a license. He'd made it harder and harder for low level families to have children. Only those within his circle were allowed.

He hadn't even fathered his own children. He couldn't pick an ordinary woman to have a child with to continue his line. She had to be of great respect to his people as well as loyal to the Ursid family, but he couldn't simply trust just anyone, nor could anyone live up to such standards. He needed three children yet all he had was his dead sister's common born son for an heir. He couldn't leave the responsibility of a lord to his ungrateful nephew. Three children would make the perfect number. The eldest would of course rule over Neroso, but the other two... Well, he had plans for them as well. Not as spares, but for their own rule.

Gideon needed more space. More land for his people so not only they would prosper, but the sigil of his family. Across the Westim Ocean, he knew there was more land, ripe for the taking. His father had started to venture to the new land with their ships expecting to find a new world with a plethora of resources, but instead, they found the Vardyians. Vile mongrels.

A continent of two warring countries, Austerland and Enross, fools who destroyed their own pitiful excuses for economies and left their lands in ruin all because they could not stand the other. He couldn't imagine living in an uncivilized nation surrounded by poverty and disease. There was only one thing left for him to do. Put the scum out of their misery and conquer their lands under the Ursid rule and expand the Isle of Neroso's reach so his people could thrive. Most of all, the Sun Bears would be able to prosper and live alongside his family line. The Isle of Neroso would then be home to the Sun Bears, his family, and those he deemed worthy.

He would see to it that his two youngest heirs would each rule over Austerland and Enross. Three countries all under one family's rule. He would go down in history as a conqueror of this world.

"Uncle!" Dominic called from behind him. The teenage boy stomped his feet out of the glass sliding door from the manor.

Gideon sighed; his nephew gave him grief.

"Have you finished your training for today? If you are to be an officer of the Enforcers, you're going to have to work far harder than the reports I've been getting."

"This has to stop, Uncle!" Dominic stood nearly as tall as

he did, but his size did not scare Gideon. His nephew's eyebrows furrowed, and he held his fists clenched at his side, looking too much like his commoner father. It had been all too easy to be rid of the useless man after his wife, Gideon's sister, Rhea, threw herself out of her window in madness.

"If you are going to address me in such a manner, I suggest you make your intentions clear." Gideon sighed and rubbed his tempers. He didn't want to play this game with his nephew; he had too much work to think about. Dominic had such promise as a young boy, but he'd just disappointed Gideon since. It was times like this he was glad his sister was dead.

"You're sending Enforcers to Vardya!"

"Of course, I am." He couldn't have said it any plainer or simpler than that. "You know the pressures we are under. If I don't do something now, our people will have nowhere to go. I will not give a single inch of the Sun Bear habitat. I'd see people in the streets before our house sigil is damaged any further."

"But that's just it. You'd destroy the pride and reputation of our family if you send Enforcers to Vardya. I know what you plan to do when they get there. You are going to commit genocide on the whole continent!"

"You worry yourself with things that are not of your concern." Gideon stepped forward, reaching his hand out to Dominic, but he shrugged him off.

"The people here will no longer love or respect you if they knew what you were about to do," Dominic spat with his eyes narrowed. He reached behind his back, revealing a knife, and lunged forward, but Gideon was far quicker. He grasped Dominic's hand that wielded the knife and threw him to the ground. He pushed a knee into his nephew's chest, pinning him, and snatched the knife away.

"Love? You think I give a damn about the love of the

people, you stupid boy? Now you've made me angry. Now you are going to see what happens when someone comes between me and my rule." Gideon leaned over with the gold handled knife in his hand, hovering over Dominic's head, and pointed the knife down, pressing the tip of the blade into his forehead. Dominic cried out as Gideon dragged the blade across the left side of his face, narrowly missing his eye. He would let him keep his eye, if only to give him the opportunity to see the Vardyians fall.

A long river of crimson ran from his forehead to his chin. Gideon stared at the blade in his hand and listened to the screams of his nephew. He would make an example of him to teach him a lesson. Gideon turned the knife on himself, cutting into his own face to mirror the gash on Dominic's face. If his nephew wanted to choose the Vardyians over his family and the Sun Bears, he would let him, but not without leaving a scar. A scar that would remind them both of the betrayal. Every time Dominic saw his own face, he would see Gideon, and remember.

He didn't scream. No, he wouldn't let the pain break him. It fueled him to keep going.

"You don't know what it takes to rule a country. You are weak. You've disappointed me. Run if you want. Run from your blood and your country. But know this: no matter where you go, no matter who you meet, you will never erase the scar from your face. When you look into a mirror, you will see it and think of me and the betrayal of your blood, your people, and the Sun Bears. You don't deserve to have one. See if you can find *love* with that face."

Gideon stood and threw the knife to the ground. The blade dug into the dirt so deep only an inch of the blade remained visible. Gideon dusted himself off as Dominic rolled to his side panting, clutching his bleeding face. The sun had faded away leaving only twilight lingering over the city.

Gideon straightened his suit and pulled out a dark gray handkerchief from his pocket and dabbed away at the blood streaming down his face. In the corner of his eye, Dominic leapt over the side of the railing and ran across the open field toward the city.

He'd let Dominic go and run away to Vardya. It only strengthened his plot to take over. The people of Neroso would not think favorably about clearing out the Vardyian population, but they would change their minds if they believed his beloved nephew and heir to his reign was captured and killed by the Vardyians. He didn't wait for Dominic to reach the cover of the trees; he headed back into the manor needing a drink.

Inside, he strode through white halls dripping blood behind him. A young maid screamed seeing the red splatters. He didn't care if she was scared. Staff weren't to be seen or heard. He'd let Rowan deal with her.

"Sir?" Rowan, his most senior advisor, dashed to his side. He dropped his slate gray communication pad to the floor and his eyes widened only for the slightest second before he resumed his composure. He didn't check to see if the screen had cracked, he knew if he'd taken his attention off Lord Ursid, there would be trouble.

"Call for the doctor and have him sent to my office." Gideon waved him off. He hated when they made a fuss over him as if he were weak. He was strong, far more powerful than any man or woman on this island. His shoulders carried his people, not his advisors.

Rowan blinked several times. "Yes, sir. Shall I call on the Enforcers as well, sir?"

"No, call the tailor."

"The tailor, sir?"

"Are you deaf?" Gideon slowed to a halt. The blood streamed from the sliced skin down the side of his face, staining the fabric of his suit. It meant little to him. He'd throw the suit out and have his personal tailor craft him a new one. Possibly several.

"No, sir. Right away, sir."

"One last thing," Gideon said. "Have a watch set up around Koa, we can't have my nephew taking off with the bear. It no longer belongs to him." Gideon would not allow Dominic to take the young bear he trained. It would be released back to the sanctuary with the rest of the bear population.

"Yes, sir." Rowan left without another word.

He strode through the hallway until he came upon the black door to his office. He swung the door open wide and headed to his dark espresso bar in the corner. He preferred a neat and tidy space. Everything had a place; he didn't care for trinkets and unsightly decor. If he wanted something beautiful to look at, he could sit at his desk and watch the city below through his glass wall.

At the bar, Gideon hovered his hand over several of the bottles, trying to decide which was his poison tonight. He selected a 15-year-old triple cask scotch. Three sets of footsteps entered his office, but he didn't turn. He kept his focus on the bottle, mulling over the bright amber color and imagining the flavors. He'd tried it before and knew its taste well, but it was all part of his ritual.

"Good evening, sir—"

"Not until I've had a drink."

Gideon took an eyedropper from one of the drawers and filled it with water. He picked a short crystal glass and held it at eye level. With a steady hand, he squeezed the dropper ever so slightly, letting one lone drop of water splash into the bottom of the glass. Satisfied with the amount of water, he poured in the amber liquid. He held the glass in front of his nose and inhaled the smokey scent before taking a sip. The

7

tannins of the alcohol burned across his tongue. He let it sit there for a moment before he swallowed it, letting the warmth run through his chest.

"You may begin." Gideon took one more sip savoring the flavor and sat in his high-backed desk chair wanting the doctor to be quick. He had much to plan with sending his scouts to the foreign land of Vardya and the doctor was just another obstacle in his way. He didn't let any rage take over him, he was above that. He could wait. He was a patient man. Like fine scotch, the more time, the better. He valued the long game, something his nephew neglected.

CHAPTER 2

SATCHA

14 YEARS LATER

S atcha awoke to the ground shaking beneath her. Her bones vibrated to life as she rubbed her tired eyes awake.

Bombs?

For the love of the Hawk, not more bombings!

She had to move, but the bright sky hovered over her, and the sunlight shone in her eyes. She blinked her eyes, banishing away the black spots in her vision. The Enforcers from Neroso would arrive soon. The cruel soldiers from across the Westim Ocean only did one thing when they landed on the shores of Enross and that was to destroy everything in their path. No one knew why, and if anyone did find out, they likely were killed.

It was time for her to move on, again, forever avoiding the path of the Enforcers. There was no escape from the shadow of black smoke creeping in from the Sea River that bordered Carose. The Nerosians left a cloud of destruction wherever they went. The fishing village of Carose seemed safe enough—that should've been her first clue that danger lurked.

She forced herself up off the hard ground as screams erupted from across the village. Her back ached from sleeping against the large oak tree in the middle of the old, worn-down village. Crumbling stone buildings with fractures in their walls lined the dirt roads. She grabbed her old brown leather bag resting at her feet. Fourteen years on the run, constantly moving, had worn the bag thin. A faint smell of leather lingered when it got wet in the rain, bringing Satcha a sense of nostalgia she couldn't place, but she clung to those moments and treasured the idea she created in her head of foraging with her mother and getting caught in the rain. Cracks ran along the edges of its seams. It was a miracle they'd held together this long. She secured the bag across her chest and tried to ignore the ache where the straps dug into her shoulder.

When she'd fallen asleep, the village of Carose had sat quietly with only a whisper of the wind in her ears and the smell of salt tingling in her nose. The streets had been empty, only a few small shops were open for business, and not a citizen in sight. Whether it was a lack of money or a lack of customers, it couldn't be long before the doors would close for good.

A loud boom rang through her ears. The grocery store collapsed in a heap of smoke and rebar. It was the same shop she'd peeked in earlier before the old grocer chased her away from what little vegetables and bitter berries they had. She wouldn't have stolen them from him; she wouldn't steal from someone who also endured the deep hungry ache in their belly. Despite their low value, she still could not afford them. More explosions of black smoke and falling buildings crashed down, landing in a heap of rebar and cement around where the grocery shop once stood.

A faint whistle whispered through the air, a sound all too

familiar and uninviting. She didn't have time to look up. She ran as fast as she could. The bomb crashed down, sending an invisible wave of force from the blast knocking her to the ground. Her nose crunched against the hard ground and every joint in her body ached, but she had to push on. She staggered to her feet and looked back at the wreckage. The tree she'd slept against was gone and in its place was a twenty-foot-wide hole in the ground as deep as it was wide. Not two feet to her left was the head of the statue of the old King of Enross who'd ruled a hundred years earlier. His nose had broken off and a deep crack ran down the middle of his forehead. She was lucky it was him and not her. The rest of the statue's body lay at the foot of the cement pad, The Hawk of Enross still intact on the shoulder of the King's beheaded body. Many people believed hawks were sacred and watched over the people of Enross. She held no such belief.

Satcha sprinted across the park. Overgrown grass and rotted flowers lay dead in once-cared-for garden beds. An hour or two worth of rest wasn't enough to keep her going for too long. Escaping and finding shelter was her goal.

She didn't have the time to stop and look at the damage. They were coming. The Enforcers. Over her shoulder, they marched into the village from their large black ships. Women and children ran from buildings in one direction while men grabbed what weapons they could and headed toward the marching army.

Lot of good that will do them.

Bows and wooden planks for shields were no match against the armor and technology of an Enforcer. Their blasters melted skin straight to the bone with one hit.

There wasn't much left of the village behind her. Just a handful of buildings stood while the rest were blasted to nothing. She imagined them once standing tall and proud, but now they lay scattered among broken concrete and iron. A village surrounded by forest on all walls except the one facing the Sea River to the west. Only one dirt road led out of the city, barely wide enough for a horse and cart to make its way through. There were more roads once, but they had long grown wild after the war of all wars—the Old War that had ended more than a hundred years ago.

A war as old as time itself. Enross and Austerland hated one another. No one remembered why.

Once out of the open, she ran alongside a row of small stone houses and took cover where she could. The smaller the houses, the closer to the edge of the village, closer to the cover of the forest surrounding the village, and closer to escape. Satcha ignored the ache in her feet. Her brown makeshift shoes were far too small and tied together with a quarter inch of rope that cut into the bottoms of her feet.

The crunch of boots marching along the rubble sounded close by. Too close. She threw herself over a small stone wall to avoid being caught. The wind knocked out of her chest and her bones ached against the ground. She leaned back against the wall and listened for anyone following her. Blood gushed from her nose; she touched a finger to the tip of it, but something didn't feel right. The cartilage was out of place and the nerve endings shot fire along her skin back to her brain. She didn't have much time to waste, but she couldn't leave her nose broken like that. She grabbed a stick from the ground next to her and clamped it between her teeth.

She lined her thumbs along the sides of her nose and took three deep breaths before pressing them together, hard. She bit against the stick and tried not to cry out in pain. She wasn't sure which was worse: breaking her nose back in place, the sound of snapping cartilage, or the feeling of her nose bending under the pressure of her thumbs. The bleeding would stop soon enough, but the pain would linger.

She spat out the stick, hearing the marching of boots

drawing near her. She peeked over the stone wall to get a good look at what trouble lay behind her. Two dozen soldiers dressed in slick gray armor, with shiny silver helmets in the shape of a bear's head with black shield visors in its open jaws, searched through the wreckage not fifty feet from her, looking for survivors. Sun reflected from their helmets and uniforms, shining bright light in her eyes, blinding her. She ducked before anyone could catch a glimpse of her.

Survivors.

It was the wrong word for these people. They were victims, new hostages and more slaves for the war factories. If caught, they'd either be deemed fit enough to train as a slave soldier or forced to build weapons. Death was the only other option. No slaves crossed the Westim Ocean to the Isle of Neroso. That was reserved for their *own* kind.

She crawled along the cover of the wall and squeezed herself through a gap between what was left of the front and side walls of a house. Here, the air hung thick with smoke and choking dust. She pulled her black bandana from her neck and tightened it around her nose and mouth.

She didn't know how long she'd been on this Earth; maybe twenty-four years? Did it even matter anymore? She'd never known a home or family, or a name beyond Satcha. She didn't even know how she'd come about her name, but it had been the only name she'd known. If she had a family, she couldn't remember them. The only explanation she had for her lost time was the scar on her scalp. Out of habit, she combed her fingers through her hair and felt the bumpy scar. She didn't know how she got it, which only reinforced her theory.

She thought she could remember a family, but she could only picture a man and woman with the same color hair as her with blank faces. No lips, eyes, nor nose. She'd wandered a long time before she found Agatha. It was Agatha who taught her to survive and defend herself—and how to be a second set of hands to steal supplies—but nothing she taught her could stand against the weaponry of the Nerosians. Not even enough to protect Agatha.

Satcha slipped inside the cracks of a broken house. Enforcers were around the corner on both sides of her, with no escape. She leaned her head back cursing at the smoke in the sky. Above her head sat an open window with enough room for her to squeeze inside, but too high for her to climb. The house had been long abandoned and cleared of any valuables. A table had been knocked over and chairs lay broken around it. She spotted a window on the far side of the small room that faced the forest. Through the dust covered glass, a clearing opened up where the village ended. She pushed the window open and climbed through the concrete open space ready to sprint across thirty feet of open space to reach the tree line. She sank to the ground and crept along the last row of stone houses. An Enforcer stood firing their blaster at people trying to make a run for it. Bodies fell in a pile so close she could see the whites of their eyes and blank stares. If she didn't act quick, she would be one of them. She picked up a jagged rock and chucked it as far as she could throw in the opposite direction, hoping to draw the Enforcer's attention away.

Footsteps headed toward the rock. Satcha darted for the cover of the tree line on the edge of the city. She couldn't be caught. Not again. Her wounds had barely healed and no longer scabbed from her last run in with the Enforcers. She and Agatha had been so hungry, she had to do something, but they both ended up getting caught. Satcha was flogged for stealing an old piece of cheese no bigger than her pinky finger while Agatha... Poor Agatha couldn't take it any longer. Her frail heart gave out as Satcha fought not to scream as the Enforcers whipped her. Satcha remembered the tears burning hot against her cheeks as she watched, bound to a tall wooden pole while they tossed Agatha's body on to a cart and hauled her away like garbage.

Ten yards... Five yards...The forest...

She panted, leaning her back against an oak tree, and listened for any pursuers. Giant metal treads carried armored vehicles over the remains of the stone houses she'd slipped through. Twenty Enforcers marched behind the steel vehicle, their gray military uniforms blending in with the concrete. She'd only been able to notice them from the shiny silver helmets they wore. The sunlight caught the reflective helmet of one patroller and shone in her eyes.

She'd been so reckless staying in the city for so long, but she needed supplies. She'd only found a few rations for her aching belly; half a loaf of stale bread and one lone piece of jerky. She didn't know what kind of meat it was, but she wasn't picky. She couldn't be picky in her state. Her skin clung tight against her ribs and her cheeks sunk in under her eyes. She couldn't remember the last time she'd eaten a decent meal. There were far too many Enforcers for her to manage to go back and steal anything worth taking. She'd only steal from them, not the refugees. The Enforcers continued to bomb cities and create their compounds across Enross and Austerland.

Austerland was where she was headed next. She needed to reach the port on the west coast to cross the Westim Ocean and reach the Free City in the heart of the Isle of Neroso, the home of the Nerosian Enforcers. The one place she'd hoped she would be free and not have to live under their attack, but within the safety of their own people. It was rumored among the people of Enross to be a paradise, a haven on this Earth deemed safe and unplagued by war. Only the wealthy could afford passage, but she planned to sneak onto a ship. To create a home for herself.

She'd never been to the Free City, let alone across the

Westim Ocean, nor had she laid eyes on it. She'd heard stories about the land beyond the gray waters. Endless flowing plates of food, never a cold night resting deep within your bones, and best of all, peace. But as the Enforcers leveled city after city, and built their compounds across the land, talk of the Free City had tapered off. Peace was the prize waiting in the Free City, but it was forbidden to leave unless you had the money. Money was one of the many things she didn't have. She'd hoped her fortunes would change once she stepped foot on the shores, but it was a fool's dream, and she knew it.

Peace was not her only goal in the Free City. What better way to take her revenge than to attack from within and avenge Agatha by killing the Masked Man, the leader of the Nerosians? She didn't know him by any other name, she'd only heard whispers of the man behind the Enforcers. It didn't matter what his name was, all that mattered to Satcha was her dagger, Agatha's dagger, slitting his throat and watching him bleed.

Her stomach rumbled and a burning crawled up from her belly into her mouth. A sick bile. She slipped through the trees furthering her distance from the foot patrols. No longer could she hear the pained cries of those captured. She was glad— there was only so much of it she could take, but she couldn't dwell on the loss of others. It only brought back painful memories, but she couldn't let the nightmares of Agatha's death haunt her now, she needed to focus on her own survival. Her stolen food would have to last the journey. Who knew when she would find more.

The hot sun blazed upon her back. Satcha didn't stop until she was a league away from the burning village. Exhausted from walking, the heat of the sun and no food, her knees buckled and she slumped forward onto the hard ground, cutting her cheek on a sharp rock. The warm drip of blood trickled down her face. Starved and dehydrated, she lay on the ground and managed to muster enough energy to reach in her bag for the small canteen. She'd stolen it from her last camp raid not two weeks ago. Only two drops moistened the tip of her tongue, but it gave her enough will to chew on some dried jerky.

She rolled onto her side and dragged herself across the ground, propping herself against a tree trunk. She couldn't stop here, she needed to keep pushing, but her body could take no more. She'd been this hungry before, but never so thirsty. Her throat was dry as the Austerland desert and she longed to quench her thirst. The world spun round and out of focus. Her eyes deceived her with visions of white sails gliding across the sea, headed to the Free City. Her ears rang, but through the ringing, she heard the distinct gallop of horses racing toward her. Figures in dark blue cloaks approached her, but she couldn't move, her body too weak to run away.

Strong hands grasped her shoulders, picking her up as if she were but a mere child. She didn't care who it was. Let them kill her. At least her suffering would be over. Besides, as weak as she was, there was nothing she could do. The Enforcers had found her. They'd either kill her or take her to the refugee camps where she'd be forced to dig through debris after the bombings and build more Enforcer camps. She'd rather have death. At least she would be free. But with her luck, she'd end up a lost soul wandering these lands forever.

Satcha tried to open her eyes, but the bright light from the sun glared down. She lay back, trying to block the light with her hands, and saw two figures standing over her before the world went dark.

CHAPTER 3

DOMINIC

Dominic wanted nothing more than to scream at the top of his lungs. A fire built up inside of him that he fought hard to contain. Every step forward he took, the Enforcers were three steps ahead.

They'd lost the Sea River right before his eyes. Again, his uncle had landed another blow to Enross. The smell of smoke hung in the air and swept across the sky unleashing the impending doom of what was to come. The black ships anchored in the port and brought forth a fury of which the villagers of Carose had never seen before. With Direct Energy Weapons at their disposal, no one stood a chance against them, but that didn't mean he wouldn't try.

In his arms, an unconscious young girl slumped against him. He had no doubt in his mind she was a survivor from the attack in Carose. Dried blood covered her face and matted in her hair. Brunette, blonde, or redhead? So much blood and dirt had caked her scalp. The girl was frail and thin from hunger. How many more suffered the life of poverty like she did? The Enross Army barely fed itself, let alone be able to help the surrounding towns and villages, no matter how much he wanted to share what little resources they had. It wasn't up to him.

Guilt sank deep into his stomach remembering the last time he'd seen his uncle. Thirteen? Fourteen years? He couldn't remember. The time between landing on Austerland and the journey to Enross seemed a blur. So much time had passed, it almost didn't feel real, but it wasn't a nightmare he could wish away and hope to stop haunting him at night. It was real. Gideon was real. If only he'd been able to convince him of another way to help the Nerosians without the cost of lives in Vardya. It would have been a long shot if there was any point of negotiating with him, but it was a better alternative to killing Gideon. If he hadn't fumbled and regretted his attack at the last moment, he knew what would've happened. Gideon would've died at the hands of his nephew, and he would've been sentenced to death with the knowledge that Hector, Gideon's right-hand man, would carry on the torch in his stead. Gideon had molded Hector into the perfect loyal follower who never questioned him. Hector delivered results, something that Dominic was never able to accomplish for his uncle, nor wanted.

"Lennox, take the girl back to base. I'm going to see if I can find any more people who've escaped," Dominic said, as he carried her to his trusted friend and lieutenant. It'd been twelve years since he made his way into the hidden village of Rios to find not only a friend, but a brother.

"Not a chance!" Lennox rolled his blue eyes. He ran a hand over his short blond hair and groaned in his typical act of defiance, but Dominic liked that. He needed someone to contradict him and make him see things in ways he couldn't. "Are you crazy? You can't go back there alone. Not even if the whole Enross Army was at your back. We don't stand a chance against them."

"I can't stand by and watch them kill more people."

Dominic bit his lip and debated grabbing the reins of his chestnut stallion from Lennox and riding back to the village, but he knew Lennox would stop him. He was too loyal to let him go alone.

"That's not what we came here for. Recon my ass! Or do you not remember? You told me we were surveilling the area for Enforcer movements. Well, guess what? We found the Enforcers, saw them blow up Carose, now let's go before we get caught up in this and the General tans our hides."

Dominic sighed. Lennox was right, he couldn't keep dragging him off on these secret missions behind the General's back, but he had to do something. He couldn't stay idle at the base any longer.

"Dom, you saved the girl or at least what's left of her, take that as a win and let's go." Lennox thrust the reins of Dominic's horse at him; he wasn't about to back down.

"Fine. Here, help me, take the girl." Dominic gently passed the girl over to Lennox, who was far less gentle, but the girl didn't jostle. If it wasn't for the faint rise and fall of her chest, he'd swear she was dead. Dominic climbed on to the saddle of his horse and reached for the girl again. Lennox didn't put up a fight, it was more of an offering of a promise he wouldn't do anything stupid and bolt off back to Carose.

"What are you going to tell the General?" Lennox asked when he was seated on his white mare.

"I haven't figured that out yet, but I'll think of something. He won't be back for at least a week or two. Maybe a day more if the Reeock guards give him any more trouble." He clicked his tongue and squeezed the horse with his legs and started off toward the base. The girl sat in front of him, leaning back against his chest. He held the reins with one hand and had his arm wrapped around her waist keeping her steady.

"Monroe is going to be all over this," Lennox complained.

"You have to stop that. Monroe is a lieutenant, part of the

army the same as you and me. You can't keep up this little vendetta you have against him." Dominic sighed. He was tired of hearing Lennox's gripes about Monroe. He'd never even said why he didn't like him; Monroe was a suck up and looked for a way to edge himself closer to a promotion, but it wasn't like Lennox to worry about his own rank. Sure, Monroe wasn't Dominic's favorite person, but he was on their side. Any enemy of the Nerosians, and his uncle, was a friend to him.

"Yeah, yeah, whatever you say. Let's just get back before nightfall."

"Not much chance of that, but yes, let's pick up the pace." Dominic coaxed his horse on, never taking his guard down. His eyes scanned the trees around them as they made their way back. Night Raiders would be roaming the woods, especially after an Enforcer attack, picking off the victims as they made their escape. He couldn't help but look at the girl leaning against his chest wondering what horrors she'd faced. He needed to get her back to the base, safe and sound. He couldn't help everyone, but he could help her.

"You know, you can't take on the Nerosians yourself," Lennox spoke after a moment of riding through the woods in silence. "It's not your fault nor is it your burden to bear. You may have signed up for this, but you are taking it too personally."

Dominic didn't know what to say. There wasn't anything he *could* say. After all these years, he'd still never told Lennox where he came from, or at least the true story. For all Lennox knew, he was an orphan from the village of Torta to the far south, his family lost to sickness. It was an easy enough story to believe. The sickness had plagued both Enross and Austerland for years, taking people with a red fire from within, burning them from the inside out.

Lennox would never understand. He couldn't tell him the

truth of where he came from or who he was. Hell, the army would never understand. Dominic imagined the General finding out his true identity and attempting to use him as a bargaining chip, but it would be no good. Gideon never cared about him. He was a chore to take care of, a burden of his mother's doing. He could barely remember his mother, only five when she died. What little he did remember were the funny stories she'd told him about the Sun Bears, how they talked to her and told her secrets. None of it made any sense to him, but he loved watching her face light up and smile at him, but none of that mattered anymore.

"Let's get back to the base." Dominic took a deep breath and urged his horse on, but the demons of his past, didn't let up in his head. All he could think about was every step he took away from Carose was a life lost that could've been saved.

CHAPTER 4

SATCHA

The sun glared down, hot on Satcha's face. Her body swayed side to side in rhythm with the gait of a horse.

A horse? How did I get on a horse?

She'd seen many of them before, but never sat upon one. Her bottom ached with her legs spread over the hard leather of the saddle. Her back leaned into the chest of a stranger who had a firm arm around her waist. She kept her eyes closed, using her other senses first. The cricketing call of cicadas and the snort of two horses broke the silence in the air.

She couldn't remember what happened. Her head weighed heavy and ached as she tried to piece together the forgotten, but there was a more pressing matter. She needed to keep up the facade and pretend to be asleep. She needed to find out what she could about these riders before she made her first move. She was in their possession. Who knew what they would do to her if they knew she was awake? Give her lashings? Cut out her tongue? Rape her?

"What are we going to do with the girl, Cap?" a rough voice said—a man, by the sound of it. The sound of the second set of hooves approached on the right. She debated flinging herself off the horse to the left and making a break for it, but in her weakened state she doubted she could break free of the stranger's grasp. She listened for more horses, but she was sure it was only the two. She'd escaped the Enforcers once before, and she could do it again. She just needed to wait for the right moment.

Something wasn't adding up in her head though. Enforcers didn't use horses; they used armored vehicles. Only Nerosians held any great power of technology. After years of fighting in the Old War between Austerland and Enross, only a ceasefire agreement kept the two countries afloat. All knowledge and technology either country had was lost in the Old War along with the loss of resources and manpower. The stranger she was leaning against didn't feel like they were wearing the hard armor the Enforcers wore... In fact, they wore no armor at all. The roughness of a uniform chafed against her bare elbow. Who were they?

"We'll bring her back to camp."

"She looks awfully scrawny. She'd be another mouth to feed—"

The rider stopped his horse. Satcha didn't dare move, there was too much unknown for her to attack yet. She set her focus on the stranger and waited for a lapse in the grasp around her, but it was iron tight.

"We'll make do," the one called Cap answered. The other voice sighed but didn't mention it any further. The rider clicked his tongue, and they were off again.

Not able to stand the unknown any longer, she looked through her eyelashes at the arm around her waist. It was not the color of an Enforcer uniform, it was dark blue. She'd been right, these men couldn't be Enforcers. She suspected they were part of the Enross Army; no Austerland forces would be this far east.

24

Yes, the Enross Army wore dark blue uniforms. She'd seen them once or twice before in her travels. They'd tried and failed to save many cities from the Enforcers but didn't have the weapons nor technology to keep up with them. They only had the blind pride for their country and the will to fight.

Idiots.

Regardless of who they were, they were still her captors. Moving slowly, Satcha felt for her knife, hidden at her left ankle by pressing her leg against the horse's side. The steel hilt pushed into her and she fought to hold in a sigh of relief. She imagined the motions of grabbing it and stabbing it into the neck of the man behind her. She could push him off the back of his horse and take off at a gallop straight to Austerland. She tried to imagine sliding back in the saddle and grabbing the reins but wasn't confident in her ability to stay on without the hold of the stranger. She also had to worry about his companion. Maybe if she'd been an experienced rider, she could've out ridden him and lost him in the trees. If she could make it to the port, the horse would sell for enough money to get her some new clothes and food for the voyage, but she'd need twenty horses to buy passage.

But there was no route for escape yet, she would need to wait to get to their camp and then slip away. A full-on frontal attack wasn't her style. She relied on her stealth and speed to sneak up before striking. She peeked through her eyelashes again; orange skies glowed from behind the mountains as the sun set. It was dangerous to travel at night—the Enforcers were too quick in their armored vehicles and they were on horseback—so if there was an ambush, these two soldiers would stand no chance.

It took everything in Satcha not to squirm. She didn't dare sneak another peek; she'd play dead until the time was right. She'd have to stick to her plan and escape at the camp.

Despite the impending danger of the dark, her captors

continued riding. They only stopped every so often to listen for anyone who might be following. The two men seemed content in the silence and didn't speak again for a long time. Satcha dozed in and out without quite meaning to. She felt awkward leaning into the stranger but didn't want to reposition herself to let him know she was awake.

"Look out!" the other man shouted.

The horse reared, throwing Satcha and her captor onto the ground. The impact knocked the wind out of her, and she fought to choke down gasps of air. She opened her eyes to see her captor jumping to his feet. A man dressed in all black lunged toward him.

Night Raiders!

Bandits of the night stealing anything they could get their hands on from those foolish enough to travel in the dark. This was her chance to get away. She'd grab a horse and ride off into the night. She rolled on the ground away from the two men and toward the neighing horses, but they were off at a gallop, riderless into the woods. She pounded her fist on the ground and fought back a scream.

Her frustration captured the attention of a new assailant. A dark figure stood over her and grasped her by her hair. She gritted her teeth against the pull on her scalp. Reaching out, she grabbed the man's hands and pressed his fingers against her skull forcing him to release her. He took a step back flexing his knuckles.

Greasy, dark brown hair hung out of the dark hood. She knew she didn't smell great, but this man was no bed of roses either. He smelled of rotting fish. Bile pooled in the back of her mouth making her fight to keep her stomach calm. The man charged at her, giving her only seconds to react. She dodged his charge and grabbed his neck from behind with her left hand. With her right she grabbed her concealed knife. She pulled his head back to reveal his neck.

With a steady grip on the blade, she dragged it across his throat, just like Agatha had taught her. Blood sprayed out and a gargled cry escaped his mouth. She let his body fall to the ground.

She looked back at her riding companion. He'd thrown the attacker on the ground and drawn a gun from the small of his back. He breathed in deep heavy breaths but wasted no time. He grabbed the man by the hair, pulled his head up and pressed the barrel against his head. The shot rang out, no doubt alerting anyone else in the area of their presence.

The other man straddled another Night Raider and placed his hands on the sides of the attacker's head. With a swift motion, he snapped the man's neck. He shoved the slumped body aside like a piece of garbage.

Satcha knelt on the ground to try and gather her bearings. The two men dusted themselves off and looked around for the horses. She picked herself off the ground, watching them. She held no loyalty to them, she needed to slip away before they could notice. She stepped toward the tree line when one of the men pointed a gun at her.

She froze in place, staring at the end of the barrel. The man pulled the trigger sending the bullet flying. The sound of the shot rang in her ears, but she felt nothing. Where had the bullet hit her? She wanted to look and examine herself, but she couldn't take her eyes off the man standing not fifteen feet from her. There was a gargle from behind her and a thud. The man lowered his gun and turned to the other man and smiled. She looked behind her and saw another Night Raider laying dead on the ground.

They protected me?

Not twenty feet behind the two men, another Night Raider lurked in the bushes toward the one called Cap. Satcha gripped her knife in her hand as she swung her arm back and aimed. She launched the knife and watched it fly through the air directly into the throat of the hiding man, bringing him to his knees before collapsing in a heap on the ground.

Both Cap and the other soldier turned to face her with jaws dropped. It was the first time she could properly see either one of them. Two tall figures dressed in dark blue military uniforms with the same color cloaks covering their backs. Both were young men, in their late twenties, she guessed. The nameless soldier's face was hard and clean shaven, with blue eyes and short blond hair. He looked ordinary, like any other soldier she'd come across. Cap's appearance was far different from his companion. His black hair was a little longer than the other soldier's and matched the night sky. His jaw was angled as if it'd been chiseled to look that way. A long thin scar tainted his olive skin, from his left eye into the scruff of his short facial hair. His dark green eyes pierced through her, sizing her up. She stood ready, waiting for them to attack, but they made no move.

They could've taken their chance to harm her when they found her unconscious, but they didn't.

Satcha crept forward, keeping her eyes on the men as she went to retrieve her knife. She yanked the knife out of the man's throat and wiped the blade on the man's back. Once she was satisfied it was cleaned, she returned it to its hiding spot at her ankle. She avoided looking at the face of the dead man; she didn't want to humanize him. It wasn't the first time she'd taken a life and it wouldn't be the last. She didn't like doing it and she'd only ever done it in life-or-death situations.

"I think she just earned her rations." Cap clapped his hand on the shoulder of the other soldier and laughed. Cap took two steps toward her with his hand reached out. "I'm Captain Dominic Lightwood."

Satcha took a step back. Just because she'd saved him didn't mean she trusted him.

He dropped his hand and stepped back, giving her space.

"Are you a mute?"

She shook her head no. He looked at her with curiosity sparked in his eyes as if she were an artifact from a foreign land.

"Will you tell me your name?"

Satcha pondered this. It had been so long since she'd talked to another, she wondered if she'd forgotten how to use her voice. She tried not to think of Agatha. How long has it been since she died? She wasn't sure, but every time the old woman's face crept into her thoughts, it was as if she witnessed the Enforcers beat her to death before her eyes all over again. Being the distraction long enough for Satcha to escape—but she didn't know Agatha not escaping with her was part of the plan.

Satcha blinked her eyes and tried to not let the tears well. "I'm Satcha." Her throat tickled as the words rose out of her and into the world. She couldn't remember the last time she'd heard the sound of her own name.

"Well, then Satcha, nice to officially meet you."

She nodded. She didn't trust him, but she found herself curious about him. She wanted to know why he was so friendly to her when he had no reason to be. He could have let her die on the road like the other had wanted, but he didn't. He must've pitied her.

The other soldier didn't take his eyes off Satcha. He glared at her. The men in black had been dealt with, she was the new risk.

"Where are you headed?" Captain Lightwood asked.

"West." She didn't feel like getting into her plans. These men were strangers.

"There's a lot of places in the West," he challenged.

She tried not to narrow her eyes at him. What did he care about where she was headed? This stranger was far too bold to be asking these kinds of questions. Her hands clenched at her sides, biting her lip.

"The Free City."

"The Free City?" Captain Lightwood turned to her, surprised.

Had he never heard of it before? She thought for sure everyone knew of the paradise. He glanced back at the other soldier who shrugged. Satcha didn't understand what their looks meant.

"Just let her run off if she wants. We don't have time for this, Cap!" the other soldier said. His eyes darted off around the woods as if he waited for another attack to happen at any moment.

"That's enough. We don't leave people behind." The lieutenant muttered under his breath but didn't put up any further argument. The captain turned back to her. "Unfortunately, Lieutenant Lennox is right. We don't have time to stand here. You can come with us if you like, our base is well-hidden and safe."

Satcha looked back and forth between the two. Lieutenant Lennox didn't like her, it was obvious, but the captain seemed keen on keeping her safe. Safe sounded nice. Safe was her goal in the Free City, she could make a stop along the way. It would give her a chance to rest before for the rest of her journey. Satcha nodded; she still didn't trust them, but they were all she had.

"Okay then, it's settled." Captain Lightwood clapped his hands together and headed off through the trees. "Follow us."

Lennox motioned for her to follow the captain, while he trailed behind. Satcha didn't blame him, she wouldn't have trusted her either, but saving his captain should have counted for something.

They walked through the night in silence, listening for any more attackers. Satcha struggled to keep up with their pace.

Lieutenant Lennox scoffed every time she tripped or fell back. Her empty belly groaned, roaring for food. She clutched her bag close and snuck her hand in searching for the piece of stale bread. She broke off a piece and shoved it into her mouth. She didn't mind the crunch of the bread; she'd never known the taste of bread fresh from the oven but had smelled it many times. As she chewed, she lingered on the memory of the aroma of baking yeast. It filled her with hope. She longed to taste soft, warm bread, and as she followed the soldiers she daydreamed about the Free City and what other foods she might get to try.

Chapter 5

Satcha

The unlikely trio trekked through the forest for what seemed like hours to Satcha. Never did she think she would make herself acquainted with the Enross Army. She did her best to avoid the war and it wasn't easy. Every day, more and more Enforcers arrived on the shores, pillaging towns and villages, taking what useful prisoners they could find while leaving the bodies of those deemed unworthy of even slave labor.

She couldn't place where they were or where they were headed. Everything looked the same. Tall oak trees covered the sky above them, thick with foliage and no gift of light from the sun to map her way. She didn't speak to either Captain Lightwood or Lieutenant Lennox and they didn't speak to her either. Every once in a while Lennox would watch her with accusing eyes. She did her best to ignore him but was wary of where he was at all times. He seemed like a loose cannon and the bigger risk of threat than the captain. Captain Lightwood didn't glare at her like Lennox, but he kept an eye on her movements all the same. She couldn't blame him; she did the same to him.

The captain held himself differently than Lennox. He stood taller, but not prouder. The constant grimace on his face spoke the words he didn't voice. He'd seen things, and probably done things he wasn't proud of. She wondered if that was part of the difference in rank, but something deep down told her that there was more to him than what appeared. A damaged soul could recognize another with ease.

Her feet ached and her stomach still rumbled. The taste of the stale, slightly moldy bread lingered in her mouth. The soles of her makeshift shoes were worn and two sizes too small. She had little trouble imagining open blisters oozing under the fabric. The cloth tied around her feet was more for warmth than protection, but it lacked in every way. If only she'd had enough money to buy herself a proper pair of shoes.

She often wondered what her life would've been like growing up with her mother and father to care for her. Would her mother have taught her to cook and sew clothes? Would her father have come home from a long day of work as a blacksmith and greet her mother with a kiss on the cheek before giving Satcha a present he'd made that day?

Satcha let out an audible sigh drawing attention from the captain who raised a dark eyebrow at her. She jerked her gaze away from him and stared toward the never-ending maze of trees before them. As much as she wanted to picture what her life would've been had her parents not died, or abandoned her, this was the life she was given. A life where she didn't know her age, the love of a parent, or even a friend. Agatha was different. She took care of Satcha after finding her half-dead along a riverbank with a nasty gash on her head, but the woman was brash. There was no warmth and fuzziness with Agatha, even in death.

She blinked hard, trying to focus on her feet and banish the thoughts of Agatha and any resentment she held in her heart for her lack of emotion—for sacrificing herself to let

Satcha escape. She should've found another way for them both to escape.

She clenched her hands at her sides, noticing how hard she'd been stomping her feet as she walked. In an attempt to slow her pace, her foot caught on a vine and forced her forward into a large oak. Her hands reached out and caught herself along the rough bark, scraping the skin of her fingertips raw. Satcha rested her hand against the tree and tried to catch her breath. She couldn't hold up her facade anymore; she was too exhausted to walk.

"Are you kidding me? How long are we going to drag her along?" Lieutenant Lennox rolled his eyes.

Satcha couldn't help it as much as her brain told her body to move. She didn't have the energy to argue. She wouldn't have helped her if she was in their shoes.

"Go on ahead, it's not much further. I'll help her the rest of the way." Captain Lightwood sighed.

"But we're not past the barrier yet—"

"Lennox, I know, it's fine," the captain cut him off. "Send word ahead to the medical wing."

"Fine," Lennox mumbled under his breath as he stalked off ahead.

She was glad to see him leave, one less person to worry about seeing her break. She couldn't hold onto the tree anymore and dropped to the ground. The captain stood over her looking as if he might scoop her into his arms and carry her the rest of the way, but she couldn't have that. She wouldn't be weak; she couldn't afford to be. All her life she only relied on herself to get her through the harsh realities of being a nomad and she was not about to fall at the feet of someone more fortunate than her for help.

"I'm fine." With every bit of strength she could muster, she picked herself off the ground with an iron will. She was glad Lennox was gone. She didn't have the energy to endure the heat of his gaze on her back.

"Would you like any help? I meant what I said, it's not much farther." The captain stepped forward and offered his hand.

"I said, I'm fine. Let's get moving." Satcha recoiled from him, making him drop his hand.

Captain Lightwood nodded to her and motioned for her to follow him and didn't say another word but kept an even closer eye on her as if he expected her to collapse at any moment. But she didn't. He was right, it was only about a twenty-minute walk before they came to a stone pass hidden by crawling ivy.

"Welcome to the Enross Army Base," Captain Lightwood said to her as they approached. "It's not the most comfortable space, but it meets our needs for the moment."

Satcha didn't respond, she'd never known proper comfort, not that she'd been in a cave before, but she'd imagine she'd been through worse. Always on the move with Agatha and never spending more than a few days in any one place. She'd never owned more than the bag she carried and her knife. She asked Agatha many times how she got them, she couldn't remember, but Agatha said the same thing every time: she found a young girl covered in blood, unconscious, along the bank of the river, with not a soul in sight. Not a soul ever recognized her either, no matter where she went. Agatha used to joke that Satcha caused such a ruckus that the river spat her back out to be rid of her.

A soldier stood guard next to the entrance, dressed in the same uniform as Captain Lightwood, holding a rather large gun. He straightened himself before offering a salute to the captain as they passed and continued following the path. On either side of the tunnel, every ten feet, a torched glowed with fire, flickering a yellow glow against the dark walls. Wooden beams ran along the walls and ceiling of the tunnel. The further they ventured into the tunnel the worse in shape it got. The ceiling and walls were only supported by poor looking logs that had long since seen their glory days standing as proud trees in the forest. Some were on the verge of falling apart from root rot. She wasn't sure she trusted the Enross Army's tunnel digging skills. The tunnels looked like they'd been dug with hand shovels.

She'd wondered if there were ever any cave-ins. She shuddered to think that she might get stuck here never to see the light of day again.

The tunnel grew wider and sloped, growing so wide it became a large cavern and the ten-foot ceiling of rock grew to thirty feet. Soldiers clamored around in a circle watching two bare chested soldiers take swings at each other. When Captain Lightwood entered the space, the soldiers scampered to their feet and stood with a salute to him. He looked unimpressed but didn't speak a word of it.

"Private, take this girl to the medic. She'll need a good meal and a wash," Captain Lightwood called out to one of the soldiers trying to make an escape.

Girl? Wash?

He thought she was a dirty child! Of course, that's why he was so nice to her. He assumed her a young girl lost in the woods, needing help. She hadn't realized with her famished figure he wouldn't have known she was a full-grown woman. Maybe it was to her advantage he thought she was so weak and incapable. She barely realized he also said she needed a good meal. She wondered what that would be for a soldier in the Enross Army? Something hearty for the war driven soldier?

"Yes, sir!" The private tripped over his untied boots and fell on his face. "My apologies, Captain."

Captain Lightwood passed her off without so much as a goodbye before scolding the soldiers and assigning extra guard duties. He didn't look at her, spinning on his heels toward the path the soldiers exited through.

The private motioned for her to follow him with a dramatic swing of his arm. She bit her lip trying to hold back the urge to make a snarky remark. She wouldn't be told to follow like some dog, but she followed all the same with her mind set on food.

Chapter 6

Satcha

The tunnel went farther into the earth than Satcha expected before it opened up to yet another cavern, but instead of wrestling soldiers, about twenty hospital beds lined the rocky walls with sick and injured soldiers. Three nurses dressed in white scurried from one patient to the next checking bandages, temperatures, and giving medications.

"Ms. Alba," the private called to one of the nurses sitting at the far back of the room at a small pine desk. Satcha's heart sank to her stomach when the old nurse lifted her head up. A chill ran down her spine as if she'd seen a ghost. The nurse's silver hair was pulled back tightly in a bun and her tired eyes hid behind thin round glasses. Had she not seen Agatha die with her own eyes, she would've sworn she sat alive and well in the medical unit of the Enross Army. "Captain Lightwood asked me to bring this girl to you."

Ms. Alba raised an eyebrow at him before flickering her glance to Satcha. She felt the heat of the woman's gaze upon her face. Satcha wasn't sure why she looked at her with a curious eye; maybe she was surprised to have someone other than a soldier be a patient, or maybe she was like Lennox and didn't want to waste medical supplies on a nomad.

"Yes, yes. Find a clean bed and I will tend to her momentarily," Ms. Alba called from her desk and began sorting the paperwork before her. Satcha couldn't take her eyes off the woman, not just of the resemblance, but the voice as well. In all the years she spent with Agatha, she'd never mentioned a family or really much of anything about her past. She avoided questions about herself at all costs, which was a trait Satcha had adopted.

"Yes, ma'am!" The soldier smiled and bumped Satcha with his elbow as he walked with his arms swinging off beat from one another. Satcha guessed he wasn't assigned many meaningful tasks.

He bounded toward the closest bed, near the entrance, away from the others. She didn't need this puppy dog personality near her anymore as she was quite capable of making it to the bed on her own. She sat on the bed and leaned back, bracing herself for a hard impact, but sunk into a soft mattress with white linens. She imagined it must be what it was like to lay on a cloud. She'd never been fortunate enough to experience such comfort.

"Back to work for me." He smiled and nodded in farewell before taking unnecessary long strides out of the medical wing, as if he was afraid he might miss something back with the other soldiers.

Satcha stared up at the dugout ceiling of rock. A giant wooden beam held in by spikes was directly over her, holding the ceiling in place. She tried not to think of it breaking loose and falling on top of her, crushing her small frame into bits. Not now. She couldn't think like that, not when she finally had a moment to rest. Ms. Alba came into view and hovered over her, holding a tray with a steaming bowl. Saliva pooled in her mouth as she inhaled the scent of unknown herbs and meat.

"Let's get some food into you first, and then you can go wash up, so we can have a good look at you."

A second wind picked her spirits up and helped her find the strength to reach her hands out to grasp the bowl. She ignored the burn of the hot metal against her lips and drank as many gulps of the scalding broth she could manage.

"Now, now! Slow down or you will make yourself sick!" Ms. Alba pulled the half empty bowl from her, but Satcha didn't care. She craved the hot broth and so did her belly. A blister swelled on the tip of her tongue and stung against the back of her teeth. Never had she had anything so flavorful and delicious.

Ms. Alba picked up a spoon and fed Satcha, far too slow for her liking, but she didn't complain. She let the liquid sit on her tongue tasting the savory flavors and ignoring the further burn on the blister.

"Come with me," Ms. Alba commanded, putting the bowl and spoon aside.

Satcha sat up from the bed hoping there would be more food. She nodded to Ms. Alba, trying not to make eye contact with those narrow blue eyes, not unlike the familiar gaze of Agatha. She followed her, wondering what foods might await to fill her belly next. If the broth tasted this good, she couldn't imagine what the taste of warm bread would be.

Oh, please, fresh bread!

Ms. Alba didn't speak to her as they walked through the tunnel and that was okay by her. She preferred her silence. Silence was the only thing that had kept her safe for this long. She'd been able to sneak into Enforcer compounds many times with Agatha, successful for all but one attempt. The last time. The sting of the scarred lashes on her back reminded her she could never risk being caught again. She tried not to think of

Agatha lying dead, face in the mud with the Enforcers standing over her body.

As soon as she regained strength here, she planned to sneak away and never be seen by the Enross Army again. She still had her mission: get to the Free City and kill the Masked Man. For her parents, whoever they were, and for herself, but mostly for Agatha.

Ms. Alba led her to a private area at the end of the tunnel. The walls were surrounded by a white curtain. In the middle of the makeshift room was a large, round, metal tub with steaming water, vapors rising from the surface. Satcha never liked having to wash. Agatha certainly never cared much for hygiene when the constant threat of survival loomed. She'd let Satcha splash in the water on hot days when they could afford a break, but it became less and less frequent as she grew older. She would wash her face quickly if given the chance or take an efficient dip in the shallow end to loosen the dirt. Since Agatha's death, she'd only ever swam in cold rivers to rid herself of dirt. It took too long for the cold to leave her bones.

"There's soap for you to use and a clean cloth. I'll be back with some proper clothes." Ms. Alba ushered Satcha into the room and pulled a clean towel from a white metal trolley against the wall.

Satcha nodded to her but kept her eyes on the tub of water. Tearing her eyes away, she hid her knife in her bag and set it next to the tub within arm's reach. She didn't wait for Ms. Alba to leave before stripping off the torn, rugged coat, and earth-colored shirt and pants. Ms. Alba gasped—she'd probably noticed the scars on her back—but said nothing.

The hardest part was yet to come. Satcha lowered herself to the ground, ready to take off her makeshift shoes of brown scraps tied together. She untied the rope and winced when the fabric rolled away from her raw skin.

Ms. Alba didn't say a word as she watched Satcha haul

herself back off the ground and peer into the tub of hot water. She collected Satcha's dirty clothes and left the room.

Satcha dipped her fingers into the warm water before hoisting herself over the edge and lowering herself in. She sighed and rolled her shoulders back, feeling her muscles relax. The warm water stung against the cuts and scrapes along her body. Her long, matted hair floated in a clump at the nape of her neck. She tried to comb her fingers though, but it was a lost cause. She reached for the small piece of soap and held it to her nose. Sweet scents of flowers filled her nostrils and with it came a deep-seated envy of anyone who'd had the privilege of bathing in such fashion.

It'd been weeks since she'd last found a safe spot to bathe. The Enforcers set up most of their compounds near lakes and the Sea River for the control of the water supply, further denying the Enross Army of resources. Several villages counted on the Sea River to provide sea travel for trade and power, but as the Enforcers took over, the water mills were either destroyed or diverted to the compounds, and normal civilians lost easy access to the water.

Ignoring the ache in her joints, she scrubbed the little bar of soap against her skin starting with her arms and moved to her chest. The clean water turned into a muddy brown, especially when she coated her hair in the soap. Broken pieces of twigs floated along the surface as she tugged against the knots in her hair. She tried her best to untangle it, but only made it worse. She didn't care about the luxuries of having well-kept hair, she would've cut it short if she could, just to avoid having the routine care for it. Ms. Alba and the other nurses were neat and tidy, despite their dirty job of tending to wounded soldiers. She chewed her lip, thinking about how lucky they were to not only have the safety of a roof over their heads, but the luxury of being clean and wearing clothes that fit.

She continued to scrub a little too rough, making her skin

glow red, but it was all she could do to focus her anger on herself for not caring for herself better. Nor having the capability of doing it by herself. She didn't want to be a burden on anyone, she was the only one she could rely on, and the fact she'd been only able to do the bare minimum of staying alive angered her.

How long had she dreamed of going to the Free City and been nowhere closer to making it there? She needed to make her move and now seemed as good as anytime. She needed to use what resources she could from the Enross Army and get herself out of Enross. Out of Vardya and make her way to the Free City, kill the Masked Man, and find peace.

Chapter 7

Dominic

Dominic didn't waste any time when he returned to the base. He hadn't even bothered to reprimand the two privates fighting in the mess hall, let alone Private Archer, who'd slipped away while stuffing his notebook of wagers into his coat. He'd have to deal with that later. There was far too much work to be done and far too much to plan.

He saw the girl off as far as he could before he had to get back to work. A slight tinge of guilt riddled him for being so harsh to her when they parted ways, but there was much on his mind. The Enforcers had taken over Carose on his watch. He was in charge of the base since General Ballard had left to negotiate a supply trade between the army and the Capital, Reeock, to the south.

He didn't have the General's permission to do his little recon mission on the Enforcers in Carose. Another village lost to the control of his uncle and his Enforcers. He knew the General didn't approve, but he had to try. He couldn't let the army fall further behind in the war. There was no time for stopping at his private quarters to change nor for rest. He quickened his pace, heading straight for the war room.

He opened a heavy steel door to the tunneled-out room with a large conference table sitting in the middle, giving barely any space for two soldiers to walk side by side around it. Lennox had gone ahead and gathered the other officers to wait for him to debrief their scouting trip.

"Thank you for gathering on such short notice." He took his place at the head of the table but didn't sit. Not because he wanted to be above them and show his rank, but if he sat, he wasn't sure he could get back up again with the ache in his legs. He used the ache to fuel his deep desire to put a stop to the Enforcers and push them back to the Isle of Neroso. He wanted the other officers to be as mad as he was and avenge the fallen city. "Carose has been taken by the Enforcers, giving them further access to Enross through the Sea River. We can only assume it was a strategic move in their plan so they can provide reinforcements and supplies to the Tower east of here."

"Were you able to rescue any survivors, sir? We heard you brought back a girl," Corporal Fuller asked. He sat at the far end of the table. Dominic liked Fuller; he couldn't help but root for the underdog. Fuller worked harder than most of the other officers, but he wasn't lining up to kiss the General's ring in support, so a corporal is where he found himself. Stuck and going no further despite how many times Dominic had vouched for him.

"We recovered one survivor, a girl starved to the brink of death. We found her north of the city. We have no idea how many fatalities or slaves were taken by the Enforcers." He flexed his hands behind his back. If there had only been a sign or a piece of intel, he could've gotten together a team and tried to defend the village, but again, the Enforcers slipped through his grasp.

"We should send word to the General." Lieutenant Monroe rose from his chair and snapped his fingers at an aide standing back near the door.

The scrawny aide with bright red hair gulped and scratched notes on his clipboard. Dominic raised his hand to silence Monroe.

"I've already sent one of our fastest riders with a message to the General," he lied. The last thing he needed was Monroe sneaking off to share intel with the General behind Dominic's back. "Until we hear back with more orders, I want our perimeter checks to be doubled and have troops prepared for an attack. We won't get much warning if the Enforcers find us here."

Monroe set his jaw and narrowed his eyes but sat without arguing any further. Dominic didn't quite trust the lieutenant as much as he would've liked to. Monroe was too concerned with sucking up to the General every chance he got, meanwhile stepping on the toes of the other officers to see to his own personal gain.

"Lieutenant Lennox and I have also been able to gather further intel that the Neroso structure to the west has proof of the bloodline of Vardya."

Several officers rolled their eyes while Monroe scoffed. He knew he would get this reaction from them. He seemed to be the only one keen on uniting Enross and Austerland against the Enforcers. It was their last chance to beat them. Combine the armies and share the resources. Lennox kept his head low and made no move to step in. Dominic knew he had Lennox's loyalty, and the other soldiers knew it too. They'd joined the army together as boys.

"The Blood Scrolls? Again, Captain? Does the General know this was your little mission?" Monroe stood and headed toward the door.

"I haven't dismissed you yet, Lieutenant." Dominic

couldn't help but stop him. He couldn't risk losing control of those beneath him. He needed them to come to his side and help him—otherwise, they were done for.

Monroe stopped in his tracks before turning the door-knob to leave. He didn't turn back right away, Dominic figured he must've been trying to control the emotions on his face. He needed to keep up a good appearance to avoid any negative feedback getting to the General. Monroe turned with a blank look on his face and sat back in his seat at the table.

"Now, back to our next move—"

A knock at the door interrupted Dominic. A brunette nurse peeked inside the room but made no further move to enter.

"Pardon my interruption, Captain, but Ms. Alba needs to speak with you at once." Her wide brown eyes, much like a doe, darted around the room looking from officer to officer before settling back on Dominic again.

"I'll be down to see her shortly. Thank you." Dominic sighed and turned back to the officers, but the nurse didn't leave.

"Actually, Captain, this is of great importance, and she urged me to make sure you came straight away." She gulped and brushed a stray hair back behind her ear.

"Fine." He had to put the poor girl out of her misery. She'd done her job and delivered the message. "Let's adjourn for now but meet back in an hour to go over our next steps."

Ms. Alba wasn't the kind to intrude on officer meetings, so it had to be important if she called on him. Especially during a mission debrief. He could only assume it was about the girl, Satcha. He couldn't imagine what trouble may await him in the medical wing. He hoped she hadn't attacked anyone with that knife of hers. Perhaps he should've taken it away from her before sending her off to the medical wing with Private Alderson. In any case, he knew whatever waited for him, it was to do with her.

He'd never seen such feral eyes before, constantly shifting, searching for any threat of danger. He couldn't help but sympathize with her. What had she seen? What had she experienced in this life to develop such an untrusting fear even to those offering their aid? Guilt riddled him like a virus racing through his veins. It ate away at any of the good he'd done to protect these lands and the people, leaving only the constant reminder there were plenty out there suffering like her.

To his surprise, Ms. Alba strode into the room with her lips pursed. She stood to the side of the room watching the officers file out, along with her messenger nurse.

"What's happened?" He couldn't take the silence any longer as they waited for the soldiers to clear out of the room.

"I think it is best if you see for yourself." Ms. Alba lowered her voice to a whisper, "The girl may have some information that could be useful... to your cause."

"Let's go." He didn't need any more convincing. He trusted Ms. Alba and though she would never admit to anyone, he knew she was on his side for the good of both Enross and Austerland. For Vardya.

"I must warn you, Captain." She touched his arm, bringing him to a stop in the middle of the hallway. "It's the girl. She bears a mark I've never seen before by that of the living."

He stared into her eyes taking in her words, but not quite understanding their meaning. What could he have missed about the girl and how did she relate to his search for the Blood Scrolls?

"What mark would that be?" he asked, not sure what to expect.

"She'd been flogged by a DEW whip," she whispered. Her eyes shifted side to side making sure no one was close, but it was only them in the empty tunnel. "No one gets away from the Enforcers with their life. How did she, a scrawny sack of bones, do it?"

Dominic didn't know how to answer. He'd never been able to recover those taken by the Enforcers. He knew well enough any prisoner deemed strong enough to work were slaves until they proved themselves useless.

"I'd like to see her and ask some questions."

"I figured you might," she said. "Let me collect her from her bath and make her presentable and I will call for you."

"Thank you." He nodded to her.

Ms. Alba gave him a grim smile before heading down the tunnel toward the medical wing. Toward the girl who could give him the answers to the questions that kept him up, sleepless night after sleepless night, staring at unanswered letters he'd received from people around Enross asking for help to locate family members—even if it was just a body. He didn't know how to tell them there was no point in looking; once the Enforcers decided they were done with a slave, they were disposed of without a trace... Likely with a technology developed after he'd escaped Neroso, something that Satcha might have seen.

Chapter 8

Satcha

Ms. Alba returned to the bathing room carrying folded clothes in her hands. Satcha crossed her arms over her chest, despite undressing in front of the nurse prior. With the added layer of dirt covering her skin, it left her more exposed than before, but Ms. Aba didn't shy away from the sight of Satcha naked in the tub. In fact, Ms. Alba pushed her thin gray eyebrows together and scoffed at her.

"Oh, this won't do. Stay still dear," she grumbled and set aside the clothes. She marched over to the tub with no concern for Satcha's nakedness while shaking her head and muttering under her breath.

Satcha froze as Ms. Alba took the cloth from the edge of the tub and began cleaning her back. No one had bathed her before; she didn't know what to do. She held her breath, not able to stop thinking about all the ways Ms. Alba could drown her. It was a reflex she couldn't stop. Her eyes darted around the room looking for anything she could use in case the old nurse turned on her, but the woman hadn't given her any reason to think that way. Satcha tried to quiet her anxieties and tell herself Ms. Alba had only helped her, whether she was happy to do it or not. And Ms. Alba didn't hurt her—instead, she carefully untangled Satcha's hair and massaged in the soap gently, making her eyes close, if only for a moment. Her shoulders relaxed and she sighed.

Was this how a mother would bathe her child? Every time she tried to remember her parents, the scar on her scalp ached as if it was a fresh wound.

"We have to make you presentable for the captain. He will have some questions for you about how you got those scars on your back."

"No!" Any sense of calm Satcha had gained was stripped away like a rug pulled from under her feet. Satcha pulled away.

Presentable for the Captain? What does he want with me? Why do my scars matter to him?

What would Captain Lightwood want to see her for? Nothing good, of course.

"Oh, come now. We know who did that to your back and want to know how you escaped." Ms. Alba pulled Satcha back within her grasp and brushed through her hair no longer gentle. Satcha winched at the tugging on her scalp.

She didn't want to be dragged into other people's problems. It wasn't her war.

Satcha couldn't remember which side of the curtain wall she'd come in; it all looked the same, but there was only one way out—back through the tunnel she came. She could sneak along the back of the cavern, but she wouldn't be able to make it past the soldiers presumably at every entrance, let alone navigate through the tunnels. Any memory she had of arriving was blurred, despite it having not yet been an hour.

Ms. Alba didn't stop until every strand of hair was untangled. Satcha wanted her to go back to the gentle head massage and carefully brush out her tangles, but she didn't want to give in. So, she let her continue pulling. Her scalp ached, and she fought the urge to yank on Ms. Alba's neatly tied bun and run off. The warm water was now lukewarm, and so filthy Satcha could no longer see her limbs through the water.

"You could probably use another scrub down, but I don't think we have the time." Ms. Alba snapped her fingers at Satcha to get out of the tub. Satcha's limbs protested and she could barely hold back the yawn wanting to burst out of her, despite the fear that riddled her knowing the captain was coming to see her. Ms. Alba yanked her up, wrapping a towel around her and rubbed the rough fabric against her skin to dry her. Satcha stepped out of the tub and away from Ms. Alba's grasp.

"I'll do it myself."

"Good. Once you're dry, get dressed quickly. The captain will be on his way." She was curt with Satcha, as if she'd been annoyed having to care for her. She left Satcha alone to dress. Satcha rummaged through the clothes without too much care, pulling on the dark blue army shirt and pants. It must've been all they had. Underneath the clothes, Ms. Alba left a small round mirror. Satcha picked it up and stared at the stranger's face looking back at her.

Her long blonde hair was damp, pin straight and untangled with the ends just past her belly button. She'd never seen her hair so long or straight before. If she was capable of the upkeep it would've changed her mind about wanting to cut it. For the first time ever, she considered herself to be pretty. Pretty if it weren't for the feral blue eyes that stared back at her, not unlike a cornered wild animal. The roughness of her skin had been washed away with the mud and was left in red splotches.

She didn't want to look at herself anymore. She looked too much like a stranger, like she'd almost forgotten what she looked like. She had only ever known the dirty nomad in the reflection of lakes and rivers.

The fabric of the dark blue uniform hung off her frame, but it didn't itch like her old dirty clothes. At her feet were a pair of gray socks and black boots. Her feet ached remembering the tightness of her too small shoes. She slipped on the socks and slid her feet into the boots that fit perfectly. They were not too big, and not too small; she had room to wiggle her toes for the first time in a long time. She left the laces undone, not knowing how she should tie them.

She heard footsteps approaching from outside the curtained room. She'd been so distracted by her appearance and the boots that she'd forgotten the captain was on his way to question her. It was too late to escape.

There was nowhere for Satcha to hide, there was only one way out of the room and that was back the way she came. She could only sit in the lone chair of the curtained room and wait for Captain Lightwood to question her. She pulled her brown bag onto her lap and fidgeted, playing with a ripped seam she had yet to fix. Outside the linen walled room, she heard voices approaching.

"You're sure the Enforcers were behind it?" Captain Lightwood's voice sent a jolt of apprehension down her spine.

"Yes, sir," Ms. Alba answered.

"Who could do that to a young girl?" Captain Lightwood snapped at no one.

"Young woman. She's malnourished for sure, but I assure you, she's a fully developed woman."

Satcha didn't like them talking about her. She liked even less he'd thought she was a young girl. What kind of young girl carried a knife and would slit the throat of a stranger with no hesitation? She reached her hand into her bag feeling for her knife.

Where is it!

She looked around the tub, but there was no sign of it. How could the old nurse have taken it without her noticing?

She should have waited until the nurse gave her some privacy to undress and hide her knife.

She couldn't sit idly any longer. She got up from the chair, nearly tripping over her untied boots, and stood facing the entrance against the back wall. If there was any risk of being attacked, she wanted the extra distance to allow her time to react in her weakened state. Her heart thumped in her chest so loudly she had to close her eyes to focus on what the voices were saying.

"I'm not sure what you will find out from this girl, but I think it will be worth your time," said Ms. Alba.

"I appreciate you coming to me with this. I'm looking into every possible lead to recover the scrolls," he replied.

Scrolls? Satcha's ears perked up and opened her eyes. *Interesting.*

Captain Lightwood and Ms. Alba entered through the curtain. The captain looked surprised to see Satcha standing on her own and eyed her closely. She didn't like him studying her, but knew she was even far more threatening than he gave her credit for. He looked at her differently than before. He didn't look threatened by her, which annoyed her, but he watched her with a new gaze. Amazement? She squinted at him trying to read his face, but she couldn't place his expression.

"Satcha, I'm not here to hurt you. I told you I'd get you here safely. I just want to ask you a few questions about the Enforcers—their compounds." He held his hands up and took several steps forward.

Satcha eyed Ms. Alba. She didn't trust her and didn't want to talk with her in the room. The fewer people, the better, and the easier it would be for her to escape. She'd make it a lot farther in new boots and warm clothes. Captain Lightwood seemed to notice Satcha glaring at Ms. Alba and nodded to her. Ms. Alba's lips flattened across her face as she strode out of the room.

"Satcha, I know you don't want to trust me, but I assure you, you can. How did you escape from the Enforcers?"

"Which time?" She wanted to play dumb, but she also wanted to show off and prove she wasn't the child he'd expected. She wanted him to know she was dangerous, that she could take care of herself. That she wasn't a little girl needing rescuing.

Captain Lightwood blinked a few times. "What do you mean which time?"

"Well, I only got caught once, and I've got the lashings to prove it. All the other times, I've managed to slip through, steal some supplies, and get out." She flicked her damp hair over her shoulder, brushing past him, and sat in the chair. She leaned back, trying to show off and be nonchalant. It wasn't like her, but she wanted to impress him. She didn't know why. In any case, an ego would help her with her plan. "I could help you get what you're looking for."

Captain Lightwood raised an eyebrow. "And that would be?"

"These special scrolls you need. I could help you get them. For a price." She leaned forward, resting her elbows on her knees and stared at his dark eyes, not blinking.

"What do you know about the scrolls?" He eyed her up and down, sizing her up, with narrowed eyes. He had no idea what she was capable of. Years being on the run and only relying on her wits to keep herself alive had served her well. Her gut told her he would be very willing to retrieve whatever these scrolls were, and she would use that to her advantage.

"I know you need them, and I need something too." She ran her fingers through her wet hair, pushing it back behind her ear, and waited for him to make his move.

He chewed his lip. She had him right where she wanted

him. She'd play along with him in this game. She didn't care about pieces of paper, but if he could give her what she wanted, she would find them.

"What do you want in return—"

"Sir, the General needs you." Lieutenant Lennox strode into the room with a radio and handed it over to the captain .

"Thank you, I'll just be a moment." He slipped out of the room, leaving Lennox and Satcha staring uncomfortably at each other.

"I see you're still leeching off us."

"Not for long. As soon as I get you those scrolls you want so badly, you'll be sending me off on a ship to the Free City as payment."

His eyes widened in surprise, but he recovered quickly. "What makes you think we would ever trust someone like you? Little Neroso lover."

She narrowed her eyes at the remark but didn't intend to acknowledge it further. She was no Neroso lover. "As long as I'm not in the way of their blasters, I have no issue with the Nerosians. It doesn't look like you have anyone else standing in line to help you, Lieutenant."

Lennox raised his eyebrows at her. "I'm not going to sit by while we have a spy in our grasp. I'm sure it wouldn't take long for me to squeeze some secrets out of you."

"I'm no spy, nor am I on anyone's side. I look out for myself."

She didn't like the way he spoke to her. He was a liability to her plan.

Satcha reached for the mirror Ms. Alba had left for her and threw it on the floor. She followed it down, her boots flying off her feet, and clutched a jagged piece of glass in her hand. She lunged at Lennox, but he saw her coming. He grasped her wrist and flung her past him onto the ground. The air knocked out of her chest, and she squeezed her fist too tight on the glass shard. It dug into her palm and fingers, blood seeping through and soaking her hand, but she didn't let go. The lieutenant stood over her and kicked at her hand. The rubber sole of his heel made her knuckles crunch, and she lost her grip on the glass. She breathed heavily, seething with hatred for him.

Lennox sneered at her, muffling a cruel laugh. He leaned over her and wrapped his hands around her neck.

"You little bitch!" He squeezed off her airway with little trouble.

Her heart beat so loud her pulse rang in her ears. She tried to kick her legs against him and pry his hands off her with her own. She kicked her feet out again, this time sweeping her right foot behind his knees, knocking him to the ground. She rolled to her side and grasped the glass once again before she pounced on him, straddling him like she had the man in black in the woods. She held the shard to his throat—

"Enough!" Captain Lightwood charged back into the room. He pulled Satcha off his lieutenant and grasped her arm. Lennox rolled to his side gasping for air while Captain Lightwood thrust her to the ground and pinned her, his knee digging into her bony chest.

"She can't be trusted, she's a Neroso spy! I swear! She tried to attack me," said Lennox. Neither Satcha nor Lennox looked at the captain. They glared at each other. If looks could kill, they'd both be laying dead.

"Enough! We need her, we don't have a choice." Captain Lightwood didn't yell, but the fury in his voice put Lennox in his place.

"Yes, sir." Lennox backed down, but fire still raged in his eyes. Satcha smirked at his chest, heaving up and down, straining to catch his breath.

Captain Lightwood turned his focus back on Satcha, still pinned to the floor beneath him. "I need you to be on our side for this. I don't care where you're from or what you want. I need to know if I can trust you."

She gave a single nod and dropped the glass from her hand. With that show of trust, he released her. Satcha scooted away from them until her back touched the tub and clutched her bleeding hand. She couldn't get caught up in this mess, but there was no way she could get to the Free City on her own. She watched as Captain Lightwood held out his hand to Lennox and hauled him up.

"We will give you two weeks to recover, but we can't spare any more time than that. That is, if you even need it after the display you just showed. You'll stay and work in the medical wing under Ms. Alba's instruction. Don't make me regret my decision." Captain Lightwood nodded to her, once, brisk and business-like, and left the room with Lennox in tow.

Ms. Alba came back into the room muttering about the mess they'd made and led Satcha back to her hospital bed to get her hand cleaned and stitched. Ms. Alba wasn't gentle as she bandaged her up. Satcha tried as best as she could to breathe and calm herself. She had to prepare herself for the next time she'd run into Lennox. Next time she would be ready. She'd gather her strength and fill her belly.

CHAPTER 9

LENNOX

"Dom, how can you let her stay? She wants to go to Neroso!" He couldn't understand how Dominic could be so stupid as to trust this girl. Lennox paced back and forth across Dominic's small office. It wasn't much, just an old tunneled-out room with wooden beams supporting the structure and a small desk with a few chairs. There were no personal items nor decorations covering the dark walls. Dominic only used it for paperwork, so he never spent much time there. Lennox knew how much he hated being stuck underground. If Lennox couldn't find him in the tunnels, he was out patrolling the army border either on foot or horseback.

"She knows how to get in and out of a Nerosian compound. How could I risk losing this opportunity?" Dominic leaned his elbows on his desk with his head in his hands, massaging his temples.

"That's another thing! You don't have the General's approval for any of this! If he finds out that you are after the Blood Scrolls again, he will demote you—or worse."

How many times had they been through this? Lennox

couldn't let Dominic go through with this. He couldn't risk losing him, especially when Dominic was all he had. Lennox knew the General was easy to sway and Dominic wouldn't hold his favor forever. Especially not with Lieutenant Monroe snooping about. He'd made a special effort to keep tabs on him at all times, it wouldn't be long before Monroe would make his move against Dominic, and Lennox wanted to be ready.

"The General doesn't have to know. All he needs to know when he gets back is that we found a way in and out of the building."

"You expect a lot from this nomad scum." Lennox gritted his teeth and tried not to spit the words out but failed. "I wouldn't be surprised if this is a plot set up by the Enforcers to toy with us. They've been growing strong in recent months and we haven't even come close to holding them off, let alone pushing them back to their ships."

"Noxy, trust me, I know this seems rash, but we have to try. You know as well as I do, we can't beat the Enforcers on our own. The General will fight to the last man before we can make a dent in their army. We can't risk that."

Lennox sighed at the use of Dominic's nickname for him and slumped in the chair, defeated. He knew that Dominic was right; the General wouldn't back down even if it came to the demise of the whole Enross Army. Everything in his training told him to try and stop Dominic and follow the orders of the General, but his loyalty to Dominic got in the way of that. How could he ever let Dominic do this alone? He wouldn't. Not once in the years that they'd known each other had Lennox ever won an argument. He gave in to Dominic, every time, but grumbled his concerns. It was probably why Dom was promoted to Captain and he was still a Lieutenant. Not that he minded. He would gladly step aside and follow Dominic anywhere.

"What do you need me to do?" Lennox sighed and gave in, like always.

Dominic let out a sigh of relief of his own and gave a small smile. "I can always count on you, my friend."

Lennox nodded and tried to hide his grimace at the word *friend*. He knew that was all he was to him. Many times Lennox had chastised himself for thinking such thoughts. Was there something wrong with him? Why did he feel this way? He'd tried many times to distract himself with one of the nurses, but he never seemed quite satisfied. For the most part, he did it to try and make himself be what was considered normal and to put a stop to the other soldiers sneering at him. *Boy lover. Lady Lennox.* But worst of all was the *Captain's Bitch.* Dominic seemed to be the only one who didn't know and that meant he was safe with him. If Dominic wanted a friend, he would play that part and play it well. They'd been friends since they were teenagers, after all.

There was a part of him deep down that hoped Dominic was like him. He never ran around wild with the nurses the way the other officers did. The only woman he'd ever seen him with was Rosalie and that was short lived. Plus, Dominic was more annoyed with Rosalie than friendly to her. That kept his hope alive. He couldn't be the only one who had such feelings.

Lennox breathed in deep and let out a heavy sigh. "What's your plan?"

"I need you to get a crew of ten soldiers to go undercover with us for reinforcements or rescue if need be. Satcha and I will go in alone and search for the scrolls while you keep an eye on things outside. Strictly covert."

"There's a lot of holes in that plan. Number one is the fact you are trusting the girl so much."

"I have a feeling about her."

Lennox narrowed his eyes. "What about our end of the

bargain? I told you; she wants passage to the Free City. Are we really going to hold up that part of the deal?"

"Let me handle that. You just handle getting the team ready."

Lennox set his jaw and didn't argue. There was no point, but for the first time ever, Dominic wasn't telling him the whole plan. It'd never been that way between them before. What about this nomad fascinated his Captain so much? He couldn't let him be blinded by the tricks of this woman. Not on his watch.

"Promise me you will have surveillance on the girl."

"You worry too much, but I'll see to it myself." Dominic smiled before returning to the papers on his desk. Lennox couldn't return the same aloof feeling.

Lennox rose from his seat and left the office without another word. He would plan this mission for his Captain, but he also had his own to attend to. He needed to watch this girl and find out more about her. Something told him he couldn't trust her. There was something about her he couldn't shake off. She wasn't familiar but there was an uneasiness in his stomach that screamed danger. For once, he couldn't trust Dominic to do his due diligence. This girl had her own plans and he needed to make sure the captain wouldn't be at the wrong end of her blade.

The damp tunnel offered no comfort or warmth as Lennox strode toward the medical wing, not able to let it sit. He wouldn't let any harm come to Dominic at the hands of this nomad. He needed to find out what the real reason was she was there and why she wanted to get to the Free City so badly.

"Lady Lennox, what a surprise!" Monroe matched step with him and wrapped an arm around his shoulders, which Lennox was quick to shrug off.

"Shouldn't you be off sucking the General's dick?" Lennox grumbled.

"I think you would know a lot more about that than me, *boy lover*."

Lennox clenched his fists at his sides, knowing what was coming. Corporal Green and Sergeant Walis stepped out from whatever depths of hell they'd slithered out of and blocked his path. They towed along with them a doe-eyed nurse he didn't recognize. She ducked her head, letting her chestnut hair cover her eyes.

"Lenny, have you met Jessa yet? She's a brand-new nurse all the way from the island of Allos. Not often we get a chance to have an offshore visitor from someone other than the Enforcers."

Lennox bit his lip. The two soldiers stood on either side of the nurse and she seemed to shrink under their height. He wasn't quite sure what they'd done to her, but he had an idea. He hoped he was wrong. So often nurses fell victim to abuse from not just soldiers but officers. It made his gut twist in knots. Some of the nurses seemed to like the attention, but Jessa didn't seem like part of that group. She was scared.

"Welcome to the Enross Army," he said between his teeth, but the nurse never looked up.

"We were showing her around, why don't you give her a proper welcome and take her to Sub Lake?" Monroe suggested while the two soldiers snickered. "Surely, you've got the time and willingness?"

There it was. The real evil behind this game with Monroe. He wanted Lennox to rape this young nurse as punishment. Bile filled his mouth and he fought to settle his stomach.

"I don't have time for this." He backed away and reached for his radio, but Monroe was too quick and swiped it off his uniform, leaving him no chance to call Dominic for help.

"Well, if you don't, I'm sure Green and Walis would be

happy to show her the lake," Monroe sneered and nodded to the two soldiers who grinned.

"Fine, I'll take her," Lennox said in a rush. He couldn't let those two monsters assault the poor girl. Jessa let out a cry and tears streamed down her cheeks, but she didn't look up.

"Great! Green, Walis, escort them down and see to it that Lenny gives her a proper tour. I've got to get back to work." Monroe smiled and clapped Lennox on the back. "Enjoy, Lenny Boy."

How am I going to get out of this? How can I get her *out of this?*

Monroe headed back up the tunnel while Green and Walis ushered Jessa through the path, Lennox following with heavy footsteps. Each step, his feet grew heavier than the last. They weaved through the passes as the tunnel became narrow and dark. There was only one reason people went to Sub Lake and that was to screw.

A thin fissure in the wall led through to an open space where the cavern housed a lake of crystal-clear water which supplied the army with its drinking and bath water.

"Climb on in and enjoy. We'll wait out here." Walis pointed to the crack in the wall.

Jessa's hands shook as she stepped through, seeming to just want to get it over with. Lennox wondered how the two soldiers managed to sneak her away from Ms. Alba. She would've been furious to know what they were up to. He believed she stayed as an army nurse just to try and protect the nurses under her watch, but her best wasn't enough sometimes.

"Here, take this." Green passed Lennox a flashlight and waited for him to follow the nurse.

Lennox took a deep breath before he slid through the fissure and into the cavern. The two soldiers stayed by the entrance, not moving away.

"Follow me," Lennox said to Jessa as he turned the light on but made no move to usher her along like the Green and Walis.

She let out another sob but followed him against whatever in her head told her not to. Even in the dark, he could see the fear in her face.

"I think we're far enough." Lennox sat down and leaned against a boulder. He brushed the back of his hand across his forehead.

Jessa stood in front of him shaking and began to unbutton her dress. Lennox threw his hands up and averted his gaze.

"No! You don't have to do that. I'm not going to touch you. I only brought you here so they wouldn't," Lennox said. "I'm... not like them."

Jessa fell to her knees in front of him. "Thank you," she sobbed in between her words.

"We can stay here for a little while and let them think what they want, but please know, this is not going to go unpunished. The captain is a good man and a friend of mine. He will not let this go."

She controlled her sobs and sat back against the boulder next to Lennox. "How can they do this? I came here to help my country, not be used like a dirty rag for the soldiers to play with."

"Unfortunately, the captain can't be everywhere, and neither can Ms. Alba, but that doesn't mean you aren't safe here."

"I haven't even met Ms. Alba yet. Those two told me they were bringing me to her, but they brought me to Lieutenant Monroe first—" She started crying again, not able to finish the sentence.

"I'm sorry for what he's done to you... There's some good people here, then there's Monroe and his little band of weasels."

"You sound like they haven't been the best to you either." She hiccupped.

"I told you. I'm not like them... They don't like that." Lennox didn't know what else to say. He'd never told anyone his true feelings. He hadn't come right out and said it, but it was the closest he'd ever come before. He couldn't imagine what it would be like to be Jessa.

Jessa hugged her knees close to her chest, careful to cover her legs with the skirt of her dress. She'd stopped crying, but her eyes were still puffy in the low light of the flashlight resting on the ground between them.

"How long do you think they will wait outside?" she asked.

"I think we can give it a few more minutes." Lennox sighed. "I'm Lieutenant Lennox, by the way."

"Jessa," she replied. "I don't usually meet people this way."

Lennox couldn't stop his laughter from escaping his chest. "I can honestly say the same. Once we're out of here I'll make sure you get to Ms. Alba safely."

"Thank you, Lennox." She smiled.

"I'm sorry you had to go through with that. I'll do what I can to make sure Captain Lightwood has the three of those idiots dealt with. That never should have happened. I'm sorry they did that to you."

"Oh, my Hawk! No! They didn't touch me. I thought they were going to, but they brought me to you instead. Monroe didn't touch me, neither did the other two."

Lennox breathed a sigh of relief. "Thank the Hawk."

"I've never been so scared before, I thought for sure *you* were the one who wanted me, that is, until we met up with you in the tunnel. They said such vile things about you..."

Lennox groaned; he could only imagine what they'd told her about him. None of it would've been good. No wonder she was terrified. He stood, brushing off his pants before he held his hand out to Jessa.

"Let's get you to Ms. Alba in the medical wing. She's a tough old woman and she will work you to the bone, but she is a good person who looks out for her nurses."

Jessa placed her hand in his and let him help her to her feet.

"Thank you, Lennox. If there's anything I can do to repay you, let me know."

Lennox couldn't help but grimace. "For the love of the Hawk... You don't need to repay me for not being a disgusting monster..."

"I guess you're right... That's so stupid of me. My mother would've slapped me if she ever heard me say such things."

"If you ever need any help at all, please come find me. I mean it." Lennox walked Jessa back to the fissure in the wall expecting Walis and Green to be waiting, but they'd already left.

"Thank you. I will remember that." She smiled as they made their way into the main tunnel.

"I would caution you not to wander alone. They may not have done anything this time, but I wouldn't put it past them next time."

"I don't think I want to explore these tunnels any more than I need to. I'll be working in the medical wing with the other nurses and try to make some friends."

Lennox nodded along, taking in her words. Making friends with other nurses could be a blessing or a curse depending on the nurse. Not to mention that wild girl spending time with Ms. Alba now that Dominic struck that deal with her.

"Promise me something." Lennox stopped and touched his hand to Jessa's elbow just as they reached the doorway to the medical wing.

Jessa watched him with those wide doe eyes and a slight smile in the corner of her lips, not like the flirtatious nurses he'd come face to face with, but the smile of a friend. Or someone he could see himself being friends with.

"Please be careful around the girl named Satcha. She's a nomad and we don't know much about her. I'm not sure she can be trusted," Lennox whispered.

"Okay, I'll be careful." She smiled again, looking rather confused, but didn't press it.

"Well, let's introduce you to Ms. Alba. I'm sure she has lots for you to do." Lennox forced a smile and hoped Jessa didn't come into other trouble—Monroe or Satcha, or otherwise.

CHAPTER 10

SATCHA

Three days passed, and with a full belly after every meal, Satcha gained a few pounds, giving her a healthier figure. Not that it was hard to look healthier than the skin and bones she had been. Her cheeks didn't seem as hollow and sunk in as they once had, and her face was flushed with a healthy pink.

The nurses, especially Ms. Alba, were surprised at how quick she'd bounced back and gave her chores to help with the other patients.

She wasn't fond of being given orders.

She made her way through the tasks as fast as she could to be done with them; she changed bed sheets and fed the injured soldiers who couldn't feed themselves. When she wasn't cleaning, she would venture through the tunnels for a walk, each time learning a new path, but never finding the exit from the underground army base. She'd made a small map on a piece of paper she'd hidden in her bag. Just in case there was a shift in their agreement, and she needed to escape.

Neither Captain Lightwood nor Lennox paid her any visits. She wondered if perhaps they'd forgotten all about her and their deal, but that was unlikely. Whatever scrolls the Nerosians had, they were needed desperately. Desperate enough to strike a deal with a stranger they'd pulled from the steps of death. At what cost would they go to get these scrolls? Satcha wasn't ready to lay down her life for the Enross Army —or anyone else for that matter. If it came to it, she would let them suffer the consequences of messing with the Nerosians and try to find another way across the ocean.

Satcha roamed about the tunnels, counting soldiers in her head and trying to keep track of their locations. No one paid any mind to her, not that they would've noticed as she took extra care not to stand out. She found her way into a large open space with thirty or forty soldiers going through training drills. Similar to the tunnels, wooden beams supported the ceiling, but it was lit with natural light. Satcha tilted her head back, looking for the source of sunlight. In the middle of the ceiling an open panel let in the rays of the sun and filled the cavern with a cool breeze.

Lennox screamed out orders and the soldiers responded like dogs, following his commands with great obedience as he made them face this way and that. A silly dance of sorts. She stayed in the background and out of sight but could feel the heat of someone's stare on her back. She scanned through the faces of the soldiers until she locked eyes with Captain Lightwood. He stood around a table with several soldiers looking over maps. The soldiers didn't seem to notice his focus was elsewhere. He didn't smile at her nor offer any means of a greeting, it was as if he was trying to read her mind from a glance. She couldn't hold his gaze any longer; she ducked her head down and started toward the medical unit.

"Well, you're looking better!" a familiar voice called to her, stopping her in her tracks.

Satcha turned to see the private who'd taken her to the medical unit when she first arrived. Young and eager. A child-like grin was plastered across his face and his short blond hair seemed too unkempt for a soldier, sticking out in every direction. He bounded over to her with his lanky arms and legs like a puppy still experiencing growing pains.

"Thanks." She looked back to see if Captain Lightwood watched her still, but he was gone.

"My name's Tom. Private Thomas Alderson."

She didn't look at him, instead searched for where the captain went, muttering, "Satcha."

"Nice to officially meet you, Satcha." Her attention swung back to him when he thrust his hand out to her, but she stepped back, glaring at him for his overt friendliness. He didn't seem to be offended by her, too naive to see she was annoyed by him.

"Private, back to your duties," Captain Lightwood cut in, stepping beside Satcha. She looked up at him, not realizing how tall he was before. He towered over her.

"Yes, Captain." Tom gave a clumsy salute and jogged off.

"You're distracting my soldiers," Captain Lightwood said, looking put out.

It almost brought a smile to her face, but she kept herself composed. "I think that one probably gets distracted at the smallest of things."

"We all have our strengths and weaknesses." Something in his voice made her look up at him, and when she did she was shocked to find his eyes scanning her face. She ducked her head, feeling as if the seams of the Enross uniform gave way and left her standing naked in front of him. She felt too exposed. His bright green eyes flecked with gold stared into hers, and like before, she felt like he was trying to read her mind. She didn't want him to tear down her walls. She wanted to keep her thoughts to herself.

She shifted back and forth on her feet and sweat pooled in the palms of her hands. She wiped them on her pants before she slid her hand into her pocket and covered the map, protecting it. He couldn't find out about her backup plan. They stood watching each other, as if waiting for the other to speak first and fill the void of silence. She didn't want to stand around any longer and headed toward the tunnel back to the medical wing.

She kept her eyes straight ahead, careful not to look back at him. She couldn't bear to fall victim to the trance his eyes put her in. She couldn't risk getting lost in the eyes of a stranger, let alone a soldier.

"What's in the Free City?" he asked, falling in step with her.

Who wouldn't want to go to the Free City? What a strange question. The Free City was a paradise. Outside the glittering city was a lush tropical jungle with plenty of fruit and warmth from the sun. Hadn't he heard the stories? Sure, the Nerosians were cruel to anyone outside of their lands, but within the Isle of Neroso, they were safe and peaceful. She couldn't control her confusion, she stopped and looked at his curious eyes, falling back under a spell. She found herself not being able to look away from him. Despite the dark green of his eyes they danced with light. Why did he find her amusing?

"I don't know yet." She'd only planned on how to get there; the rest of her plan was still to be written. She didn't know what the inner-city looked like, what the people were like outside of those uniforms. All she wanted was her revenge and to find peace. Kill the Masked Man and if she survived... Well, that was a mystery.

"You would risk your life to go to a place you know nothing about? A place where the enemy sleeps?" He looked amazed by her, as if she was a mythical being, but she was just Satcha. Lonely, wandering Satcha.

"You would risk your life in a *war* for people you don't even know?"

"It's an easy decision when you've seen the things I've seen."

"If you've seen the things *I've* seen, you might consider hiding and not storming an Enforcer compound." She stopped in her tracks, trying not to remember Agatha's limp body on the ground, covered in blood, but nothing could stop the images from flashing through her mind.

"That may be the case for you, but I've also seen things that would make the bravest of soldier's skin crawl," he said.

They stood in silence, lost in their own haunted memories. Satcha couldn't imagine he'd seen anything worse than she. Afterall, he had an army behind him. She had no one.

"When are you going to talk to me about the plans?" Satcha broke the silence, not able to stand it any longer. Three days and nothing. What had they expected her to do, other than offer free labor in the medical wing?

"The plans are being taken care of."

"I assumed you might want to include me on those plans, seeing how you expect me to help you find these scrolls. How am I supposed to trust you?"

"I think the better question is, how am I supposed to trust you?" he countered.

"You really should've thought that part through before you struck a deal with me." Satcha rolled her eyes, not caring if he saw her annoyance.

"Maybe so, but you will be on a need-to-know basis, even if it is only to appease my lieutenant's suspicions of you."

"That seems like a death sentence if I ever heard one."

"Well, it sounds like without us, you face the same, so if I was a betting man, I'd say your odds are better with us." He stood with his arms crossed his chest, staring at her, not shying away from the truth their upcoming mission would be danger-ous. But she'd known that long before he ever said the words.

"If you're going to keep me at an arm's length, I want to

work with your troops and train. You've taken my knife; how do you expect me to defend myself otherwise?"

"You want to train with the soldiers?" His green eyes lingered on her skinny arms and the lack of muscle.

She couldn't let him push her aside just because he wouldn't let her in on the plan. She stood her ground, jaw set. She watched him think through her request, her demand, and wondered how he'd gotten the scar on his face. A blade had carved that line down from his forehead and into his facial hair. For someone to get that close to him, she knew he'd seen terrible things too. She knew he'd fought to survive, just like her. The only thing that kept her alive without Agatha's experience was her wits and drive to survive. She imagined he must be the same.

"Yes." She straightened her shoulders trying to make herself seem bigger, but it only gave notice to the bones poking through her skin.

"I'll consider it and get back to you."

"Fine, but the clock is ticking." She turned away from him and headed to the medical wing.

"Satcha," he called.

She turned back to see him still standing there in the middle of the tunnel, his arms no longer crossed, but hanging at his side. Something about his face was different, his jaw flexed as if it fought the words his mind wanted to say.

"Try not to wander too far." He spun on his heels and walked away, his back ramrod straight. There was something about him that looked more like a captain than usual. She gulped and crossed her arms across her chest.

His disappearing figure made her wonder again about the scrolls. What did they mean for the army? She'd never chosen a side between Enross and Austerland—it hadn't seemed right for her to make a choice when she didn't know why they went to war in the first place. After the war and the continued cease fire, did anyone know? It was hard to even think about the Old War with the Nerosians taking over.

She could never side with the Nerosians, but she would hide and live among them to keep safe. Death-and-destruction was not a path she would take nor leave behind her. She'd done nothing but try to avoid them. A quiet, simple life was all she longed for. Before her and Agatha were captured, it was what they hoped for but never found.

If she stayed and helped the Enross Army, would the scrolls help bring down the Enforcers? She didn't think it was possible. The Enforcers were far too strong and powerful compared to the rebuilding armies of Enross and Austerland. She chewed her lip on the way back to the medical wing, playing out the scenario of staying and helping the army. She knew she could get into a compound. Getting out was the problem. And... Would helping them even get her to the Free City? Captain Lightwood must have some sort of pull to get her passage; he was an officer!

But what she didn't know was if she was ready to risk her life just for a chance at getting to the Free City. She had so much to think about.

"There you are, Satcha!" Ms. Alba called. "I expected you back a half hour ago—we need these sheets cleaned before more wounded come in!"

Satcha sighed. She almost wished she could break into the Nerosian compound now, just to avoid Ms. Alba's long to-do list. The other nurses seemed all too willing to add to her cleaning duties as well. She gathered the soiled linens and dragged them off to the laundry tub, going through the motions of what Ms. Alba expected of her.

CHAPTER 11

DOMINIC

It was one thing after another it seemed. Dominic leaned against his desk with his head in his hands, dreading having to convince Lennox to let Satcha train with the soldiers. He knew Lennox would undoubtedly cave and follow orders, but it wouldn't be without protest. He would hear about it for days, and the protest would probably continue after they completed their mission. He even imagined that if they should die, Lennox would find a way to defy the afterlife and make sure Dominic knew that he didn't approve.

There was a much bigger concern to be addressed than having to worry about Satcha and Lennox killing each other during the training sessions: Monroe, Green, and Walis harassing the nurses. Lennox had confirmed they hadn't touched the new nurse from Allos, but that didn't mean there weren't others they had already gotten to.

He couldn't help but feel he was wasting his time with the Enross Army when incidents like this came up. He never wanted anyone to have to experience a violation to their body, and he wanted to make sure it never happened again, but he kept getting distracted by the war. Guilt riddled him thinking thoughts like that, but there was a much bigger picture to see. One obstacle after the next, always something delaying him from making his move. He was nowhere closer to uniting the two kingdoms than he was when he'd discovered the whisperings of the lost royal bloodline.

It'd been years since he discovered the truth, and he hadn't been able to do a single thing about it. Word had come from Reeock that someone had broken into the archives in the lost city, Novo, and stolen scrolls of the Vardyian histories. He'd traveled to the southlands, all the way to Novo himself with Lennox before they joined the army.

He wasn't prepared for what they found there.

Stone buildings crumbled in mounds and not a living soul in sight. Flies buzzed through the decay as vultures and wild dogs tore through whatever flesh remained on the bones of the chroniclers who lived there. What little remained in terms of books and scrolls had been burned, but in the rubble he managed to find the mention of the Blood Scrolls. It took him months to piece together what the Blood Scrolls even were thanks to his research in Reeock, but he still was no closer to finding out what had happened to the royal bloodline, and that scared him most of all.

It haunted him. What if he was on a wild goose chase and there was no longer a royal bloodline? What if the bloodline truly ended with the Princess of Enross and the Prince of Austerland? Then all this searching was for nothing and there was no other way to unite the two kingdoms against the Nerosians. The Enforcers would continue to make their way through the continent destroying everything in their path and then his uncle would win.

It had been so long since he'd given his uncle so much thought and years since he'd seen him. Fourteen years since he'd carved the line down his face before turning the blade on himself. Out of spite, just to make sure he would never forget.

It was hard in those first five years. He never gave the real answer when people would ask him how he got his scar. He couldn't reveal himself and he couldn't admit to anyone the great shame behind being Lord Gideon Ursid's nephew.

The Masked Man.

Shaped like the head of a black bear, Gideon had taken to the mask not long after Dominic had escaped. It surprised him more than anything, the whispers from across the Westim Ocean about the Masked Man. For a time, Dominic wanted to believe Gideon had been killed and someone else had taken over, but he knew it had to be his uncle. Gideon would've never disappeared or died that quietly. It was almost ironic Gideon would give himself the same scar but then hide it behind a mask. It left Dominic with the shame of seeing his own reflection. He never looked into mirrors anymore and avoided the opportunity to see his face. Despite his captaincy, he kept his facial hair long enough to cover the skin of his face but trimmed enough to follow protocol.

He was due for a trim soon. Had General Ballard been at the base, he would've shaved it clean every day, but he used his absence as an excuse to go a few days longer without having to see the reminder.

As much as he could've sat and sulked, he couldn't put off speaking with Ms. Alba anymore. He needed to let her know what happened with the Allos nurse and to be on the lookout for any of the soldiers getting too familiar.

Soldiers saluted him as he walked through the tunnels; normally he would've saluted back, but he only nodded in acknowledgement. Too much weighed on his mind.

He made it to the medical wing, but almost lost his nerve when he saw Satcha changing the bed linens. He'd nearly forgotten the nomad would be there. It made him realize how many things in the base could be dangerous for the nurses.

She caught his gaze and raised an eyebrow at him, but he

ignored her and made his way to Ms. Alba's desk where she went through paperwork.

"Ah, Captain! Perfect timing. We're running low on inventory." She huffed. Her glasses rested on the tip of her nose as she peered at him. This was a common complaint from her. There weren't many rations or medical supplies, and too many mouths to feed and wounds to mend.

"If you can prioritize a list, I'm sure we can have someone sent to Reeock to gather some things."

"I wished you'd have a different answer each time I asked," she grumbled.

"I do too, but it's all we have to work with." He grimaced, shifting back and forth, and surveying the nurses around them.

"Is there something troubling you, Captain?" Ms. Alba lowered her voice and pushed her glasses back up her nose.

"I was wondering if we could discuss something in private. There's been some concerns with some of the nurses."

"I see." Ms. Alba gathered her paperwork in her hands and pushed away from her desk. "Why don't we go to the storage room and speak further while I continue my inventory checks."

Several of the nurses watched them with fascination. "Back to work ladies, those linens will not change themselves," Ms. Alba barked.

In the corner of his eye, Dominic saw Satcha among those watching. He knew before he left the medical wing she would try to speak with him again. Whether it was about training or the Blood Scrolls, he didn't know.

Ms. Alba held open the door to the small storage room. Dominic couldn't help but notice the sparse fillings of the metal shelves. He'd never seen it full, but he'd also never seen their medical supplies so low before. His only hope was that when the General returned, he'd brought more with him from his travels in Reeock.

"Now Captain, what do I owe this pleasure?" Ms. Alba didn't look at him, keeping her focus on counting out bagged metal tools he had no idea the names of.

"I have been told that some soldiers have been attempting to sneak off with nurses to Sub Lake," he said. He didn't know how to put it delicately but wasn't willing to avoid the topic in General. But Ms. Alba didn't like that; she'd rather him just come right out and say it.

She stopped and raised a gray eyebrow at him.

He sighed.

"Lennox caught Monroe, Green, and Walis trying to take advantage of the new nurse from Allos and bring her to Sub Lake. Thankfully Lennox was there and... the nurse was not... compromised."

"Why was this not brought to my attention immediately?" Ms. Alba asked, an edge of anger in her voice. He couldn't blame her.

"That is my fault, completely," he admitted. "I wanted to be sure nothing happened, and also be sure that what Lennox told me was the truth."

"You doubt Lieutenant Lennox?"

"No... Of course not. I doubt whether or not the nurse herself lied to protect them." He was not enjoying any part of this conversation. "I can't exactly take it higher—to the General—without the facts." He paused. "And you know as well as I the General is too familiar with the nurses as it is."

Ms. Alba scoffed and went back to counting; this time the box was filled with a variety of scalpels packed in clear plastic bags. "What I wouldn't give to stick one of these in his throat."

"Mind who you say that to. I might not be a fan of the General, but he is still my superior," Dominic cautioned. He looked back at the closed door and worried if someone could've been listening on the other side. He wouldn't risk losing Ms. Alba as an ally if the wrong person had heard her.

"You have much more restraint than me. I can't lie and say that my hand may just slip one day."

"Then another would fill his shoes and take on his role and probably do the same. It doesn't make it right, but it's an unfortunate reality."

"Not if you were to take over."

"I can't start a mutiny, not with how volatile things are. We're short on well-trained men, supplies, and leadership. It would be a disaster." He'd been through this with her many times before. There was no easy path. He didn't want any more responsibility in the army, it took away from his real mission. He was comfortable with his current rank as it gave him enough leeway to slip away to his own devices. The higher his rank, the more eyes on him. "Keep an eye out. If you notice anything odd, please let me know at once, and I will do my best to protect them."

"A time will come when you are forced to make a decision, Dominic." Her voice softened, becoming almost maternal. She'd on rare occasions called him by his name instead of his rank and each time it was about the same thing: his role in the army. "Mark my words, the longer you wait, the more damage will be done. I fear for your life as well as my nurses. Lieutenant Monroe will weasel his way around you, and the General will not be kind to your *cause*."

"How're things working with Satcha? She's been here a few days now and you seem to be keeping her busy." He couldn't help but change the subject. They would go round and round otherwise. They both knew that.

"She's got a bit of an attitude and she scares some of the other girls, but she's proved herself to be capable."

"Could you spare her for a few hours each morning? She's

asked for some training... I was hoping Lennox would work with her, but after the last time they interacted, I can't imagine both of them making it out alive."

"Yes, but I need her back after breakfast to help move patients and clean. I hope you know what you are doing with her." Her face grew grave. Her lips were unsmiling, not that it was out of the ordinary, but he could tell there were words she wasn't saying. Words Lennox would say enough for them both.

"I'll be careful." He nodded to her and left, striding out of the medical wing before anyone could stop him.

He needed air before jumping into yet another task. It'd been over a day since he'd been outside. He needed to stretch his legs and get his thoughts together. Tomorrow he would train Satcha against all the warnings he'd been given. She was the last shred of hope he had of getting the Blood Scrolls. He was willing to take the risk.

CHAPTER 12

SATCHA

S atcha couldn't sleep. She lay on her back staring at the rock ceiling and held out her hand, pretending to twirl her knife over the side of the bed. She wished she could feel the cold steel of the hilt in her hand. She wondered if she would ever see it again.

She tossed and turned, but her mind raced thinking about the scrolls. What were the Blood Scrolls and why did the Enross Army want them so bad? She played through different scenarios, but they all ended with her getting captured and killed by the Enforcers. Had she made a bad deal? Captain Lightwood had ignored her back in the medical wing; maybe he regretted making the deal.

An overwhelming dread loomed over her—she couldn't stay here any longer. She would rather die out on her own than in an Enforcer compound.

Soldiers snored on either side of her, sleeping peacefully. She needed peace and quiet. She needed to breathe fresh air.

She swung her feet to the floor and pulled on her boots, grabbing her bag from under the bed. The snoring soldiers were the only ones making any noise. She carefully stepped around the beds and made her way to the exit.

She knew the guards would stop her, there was nowhere to hide or slip through without being detected, but the guards were not at their regular posts. Strange, she'd never seen it unguarded before. Everything was unusually quiet, only the sound of her breathing filled her ears. She crouched, crawling behind wooden crates at the end of the tunnel. She peered around them to see the open area empty with no soldiers guarding any of the other tunnel entrances.

She didn't need to look at her map. Of the three tunnels she faced, there was only one she hadn't taken yet. She was sure the path on the left would lead outside. She wasn't sure if she would make it to the end undetected, but she was determined to try. Quiet as a mouse, she slipped around the crate and hugged the wall. She stood in the opening of the tunnel, but there was no light past the third torch. She tried to piece together her memory from a week ago when the captain had escorted her through the entrance.

Creeping along the tunnel, she stayed on the lookout for guards, but nowhere did she see the dark blue uniformed men. She wondered where they'd all gone. There couldn't have been any danger; the medical unit still slept. If there was any attack, they would've been busy with the injured. A breeze drifted across her cheek and cool air filled her lungs as she traveled further through the tunnel. This was the exit.

Crawling ivy hung over the walkway, she peeked through the leaves looking for any guards or signs of danger, but there were none. She didn't let down her guard,

Something was wrong. As much as she wanted to run out of the cave, she couldn't. It seemed too perfect the guards were off somewhere else. She was sure this was a trap... but she still had to try.

The sky was dark. Clouds covered the moon and shielded

any light from revealing her standing out in the open. She took a few steps toward the trees, longing to slip away into the night and not return, but she couldn't help but look back at the tunnel.

They'd kept their word and kept her safe and fed her well. Sure, she had to keep her end of the bargain, but who knew how long she could keep this up? What if she failed to get the scrolls and this was her only chance at truly getting to the Free City? She went back and forth in her head to leave or to stay. If she got them the scrolls she would have their help getting to the Free City, but who was to say Lennox wouldn't dump her off a cliff and tell Captain Lightwood she'd safely arrived?

"I was wondering if you'd try to escape."

Satcha gasped and turned to see Captain Lightwood leaning against a boulder by the cover of the ivy. He stood alone, as if he were waiting for her. Maybe he was, it seemed as good of a trap as any. Leave the door open and let her reveal herself.

"You set me up." Satcha clenched her fists at her side.

"I had to see if I could trust you." He closed the space between them. He stood a foot away and in the dark of night, his eyes still gleamed.

"I needed air." She ducked her head, avoiding his gaze. "One can only hide underground for so long."

"I'll pretend to go along with that theory."

"What's so important about these scrolls anyways?" She couldn't take the secrets anymore. If her life was at risk, she needed to know what she fought for. He studied her face, but she wasn't going to yield.

"How much do you know about the Old War?"

"Austerland and Enross fought against each other." She groaned. "What does the Old War matter?"

He sighed. "There's obviously a lot more to the story than that."

"I haven't had a lot of time to brush up on my war history," she said sarcastically.

"The countries Enross and Austerland have been fighting long before the Old War, for hundreds of years. The Old War was never supposed to happen. The King of Austerland and the King of Enross decided to call a truce and unite the two kingdoms under one rule. The Prince of Austerland would marry the Princess of Enross and bring the two countries together in harmony."

Satcha scoffed. "That worked out well, didn't it?"

"Well, for many it did, but after the two married, the prince was assassinated, and the princess went into hiding never to be seen again."

"Was it the Nerosians?"

"We'd like to believe so—at very least it was the start of when their voyages across the Westim Ocean began. For all we know, it could've been rebels from either country that killed the prince. Unfortunately, no one knows for certain."

"So, what's the point of getting these scrolls? Both royal families are long dead."

"It's believed the princess was pregnant and the royal line from both countries lived on. The Blood Scrolls are proof of the lineage. Finding them could bring the two countries together to fight off the Nerosians. For good. It will help everyone in Vardya."

"Such a loyal soldier." Satcha laughed and Dominic eyed her suspiciously.

"Why do you want to run away so badly, to a place you've only heard rumors of? What's so bad about calling Vardya home?"

She'd never been asked that before. What *was* wrong with calling Vardya home? The easiest answer, or maybe it was an excuse, was that she'd never even known a home. The farthest memory back she had was Agatha pulling her out of the river, with blood running down the side of her head. She was only a child. If it wasn't for Agatha, she would've had no one to teach her how to protect or care for herself. Sometimes she wondered if her parents weren't too fond of having a child and threw her in the river, left for dead.

But she survived.

She couldn't remember faces, didn't recognize anyone, or any place she'd ever been. She only had Agatha, a grumpy old woman who had been on her own for decades.

"It's never been a home to me. I've never stayed in any one place for too long. The people here are weak and helpless. I've made myself strong; it's the only way I've been able to survive this long."

"That's the kind of thinking the Nerosians have," Captain Lightwood scolded. "Just because I'm a soldier doesn't mean I want there to be war. This could end it once and for all."

"You honestly expect two countries who've hated each other for as long as time itself to come together with this unknown heir, *if* one exists, and beat the big bad Nerosians? The ones who may have killed the prince thought to unite them? Good story, did your parents have the wet nurse read it to you every night?"

"Some of us still have something to believe in; not a fantasy, but true belief." He narrowed his eyes at her. "My father was never in the picture and my mother died when I was young, just so you know. I have also had to find ways to survive."

"Oh." There was nothing for Satcha to say; she knew she crossed a line. She knew what it was like to not have a family. He was like her, an orphan. And he was right—she didn't believe in anything except a safe sanctuary far away from here that she had never seen with her own eyes. The wind gained momentum, sending a chill down her spine.

"I suggest you get back to the medical unit and get some sleep. Tomorrow will be a big day."

"Why?"

"Tomorrow, you start training with me," he said, keeping his eyes on the woods, his back to her.

Satcha didn't say a word. She'd never expected him to let her train, let alone train her himself. She looked wistfully into the woods, wondering if she should have made her escape, but turned and made her way back down the tunnel. As she climbed into bed, Satcha vowed to help him get the Blood Scrolls and fulfill his weird royalty obsessed dream. Just as long as he helped her fulfill her dream of the Free City.

CHAPTER 13

DOMINIC

Dominic watched Satcha descend into the tunnels. He wasn't sure what to think of her, but he knew there was something different about her. She wasn't like the other women he'd known. Most of them were nurses for the army, slinking off to dead end routes of the tunnels with soldiers—willingly, of course. Not like what happened with Jessa.

Satcha wasn't like the women he knew back in his adoptive home, Rios, either. She took care of herself and trusted no one. He was used to being able to tell what the women around him wanted. Marriage. A means for children. A provider. But he had more important things to concern himself with than finding a wife. He didn't understand how the men and women all around him were ready to commit to one another in the middle of a war. Nobody knew what could happen— here today and gone the next, but he guessed that was the point. To have someone to share what little in the world there was to be happy about.

He thought of Rosalie back in Rios. She wasn't unlike Satcha in appearance, but instead of smooth blonde hair,

Rosalie's was so wavy it was almost bushy. She was beautiful, but he couldn't give her what she wanted. He'd felt bad for her and hoped she would find someone to be the rock she needed, but it wasn't him. He didn't like the way she'd looked at him with hurt eyes. He'd told her time and time again they couldn't be together. Nothing could get in his way of his mission. He needed to stop his uncle and the Enforcers if it was the last thing he did.

Why did Satcha want to go to the Free City? Surely, she couldn't have known what awaited her there if she ever got across the Westim Ocean. He needed the Blood Scrolls, even if it meant lying about getting her there.

He leaned back against the stone wall scolding himself for feeling guilty. He couldn't let the feelings of one affect the lives of many. This was far bigger than Satcha could ever imagine. The continent of Vardya and all its people were at risk. If he couldn't unite the people of Enross and Austerland, then there was no hope left.

He'd tried many times to contact the Austerland Army behind the General's back, but there was never a response. He'd sent letters in secret to try and form an alliance, knowing if he'd been caught, he was good as dead. He'd tried to make small hints to the General and the other officers to reach out and call a truce with Austerland, but no one would consider it. The only option left was to find the heir of Vardya and unite the two countries' capitals, Reeock and Hortus. Only then, maybe people would listen. Maybe people would band together and join arms. He knew it was a long shot, but he couldn't risk not putting in every effort. After all, it might have been partly his fault his uncle caused so much destruction. What would've happened had he stayed in the Free City and attacked his uncle from within the city walls? It was a question that kept him up at night.

Dominic rolled his shoulders and stretched his arms out

behind him. He didn't think Satcha would make another escape attempt, not after catching her. She was too smart to try anything again. He whistled out into the trees and three soldiers revealed themselves from their hiding spots.

"Keep an eye out for any movement. If she tries anything again, call me immediately," Dominic ordered.

"Yes, sir," the three responded in unison.

Dominic took one last look at the dark sky before heading down the tunnels once again. He hated hiding underground. He missed the open air of Rios. The sound of the river in the night running around the bend. He often went for long hikes and explored along the riverside to a great waterfall. The sound of the water crashing into the river from above drowned out the constant voice in his head blaming him for not doing enough. For not helping more people. How many lives could he have saved had he done something sooner? He didn't want to know the number.

He ignored the soldiers saluting as he passed and made his way to the war room. He needed to find Lennox and plan for the invasion of the Enforcer Headquarters. He needed to consult with his team before anything was set in stone. He didn't know if he could trust Satcha with any of the information. He opened the door to the war room to ten soldiers seated around a long conference table, waiting for him.

"I told you she would try to escape." Lennox leaned back in his chair and put his boots on the table.

"I have it handled."

"I'm not going to sit by while that rogue wanders around these tunnels with her little piece of paper making a map any longer. We need to get rid of her."

Dominic didn't say anything. He'd also seen Satcha scratching out a layout of the tunnels. And he'd also seen her in action, fending off the Night Raiders and attacking Lennox, but something told him to hold off. He believed if she wanted him dead, he would've died the night he brought her to the base when they walked back alone. She was a survivor of the Enforcers. As far as he knew, before Satcha, he'd only known himself as the only person to have ever escaped their grasp. It wasn't easy. The lashings on her back showed the true evil behind their forces; they only took what they wanted and destroyed the rest. He fought the urge to touch the prickling scar on his face.

"If she can get us into the headquarters, we can steal some intel and maybe take out the tower."

Lennox laughed. "Is that what you tell yourself we are doing?"

Dominic narrowed his eyes. Lennox saw right through him; he knew what he wanted to do. Lennox had tried to talk him out of this many times before and mind his rank in the army. He didn't dare look around at the soldiers watching him and Lennox argue. He'd let Lennox have too much leeway and couldn't let him disrespect his authority any longer.

"Enough, Lieutenant. You are all under orders to complete this mission. I only need you to set up a perimeter. I will be going in alone with Satcha."

"Dominic, no—"

"Lieutenant, if I have to tell you one more time, you will be reassigned. Got it?" He hated having to discipline his friend, but he had no other choice. The General would be back soon from his travels, he had to act now. He didn't know if there would be another chance.

Lennox didn't say a word, his mouth clenched shut and a muscle twitching in his jaw. The other soldiers sitting around the table looked uncomfortable, their heads down and eyes avoiding Dominic's. Most of them knew Dominic and Lennox had signed up together, but only some could tell that Lennox was jealous of Dominic's expedited climb up the ladder of command. Dominic hated to remember it, since they were such good friends, but Lennox was only a lieutenant because Dominic had taken him under his wing back when he had been acting out. He'd never followed orders, made several childish outbursts, and had even stolen whiskey from the General. If it wasn't for Dominic cleaning up after him, Lennox would have been reprimanded long ago. If it wasn't for the fact he was a good soldier on the battlefield—not to mention a close friend and ally—Dominic would have sent him packing long ago.

Dominic turned to face the other soldiers. "I want two teams to recon on the west and east sides of the building. Get me a patrol log and be back within two days. We're running out of time." They made no fuss like Lennox.

"Yes, sir!" the soldiers chorused. Lennox scowled at them.

"May the Hawk watch over us," Lennox muttered under his breath. Dominic held in a sigh, knowing Lennox was trying to bait him further into an argument. Lennox didn't care about the sigil of Enross. The hawk had been long worshiped like a God of Enross—just like the elk in Auster-land. Dominic didn't believe in gods—he couldn't help but think of the Sun Bears and how far his uncle would go to protect them—but he could admit it was a nice thought to believe in something bigger than themselves. Had there been any way to confine and care for a hawk, he couldn't imagine wiping out an entire population for a hawk, let alone a Sun Bear.

Dominic ignored Lennox's prodding; he needed to rest. He turned on his heel and left Lennox to his muttering.

Ten minutes later he lay in his small cot staring at the wall while he waited for sleep to take him. He couldn't trust Satcha with Lennox so the best-case scenario would be to set the perimeter and then sneak inside the headquarters with her. Just the two of them. He couldn't risk the rest of the team for a mission he didn't have approval on.

He played through all the scenarios in his head of what could happen, but he was sure there would be no planning for what was to come. For good or for bad. He closed his eyes and twenty minutes later, a knock came to his door. Another long day ahead after a sleepless night.

CHAPTER 14

LENNOX

L ennox stared out across a sea of soldiers getting their fill of morning rations. Mealtimes were his least favorite time of the day. It meant suffering through the snide remarks and occasional elbow to the gut. Once, Monroe had stuck his foot out to trip him. There was nothing he could do to stop any of it. They never backed off. He'd thought about going to Dominic, but in the end, it would only make things worse.

Captain's Bitch running off to cry. Monroe and his morons would have a field day.

He debated skipping breakfast and leaving his tray of dry overcooked eggs and burnt toast on the table, but what little they had were to hold him over to lunch and then dinner. His stomach growled, a reminder that food was not to be wasted. It was all he would get.

"Mind if I join you?" Jessa stood next to him with a kind smile, holding her own tray.

"You don't want to sit with the nurses?"

"It's only been a few days but working, living, and eating

together is getting under my skin a bit," she said through a laugh.

He breathed a sigh of relief and followed her to an empty table, very aware of Monroe watching him from across the mess hall with a cruel grin. At least in the mess hall with Jessa and plenty of witnesses, it was less likely Monroe would bother him. Less likely, but not unlikely.

Lennox slid into the seat across from Jessa, careful not to have his back to Monroe and his group of morons.

"How're things going in the medical wing?" Lennox asked as he pushed his eggs around on the tray. He might've been hungry, but he still had to work up to putting the pale-yellow mush into his mouth.

"Good, I think." She shrugged. "Ms. Alba is certainly a work horse and expects everyone to keep up."

"That she is. You'll get used to her routines soon enough."

"I hope so. There's a lot of focus on the other girl, Satcha."

Lennox's ears perked up.

"What do you mean?" He leaned forward, keen to know what the little nomad scum was up to.

"She's kind of odd. She scares the other nurses." Jessa took a small bite of eggs and from the look on her face, it took everything she had in her to swallow it.

"They are scared of her?"

"Well—she's just so intense. That wild look about her, you know? She's constantly watching everyone as if she's expecting to be attacked at any moment."

Lennox nodded along, pulling back the peak of his interest. He'd seen firsthand that others were weary of Satcha. They had good reason to be; he'd seen her skills with a knife. Plus, he couldn't ignore the fact she wanted to get to Neroso. He couldn't fathom why someone would ever want to go there. The Nerosians only brought death and destruction.

"I kind of feel bad for her. It makes me grateful for what I had growing up. No matter how little we had, it was still more than that poor girl." Jessa's eyes flickered to the soldiers and nurses waiting to get their morning rations, Satcha standing in the middle of the long line, anxiously shifting back and forth, waiting to be served.

"What part of Enross are you from, Lennox?" Jessa asked, pulling his gaze from Satcha.

"Northern. Not far from the Village of Velha," he lied. No one knew that he and Dominic came from Rios and they would keep it that way. The only way the village stayed safe for so long was the secrecy of its existence and whereabouts. It was the one rule everyone had to follow at all costs if they ever left the village.

"Hmm... I can't quite picture you as a fisherman," she said, laughing.

"Maybe that's the reason I left," he said. He found himself smiling at her; he barely knew her, but he liked her company.

"Left or asked to leave?"

"It was probably a bit of both." Lennox laughed, realizing at the same time he lived such a tense life. It was nice not to have to hide his feelings around Dominic or be scrutinized by Monroe and his morons. He couldn't remember the last time he'd relaxed.

But then he caught sight of Monroe watching him and his happiness slipped away.

"I'm not sure I like him either." Jessa nodded her head to Monroe but didn't look at him.

"He's not someone I would go out of my way for." Lennox didn't want to make a big thing about it. There were too many ears around—anything he said could make its way back to Monroe.

"The captain seems like a nice man. Whenever we pass each other in the tunnels, he smiles and asks how I was doing. He's been in the medical wing the last few days with Satcha...

I'm not sure what they do together, but she's always tired and in a worse mood after he leaves."

"As far as Satcha goes, I don't trust her. The captain is too trusting for his own good." Lennox scooped the last bit of eggs into his mouth and swallowed it as fast as he could without the taste resting on his tongue. "Just be careful around her."

"I'm sure she's not all that bad," Jessa said.

"Let me know if she, or anyone else, bothers you." Lennox stuffed the dry toast in his mouth while gathering his garbage on the tray. He barely was able to muffle out, *I'll see you later* with the toast hanging out of his mouth. She laughed and waved to him as she collected her own things and headed off to the medical wing.

Lennox had to find and check in on Dominic. It'd been a few days since they really talked more than a few words.

Luckily for him, Dominic came his way. Or so he thought.

Dominic walked past him without a single glance. It was as if everything was in slow motion. Lennox turned back to see Dominic taking a seat next to Satcha, who even offered him a slight smile.

It wasn't the unappetizing eggs that stirred in his belly. The pit in his stomach was a black hole, ready to eat him up from the inside out. He didn't want to see them together, but couldn't look away either. All the fears that haunted his dreams were coming true. The fact that Dominic might like someone and that someone wasn't him.

Why does it have to be her?

It could've been a nurse. It could've been Jessa for all he cared. The only thing that would've made the situation worse was if Dominic had found another man to call his own.

He stood there like stone watching them chatting, not able to hear their words, but able to see the crooked smile on Dominic's face.

"Looks like you have some competition, Lenny," Monroe

sneered as he leaned against the table next to Lennox. "The captain isn't interested in you and your *kind*."

Lennox couldn't hold back. Without warning, he swung his right fist back and struck Monroe's nose. Not once. Not twice. He didn't know how many times his fist collided. Monroe fell back on the table and Lennox pinned him down, not stopping his assault. Sometimes he hit him, sometimes his knuckles met the wood of the table. He wasn't sure if the sound of cracking bones were his hands or Monroe's nose before the shouting got so loud he couldn't hear. All he could see was red.

"Lennox! Enough!" Dominic gripped his shoulders and tore him away from Monroe, who was sputtering blood from his mouth, only half-aware of what happened.

Lennox wasn't done yet. He threw one final punch without meaning to. His brain couldn't stop his fist before it connected with Dominic's jaw. The moment the two connected, the red washed away from his eyes, and he saw what he'd done.

Dominic stumbled back, shocked. Before he could say anything, apologize or grovel, the butt of a gun whipped across Lennox's face. Everything went black.

Chapter 15

Satcha

Satcha didn't care to stick around and watch the soldiers fight in the mess hall; she knew there would be plenty of work to do in the medical wing with all the blood spilled. She wasn't sure what provoked Lennox into a rage, but whatever it was, she found it ironic that they couldn't trust *her*, yet someone like Lennox held power within the army.

How in the world can the captain trust him?

She thought the two of them were friends, but didn't know how they still could be after this.

"Satcha, there you are." Ms. Alba sighed, holding a radio in her hand, followed by two of her little minion nurses and the new nurse, Jessa. Wherever Ms. Alba went, her little minions were right there, sucking up. They'd stayed away from her but kept a keen watch on her and were the first to report any mistakes she'd made in her work. "There was a fight in the mess fall, help Jessa get some clean beds made and stay away from Lieutenant Lennox."

"Won't be a problem," she said, fighting hard not to roll her eyes. She didn't want to be anywhere near him if she could help it. She'd enjoyed the past couple days without his hateful eyes following her every step.

Ms. Alba gave her a curt nod, more of a warning than anything. She knew that Ms. Alba reported to Captain Lightwood, but she had nothing to hide—other than her little map, but she wasn't about to make another escape attempt. Not after he'd caught her outside the tunnels. He hadn't even mentioned it in their training sessions.

"Hi, Satcha!" Jessa smiled, but it didn't match her eyes. Satcha nodded to her as she began changing sheets.

Two stretchers were carried into the medical wing, one carrying Lennox and the other carrying another lieutenant she didn't know. Dominic followed the stretchers, his right eye swollen and started to bruise already. Jessa gasped at the sight.

Despite being given orders by Ms. Alba, Jessa rushed to Lennox's side and helped the soldiers get him off the stretcher and into a bed. Satcha rolled her eyes and kept her head down at the task at hand. She wasn't any good at making the beds to Ms. Alba's critical eye. She didn't know why they had to be tucked in so tightly if bloodied men were just going to mess them up again.

"Need some help?"

Dominic stood next to her. He looked frustrated and distracted. He started tucking in the corners without a response.

"I think you're the one who needs help." She nodded to his bruised eye. "That's some lieutenant you have there."

"He's not normally like this," he snapped, eyes dark and his fists clenched the sheets.

Satcha didn't know what to say to him. She wasn't good at this kind of stuff, comforting people, or even being around others in general. There'd never been time for a heart-to-heart with Agatha—they'd always been doing what they could to survive, to make it through another day. She turned away from him and headed for the next bed.

"I'm sorry," Captain Lightwood said. "I'm dealing with a lot right now."

"Why do you try so hard?" she asked. "It's not as if everyone else is breaking their backs around here."

"Maybe that's why I do it."

Satcha chewed her lip, thinking the army didn't deserve him—or rather, Vardya didn't. "I'll get you some ice for your eye."

"It's fine," he huffed. "I'm fine."

"Don't worry, Captain, I'm not trying to coddle you. It's strictly for my own benefit." She smiled at him—or tried to, anyway. It could have also been a grimace. "We have training this afternoon and I want you at your best. It doesn't feel like a win if you can't see me coming."

Dominic laughed with a rare smile that Satcha couldn't not smile back at. "Fine."

Satcha strode across the room weaving her way past the hustling nurses tending to Lennox and the other soldier. She caught sight of Ms. Alba watching her from the corner of her eye, but the old nurse made no effort to stop her as she headed back to Dominic.

Satcha handed him ice wrapped in a towel and a damp cloth to wipe his brow. He took them with a smile.

"What?" she asked.

He chuckled. "Maybe you're not as suited to work in the medical wing as we'd hoped." He sat on the bed they'd just made and pressed the ice pack on his cheek.

Satcha narrowed her eyes at the comment. The other nurses tended to their patients on their own rather than giving them bandages to do it themselves, which is what she usually did. They'd got themselves into the mess, they could heal their own wounds as far as she was concerned. But the other nurses just looked... natural.

"If you can't take care of yourself, you'd never make it outside of this place." She sat next to him and stretched her legs out, feeling the pull of her aching muscles from training.

"That's why I don't think you are suited to be a nurse. You'd be a far better soldier."

She scoffed. "Don't think I'm here to sign up after we finish the job. I've got my own plans in mind."

"The Free City," he stated. "What do you think is waiting for you there?"

She chewed her lip not knowing what to say to him. How does one admit to wanting to hide amongst the enemy while others die at the hands of their forces?

"You steal from the Nerosians, so you seem to have no interest in joining them, and you don't approve of their takeover. Why do you want to live amongst them?" he challenged her.

"I never said I wanted to live with them, Captain Lightwood."

"So, it's revenge then." He nodded, thinking he'd figured her out. "They killed someone you loved."

"Not so much love, but owed a great deal to," she muttered. She stood up abruptly. "I have to get back to Ms. Alba. Will you be ready for this afternoon?"

"I'll be there." He nodded, the smile from earlier long gone from his face. The strict soldier who carried Vardya on his shoulders sat in front of her.

She could feel his eyes on her back as she walked away. She wasn't sure why she'd shared so much with him or why he was even curious. Hearing her own words out loud only reaffirmed her drive to get the job done. She'd help him find the Blood Scrolls, then it was his turn to help her avenge Agatha. She didn't know if she would make it out alive once she took down the Masked Man, but she didn't care one way or the other.

CHAPTER 16

LENNOX

L ennox woke with a dull ache in his head. He squinted his eyes at the bright light. The hum of fluorescent lighting rang in his ears, as if to shake his brain awake. He could tell from the noises around him that he was in the medical wing. Everything came back to him in a flash. Satcha and Dominic. Monroe. The fight. He rubbed his forehead with the back on his hand, feeling the ache throb under the pressure. Dom always told him he had a hard head; the gun he was hit with was harder.

"Fuck," he groaned under his breath. He'd hit Dominic. He knew he fucked up, knew it was bad, and he wasn't sure how he could fix things—if he even could.

"Lennox! Thank the hawk!" Jessa rushed to his side and began fussing at the bandages over his eye.

"How long was I out?" He pushed himself up and rolled his shoulders back. His entire body was stiff.

"About ten hours. It's nearly six in the evening."

"Shit. Where's Dominic?" he asked, trying to get off the bed, but Jessa placed a hand on his chest to stop him.

"Hang on! You have a concussion, you should rest!" She

wasn't strong enough to stop him, though, and he stepped around her, fighting the dizziness in his head.

"I'm fine. I need to find Dominic, now." A clean uniform and boots sat at the foot of the bed, and he slipped the pants and boots on under his hospital gown.

"I know I don't know you that well, but you're someone I would like to call a friend. I'm worried by what happened today."

Lennox stopped buttoning up his shirt to look at her. Her eyes were full of concern, which took him by surprise. No one looked at him like that. He'd grown used to always running after Dom and voicing his concerns to him, but not once had Dominic stopped to worry about him. That didn't mean they weren't friends, but it made him suspicious their friendship meant more to him than Dom.

"I appreciate your concern, I do. But I need to work this out with him." Lennox tried to come across as sincere as possible, but it sounded a little too harsh. It would be another conversation to make up for later, but he had other things to worry about. "I'll come back afterward, and you can check my head again, if it'll make you feel better about me leaving."

Jessa tilted her head, debating. "Fine. Make sure Ms. Alba doesn't find out I let you out."

"Thank you," he said, patting her shoulder as he passed.

Lennox strode out of the medical unit and beelined to Dominic's office. All the soldiers he came across in the tunnels gave him a wide berth and stared as he walked by. News traveled fast in the army, and he wouldn't be surprised if he'd be demoted from lieutenant. He should be for hitting a superior, whether that superior was Dominic or not.

He knew each soldier that watched him and whispered would only be waiting for a safer job. It would only ensure a front row seat to watch men they trained with die while under their command. Aside from dealing with Monroe and the harassment, it was the part of the job he hated most.

Every time Dominic put himself in harm's way, Lennox was right there following him, covering his back, which made his betrayal even worse.

Lennox rounded the last turn and found himself outside Dominic's office. He stared at the door, not able to raise his fist to knock. He didn't know what to say. Apologizing was a good start, but he didn't think that would be enough. He rested his forehead on the door, the cold of the steel soothing his aching head, not caring if anyone walked by and saw him like that. He didn't care what they thought; they ridiculed him enough already. He only cared what the man on the other side of the door thought.

Just open the door! Knock. Do something!

He took a deep breath and lifted his hand, ready to take that plunge—

The door swung in, making him stumble forward, but he caught himself at the last moment by grabbing the door frame. Standing in the doorway, Dominic stood with his arms folded across his chest, trying to muffle a laugh.

"What are you doing?" he asked, no longer able to hold back from laughing. "You know I can see you on the camera."

Dominic pointed behind Lennox at the camera on the tunnel wall. Lennox felt the color drain away from his face. He stepped back, finding himself speechless.

"Er... I..."

"This is entertaining." Dominic raised an eyebrow at him, smiling at his loss of words. Lennox scoffed and tried to compose himself. "I'm not sure I want to get a black eye again, but it's almost worth it to see you lose your head."

Luckily for Dominic, the bruise under his eye wasn't bad, but it did draw attention to the long scar on his face. Lennox had attempted in the past to ask him how he got it, but

Dominic would always change the subject. He seemed to shut himself off when anyone asked about it or stared at him too long.

"I'm sorry. I won't do it again," Lennox said quietly.

Dominic took a deep breath and sighed. "You're lucky the General isn't here. I won't be able to hold off Monroe forever, but luck is on your side today."

"Why is that?"

"The scouts came back from the tower. We need to move tonight; they got intel there's going to be a supply shipment—and likely more Enforcers—arriving in two days." Dominic stepped back from the doorway and motioned Lennox into his small office.

"We're not ready." Lennox couldn't put it any plainer than that. Dominic was a fool to think they had any chance of breaking in, especially on such short notice.

"I know, but I don't think we're ever going to be. This is our only chance. There's too much movement and we can't risk losing this opportunity, not when we can get two days head start on them before the ship arrives in Carose."

"Dom..." Dominic looked up from tidying his paperwork. You're going to get yourself killed. No, actually, you're going to get us all killed. This is absolute bullshit!" Lennox plopped himself into the chair across from Dominic's desk, staring blanking at the map of Enross splayed out before him.

"Noxy..." Dominic groaned, rubbing his thumbs against his temples.

"No. Don't *Noxy* me. You need to put your feelings aside and look at this from a soldier's perspective. Before this girl came along you always leaned toward planning and logic, but now that all seems to have been thrown out the window!"

"I know you don't trust Satcha, but I have a gut feeling this is what we need to do."

"I can't let you go through with this. This is not some game, the Enforcers are here, and we cannot out-power them."

"That's my entire point!" Dominic threw his hands up and gestured to Lennox as if this was some big breakthrough and not the ramblings of a madman. "We don't have the weaponry they have, but we do have our training—and someone who has been in and out past their security—on our side."

"You're forgetting we don't know her," Lennox exclaimed. "How do you know she's done the things she's said? She is covered in scars from lashings. It may have been by some dumb luck she got away from them once, but I can't see this ending well for us."

"You don't have to come," Dominic spat. "I'll do this myself."

"Now you are really going crazy. I'm not going to let you walk in there with that little bitch and get yourself killed!" Lennox yelled, shooting to his feet. He was shaking.

"We're going to be fine," Dominic said through his teeth. He stayed seated and stared hard at Lennox.

"I'll go with you, but don't expect this to turn into a successful mission. I don't want to end up saying I told you so, but I can't see this ending any other way," Lennox said evenly. He took a deep breath and tried not to let the rage in his chest burst out.

"Gather the team and let Satcha know we will head out soon." Dominic looked away from him and started folding the map, smaller and smaller, until he could tuck it into his shirt pocket.

"I hope you know what you're doing," Lennox said softly. Dominic ignored him, but he knew the conversation was over. There was nothing left to say.

CHAPTER 17

SATCHA

Satcha tried to focus on her breathing. Her body was exhausted but her mind raced. Her training with Captain Lightwood was working on hand-to-hand combat. Out of all the sparring she did with him, she only managed to pin him once and that wasn't good enough for her. He'd been holding back on her in the first few days which set a fire burning deep inside her.

She had to be better. She *needed* to do better. It was the only thing keeping her from a fit of panic. She couldn't let herself lose control of her mind, because if she did she'd think too much about the rock ceiling and how far underground she was. It'd been nearly two weeks since she'd seen the sun. Since she'd breathed fresh air.

Inhale... Exhale... Inhale... Exhale...

"Get up." A heavy black bag landed directly on her stomach, knocking the wind out of her. She glared at Lennox as she coughed, trying to catch her breath.

"What do you want?" Satcha wished the captain hadn't taken her knife, she could've used it to go round two with Lennox.

"We will move in on the compound tonight. Captain's orders." He tapped his foot impatiently at the foot of her bed. "Come on."

"Now?" Satcha groaned. How could they possibly think this was a good idea? No wonder they'd never won a war.

We haven't even gone over a plan!

He rolled his eyes and walked out of the medical unit just as he came in, without a sound and a chip on his shoulder. She sighed and flipped open the bag's flap and peered inside. A pair of black boots sat on top of a neatly folded Enross Army uniform. She scoffed. They'd make her wear their uniform, wear their brand, but not let her be a part of the plans.

The rest of the medical unit slept soundlessly. She slid out of bed and dressed in the uniform. She couldn't risk her chance of getting help to the Free City. The thick fabric chafed her skin as she pulled the pants up. The uniform hung low on her hips, she had to tighten the belt to the very last hole to keep them on. She laced the boots; they were slightly worn and she couldn't help but wonder who they'd belonged to. Was it a child soldier who grew out of them? Or worse, were they taken off a fallen comrade? She didn't want to think about it.

She sat on the bed for a few moments, forcing her body to wake up. What little bit of muscle she had ached against her bones. She longed for a quick meal—bone broth came to mind, light on her stomach but filling enough for the journey.

She couldn't put it off any longer, she had to go. She looked around the medical unit, wondering if she would make it back or not. Almost as if to make a promise to herself, she stowed her brown leather bag under the bed. She'd have to come back for it. Dressed in the uniform and her knife still missing from her right ankle, she made her way through the tunnels to the exit.

Satcha let the cool night air fill her lungs. Outside the entrance, soldiers hurried to pack their horses with supplies and weapons. They paid little attention to her as she stood by, as if she didn't matter. She shook her head; she wasn't sure why it even mattered to her. Soon enough, this would be over and she would be on her way to the Free City.

"I don't like the idea of this, Cap. We can't trust her," Lennox said as he climbed onto his black and white speckled horse.

Satcha couldn't help but roll her eyes at him. How could she trust *them*? Lennox had attacked Dominic the day before. This wasn't a one-way path. There was a tenuous trust unwillingly bridged between them. But Satcha preferred Lennox's outright distrust of her compared to how Captain Lightwood treated her. She knew Lennox didn't like her, despised her even, but the captain was a mystery. He hadn't spoken to her since their training that afternoon and it hadn't been about leaving tonight for the compound.

"That's enough, Lieutenant." Captain Lightwood didn't look happy. She wondered if he would speak to her, but he passed by her to speak to a group of ten soldiers.

She couldn't let it go, she had to know the plan. There was no way she could sneak the whole group in. Maybe one or two, but certainly not ten. The captain seemed capable enough, but was he able to disappear into a crowd like her? Able to squeeze through small places and run like his life depended on it? Probably not. She had a lifetime of experience behind her of going unnoticed. He wore a uniform that marked him for all to see. The fabric on the same uniform clung to her skin and reminded her she too was marked by it, and anyone who saw her would automatically assume allegiance to Enross. It was a giant target on her chest.

"What's the plan?" She fell into step next to him.

"We are gearing up the horses and heading out in ten minutes."

She made a strangled noise that came from deep in her

throat. She cut ahead of him and spun on her heels, making him stop dead in his tracks. "Do you seriously expect me to follow along blind? This is not a time for mind games or power plays! Not with the Enforcers." He studied her for a moment as if trying to figure her out like an intricate puzzle.

"We got some intel," he said finally. "They are receiving a shipment of supplies tomorrow evening. We need to strike now, before they get reinforcements. We've planned what we need to do to get in and set a perimeter. The rest is your responsibility and the skills you've told us about to get in and out." He looked at her, seeming unsure of this plan as well. "Unless you want to go back on your word."

"No, I can do it. Just keep your men out of the way, Captain Lightwood."

"You know, you can stop being so formal. You aren't part of the Enross Army." Dominic set his jaw as if he strained to hold something back. "You can call me Dominic."

Satcha eyed him, not sure of what to make of his request. She was still fired up from snapping at him and didn't know how to respond to his peace-offering. Calling him Dominic would break down a wall between them.

"Don't worry, Dominic," she said, "I'll get us in and out."

She wasn't sure how she felt about it, but she relished the thought of seeing Lieutenant Lennox's face when she addressed the captain next. He wouldn't like that at all. Driving a wedge between the two of them might be the easiest way to gain the captain's—Dominic's—trust and ensure her passage to the Free City.

He stared at her for a moment, but she wasn't going to be the one to look away. She set her jaw.

A soldier walked over with a large, chestnut-colored horse in tow. Dominic broke their stand-off and stepped around her to take the reins. He patted the horse on its head and whispered something to it. Satcha had never interacted much with horses before—as evidenced by her lack of riding skills—nor any animal, other than hunting birds and rabbits for food.

Dominic checked the bags before climbing onto the horse's back with ease. He clicked his tongue and the horse stepped toward her.

"Satcha, you're riding with me." Without notice, Dominic reached down and pulled her onto the horse. He swung her up with ease. Her stomach swooped as she moved through the air, settling in behind him. "Hold on."

She didn't realize he was *that* strong. He really had been holding back during training. If things went badly and she had to escape, she wouldn't be able to overpower him. Maybe she could outsmart him and get away with her knowledge of the forest.

Lennox's horse trotted up next to them. He watched her with his narrowed eyes as she wrapped her arms around Dominic's waist. His stare was hot on the side of her face. She stuck her tongue out at him; it was immature but she enjoyed seeing how much it bothered him that she had her hands on his captain. He scowled at her.

It surprised her, but she couldn't help but notice the hard muscle that lay beneath her hands and the fabric of his uniform. She loosened her grip, but kept her arms wrapped loosely around him to stay seated—and also to annoy Lennox, who fell into line behind them. She could feel his eyes locked on her.

"Lennox, scout ahead," Dominic commanded.

Satcha smirked at Lennox as he passed, enjoying his scowl. He didn't complain about the order, but he made sure to nod to one of the other soldiers following. The soldier returned the nod and moved his horse into Lennox's previous position where he kept an annoyingly close watch on her. Were they stupid? Dominic was the one who would help her to the Free

City; she wouldn't risk hurting her chances of losing her utopia.

A blanket of dark clouds covered the night sky, hiding the moon and stars. Satcha's thoughts turned to the Free City. Surely such dark clouds never spoiled the sky there. She tried to imagine what it must look like, with the towers of glass and steel, and what it was like to wake up in a building. Not under a tree or in a ditch, or in an underground army base. But somewhere with windows, where she could see the sun filter through in the early morning. Maybe even the ocean. The quicker they found the Blood Scrolls, the quicker she would be on her way across the sea.

They rode for hours in the dark of the night. Satcha stifled a yawn. No matter how on edge her nerves were, there was no denying she could've used another hour or two of sleep. The sound of the horses' hooves became an unbearable drum in her mind. Every clop of a hoof meant she was that much closer to the Enforcers. Satcha found herself leaning against Dominic's back half-asleep. He didn't seem to mind.

The quickening ease of her ability to find comfort with him surprised her. She'd never leaned into a stranger before. What made him different for her to let her guard down, even just a fraction? She didn't know, but she had to be careful; he was still a potential threat.

She sat up straight and tried to shake off her curiosity about him. She had a job to do. She'd never entered a compound with anyone other than Agatha before and she didn't want to get caught on account of someone else's mistakes.

"Listen up!" Dominic spoke loud enough for the team to hear. "Hitch your horses in the cover of the trees. We'll have to walk the rest of the way. Team One, you take the left flank, Team Two, you're on the right. We'll take the middle. Keep your eyes open and don't get caught." The ten troops split into their teams while Lennox waited for Dominic and Satcha. Dominic pulled out Satcha's knife from his saddlebag and handed it to her.

She took it without hesitation, brightening immediately. She caressed the hilt like she was welcoming an old friend home. It had bothered her, not being able to feel it against her skin. It was her only weapon of protection; without it she had felt exposed. Dominic watched her carefully as she pulled her pant leg over the knife, concealing it. It looked like he wanted to say something but decided against it.

What does he expect? I'm not going to thank him for returning something that's mine!

"I have a bad feeling about this, Cap," said Lennox, still eying Satcha, like she might draw her knife at any moment and attack. To be fair, it wasn't a far-off thought when Lennox was around.

"Enough, Lieutenant. You've told me your concerns, now drop it. The Enforcer compound isn't far. I don't need you two getting us caught." Dominic grabbed a rifle and swung it over his shoulder. He reached into the saddle bag again, this time pulling out a black handgun. He turned to Satcha. "Do you know how to use one of these?"

She stared at the black barrel. She'd had guns pointed at her before, but this was different. Despite the unease of seeing the gun in his hand, her gut told her he wasn't going to hurt her. He twirled the gun around in his hand, facing the handle out to her to grasp, but she didn't accept it. Her vision whited-out at the corners as she stared at it. She couldn't force her fingers to move and take it. They hadn't gone over guns in their training; she had no experience with a weapon like that.

"You've got to be kidding me? You let her keep the knife and now you're going to give her a gun—"

"A knife she used to save my life!" snapped Dominic, flaring up.

She'd never seen Dominic react in such a way before and backed away from him. It wasn't like she had much experience of his moods, but this seemed different to her. It was as if she could feel the weight bearing down on his chest. The pressure he was under. She looked back and forth between the two soldiers, watching them throw daggers at each other with their eyes. Dominic was the first to move. He took Satcha by the hand—she couldn't help but flinch under his touch—and pressed the gun into her hand. She tried to pull away but he didn't let go. She looked up at him, nervous, and shrunk under his height.

"If worse comes to worst, I hope you'll be on my side once again," he said. His green-eyed stare burned hot on her face.

She took a deep breath and tried to ignore the electricity of his skin touching hers. She pulled her hand away, taking the weight of the gun with it. It was heavier than she expected. She turned it side to side, examining it. She hated it. Bile flooded her mouth.

She held death in her hands.

"Do you know how to use it?" Dominic asked again. He didn't step back, leaving little space between them.

She needed space.

She stepped back and released a shaky breath, feeling the cold metal in her hands. She hefted the gun and aimed the barrel into the trees, the way the Enforcers had done many times to her. "Pull the trigger, barrel goes boom. Bodies fall."

"Just make sure they're Enforcer bodies. I'm trusting you."

She nodded to him without another word, and concealed the gun in the small of her back. Lennox swore under his breath in frustration. Normally Satcha would've laughed at him or made a snarky comment, but she was preoccupied with the weight of the gun and their mission. They were too close to the compound for her liking for any goofing around.

They made their way through thick trees in silence. A dark green moss glistened, moist with the scent of rotting wood wafting in the breeze. She'd traveled all along Enross, but never so far north before. Above her, the clouds broke apart and tapered into small wisps. A tall, mirrored glass tower poked through the treetops into the night sky unlike any Enforcer compound she'd seen before. The ones she'd come across were mostly ruined buildings. The tower reflected the forest back at her, camouflaging it to anyone who stood more than a hundred yards away. If it wasn't for the moonlight she wouldn't have even seen it. It must've been how they kept it hidden, but under the moonlight it was a forest shaped as a building. This wasn't a compound. This was much more.

Oh no...

"Ten guards," said Dominic. He peered at the border of the tower through a pair of small black binoculars. "Which way would you take?"

"What do you mean which way?" *Shit.* Satcha's stomach dropped as she realized what he was asking her. She had no idea what their plan was—since he hadn't told her anything—especially once they got inside. *If* they got inside. "I've never been here before."

"For fuck's sake! I told you this was a bad idea!" Lennox kept his voice low, but his eyes were full of rage, making him look as if he wished he could throw daggers at her.

Dominic's face fell. "You said you've broken into compounds before."

"Yeah, *compounds*. But this... This isn't a compound! I don't even know what this is!"

This place, whatever it was, was way above her skill and experience. She stole cheese and cured meats, not highly confidential scrolls containing information on a lost bloodline.

"It's too late now. We might not get another chance for months and it'll be too late." Dominic stowed his binoculars and picked up a small radio. "Team one, take out the two west guards."

"We can't do this, Dom." Lennox grabbed the radio from him.

"I have a plan." He pulled the radio from Lennox's grasp and hooked it back on his uniform. "You stay here and keep a lookout. Satcha and I will go to the west entrance and meet team one. Satcha, let's go."

She wanted to run. This was not a compound, and that meant there was only one thing it could be. It was a headquarters. She couldn't sneak into an Enforcer Headquarters, but she also wasn't about to stay with Lennox and end up with a gunshot to the head. She looked at him out of the corner of her eye and swore she saw his hand twitch by his holstered gun. She followed Dominic through the cover of the trees. Dominic went still, slinking low, far too fast for Satcha to stop herself and collided against his back.

"Wait," he whispered. He held his hand up in front of her as he listened. He whistled a two-tone note. Three seconds passed before there was an answer of three notes. He sank lower and motioned for her to follow.

Three of the Enross soldiers took cover in the trees with two dead Enforcers at their feet as they rummaged through the Neroso tech the soldiers had carried. Satcha stared at the building before them; it was much larger than she'd expected, standing taller than the trees and up into the sky. She wondered how much of Enross could be seen from the top. She walked toward the building, hand reaching, fingertips almost grazing the structure, before Dominic pulled her back.

"If you touch it, it will set off an alarm."

She pulled her hand back and turned to look at him, startling herself. He'd taken his shirt off. Her eyes lingered on his abdomen; she'd never seen someone who looked so strong. His muscles caught her off guard and she tried her best not to stare, but she thought she heard one of the soldiers snicker at her. Dominic took the uniforms off the dead guards and threw a shirt at her. "Put these on."

She tore her eyes away, not wanting him to catch her looking. She turned her back on him and the guards before removing her jacket and shirt revealing the scars on her back. No one laughed nor said a word. She didn't like them seeing her scars, but it was better than the alternative of her bare chest. When she turned back to face them, Dominic held out a shiny metal helmet from one of the dead guards. It was heavier than she expected and too big, as were the shirt and pants. She rolled up the hem of the pants and arms, and tightened the belt. The Enforcer uniform was much larger than the one she wore from the Enross Base.

"You ready?" Dominic asked her, slipping on his own helmet, looking intimidating standing over her.

"Yes," she lied. She was terrified this would be the last time she'd see the moon. She stared at it through the night vision display on the helmet, taking in every last detail she could of the milky white circle in the sky.

CHAPTER 18

SATCHA

" I really don't think we should be doing this," Satcha said. Her gut told her to get out of there, but she followed Dominic just the same. It was a suicide mission to think they could get into the Enforcer Headquarters, even if they had the stolen uniforms. It was only a matter of time before one of them slipped up and they would be captured and killed. If they were lucky.

Dominic kept a steady pace heading toward the building and didn't show any sign of slowing. Satcha sighed.

Two guards stood by the front entrance, but Dominic turned to go around the left side of the building as if feigning doing a foot patrol. Satcha tried her best to keep up and look natural, but in the oversized uniform, she imagined herself looking like a child at play. Her pant legs began to unwind and drag around her boots as she tried to match his step. Once out of sight past the guards, they ran alongside the tower, realizing only then the structure wasn't glass, but reflective metal.

They came upon a gray door with no handle. No way to get in, only a way to get out. Dominic pushed against it, careful not to touch the glass on either side, but it didn't budge. He beat his fist against the door and swore under his breath.

"We have to get out of here." Satcha's eyes darted around looking for any signs of danger. She couldn't help but picture Enforcers taking them by surprise and capturing them. She couldn't be caught again. Her scars burned as she remembered the pain of the whip tearing into her.

Nothing about it seemed right. If she'd known it was a headquarters, she never would've agreed. She kept her back to the building and let her eyes wander along the tree line, searching for patrols. The night vision visor disoriented her eyes and she fought to focus on any one thing. Everything looked wrong, including Dominic in the Enforcer uniform. She kept having to remind herself it was him and not reach for her knife. Or the gun.

"Come on, we have to get out of here." She grabbed his arm and tried to pull him away. He looked back and forth between her and the building, and for a moment she thought he might run right through the front door.

"Come in, West Gate. Do you copy?" a voice said in Satcha's ear. Satcha froze, the built-in radio in her helmet scaring her. She pulled it off her head and took a deep breath of fresh air.

"If we don't go now, we're as good as dead. They're radioing the guards." Satcha held up her helmet and was about to smash it before he caught her wrist.

"No, we need it. We'll take it back to the base and we can try hacking their communication systems."

"Fine, but you take it. Let's go now!" They didn't have time to argue. She handed the helmet to him—she would let it drag him down, but she wasn't going to be caught stealing it.

She didn't want to wait for him any longer and took off toward the forest. It only took him a few strides to catch up with her as they reached the cover of the trees. She didn't know which way she was running, but the opposite direction of the tower seemed as good as any. Her pant legs finally fell over her boots and tangled in her feet. She tripped, falling over with a thud. The impact stunned her, and she fought the urge to roll onto her side in pain.

Suddenly, a loud siren rang, and a bright red light flashed through the sky.

"Get up." Dominic pulled her to her feet.

"Wait." She pulled out her knife and cut off the excess uniform fabric. She kicked the pieces away and dusted herself off.

Gunfire pelted through the sounds of the siren. Dominic tossed the Enforcer helmet to her before he unholstered his gun and fired into the trees. The helmet hit her square in the stomach, making her gasp. She sat back in the bushes watching him as he skillfully fired a few rounds before taking cover.

"Are you hitting anything?" Satcha leaned against the base of the tree, curled by his feet. There was nowhere else for her to hide.

"Yes! Stay low."

Two shots sounded off, one hitting a tree not five feet from her. The bark splintered off but there was no bullet, just a scorch mark burned into the tree. She didn't know what kind of technology was behind the blasters, but she knew well enough that one hit would burn a hole right through her chest. Dominic stepped out from behind the tree, and fired two more shots. No shots were returned. He knelt next to Satcha and listened. Silence.

He looked more dangerous than the Enforcers. No bullets could penetrate the armor of an Enforcer. There was only one spot she knew of where their suits had a weakness. Their necks. As a witness to Dominic's aim, she vowed not to make herself an enemy of him.

"Follow me and stay low."

She panted hard running after Dominic, who seemed unburdened by the sprint. He dove behind a tree and motioned for Satcha to hide. She lay on the ground beneath a thorny bush, hugging the Enforcer helmet to her chest, fighting to control her heavy breaths. Dominic whistled a strange call and after a moment, through the trees, someone whistled back.

"Cap?" Lennox called softly. He stumbled through the bushes with a limp, blood dripping down his left leg as he clutched his right arm. His pants had melted into the skin of his leg. He was lucky it wasn't a direct hit. If he'd been hit, Satcha was sure there would've been no leg left.

"Noxy, where are the rest of the soldiers?" Dominic asked. He helped Lennox sit at the base of the tree, the lieutenant wincing all the way down to the forest floor.

"Dead. They knew we were coming."

Dominic took his belt off and clasped it around Lennox's thigh. Lennox clenched his jaw so he wouldn't cry out. "Satcha, I need your help."

Satcha stayed low to the ground and quietly revealed herself from her hiding place. Everyone but Dominic seemed to know what a risk this mission was and advised against it, but he'd pushed on. Satcha couldn't help but wonder what drove him to act so rashly. Surely, a captain of an army wouldn't have gotten to his post by making such decisions. There must've been more to it. It couldn't just have been about the Blood Scrolls.

"What do you need?" Satcha stood over Lennox, who scowled at her. She wondered if he'd hoped she would wind up dead in all the commotion. It wouldn't have surprised her if he had.

"We can't get back to the horses from here. We're going to have to go north to Rios and hope the Enforcers don't beat us there." She'd never heard of Rios, but before she could ask about it, Lennox shook his head vehemently and tried to stand.

"No! She can't be trusted—"

"There's no time for that now. We have to move," said Dominic. He hoisted Lennox up and waited for Satcha to take Lennox's other side. Reluctantly, she slipped under his other arm, but she was shorter than him and most of his weight leaned toward Dominic. She hated having to help Lennox, and it seemed the feeling was mutual. Hate radiated off him.

They limped away from the tower as fast as they could to the mysterious Rios.

CHAPTER 19

SATCHA

Satcha's stomach rumbled as the three of them made their way through the lush forest toward the promise of safety. Her feet weighed heavy as she fought to not only hold herself upright, but the weight of Lennox. She'd nearly tripped several times over roots that stuck out of the ground. She wondered if perhaps there was no more room for them to spread the length of their limbs or if they just got tired of being underground. In the short time she spent with the Enross Army at their base, she certainly didn't enjoy the dark and dampness of the tunnels.

As much as she complained to herself about the blisters on her feet, they had bigger problems. They'd failed to get into the Enforcer Headquarters. None of this would've happened if they included her in the plans ahead of time. An Enforcer compound would've been easy, but the building they took her to was a fortress. There was no telling what resources they had inside. Anger crept up inside her and leaked off in waves, hanging in the air with the humidity.

The forest looked untouched by humans, growing wild

and untamed, just as it was intended to do. Overgrown foliage covered the ground and green moss climbed up tree trunks. The moonlight dimly lit their path, only letting a pale glow through the high tree branches. The only noise was the hoot of an owl and the whisper of the wind.

A chill ran up Satcha's back in the eerie silence. It'd been hours since any of them had spoken. She wondered about where they were headed. She'd known of the river named Rios, but never heard of a village. She wasn't sure if they were telling the truth or not; it wouldn't be the first time they'd kept her in the dark.

Her stomach growled again, rumbling deep from within. She'd been spoiled by her time with the Enross Army getting three full meals a day. The soldiers complained about the small portions, but she had no grievances. The growl in her stomach was hard to ignore. She hadn't eaten since dinner the night before. She scolded herself for getting too comfortable eating regularly. She should've tried to space it out, but it was too good to pass up. She didn't care what the food was, she took it gladly. She even happily drank the bone broth the soldiers choked down.

Every now and then Lennox would groan and need to stop. She was happy when he released his grasp around her. He only took aid from Dominic, not that she would've helped. She'd been surprised Lennox had kept up as well as he did, and she didn't put it past him to grin and bear it through the pain. She would've done the same. She stretched her arms out behind her and stalked off to a comfortable spot beneath a large tree. She sat at the base of the trunk which gave enough space away from the two soldiers without being out of sight. Despite the extra distance between them, she could feel Lennox's hatred for her through the air as if a laser had fired through her chest.

Dominic held a canister to Lennox's mouth for him to drink since he wasn't able to hold it on his own, his arms laying limp at his sides with his hands shaking. Satcha couldn't help but gaze at the woods. This was her chance. In those thick trees she could disappear within seconds. It was a risk, but it was a risk she was willing to take. Anything to get away. She stood slowly, trying not to attract their attention. She wandered toward the thicker cover of the trees, but something told her to stop in her tracks and peeked back at them. She couldn't shake the gnawing feeling. Should she leave? Or should she stay? She held her breath, watching Dominic tend to Lennox's leg, but as if he sensed her, he turned and locked eyes with her. His green eyes held her gaze, and she was unable to look away, frozen in place.

"What's wrong?" Lennox asked. He looked back and forth between them, but Satcha and Dominic didn't break eye contact. He knew she was thinking of escaping, but wasn't doing anything to stop her. For the first time in her life, someone saw her. It was as if he could read her mind.

His gaze held her captive. He was a stranger. But this stranger saw her for more than the nomad she was. He'd recognized her abilities and accepted help. He needed her stealth to get into the Enforcer compound. As much as she hated the idea of it, she took pride in the fact she could, and they couldn't. It would have been nice had they trusted her enough to let her in on the plans, but she would've done the same thing too. Kept her cards close to her chest. Wasn't she doing the same thing with her plans for the Masked Man?

"Nothing, let's keep moving." Dominic forced Lennox off the ground and started toward her. She was relieved when they passed by, and she was free from his watchful eyes. She sighed and followed. It was obvious she stayed to use them for their food and shelter, plus the added promise of passage to the Free City...

But why did *he* fascinate her?

Sweat dripped from Satcha's brow from the thick humidity. The sun's hot rays peeked through the treetops sending heat waves upon them. In the light, Satcha saw it wasn't a forest at all, but a jungle. New jungle-type trees replaced the oak trees of the forest. She didn't know what they were called, but their size put the oaks to shame. They stood three times as tall and wide as a small hut. Bright green ferns covered the floor of the jungle and fanned out across the path, making it hard for Dominic to maneuver himself and Lennox.

"How much farther?" Satcha asked. Her empty belly and the rising temperature made her dizzy. She'd long given up wearing the Enforcer helmet and tied it to her belt. The sun reflected off the shiny silver helmet and sent beams of sunlight in every direction. Whenever she stumbled the rays shone into her eyes making black spots cloud her vision.

"We should be reaching the river soon," said Dominic. Sweat dripped down his face and his dark hair stuck against his head.

"Watch where you point that thing!" Lennox snapped as the light from the helmet reflected directly in his eyes.

She grinned, enjoying any displeasure she brought him, but moved the shiny helmet's glare from his face. Dominic shook his head like he was too exhausted to scold them.

They'd gotten into a routine of stopping every half hour to give Lennox a chance to rest, but after all the long hours of trekking through the forest, Satcha's feet had grown numb. Her socks were drenched in sweat causing the hard sole of her boots to rub uncomfortably against her feet. Her toes and heels were covered with bright red blisters. The soldiers made no complaint, so neither did she. She didn't want to be the baggage that slowed them down. Lennox did that job well on his own with his injured leg. The bleeding had stopped, but a fever had set in. She was glad it was him and not her under the humid air with a fever.

"We need to get to Rios as soon as possible," said Dominic. He checked Lennox's wound with a grim look on his face.

"Isn't there any place closer we could get to?" Satcha asked. She wasn't sure how much longer she could walk on her blistered feet but dipping her sores into a cold river sounded nice.

"They are friends of the Enross Army and have skilled healers. We will be able to rest easy there for a while."

She nodded, but was still unsure of this plan. It sounded like a mirage. She knew better; there was no safe place in Enross or Austerland. The only safe place she knew of was the Free City, hiding in plain sight with the enemy's own people. The farther she traveled north in Enross, the farther away she was from the west port in Austerland.

Lennox grunted as sweat ran down his face. His short army haircut glistened under the hot sun. Dominic rested him against a tree and offered him the canister of water once again. He breathed heavily in between sips of water. Satcha averted her gaze; she knew he would die before they reached the river village. There was no point wasting anymore of their water supply on him, but she didn't tell Dominic. She guessed he would be opposed to any type of mercy killing to put Lennox out of his misery. He seemed like the type to try to defy all odds and do "good" no matter what the cost. She admired him for trying so hard but couldn't help but think him naive about the world. Had he not seen and suffered the cruelty of living in this land?

Dominic nudged Satcha's side with his elbow and nodded

away from Lennox. She followed him until they were out of earshot from the groaning soldier.

"We need to stop the fever."

Satcha crossed her arms. What did he expect her to do? There was no point now in saving Lennox. He was a goner. She wasn't a healer, nor had she ever had the displeasure of being shot. She was smarter than that—well, no. Maybe she was just one of the lucky ones. She'd seen countless faces fall to the Enforcers before.

"He's going to die," she said plainly, and frankly she didn't care. He was no friend to her and if it wasn't for Dominic, Lennox would've left her to die in the road. Why should she do anything different for him?

"We don't leave people behind."

"He's not my people. I have no one," she muttered. She turned her back to him and squinted at the sky through the thick branches. The sun set high in the sky and burned hot, glaring an unforgiving blinding light.

"Please." Dominic reached for her hand and held it gently in both of his, taking her by surprise. It was the first time he touched her to connect with her. It was like when they trained together. His touch tingled along her skin and turned her blood to ice. She tried to pull her hand away, but his grip tightened, not letting her escape.

It should've scared her to have someone hold her so fierce, but it didn't. Something danced along her skin, fear or excitement, where his warm hands touched hers. She fought to keep a shiver at bay.

Neither said a single word. She was shocked they were so close—she needed to pull away, but she was unable to move. Why did he have this effect on her?

His green eyes shimmered bright and she forced herself to blink.

There. Look away. Take a step back.

With her eyes closed still, she pulled back her hand, breaking the spell. She never got attached nor stayed in one place for too long. She'd lost the only person who'd been there for her. Had she not developed a taste for revenge, losing Agatha would've broken her. She couldn't let him cloud her thoughts because she couldn't help but notice the feeling that she *wanted* to help him. And not just to get to the Free City.

"Satcha, please. He's like a brother to me; he is all I have left. We grew up together."

Satcha sighed. As much as she hated Lennox, she wanted to help him for Dominic's sake. She'd never involved herself in the affairs of others. It was too messy. Having others around seemed like a good way to get captured or worse, killed. She got Agatha killed. That weighed on her conscience. If you were on your own, you only needed to look out for yourself, but she couldn't fight off the feeling of wanting to help Dominic.

"What do you want me to do?" she asked, giving in.

"I'll do my best to clean the wound, but I need you to look for some herbs. There are these little white flowers, with little blue blossoms rising out of them. I can mash it up into a salve. It should help fight off the infection and bring down the fever long enough for us to get him to Rios."

"I know them." She didn't know the name of it, but she'd used it on her own wounds many times before. The flower had long white petals like a daisy, but instead of a yellow center, a bright blue round thistle bloomed out like a plant growing within another plant.

"Good. I'll get things set up while you go look."

She nodded but avoided his eyes. She remembered the feel of his hand on hers as if they still touched and her heart sped up. The same chill ran down her spine again. She shook it off and tried to focus.

"And Satcha..." he called to her. She turned and caught his gaze once more. "Be careful."

This time it wasn't her who broke eye contact. He ducked his head and walked back off to Lennox. Why did he suddenly have this effect on her? She wiped the sweat from her forehead and breathed in deep. She had to find the flower.

CHAPTER 20

DOMINIC

Dominic didn't watch Satcha walk away, focusing all his attention back on Lennox. He didn't look good, he knew that, but there was still a chance if they could get to Rios. Lennox just needed to hold on a little longer.

"Noxy," Dominic said. "Noxy, you have to wake up."

Lennox stirred, head rolling to the other side resting against the tree trunk. Sweat covered Lennox's face and neck and soaked through his shirt.

"Come on, Noxy. Wake up!" Dominic knelt next to him with his canteen in hand.

Dominic tore the end of the ripped leg of Lennox's trousers and unscrewed the cap of the canteen. He poured some water on the fabric and dabbed away the sweat on his friend's face. The water wasn't cold, but it was enough of a temperature change that Lennox's fluttered open.

"Dom..." Lennox said hoarsely. He squinted in the sunlight despite how dim it was under the canopy of leaves.

Dominic let out a small sigh of relief. "I'm here." It wasn't much of a sign of life, but it was enough to keep a hold of his hope. "Here, take some small sips."

He pressed the canteen to Lennox's lips, but the moment the water touched his tongue he began to choke. Dominic pulled back the canteen and watched his friend heave on his own rattling breath, helpless.

"Try to breathe slowly," Dominic said. He sounded like he was begging.

He knew the only thing, or rather the only person, who could help Lennox now was Satcha. If she could find the veneno flower, they could make it to the village.

Dominic wasn't as skilled as the healers in Rios, but he knew enough about the strange, dangerous plant. The veneno flower could either take life or give it—it was all in how the salve was prepared—but it wasn't only the flower that would help Lennox, it was the healers of Rios themselves. Helene, trained in the old ways, and with an inner gift that with the touch of her hand could heal almost any wound.

Nothing frustrated Dominic more than the knowledge Helene had the gift to heal the injured and yet stayed hidden away in the small village.

"Helene is one person, and my wife. I've lost so much already. I will not risk her as well," Aleksandr, leader of the Free People of Rios, had once said to him.

Although Dominic had been grateful for the people of Rios taking him in, feeding him, training him, and giving him a second chance to start a new life, he didn't agree with their views of the world. Time after time, he would challenge the elders to help those outside of the village, but they declined every time. He couldn't help but be disgusted by them turning a blind eye to the rest of the world. Danger crept closer every day, no matter how well-hidden the village was. The Enforcers, and his uncle, would soon come.

Dominic wasn't about to hide while his uncle destroyed

town after town, killing innocent Vardyians. He knew Gideon would one day come for him and he wouldn't be found hiding away. He would be ready. The day Dominic turned eighteen, he'd left the village of Rios against the wishes of the elders to find the Enross Army and do his part to fight for the people of Enross. For Vardya.

Dominic looked at Lennox, whose eyes had slipped shut again. He couldn't help but feel guilty for his part in Lennox being on the brink of death. Had he never stumbled across the small village, Lennox never would've followed him to the army and been laying in front of him, dying. He sat next to Lennox with his head in his hands, trying not to count the impossibly high number of deaths he was responsible for.

"Dom..." Lennox mumbled.

Dominic started, turning to Lennox. "I'm right here."

Lennox's eyes were closed, but he was still breathing. His body shook as if it had been doused with ice cold water. This told Dominic one thing: the fever was getting worse. The wound from the blaster wasn't clean; it'd blistered with infection leaking from the pulverized flesh of Lennox's leg.

Dominic stared at the poorly wrapped wound and dreaded the sight of what lay hidden underneath the torn uniform bandage. He had no other choice but to clean the wound as best as he could before Satcha returned with the veneno flower so it would be ready for the salve.

He took a deep breath, recalling what little the Enross Army had offered him regarding medical training, combined with what he knew from the healers of Rios. But this was different. He'd been able to separate himself from emotion in other situations. He'd seen his men injured and dead while operating under his orders, but this was Lennox.

His best friend and chosen family. The brother he'd always wished he had was dying in front of him. Lennox had warned him not to do this, but he'd been so obsessed with finding the Blood Scrolls, he'd lost all reason.

He peeled back the bandages as carefully as possible but that didn't stop Lennox from groaning in pain. If the sight of the wound wasn't enough to make him vomit, the smell was. If Dominic had any food in his stomach, it would've expelled right then and there. Bile filled his mouth, and he couldn't hold back the dry heave of his stomach. A burning erupted from his stomach and all the way up to his throat.

"He... can't... trust her," Lennox mumbled.

Dominic's eyes watered from the smell as he forced himself to secure the bandage over the wound and tried to focus on Lennox's words. Of course, even on the brink of death, Lennox would scold him about Satcha.

"She's coming back. I know it. She's bringing the veneno flower," Dominic said with authority; there was no doubt in his mind. Despite all he knew of her, he couldn't help but want to trust her.

"Love... you... Dom," Lennox whispered, his eyes closed.

Dominic couldn't tell if he was awake or not, but he wasn't dead, and he would take that win any day. "I love you too, but don't go soft on me now, brother. I still expect you to be fighting me every chance you get."

Lennox didn't respond. Dominic couldn't help but grimace. He took a deep breath and prepared himself to unwrap the wound again, this time fighting past the scent and turning off his emotions. He couldn't be Dominic at this moment, he had to be Captain Lightwood, the version of himself he'd created to stomach the things he'd thought himself incapable of. Sending soldiers to fight off the Nerosians, knowing full well they were wildly unprepared and outgunned and facing their death.

He did what he could to clean the pus-filled wound before

wrapping it back up. Lennox winced and sucked in deep breaths but didn't speak.

A light breeze rustled through the trees, giving the slightest relief from the humid air. Dominic stood, letting the gentle air surround him, breathing in deep, hoping it would all be over soon. The temptation of trying to carry Lennox over his shoulder to the village was hard to resist, but he knew he couldn't make it. He scanned his surroundings, looking for any sign of Satcha, but she wasn't there.

He couldn't help but wonder what was taking her so long. Wherever she was, he just hoped he was right in thinking she would come back.

Chapter 21

Satcha

Satcha weaved her way through the trees, avoiding the poisonous purple ferns that fanned out blocking her way. She'd found lots of white flowers, but not the ones with little blue blossoms rising out of them. Having never been this far north before, she had no idea what the terrain would be like nor the plant life. If she'd been asked, she would have thought the northern part of the country would've been a barren wasteland, not a lush jungle.

Sweat pooled in the small of her back and between her breasts. She shrugged off the Enforcer shirt and tied it around her waist, leaving only the oversized white undershirt she'd borrowed from the Enross Army.

"Stupid flowers. Stupid Lennox." She kicked a rock, and it flew through the bushes, landing with a thud.

"What was that?" a voice called out from the other side of a bush.

She dropped to the ground, listening for movement. Footsteps sounded closer, the soft thud of boots, the rustling of leaves, heading straight for her.

She knew that sound.

Enforcers.

As she peered through the giant leaves of the purple fern she hid under, a drop of dew-like liquid dripped from the tip of the leaf straight onto her shoulder. It splashed against her skin and started to burn across her back. She cursed under her breath as more drops fell. She was under a poison fern. She couldn't stay there any longer, not without being drenched in the poison but there was nowhere for her to escape. She was cornered.

As quietly as possible, she reached for her knife and clutched the hilt tightly in her hand.

The footsteps halted next to her. The Enforcer hovered directly over her, scanning the jungle. The Enforcer's boots were next to her. She took a deep breath and swung out her right foot to sweep their legs out from under them. The Enforcer fell on their back, gasping to catch their breath.

She jumped to her feet with the fern leaves scraping like razors across her back. With her knife at the ready, she launched herself at the Enforcer and sat on his chest holding him down. He reached for her, but she slashed her knife across his chest plate. The steel of her blade had no impact and barely left a scratch. He was too well protected by his armor; she needed to break a piece of it off. Or remove his helmet.

She spun her knife in her hand and beat the helmet with the butt of the handle. The Enforcer reached with his hands trying to block her, but she was too fast and too deliberate with her strikes. She hit the corner of the visor as hard as she could. A crack split through the black glass. With one more blow, she broke through and gripped the helmet from inside. Broken pieces of the visor cut into her hand, but she didn't stop, pulling the helmet clear off his head. Terrified blue eyes stared back at her. With one deliberate stab, the blade dug into the Enforcer's neck. Blood splattered out and his hands flew to his neck as he gurgled out his last breath.

"Hey! You!" another Enforcer shouted from behind her. "Drop your weapon!"

She turned, following the voice of the other Enforcer. With his gun pointed, he fired, narrowly missing her. Using what energy she had left and not wasting any time, she dove at the Enforcer, but he was a lot stronger. Not that it took much.

Iron-like hands caught her wrists and forced her to the ground. She tried to kick against the armor but couldn't land a single decent hit. The Enforcer leaned over her and used his knees to lock her arms at her sides. Once his hands were free he ripped her knife from her hand. She stared at the shiny helmet. Her wide, terrified eyes stared back at her.

This was it.

After all her running and fighting to stay alive, this was her end. She closed her eyes, not wanting to see her own death.

She waited for the knife to cut her throat, just as she'd done to the other Enforcer moments before, but there was a *whoosh* followed by a gurgling noise. The Enforcer crashed on her, his helmet colliding against her head. Something warm dripped from her forehead down the sides of her cheeks. She peeked through her eyelashes. Inches from her eyes, an arrowhead stuck out of the throat of the dead Enforcer.

She was alive.

She pushed as hard as she could and shoved the body off her. She fought to catch her breath as she scrambled back. Whoever killed the Enforcer could do the same to her. They'd been skilled enough to strike the Enforcer in their one weak spot. They could have been a lucky shot, but she didn't think so.

The deep itch from the poisonous fern stung her back as she rolled onto her side. She'd forgotten she'd touched it again. The tingle spread and turned into a deep, fiery, burning.

"Friend or foe?" a voice asked.

Satcha pushed herself up and sat staring at the end of

another arrow, but this one hadn't yet met its target. She skidded away from the gray-haired man whose bow followed her every move.

"Friend to those the Enforcers call foe," she answered.

"Then why do you dress as they do?" The man stepped forward, further revealing himself, walking through the purple ferns unfazed. Satcha squinted her eyes at him, he wore a plain beige shirt and matching trousers.

"That business is my own, but I'm not aligned with them, old man."

"Old man? There's no respect amongst the youth today," he said, shaking his head.

"If that's it, I'll be going now." She stood slowly, watching to see if he would attack, but he didn't. He watched her as if he expected her to do the same.

"It won't be long before the visions start. You need treatment or the poison will drive you mad."

"It's a chance I'll have to take," she said, hoisting as much confidence into her voice as she could. She had a job to do; she needed to find the white flowers—and not just for Lennox.

"My village isn't far from here. I can make you an offer. We will heal you in exchange for that Enforcer uniform and any information you might've learned in acquiring it."

Satcha chewed the inside of her cheek, doing her best to ignore the poison bubbling the skin on her back. She reached behind her back and ripped the white undershirt away from the spreading poison, but it only spread further across her back and onto her hands. If what the man said was true, she wouldn't be any help to Dominic hallucinating while looking for the flower. If they could heal her, maybe they could heal Lennox as well.

"You can have the uniform, but you have to accept my two travel companions and heal them as well."

He lowered his bow and chuckled. "I'm afraid my healers can't bring back the dead."

"Not these two. I was looking for the white and blue flower to heal one of them when I ran into these two."

"You have my word. You give me the uniforms *and* any information you have, and we will heal you and your friends."

Satcha scoffed at his use of the word friends but held out her hand to the stranger in agreement. Were they her friends? Surely not Lennox, but Dominic had been friendly enough to her. She thought for a second that maybe this was her chance to get away from them. She'd be healed by this stranger, and she could get back to her own journey. Lennox would die and Dominic would fend for himself in the jungle, but there was a rumbling of guilt in her stomach. She'd made him a promise and in turn he had promised to help her.

The old man raised his eyebrows at her blistered covered hand she held out. "Maybe after the poison is gone."

"Oh, sorry." She pulled her hand back and looked down at the bubbled skin, feeling the burn, resisting the urge to scratch. "They aren't far from here. Follow me."

She grabbed her knife from the dead Enforcer's hand and steadied herself, trying to ignore the sweat drenched fabric chafing against the infection.

"Lead the way, but I will be watching you. Don't try anything funny." He didn't relax his grip on his bow. She knew if he was skilled enough to send an arrow straight through the neck of an Enforcer, he would have no trouble piercing her with no armor.

"Same to you, old man," she said, and rolled her eyes. She was in no shape to be a danger to him. They set off back to where she'd left Dominic and Lennox. Like the stranger, she kept a grip on her weapon, just in case.

CHAPTER 22

SATCHA

"Who's there?" Dominic called as Satcha and the stranger approached through the trees. He stood tall with his gun in hand.

"It's me," she called back with her hands in the air.

"What happened to you?" He lowered his gun and rushed to her side. His hands cradled her face as he inspected the gash across her forehead before noticing the poisonous blisters on her shoulders and back. The touch of his hands tingled like before, mixing unpleasantly with her burning skin.

She stared at him curiously, unsure why he'd embraced her this way. His eyes examined her as if he took inventory of all her injuries. He must've realized how stiff she stood and released her, stepping back a few steps, giving her the space she needed.

She needed to focus, they had to get to the old man's village before she collapsed, and Lennox died. And she didn't like him coddling her. She didn't like him looking at her like she was breakable. She swayed on her feet, blinking hard and quick. She was strong, she could make it.

"It's a long story," she finally answered. "I ran into some

Enforcers, but I found help." She turned to the old man, bringing Dominic's attention to him, hiding amongst the trees. He kept his distance, watching them with his bow clutched in his hands and arrows at the ready.

"Aleksandr, it's been a long time," Dominic greeted the old man, like a friend.

"It certainly has, Captain." The old man smiled, lowering his bow, and stepped out of cover to shake hands.

"You two know each other?" She looked between them. She was relieved Dominic seemed to know the man; it comforted her knowing if Dominic trusted him, he wasn't all that bad. Though at the same time an unease crept into her stomach, reminding her of his naivety and poor judgment in planning against the Enforcers, she couldn't help herself. She wanted to trust him.

"Aleksandr is the leader of the Free People of Rios," said Dominic.

"Oh." Satcha ducked her head down, a little embarrassed she didn't know who he was, but how could she? She'd never made a point of knowing anyone.

"We can talk about this later," Aleksandr cut in. "Where is your wounded friend?"

"It's Lennox. The Enforcers shot him with DEW tech." Dominic led Aleksandr to where Lennox lay against the tree. Aleksandr bent over the unconscious man.

"His condition looks worrisome, but I have no lack of faith in our healers. Though, we must hurry." Lennox's chest rose and fell in deep waves. His sweat now soaked through the Enforcer uniform he wore, and his wound was bleeding once again, covering him in a glossy crimson.

Dominic and Aleksandr prepped Lennox to move while Satcha destroyed any trace they'd been there, covering tracks and picking up what little they had with them. They didn't need any more Enforcers on their trail. Dominic carried Lennox over his shoulder as Aleksandr led the way.

Satcha was curious about the Free People; she'd never heard of them before. How had they been able to keep themselves a secret? Were they truly free? Were they part of the Enross Army? So many questions fluttered through her head, but knew it was not the time to ask any of them.

She fell into step with Dominic and watched his back for any attackers. Every now and then he would glance over at her, checking to see if she was okay, but didn't speak. The bleeding on her head stopped, but the dizziness set in. She knew she was fading; her breath was coming shorter, and every step was exhausting. Occasionally she stopped to lean against a tree, panting heavily. The cotton of her undershirt stuck to the blistered skin on her back. She winced in pain, trying not to let it show, but it became harder to ignore. Her skin burned with a raging fire, and when she couldn't take it anymore, she fell to her knees, gasping in pain.

The green of the jungle filtered over her eyes and she could no longer see any other color. She tried to focus her vision, but the world spun around her. The sun was so bright through the leaves. The trees spun around, making her forget where she was. Her stomach lurched, but there was nothing in her stomach to heave.

Dominic's face appeared over her, spinning along with the treetops. His face spun round and round, but there was something different about him.

He was calling her name.

What was different? The scar across his cheek was gone. She reached out and touched his face where it had been. She didn't know why she did it, but she liked the feeling of his short facial hair under her fingertips.

"Focus and listen to me!"

But she couldn't. She laughed. There wasn't anything

funny, but she couldn't stop. He looked away and yelled something before taking her in his arms and lifting her up. He was so strong.

She laughed once again, unable to control it. She leaned her head against him and touched his strong chest.

"You know... You're kind of beautiful." She giggled as she petted his face. "It's so scruffy."

"We're almost there. The poison is in her blood and she's hallucinating. We need to get her to the healers at once." Aleksandr's voice filled her ears, but she didn't care. She didn't have a care in the world. She laughed and giggled,

"I'm just going to... close my eyes... and... rest..." Her eyes weighed heavily. She wanted to sleep. She rested her cheek against Dominic's chest. They had been traveling for so long without proper rest. She was so tired.

"No! Stay awake!" Dominic demanded, but her eyes fluttered, and she drifted off.

CHAPTER 23

DOMINIC

Satcha's small frame slumped in Dominic's arms. *Shit!* He couldn't help but hold her close to his chest. Despite his exhaustion, he pressed on. He had to get her to safety. She needed help and it was because of him that she was in this mess in the first place.

"I'm going on ahead. Will you be okay with Lennox?" Dominic tore his eyes away from Satcha's face and looked at Aleksandr.

"Go, I'll radio ahead for help." Aleksandr shifted so Lennox's weight leaned into him. Dominic locked eyes with Lennox; he looked pissed, but he didn't have time to deal with the petty squabble between him and Satcha.

Dominic nodded to Aleksandr and ran off without another word. He never thought he would leave his chosen brother behind, yet here he was, running through the woods with Satcha passed out in his arms. He couldn't stop himself, something inside told him he needed to do everything in his power to protect her. After all she'd been through he wanted to make sure nothing ever happened to her like that again.

He wanted to make his uncle and the Enforcers pay for the

damage done to her mentally and physically. He had no doubt in his mind the scars she bore on her back were nothing in comparison to the scars they left in her head. There was so much about her that he still didn't know, but that didn't stop him from wanting to know more. He wanted to know more than her survival skills and her encounters with the Nerosians —he wanted to know *her*. What did she like? What was she like?

Dominic didn't dare let himself answer those questions. He didn't want to create a version of her that wasn't real.

Dominic scoffed at himself. What was he thinking? Get to know her? He was supposed to be leading an army. He was supposed to be doing everything to protect those his uncle sought to destroy. His mission was to infiltrate the tower and find the Blood Scrolls, not to fall for a wanderer. But he couldn't deny there was an invisible pull between them.

In the crowded tunnels at the base it was as if he could feel her presence. No matter where he stood in a room, if he looked up, his eyes would find her face.

What was the point in even thinking these things? He had no idea if she even felt the same pull. For all he knew, she thought of him as nothing more than a meal ticket and a ride to the Isle of Neroso.

That was another thing. He'd lied to her—well, not really. He just hadn't told her the whole truth... that he was *from* Neroso. But he wasn't Dominic Ursid anymore, he was Dominic Lightwood. So, it wasn't a lie at all. It was something of the past, but no matter how much he lied to himself, he still knew she deserved to know.

How would she take the news? Surely not well. He couldn't even imagine admitting it to Lennox even after all these years. He knew it was a betrayal of their friendship and it didn't make it any easier on him. He'd wanted to tell Lennox a long time ago, but the words never seemed to manage to make it out of his mouth and into the world. There was so much hate in Lennox's heart, he was sure he'd never speak to him again. So he kept quiet, carrying the burden of his past with him and now he'd carry it twice over for Satcha.

Dominic fought the urge to look down and check on Satcha every few seconds. If it weren't for the rise and fall of her chest, he would've stopped sooner, but he had to carry on and get her to the healers. He kept an eye on his surroundings, narrowly missing a hanging vine only for a thin branch to tear the skin on his cheek under his eye, but still he didn't stop. He couldn't. She needed help.

A fallen tree blocked his path and instead of slowing and finding a way around he picked up speed and ran straight for it, leaping over it only for his pack to catch on a broken branch.

"Fuck!" He and Satcha flew through the air and hit the ground hard. The wind knocked out of his chest as Satcha's head fell on his ribs. "Satcha, are you okay?" She groaned but didn't wake.

He nudged her arm, careful not to touch the poisonous rash plaguing her skin. It had spread further down her shoulders and onto her forearms. He shrugged off his shirt and wrapped it around her; he couldn't risk the poison getting on him. Then they both would be doomed. A rosiness swept across her face and sweat glistened in her hair. Dominic rested the back of his hand against her forehead. Even before their skin touched, he could feel the heat radiating off her.

"I have you, don't worry," he whispered in her ear. He pulled her back in his arms as delicate and careful as he could. His bones ached as he got to his feet and the muscles in his legs protested, but still, he pushed on.

The lush green vegetation grew abundantly around him. He tried his best to avoid branches and hanging vines but there was little he could do as the trees grew thick as if they were forming a shield around the village. It seemed even nature wanted to protect the small village of Rios. It was a maze of fallen logs, pathways hidden by emerald-colored bushes leading to the village. The further he went, the more his memories of Rios came back to him. How many times had he wandered through the jungle, exploring the different hidden pathways? Not only by the growing foliage, but also the ones created by the villagers; the traps they'd added as another layer of protection. Some of them he'd even made himself. Trip wires, nets, planting poisonous veneno ferns to ward off intruders. Hell, it could've been a fern he'd planted that Satcha had touched.

Dominic pushed on, not allowing his legs to stop.

He would help Satcha.

He needed to.

CHAPTER 24

LENNOX

A brightness flashed in Lennox's eyes making him unable to see anything except the white light surrounded by dark edges like a tunnel. He squinted and held his hands up in front of his face, trying to block it, but it was like the light was under his eyelids and he couldn't escape it. His head pounded as he swayed and energy poured out of him like the trail of blood leaking from the gunshot wound in his leg.

"Stay awake!" Dominic yelled repeatedly.

Lennox rubbed his eyes in anger. What had that wretched bitch done now? Had she hurt Dominic? The light in Lennox's eyes dimmed and let a little bit of the world around him into his sight. All he could see was just a blurred splatter, like a painting that hadn't been completed and faded into a blank canvas. In that splattered painting and white abyss he swore he saw Satcha laying limp in Dominic's arms. Dominic stared wide-eyed at Satcha, yelling for her to stay awake.

What about me?

Didn't Dominic care about him and his wellbeing? He was his best friend and most trusted companion! Didn't he need Dominic's attention? He'd been by Dominic's side for years, always loyal—even to a fault at some times. He worried Dominic held the altercation in the mess hall against him. He wished he could go back and fix things.

The blurred images faded as the white light flashed in his eyes again. Fog flooded through his head. He couldn't remember where he was. Had they escaped the Enforcers and made it back to the base?

"Come on, Lieutenant. Let's get you to the healers." The voice was strange, but familiar. A pair of hands grasped his shoulders and pulled him to his feet. He slumped against the stranger, barely able to keep his legs steady enough to carry his weight.

The man's outline sharpened, and Lennox squinted at him. What was Aleksandr doing here? He hadn't seen him in a year.

Aleksandr stepped forward and Lennox forced himself to fall in step. As soon as his foot touched the ground he screamed in pain as if an electric current splintered from his sole, up his leg, and shot off into his body. He fell to the ground like a stone. His body shook to fend off an unwelcome cold that chilled him and sent an ache deep into his bones.

Out of all the battles he had been in, he hoped this wasn't the way he would go. Shivering like a baby while Dominic held another. Not just any other, but *her*. He couldn't let Satcha get her claws into Dominic. He wouldn't let it happen and he would fight with his last dying breath to make sure of it.

CHAPTER 25

DOMINIC

After what seemed like hours, Dominic broke through the thick jungle. The sun glimmered on the riverbank as the water flowed past the village of small houses. Home. His *chosen* home. It'd been a few years since he'd seen it, but that didn't mean he didn't long to be there. Duty called and the army came first—not his homesickness.

"It's okay, Satcha. We made it," he whispered to her as he strode across the open field. He needed to find Helene.

He made his way to the community house knowing she'd be there. The Free People of Rios didn't pride themselves in luxury, but simple comforts of home and family. The community house was a home base for all; a large dining hall, a conference room for village meetings, a medical wing, and the home of Aleksandr and his family.

Dominic rushed along the dirt path and burst through the doors to find Helene and a few of the other women chatting around a table. Their jaws dropped at the sight of him and Satcha.

Dominic didn't waste any time with a social greeting. "Helene, I need your help." Helene's blue eyes widened as she stood. Her long gray hair was braided and rested over her shoulder like it had all the years he'd known her.

"Ladies, excuse me." Helene nodded to her companions and motioned for Dominic to follow her.

"I'm sorry to barge in like this on you," Dominic apologized when they were out of earshot from the others.

"Dominic, if you of all people had strolled in here casually, I would've been worried." She smiled at him. "You've always had a habit of finding trouble."

Dominic didn't laugh but let a small smile break through the corner of his lips. In his teenage years, he and Lennox were Helene's usual patients in the hospital wing. Everything from small scrapes all the way up to broken bones from the self-training they put themselves through before enlisting.

"How long has she been out?"

"About twenty minutes. We came across Aleksandr just outside the thicket. He's helping Lennox get back. He took a Neroso blaster to the leg and he's in pretty bad shape."

"I'll have to work quickly with this girl before I can get to him. The poison is spreading fast. Luckily a fresh salve was made this morning." She led him into a private room with a simple bed against the wall and a sink on the opposite wall with a cabinet full of medical supplies. "Lay her down on the bed."

Dominic set Satcha on the bed as carefully as he could. Her face was even more red than before and shiny with sweat. He tucked a stray behind her ear and knelt at her side. He wished she'd open her eyes, but the only sign of life was the rise and fall of her chest.

"Here." Helene passed a jar to Dominic. "Start spreading the paste over her skin and it should get rid of the rash. She's got some nasty scars as well. Such a shame for a fair-looking girl to bear such ugly wounds. Do her a favor and use the salve on them too. I have plenty more jars."

Dominic didn't say anything as he took the jar and spread the salve across the raw welts from the fern. He didn't know if Satcha wanted her scars removed. The healing power of veneno salve was far more powerful than any other medicine known to Vardya, and perhaps even the Isle of Neroso.

"I'll prepare the next room for Lennox." Helene patted Dominic on the back and left the room without another word.

He stood in the middle of the room with the jar of veneno salve looking at Satcha, unconscious on the bed. Would she want her scars removed with the poison? All the years he'd had access to the salve, living in the village of Rios, he'd never once tried to use it on himself, to erase the scar his uncle left on him. The scar that haunted him every time he saw his reflection. But looking at Satcha, he wanted to get rid of her pain. Even if it was only the physical reminder.

Dominic dipped his fingers into the pale purple salve and almost spread it onto her skin, but hesitated. It wasn't his choice to make. It was hers and he'd leave the decision up to her when she awoke.

The red fever was gone from her face, but she still didn't wake. He sat on the foot of the bed, staring at the wall. Just his luck, a mirror faced him reminding him of his own scar. He set his jaw and fought the urge to smash the mirror. How long had it been since he'd last seen his face? A few weeks?

He sat the jar on the bed and took slow steps across the room to the mirror. He couldn't bear to look at the scar on his face.

"Come on! Look, you coward!" He punched the wall next to the mirror. "Just look!"

Dominic pushed hard against the wall and forced his feet to take a few steps back. He opened his eyes, expecting to see something different, but what he found was himself. Green eyes scanned the face in the mirror, unable to imagine what he would look like without his scar. He dropped to his knees, letting out a sob.

He held his head in his hands and wiped away his tears before looking back at Satcha. She looked peaceful. A stomp of boots in the hallway marched past the room. Satcha was safe and resting, only now could he shift his attention to Lennox, but not before he stood over her, at war with himself. Reach out and touch her hand, or back away.

He chose to back away, respecting her space.

"I'll be back soon," he whispered. He took one last look at her before stalking out of the room to find Lennox.

CHAPTER 26

GENERAL BALLARD

General Henry Ballard stood over his desk in his crimson-walled office reviewing a map of Vardya. For ages the continent had gone without a ruler. Austerland and Enross crumbled down to nothing, almost begging to be taken. He'd done what he could to keep what was left of the Austerland Army at bay with the help of Lord Ursid of Neroso, but now it was the Lord that stood in his way.

It'd been nearly a month since he'd been in his office after traveling south to Reeock. He'd hated every single moment of it. Having to answer to the caretakers and not be the man in charge. Everything was as he'd left it in his office. The only annoyance of his return was his missing captain.

Behind his back, Lightwood had sprinted off again with a small team and he didn't know if they were alive or dead. No one had received any radio contact with them since they'd left in the middle of the night. He couldn't ignore the anger that swelled in his chest. How many times had he told that boy to mind his place? One too many, in his books. Though if he didn't come back, it saved him the hassle of the dirty work to get his snooping nose away from his business.

Ballard sat and leaned back in his chair, tossing his glasses on the desk. He massaged his temples and blinked his eyes hard, trying to remove the imprinted image of the map of Vardya from his vision. He opened the top drawer. Sitting on top of a mess of paperwork and stationery was the communication pad.

He hadn't told a soul about the package that arrived in his office three years prior.

A small black device sat inside with instructions. A blank screen stared back at him. He'd never seen such a thing before. He took the communication pad out of the box, careful not to jostle it. A blinking green cursor appeared at the top. He stared at it, not sure what to make of it. He was sure, whatever it was, that it was broken. There were no buttons on the device, just a slate black pad. He was about to set the pad back on his desk and lines of text appeared across the screen.

Hello General.

He nearly tossed the thing across the room.

We've been watching you. We'd like to help.

He watched the words appear one after the other, trying to make sense of where the transmission came from. Below the messages, a box of letters appeared with a square surrounding the word, send. He reached a finger forth and touched the letter w.

He pressed his fingers across the pad.

Who are you?

There was a long pause. Who had sent the device? His heart raced and a chill ran down his spine, sending gooseflesh along the top of his forearms. He waited for what seemed like an hour before another message appeared across the top of the screen.

We'll reveal that soon enough. We know you and we know

what you want. Power. Help us and we will help you. All you have to do is say yes.

That was all Henry Ballard needed to see. There was only one response for him to send back.

Yes.

Excellent. We will be in touch soon. Hide this device and speak no word of it to anyone. We will be watching.

There was far too much filtering through Ballard's head to heed any warning of the message. He did not think of who messaged him, nor did he worry about who supposedly watched him. He sat back in his chair, still clutching the communication pad in his hands, and pictured himself as leader of Enross. No, not just Enross, Austerland too. Vardya. The emperor of Vardya. He smiled to himself, imagining the day he'd get out of these tunnels and sit on a throne. If his plans played out correctly, that day would be soon.

It'd been months since he'd received any new messages from the communication pad. No matter what he did to try and communicate with them, the keyboard of letters only appeared when they asked something of him. For the last three years, he'd inspected the communication pad time and time again, but never found any give to the structure of it. He had no idea what it was made of or how it was powered. He didn't dare give it to those ruddy scientists in the lab. This was for him, and him alone, to see.

Ballard knocked over the miniature tower marking the Enforcer Headquarters on the map and smiled. He picked his own marker and placed it on the old Kingdom of Reeock. As soon as the Enforcers were dealt with, he'd retake the city from the filth plaguing the streets and bring it back more glorious than ever before. Halls would be lined with his portrait; no longer would he be reduced to hiding away in tunnels like some rat scum. No, he would have his throne in the castle high on the hill, surrounded by open fields of green.

All his plans for what to do with his power excited him. He fought to contain the joyous wave running through his veins all the way down to the length between his legs. The seam of his pants tightened and with an eager spring in his step, he pressed the intercom button.

His aide's voice crackled through the speaker. "Yes, sir?"

"Have that little brunette nurse come to my quarters at once."

"Right away, sir."

The General left the war room without another word and headed to his quarters to wait for his favorite nurse. She wasn't as fair as the others, but she was willing to submit to him and had perky little tits he enjoyed watching bounce as she rode him. Once he'd taken his place as Emperor, he'd find better women to have in his bed. A whole lineup of women waiting to please their Emperor. He would pick them out himself. He would pick out his whole staff and make sure they were all beautiful women. That way he could bend over the maid dusting his desk whenever he felt like it.

CHAPTER 27

SATCHA

A cool breeze blew across Satcha's cheek and the warm sunlight danced across her skin. If there was an afterlife, she was sure this was it. She didn't open her eyes, but she knew she lay in what must be a comfy white cloud in the sky. So soft, so warm, yet cool to the touch. She didn't want to wake up if it was a dream. She was long tired of running. Getting to the Free City, which was her goal, but what if she was in the Free City now? What if death brought her to her goal? No, it couldn't be... but how could she know? All she had to do was open her eyes and surely she would find her answer.

One... two... three...

Her eyes opened wide to see the sun shining through a small window. A miniature sink sat next to a wooden chest against one wall of the tiny room. There wasn't much else. The walls were rough-cut logs, and the ceiling was covered with dried-out ferns.

The poison!

She threw off the thin quilt and touched her back. Her skin was smooth with no trace of the blisters, only the roughness of her old scars. She no longer wore the white blood-stained undershirt, nor the army pants and stiff boots. In their place was a long, flowing, blue dress that hung loosely. It was tied around the back of her neck and tapered off below her knees. She'd never worn a dress before.

Who dressed her? More importantly, who had *undressed* her?

Her stomach sank. Who had cleaned her? Her arms and legs were exposed to the world. She preferred to have pants and a long-sleeved tunic. It was much better for survival. What kind of person could survive in the wilderness in a dress? She grasped her arms, running her hands up them, feeling the smoothness of her skin. The touch of her skin surprised her. It had never been so soft before. She wasn't covered in dirt like she was used to.

Where was she? Nothing about the room was familiar to her. She swung her feet over the side of the bed and tried to stand but tripped over something. She landed on whatever had tripped her, hard, and it *moved*.

"Urgh!" Dominic groaned from beneath her. She lay on top of him with her chin digging into his chest. His eyes opened and met hers. She gasped and pushed herself off him and scooted back.

"Sorry." She looked down at her hands, unable to meet his gaze. Had everything been a dream? She couldn't remember much of what happened, just that they were trying to get to Rios when she must have collapsed from the poison.

"It's okay, I'm fine. I'm just glad you're okay." He sat next to her and leaned back against the bed. His elbow gently rested against hers, but she didn't move away. Neither did he. His touch comforted her. Waking up in a strange room with no memory of how she got there or how she'd been dressed and cleaned gnawed at her brain, sending her heart racing, but that touch of his elbow against hers made it a little easier to bear.

"Where are we?" Her hair hung forward creating a veil between them. She snuck a glance at him—the scar on his face was still there, unlike in her dream.

"We're in Rios. We got here late last night, and the healers worked on you and Lennox right away. I've been here waiting for you to wake up."

"Is Lennox all right?" She didn't care, but she knew he did.

"He's still with the healers. They are trying to save his leg, but it's too soon to tell."

"I'm sorry." She tucked a long strand of blonde hair back behind her ear, removing the veil. She took a deep breath and before she could talk herself out of it, she placed her hand on his arm. "Thank you for helping me."

His body stiffened at her touch, but he didn't pull away. She froze, thinking she'd made a mistake, but he smiled at her, making her stomach do back flips. Never had she been so close to another, nor intimate, but with him, she found herself wanting to try.

Had he ever felt this way before? Had there been someone who caught his eye? Probably. She imagined women would be attracted to a captain in the army, but how often would he have had the time to get to know someone?

It was time to admit to herself that she found him attractive. His deep green eyes drew her in. The subtle upturn of the corners of his lips in a small smile. The scruff of his beard along his angled jawline. She shook her head, shaking the thoughts away. She removed her hand and headed for the door. She couldn't allow herself to get attached to him. She had to get to the Free City. It was silly of her to lose sight of her goal. She didn't need to be dragged down by a soldier who was smack dab in the war she so desperately wanted to avoid.

"Satcha!" he called after her, but she quickened her pace, bursting out the door.

Outside the one room house she found herself in the

middle of a village. Little houses like the one she'd been in were scattered along the riverside. Children ran and played, a group of four women stood in the riverbed, washing laundry, and men fished further along the shore. It was a little community of peace separated from the warring world outside.

She stopped dead in her tracks, watching the villagers go about their day. She'd never seen people so relaxed and peaceful before. They truly were the Free People of Rios. How had they stayed safe from the Nerosians all this time? Dominic came up beside her, and stood silently, watching the villagers with her.

"This is Rios?" she asked.

He nodded with a sad look on his face. "Yes, this is where I am from."

"You grew up here? Why did you leave?" She turned away from the river to face him. How could he ever leave a place like this? But deep down she knew. The only reason he would leave was to protect it. Honorable to a fault.

"No, I didn't grow up here... That's a story for another time. I left because there's more than myself to think about. There might be a little slice of peace here, but there are many other places that will never get the chance at such happiness. And there will be a day when the Enforcers make their way through all the large towns and villages and come here to take it all away."

Satcha didn't know what to say. She'd never thought about anyone but herself all her life—Agatha, but she was different—yet he put strangers before himself. She watched a young couple walk by holding hands. She thought them naive to what horrors happened outside of the village. Surely, they had to know there were others suffering? She'd been suffering for a long time, struggling to survive, but she was the same as them... if not worse. She'd known about the war and the famine throughout the country, and she only looked out for herself.

He was so selfless. How could there be so much good in one person? She tore her eyes away from the young couple. He'd been watching her, waiting for some reaction.

"Will you take a walk with me?" he asked, pulling her from her thoughts.

The idea of being alone with him away from prying eyes sent her stomach into a spiral and her brain into overdrive. She shouldn't. She couldn't. But she nodded and followed him.

CHAPTER 28

SATCHA

Dominic led Satcha past the village and toward the riverbank. They walked in silence, and she kept a healthy distance from him. She didn't trust herself to be so close to him, afraid of the shrinking space between them. Every time she put more space between them, she found herself straying back toward him like a magnet. She didn't like how hard she had to work to keep her guard up around him.

Satcha looked back and could no longer see the village. They walked along the rocky shore covered in large white stones. Every now and then he offered her his hand to help her climb over a large rock, which she would've been able to do with no problem if it were not for the dress and sandals she wore. She cursed under her breath at whoever had dressed her.

She'd grown used to raggedy old clothes no one else wanted and threw out. There was more of a breeze than she was used to. The dress was not made for survival. It offered no protection from an attack or warmth should the night grow chilly. Anger rumbled in her stomach, memories and lack thereof invading her head. Her life was a mystery to her. She had no memories before Agatha found her on the riverbank.

The unknown kept her awake at night— and now, wearing the dress, it made her wonder even more what her life was before she'd ended up half-drowned in the river.

"You look sad," Dominic said, pulling her from her thoughts.

She took a deep breath and relaxed her face. She hadn't realized her eyebrows had been scrunched together. Rolling her shoulders back. She didn't mean to frown or get lost in her thoughts, but it was hard not to think of her past and the time she was missing.

"I'm fine."

Dominic laughed. "Yeah, I've said those words too."

Satcha glared at him out of the corner of her eye. He looked too amused for her liking.

"Really? After everything we've been through, you're still going to keep silent?" He held his hand out again to help her step from the rocks and to even ground, but she didn't accept his help.

Not being used to sandals tied to her feet, nor the slick material padding the sole, she slipped as she jumped from the last big rock toward the tall grass. Dominic reached out to grab her, but she fell with too much momentum and toppled over, pulling him with her. She twisted herself mid-fall and landed on her back only to have Dominic land on top of her. The weight of his body knocked the air out of her lungs.

"Oh, shit!" Dominic rolled to his side with a grunt.

Satcha gasped for air as she rolled herself onto her hands and knees. If she could find her breath, she would've cursed those damned shoes.

"I'm sorry. Are you okay?" Dominic knelt beside her and rested a consoling hand on her shoulder.

She nodded as she coughed.

"It's okay, nice slow breaths. Breathe in... Hold... Breathe out..."

As much as she wanted to rebel against anything he suggested, she listened. Her breathing slowed, letting her collect herself and wipe the tears from her eyes.

Dominic's face was less than a foot away from her own. Without falling under the spell of his green eyes, she pushed herself off the ground and stepped away from him, looking at the rushing waters passing by.

"Why are you so determined to keep me at an arm's length?"

"Why are you trying to get close to me?" she asked him.

He pursed his lips at her. She wasn't sure if he liked that or not.

"It's been a few weeks since we met, and I feel like I barely know you any better than the day we met. You are so quiet. Sometimes when we took a break from training, I would feel as if I peeled back a layer, but you would almost recoil into yourself. I get it. We all have shit we hide from others. Hell, I've got my own baggage; I can tell you do too."

She chewed her lip. It was a foreign idea to her that someone would want to get to know her. She hadn't realized he'd been watching and noticing each time she'd pulled back. He saw her when no one else did and it made her feel exposed. She turned around to face him, his eyes watching her every move.

"I don't know who I am." It was the first time she'd ever said the words out loud to someone other than Agatha. She tried not to think of the crying, confused child of her past, but the fear of the unknown had haunted her all her life.

"What do you mean?" He watched her as if he expected her to magically disappear into thin air.

"I know my name, but that's all I know. I don't know how old I was when Agatha found me, half-dead, covered in my own blood alongside the river just outside Plumos. I guess I'd hit my head and fallen into the river. The oldest memories I have are Agatha cleaning my wounds, nothing from before."

Dominic didn't say a word. She closed her eyes and took a deep breath, trying to collect herself. She wouldn't cry; she'd been hardened by the years she'd spent living without answers.

"What happened to Agatha? You've never mentioned her before," he said eventually.

She kept her eyes closed, not able to look at him. "The Enforcers killed her because she saved me. I got out of the compound because of her."

She expected him to be furious with her for withholding the truth. She waited for him to scold her or lash out, but he didn't. She opened her eyes, expecting him to be gone back to Rios, but he was still there. He closed the space between them and wrapped his arms around her.

She gave in, only for a moment. Her head rested against his chest; she could hear his heart beating. A steady, firm rhythm. She didn't hug him back, letting her arms dangle at her sides. She hadn't hugged someone in a long time.

"I want to show you something," he said, pulling away from her, catching her hand. "Don't worry, I want to make sure you don't fall again."

"Okay." She shifted uncomfortably as he led her onto the rocks, continuing away from the village.

After a half hour, the river sped up, roaring past them, the trees standing tall with the ground rising into a hill. The sound of the crashing water grew loud, reminding Satcha of a heavy rainstorm. They rounded the last bend and found themselves at the base of a hundred-foot waterfall.

Her pace quickened, straining against the grip he still had on her hand. He let her go immediately and she went off ahead of him to stand at the bottom of the waterfall, the mist of the water chilling her skin. She'd never seen anything so beautiful and as amazing as the rushing water rolling from the cliff and crashing down below. She looked back at Dominic; he was grinning, watching her hold her hand out to feel the spray of the water. The blue water looked so inviting. She wanted to dip her feet in and let the cool chill of the water tingle against her skin.

She had imagined waterfalls like this one in the Free City. How could something so beautiful not be in her destined paradise?

"I thought you'd like this place." He reached out, letting the water splash over his hand. "I used to come here all the time to think. It's my favorite place in the world."

"It's beautiful," she murmured. She held her breath realizing how close he stood to her. She stared at his eyes looking back at her, their bodies almost touching.

He'd broken the bubble of space she created. She couldn't look away from him. She shifted her weight, feeling the rough stone poke through the flat soles of her sandals. Slowly, he lifted his hand and stroked her cheek, almost as if testing her reaction. She stayed still despite the screaming going on in her head. She didn't know what was happening, but she wasn't about to stop it either. She swallowed the butterflies in her stomach as if it would help keep them at bay. Heat coursed through her veins, and for the first time since they'd met she knew what she wanted. She wanted him to kiss her.

This revelation brought forth a whole new anxiety. She'd never kissed anyone before, and no one had ever tried to kiss her. What if she did it wrong? What was worse was thinking about his experience and who *he* might have kissed. Was this something he did often? Rescue women in the wilderness and take them back to the base and court them? But no. Of course not. That wasn't him. Honorable to a fault, she had to remind herself.

"So, you think I'm beautiful?" He smiled and his eyes gleamed, tearing her away from her insecurities.

"What?" Memories snapped to the forefront of her head. Him carrying her to the village. Touching his chest, his face.

She groaned, her cheeks growing hot, and she covered her face with her hands. "Oh my Hawk!"

Dominic let out a laugh as he pulled her hands away from her face, forcing her to look at him. She couldn't help but smile at the warmth in his laugh and in his eyes. He leaned down, her neck arching toward him. Her heart thumped against her chest and her breath quickened. This was it; he was going to kiss her. They stopped just inches from each other. She stared into his green eyes, noticing the hazel and flecks of gold. It wasn't the soldier in him that stared back, it was a version of him she'd never seen before.

"*Captain, come in, Captain, over*," a voice called, coming from Dominic's pocket.

He groaned and reluctantly pulled back. Satcha sighed and used this interrupted moment to collect herself.

"Captain Lightwood here, over." He didn't take his eyes off Satcha, but there was an annoyance in his voice as well. She fought the urge to toss the radio into the river. What could possibly be so important right now?

"*Lieutenant Lennox is awake. Over.*"

He sighed.

She could tell he wanted to stay here by the waterfall with her—she certainly did—but his duties called. He needed to attend to his friend and soldier. Honorable Dominic... Loyal, and dependable to a fault.

"We're on our way back, over."

"*Roger that. Over and out*," said the voice on the radio.

Dominic gave her an apologetic smile and clipped the radio back to his side. "We can come back. There's still more I want to show you."

"Okay." With the moment cooling off, she stepped back from him.

"But maybe not right away, we still have work that needs to be done."

His words sobered her. For a fleeting moment, she'd forgotten all about their deal. About the Enforcers. Worse, she'd forgotten all about the Free City, and her revenge.

She scolded herself for letting her guard down and getting sidetracked. She owed it to Agatha to avenge her death. The barrier she'd built up around her had fractures and there was no telling what could send it tumbling down. She wasn't sure she could repair it—or even if she wanted to.

"Don't worry, it will be fine."

She wasn't convinced. She took one last look at the waterfall, thinking she'd never see it again. She'd never get to see what else he wanted to show her. A pit formed in her stomach and weighed heavy with every step back to reality.

As Satcha expected, the moment they returned to the village, he left her at the small building where she'd woken up. She'd grown used to Lennox getting on her nerves, but this made her furious. She understood Dominic's responsibility as the commanding officer, and checking on his soldier, but couldn't someone have radioed him about Lennox's condition? But Dominic wasn't like that. He needed to see his friend for himself.

She sank onto the bed and stared at the ceiling. She was in the wrong and she knew it. He'd told her they were like brothers, that they'd both grown up here. She wondered where their families were. She hadn't spoken to anyone but Dominic since she'd awakened—or seen anyone who resembled him, for that matter. It occurred to her that nobody in Rios looked remotely like him. Green eyes, black hair, olive skin. The people she'd seen were either blonde or had sandy brown hair.

Maybe he was an orphan like her.

She strained to remember her family, but the images that sprang to mind were foggy, vague, like paint smudged across a canvas. The rocking of a chair. A woman's blonde hair against her cheek as she fell asleep. But it was all so long ago, the memories ever fading, like waking from a dream. At this point she couldn't even be sure she hadn't made them all up.

She lay face down on the bed. She would enjoy the comforts of a nice soft bed while she could. She didn't know how much longer she'd have to rest before they were off to face the Enforcers. Again.

Chapter 29

Rosalie

Rosalie smiled at herself in the small handheld mirror as she hummed. Sparkling, big blue eyes stared back at her, excited for the new day. She brushed her long, wavy blonde hair with her fingers until she gave up the daily battle. Her thick hair gave her trouble, and the heat outside didn't do her any favors, but she made do and made sure she looked her best. She slipped on her favorite green dress and spun in place, enjoying the skirt flaring out around her.

"It's perfect!"

It was a big day; soldiers had returned from the army. This excited her, even if one of them was Lennox, but the other was Dominic. It'd been years since she'd seen him. She missed seeing the quiet man walk along the shores. He'd disappear for hours, seemingly not wanting to be found. She'd tried to speak with him many times, but he wasn't much for conversation. Most of the time she'd talked enough for the two of them. She desperately wanted him to open up to her and she took him returning as a sign it was meant to be.

She remembered when he first came to the village many years ago. He was unlike anyone she'd ever met before. She was so used to seeing the same old villagers every day that when a new face appeared she couldn't help but be curious. Where had he come from?

She'd never been anywhere outside the borders of Rios. Her grandfather never allowed it, since it wasn't safe outside their village. Few knew about their village, and even less knew how to find it in the thick jungle forest. From what she'd learned from her grandfather, she wasn't missing anything much out there. She had no desire to leave and face the harsh realities of war. She hated the Nerosians for their attacks on Enross, but she hated them more for taking Dominic away.

Now Dominic was back and there wasn't a doubt in her mind he had more stories locked away inside his head. And she hoped this time she could make him stay.

Rosalie tried not to think about the blonde girl that traveled with them, but she wondered if she was someone they'd rescued along the way. Dominic was like that. Always swooping in to be the hero.

She looked at herself one last time in the mirror and smiled, ready to muster up as much courage as she could and tell him how she'd felt all these years. There was a time she'd thought for sure he'd known, especially after they spent a night together. A dull ache in her chest reminded her of the pain of his absence. She tried to tell herself if he hadn't left for the army they'd be together, but as the years passed it became harder to believe. But he was back now, and that's all that mattered.

A knock at the door startled her. She skipped across the room and opened the door to see her grandmother, Helene, waiting for her.

"Good morning, dear. Don't you look lovely this morning." Helene smiled proudly at her.

"Thank you, Grandma."

"You seem in even brighter spirits than usual this morning. Can I assume a young captain is to blame?"

"It's a beautiful morning and this evening is the harvest feast. What's not to be bright about?" Rosalie couldn't hold back a grin, confirming her grandmother's suspicions. It seemed everyone but Dominic was aware of her deep affections.

She recalled long ago when he told her it wasn't possible to be together it wasn't exactly a *no*. She'd hope that being a soldier had changed something in him. That he would want a sense of home to come back to. She remembered his touch on her skin, so hesitant, but she chalked that up to nerves. The one night he gave into his senses. She longed for that feeling to return. After, he had acted like it was a mistake. For too long she'd born the scars in her heart, but she couldn't help but believe his return was maybe for her.

"I was hoping you wouldn't mind collecting some flowers and making those beautiful arrangements you do for the tables this evening. The flowers are in a lovely bloom."

"I'll get started right away!" She hugged her grandma close and headed out of the large clay and wooden home to the fields. She would make the largest, most beautiful arrangements she'd ever made for this evening.

The morning dew glistened along the tall grass. She was careful not to walk too quickly, for her bare feet slipped and slid along the wet ground. She liked the feel of the earth beneath her feet. Her toes curled around blades of grass as she closed her eyes, feeling the sun's rays on her cheeks. Her grandma told her many times about how well her name fit her and that her mother loved nature just as much as she did. She had no memories of her parents, who had died when she was only three. Her mother had fallen ill and even her grandmother couldn't banish away the fever that never broke. Her father left for the army and never came home; she was sure the Enforcers were to blame.

Rosalie sat in the middle of the field looking at the flowers surrounding her. A variety of flowers grew in the large field. Daisies, baby blue eyes, buttercups, black-eyed susans, and violets. She gathered many but was careful not to pick them all nor any of the plants with healing properties. She organized them into bunches for each table's centerpiece, but at the head table, where the guests would join them, she would make a special bouquet. Her own special touch. She would arrange roses of every color she could find and hope to catch Dominic's eye. She would wait for the late afternoon to keep them as fresh and fragrant as possible.

Rosalie stood, gazing over the meadow with a keen sense of pride for the nature in the village until she noticed near her feet, she had bent the stem of a daisy. She knelt, caressing the pedals gently. She enclosed the head of the flower in her hands and closed her eyes. In her mind, she pictured the stem pulling itself back and cementing the bonds holding it in place.

When she removed her hands, the daisy stayed in place, its stem no longer bent. The only indicator there was anything amiss was a light green scar across the stem where it had almost snapped. It was something she was working toward fixing.

She'd hoped that with more training she could eventually heal people like she could with flowers, but she was a long way off and her grandmother wouldn't push her. Her gift became strong each time she used it, but it took a lot of energy from her. All her life, Rosalie felt like a flower encased in glass. Plenty of sunlight to grow and watered when needed, but stuck, never able to leave her pedestal.

Her grandparents and the rest of the villagers treated her like a fragile little girl. For all she knew, she was. Sometimes it made her feel small and helpless while other times—not often

—it enraged her. Dominic was the only one who didn't treat her like a precious flower to be cherished and coddled.

Guilt welled in her suddenly, she couldn't think about it anymore—which was how she spent most of her days, ignoring the privileged and sheltered life she lived.

By afternoon, the sun set high in the sky, and she had completed a dozen large bouquets. She stood back, proud of her work, when she noticed Dominic in the corner of her eye. But he wasn't alone. He walked through the village with the girl she'd helped her grandma heal from veneno poisoning. Her smile, which had been plastered on her face all day, faded away as she watched them walk into a small guest house together. Her heart sank into her stomach, and she swayed uneasily. She stared at the door to the house trying to collect herself, trying to convince herself he'd only been helping her back to her room. Nothing else.

A moment went by before he appeared in the doorway with a grim look on his face. That thawed her. As if on instinct, she stepped forward, making her way toward him.

"Dominic! It's been so long!" she called after him. He stopped in his tracks and slowly turned around to face her.

"Rosalie." He nodded in acknowledgement but didn't hesitate to keep walking.

"I was hoping we could catch up. I would love to hear about your travels."

"Travels?" he snapped at her, turning on his heels to face her. "In what world do you live in that you think what I do is travel around on some grand adventure?"

She flinched. His face was hardened and unfriendly, like the time she'd given a bouquet of flowers to Margery, a grieving widow. To anyone else, the flowers would've been a thoughtful gift, but poor Margery's face swelled and hives spread across her skin. *Stupid girl,* the woman had scolded her.

It scared her to have someone so cross with her and the way Dominic looked at her made her insides twist.

"I'm sorry," she said softly. There was nothing else to say. She didn't mean to insult him, but he'd clearly been preoccupied with something. He shook his head and headed toward the medical camp. Tears welled in the corners of her eyes as she watched him walk away. Of course, she'd been insensitive. He must've been off to check on Lennox. She shook herself free of the sadness and tried to think about the beautiful bouquet she'd made. Maybe he'd be happier at dinner. Men were in better moods when they had food in their bellies.

She headed to the edge of the fields to find the rose bushes. She inspected each one before delicately trimming them at the right length to arrange. She'd talk to him after dinner. She smiled to herself and pushed the blonde girl out of her thoughts.

CHAPTER 30

DOMINIC

Dominic knew he'd been too hard on Rosalie and could give excuse after excuse on why he'd spoken to her so cruelly, but it didn't change the fact he did not care for her the way she wanted.

Guilt for the way he treated Rosalie wasn't the only guilt weighing heavy on him. Sneaking off with Satcha to the waterfall and not staying at Lennox's bedside was not something he regretted but carrying Satcha ahead for help was. It seemed right at the time. He couldn't stop picturing her laying in the road, dying, when he'd first found her.

He strode into Lennox's room to find Helene standing over him, her hands placed on each side of his head. Aleksandr stood close to the door watching his wife.

"Lennox," Dominic called to him when he reached his bedside, but Lennox didn't respond.

"Helene put him back to sleep," said Aleksandr. "His wounds are healed, but his brain doesn't know the difference yet."

"When will he recover?" Dominic asked, looking at Helene, who hummed to herself while using her magic on

Lennox. A white sheet covered Lennox; he couldn't see the wound but trusted Aleksandr when he said it was healed. His chest didn't feel quite as heavy and tense as it had before, but he was still filled with worry.

"There you go, sleep, Lennox," Helene whispered. She released her hold on him only to stumble and catch herself on the bedside table.

"Helene!" Aleksandr rushed to her, grasping her tight.

"I'm fine, I'm fine. It took a little more than I am used to. I just need to rest," she said, patting her husband's arm and giving him a faint smile.

"Of course, my love," Aleksandr said. "Dominic, please help me take Helene home."

Dominic looked back and forth from Aleksandr and Lennox, not knowing if he should stay or not. He owed a great deal to Helene for doing what she could for Lennox—and Satcha— and Lennox lay quiet, sound asleep. There was nothing he could do in the meantime.

Dominic nodded and took Helene's arm, letting her shift some of her weight against him while Aleksandr steadied her other side.

"Helene, thank you so much for all you have done. I don't know what we would've done without you and Aleksandr," Dominic said as they made their way out of the medical building.

"You're most welcome, dear."

Once they reached Helene's bedroom, Aleksandr opened the door and led his wife inside while Dominic waited. Aleksandr helped settle her into bed and gave her a kiss on the cheek before turning to leave. Dominic's cheeks flushed, feeling uncomfortable witnessing such an intimate moment between the two.

"Come with me, if you will." Aleksandr clapped his hand on Dominic's shoulder, leading him through the hallway.

Dominic followed Aleksandr into his office, a room he remembered well. Dominic had often found himself there, asking all kinds of questions about Rios and the people who'd lived in the village, but Aleksandr always left him with vague responses. Sometimes he even lost his patience and refused to answer any questions.

The room hadn't changed since the last time he'd been there. Tall shelves lined one wall of the study, full of books, scrolls, and artifacts from long ago. In the middle of the room sat an old desk with an uncomfortable looking wooden chair. Spread across the desk were papers and sketches of Enross. It didn't make sense for Aleksandr to have maps of the country, since as far as Dominic knew he'd never left the village. Not many had and those who did rarely returned.

"Your friend killed an Enforcer outside the boundary line. If I hadn't been out for a walk, the other would've killed her with ease and likely crept closer to the village," Aleksandr said as he sat in the chair behind the desk.

"I had no idea the Enforcers were traveling this far north." Dominic strolled over to the shelves, his eyes scanning the books, but not reading the words written on the spines. His head was back in captain mode.

"This is the closest they've come thus far. I've had our security team set additional traps around the area, but nothing has been triggered. I wasn't sure what could've led them our way until you showed up."

Dominic froze. It was another thing he'd blinded himself too: the Enforcers were looking for them.

"I'm not sure what you have done, but you've left a trail behind you and led them back here to us. I warned you when you set out all those years ago to join your precious army that this would happen. You've put my family and my people at risk," Aleksandr scolded.

"I'm sorry, I had no other choice. I never wanted to lead

them here, but we needed help and were cut off from returning to the base." Dominic leaned back against the bookshelf and ran his hand through his hair. "I—"

"I'm not done," Aleksandr said, effectively cutting Dominic off. "You have brought an outsider into the village."

Dominic winced. He hadn't thought of that. He knew the rules, but he wasn't thinking.

"You cannot bring your outside problems into Rios."

"Why are you ignoring the rest of the world?" Dominic snapped. "Do you not have any guilt for leaving people to die at the hands of the Enforcers?" He may have broken Aleksandr's rules, but he was too angry to ignore Aleksandr's blind eye any longer.

"I am responsible for the people in this village and nowhere else. I have protected them and made this place safe to not have to worry about the Enforcers or Austerland—if they even still exist. We are not equipped to help anyone but ourselves, even if we wanted to."

"I'm not saying you have to go to war, though those capable of fighting should join ranks. You have something the Enforcers don't have. You have Helene. She could make a difference in our medical wing, not just her gift, but her knowledge as a healer."

"I will not put my wife at risk! You saw what happened to her when she healed Lennox, do you think she is in any condition to use that much energy on a regular basis?"

Dominic didn't know much about Helene's gift or what its limitations were, but today proved what toll it would take on her, something he'd not considered before. Despite that, he stayed silent, unwilling to concede his own point.

"Dominic, I do not want to argue about this." Aleksandr stood from his desk. "You may remain here until Lennox is healed enough to travel, but I'd ask that you leave as soon as that time comes and take the trail of the Enforcers with you."

"Fine." Dominic narrowed his eyes at the old man and clenched his fists at his side, knowing he wouldn't get any further in the discussion with him. His history of attempts had proved that. He headed to the doorway, needing to escape before his anger took over.

"Oh, and one last thing, for old times' sake," Aleksandr called. Dominic hesitated as he reached the door. "The harvest feast is tonight. You and your female companion are welcome to join us in the community hall."

Dominic left the room without responding.

CHAPTER 31

SATCHA

S atcha stayed in the house for an hour or so, not wanting to leave. She didn't know these people and didn't want to. She already found herself in more than enough trouble getting close to Dominic. She didn't like the uneasy feeling she got being around so many strangers, but the rumble in her empty stomach couldn't be ignored.

She groaned and rolled on to her side. She didn't want to think about any of it anymore. She needed to clear her mind. She needed rest, but her mind raced.

She lay on her side looking at the skin on the back of her hand. Whoever healed her had done a better job cleaning her than she had when she'd bathed at the Enross Army Base. Who had bathed her? Knots twisted in her stomach. She didn't like the fact someone had cleaned and clothed her while she was passed out.

Was it Dominic?

Surely not. She examined the back of her hand again, looking at a few freckles scattered over her wrist and up her arm. She'd never noticed them before, always too covered in dirt and sweat to see them.

Seeing the freckles made her question herself. How well did she even know herself? She knew the nomad survivor she'd turned into over the years, but unease lingered. She wished she knew where she'd come from. She didn't like wondering; there was no point when she had no one to ask.

She brushed her fingertips along her wrist, feeling the tingle of her slight touch. Not like Dominic's touch. His was something more powerful, electric, something that left her wanting more.

Despite their walk earlier, energy pulsed through her body. She needed to move. She couldn't stare at the same four walls anymore. She needed to get out. She didn't like the thought of being reliant on Dominic. Relying on other people only got them killed. Like Agatha.

She wouldn't sit around any longer. She hopped off the bed and made her way to the door.

Just like the first time she walked through the small village, people flooded everywhere going about their day. Children played with a makeshift ball, kicking it and running after it when it rolled away, and women sat in the sun weaving baskets. A group of villagers weeded a garden and a girl picked flowers at the edge of the forest. Satcha couldn't believe how carefree the people looked. She wondered again if they were unaware of the danger lurking beyond their borders.

She watched the girl picking flowers, wondering what she was doing all by herself. Everyone else seemed to be enjoying the company of others. It gave her some relief that there were some who valued their space in this village.

Something hit Satcha square in the back, knocking her forward. She stumbled, barely catching herself, before she could fall to the ground. She whipped around, looking for the attacker, but there was no one there. Behind her on the ground lay the children's ball. The four children stood wide-eyed, looking apprehensive. She relaxed her stance and ducked her head down before stalking off.

"Not used to being around people, are you?" a voice called from behind her.

Satcha froze. She turned her head to see the blonde girl who'd been picking flowers. Maybe it was a bad idea to venture out into the village; she had no idea what to say to them since she normally didn't socialize with others in villages she passed through.

"I hope you like the dress," the girl called out again. Satcha clenched her fists at her side as she realized she must've been the person who cleaned and dressed her.

She turned and looked at the girl, noticing she wore a green dress in a similar style to the blue one she wore.

"You must've seen many places. I've never left Rios before. I'd love to see the Westim Ocean. I know it's far from here and on the Austerland side, but I think it would be—"

"You talk a lot," Satcha interrupted. She knew she'd been rude, but it just slipped out. But she didn't make any attempt to apologize.

"Yes, I've been told that before, but we don't get travelers here very often. I've read all the books we keep in the village several times, but there's still so much more to learn." The girl smiled and looked toward the forest in wonder.

Satcha didn't want to get into it any further with this girl, as she clearly had a naive perception on what lay beyond the forest, but Satcha didn't have the social skills to know how to act. She needed room to breathe. She needed some time alone; too much had happened since they'd arrived. She just needed a moment to herself to think things over.

"I'm Rose, by the way. Rosalie, but I go by Rose, like the flower." Rosalie followed Satcha and fell into step next to her. She must've been about Satcha's age, she stood at her height, but her naivety knocked a year or two off.

Satcha sighed. "I'm—"

"Satcha! There you are." Dominic strode over to her.

Rose smiled at him, but he didn't see. His gaze was focused on Satcha.

"I need to talk to you," he said. He looked too rattled to have just visited Lennox. Something was wrong. His eyes were dark, and his jaw was clenched tight. A tension radiated from him.

"What's wrong?"

"Let's go somewhere private."

Rose looked between the two of them, the smile slipping from her face. Satcha didn't care about her or her naïve questions about the outside world; she wanted to know what was wrong. It must've been Lennox. He was dead, she was sure of it. As much as she despised him, she was sad for Dominic.

"Um, I'll leave you guys alone then." Rose waved her hand awkwardly before heading back to tend to her flowers.

Dominic led Satcha back to the house with her hand grasped firmly in his. What could she say to him? She didn't know how to console someone, especially since she didn't even like Lennox in the first place.

They sat on the bed, as if in sync with each other, and Dominic put his head in his hands.

"Dom, what's wrong? Lennox?" She'd never called him that before, but it just slipped out naturally as if she'd said it a thousand times before.

"There's things about this village, these people, that I haven't told you." He rubbed his temples. "Lennox will be fine. The healers here are good, really good."

"I don't understand." She was confused, watching him intently and wondering why he didn't seem thrilled that Lennox would be fine. But his words sparked something, a question that lingered in the depths of her mind, something she wasn't sure could possibly be answered. "What do you mean Lennox will be fine?"

"Do you believe that some people may have skills beyond the norm?" he asked, avoiding her question.

The hesitancy in his voice startled her. "What do you mean?"

"Never mind." He sighed and scrubbed a hand over his jaw.

She wasn't quite sure what to make of him so shaken up, but she couldn't hold back any longer. Her stomach groaned in protest reminding her she hadn't eaten since they left the army base.

Dominic's tension thawed at the sound, and he laughed lightly.

"Come on, let's go get something to eat. We showed up on the perfect day; it's their harvest fest tonight."

She followed him with her head down, not wanting to make eye contact with the villagers, but it seemed they were all headed to the same place. The large brick building sat further down the river; she hadn't noticed the large structure earlier when she was wandering. It looked large enough to fit the entire population of the village inside. She guessed by the swarm of people heading toward it, there must've been at least two hundred of them.

Several groups nodded or waved to Dominic who nodded back in acknowledgement. Satcha couldn't help but step behind him to avoid drawing attention to herself, but he matched her step and brought her back to his side.

Double doors opened wide and inviting. The crowd filtered through the entryway. The wafting smell of cooked fish made her stomach growl even louder than before.

The villagers lined up, collecting their meals wrapped in big green leaves on clay plates before finding a spot to sit. When they reached the front of the line, Satcha took the scorching plate with a hot leaf wrap and fought off the urge to gobble it down right there. Dominic thanked the woman handing out food and grabbed two wooden utensils from the table.

Satcha hoped they would go back to the house, but he led her along toward a long table at the very front. Long wooden tables lined the hall with chairs on both sides, a dozen elderly villagers seated already, eating their dinners. One familiar face stood out in the sea of strangers.

Aleksandr sat at the middle of the table with a woman on his left and a man on his right. The man next to him looked so old, he looked as if he might keel over and die any moment.

"Dominic, thank you for joining us," Aleksandr greeted him, nodding to Satcha. "It's not often we get guests during our harvest festival, let alone yourself and Lennox."

"Thank you, Aleksandr, to you and the healers for treating Lennox, and helping Satcha as well. I owe you a great debt," Dominic said as he sat at the table across from Aleksandr and nodded to Satcha to take a seat as well.

"Satcha?" Aleksandr said, surprised. His eyes widened and he grasped the hand of the woman next to him.

"Yes?" She peered at Dominic hoping he'd explain, but he looked as confused as her.

"My, what a pretty girl," said the woman next to Aleksandr. Satcha looked at the woman, unsure what to say. No one had ever called her pretty before. Not that she'd ever been this well-groomed.

Satcha felt her cheeks grow warm. She stared at the wrap in front of her and waited for Dominic to say something. She'd never sat at a table like this with friends, family, or even a sense of community, like these people. She'd seen others do it while passing through towns, but never experienced it herself.

"I'm glad Rosalie and I chose the right dress for you. That soft blue complements your pale skin well," the woman continued. Satcha was a little relieved that a man hadn't cleaned and dressed her, an old lady seemed harmless enough, but she still felt violated.

Satcha stayed quiet. She looked back and forth between Aleksandr and the strange old woman. Her long white braided hair laid over her left shoulder with white daisies woven throughout. She wore a muted red tunic dress and despite her aging years, her beauty was not hindered by the laugh wrinkles on her face.

Satcha was uneasy, her stomach rolling uncomfortably, and despite her hunger had to force herself to eat the white fish and rice before her. Aleksandr never took his eyes off her as she ate. If it wasn't for the fact he'd helped save them, she would've at least questioned his stare vocally. Instead, she tried her best to ignore him and fill her belly.

"You'll have to excuse me; I am suddenly feeling ill. So wonderful to see you again, Dominic." The old woman reached across the table and shook his hand. She didn't look at Satcha again before she left the table, Aleksandr right behind her.

"That was weird," Satcha whispered to Dominic.

"She's had a busy day, maybe some rest will do her some good," he said in a low voice.

They finished their meals in companionable silence.

"Are you ready to go?" Dominic nudged Satcha's side once her plate was empty.

After the awkward encounter with Aleksandr and the old woman, she was eager to leave. She'd grown tired being around so many people. She stood at once and made her way back to the entrance. Dominic walked next to her with a slight smile on his face. It put her on edge. She walked quickly out of the building; she didn't like having people behind her—especially a few dozen. Without her knife, she felt too exposed.

"Where's my knife?" she blurted when they were out of earshot from anyone else.

"I have it for you back at the house," Dominic said, seemingly unbothered by her question.

But it gave her mind some relief. The knife and her worn leather satchel were her only possessions in the world. She hoped her bag was safe back at base and wondered again if she'd ever get it back.

CHAPTER 32

ROSALIE

Rosalie didn't have it in herself to eat and enjoy the feast. All her hard work arranging flowers had been for nothing. Her normal constant smile and cheery mood was nowhere to be found—not with Dominic smiling at Satcha, seated across from her grandparents. Her heart ached to see him so happy with another girl and she couldn't bear to watch any longer. With no one watching her, she made her way out of the dining hall and off to her room where she intended to have a good cry. She'd never been one to hide her tears, but she didn't want to let Dominic see any hint of sadness in her.

She wanted to be mad at him for looking so happy with anyone but her, but the fact of the matter was she'd never seen him smile like that before. Satcha, whoever she was, made him happy in ways Rosalie never could before. For Hawk's sake, he sat so close that their arms touched and every time one moved away, the other instinctively closed the gap.

Rosalie was just always going to be the mistake he'd made and a secret he would never share.

It shook her to her core. How long had she been pining

over him? Years and years without even the slightest bit of interest from him—even after they'd spent the night together. How could it not have meant anything to him when it meant the world to her?

A tear slipped down her cheek as she made her way into her bedroom and shut the door behind her. She couldn't face him after this. A great shame built up in her chest after all the years wasted she waited for him.

What if she had moved on from her feelings for Dominic? Would she have met someone else in the village? Surely she would've been an ideal wife for someone. And not only that, but she was next in line for leader of the People of Rios, to take her grandfather's place when he could do no more. She didn't like to think about that though. She knew that day would come eventually, but like everything it came with a price.

Many of her friends had already gotten married and some even had a child or two. She tried to think of someone she could possibly see herself with, but with the population being so small in Rios, everyone was either a relative or too old. Most importantly, they were not Dominic.

She sobbed quietly into her pillow, careful not to draw attention to anyone in the hallway. This was her burden to bear, and she wouldn't let her embarrassment extend beyond her own knowing.

"Aleksandr, what are we to do about the girl?" Her grandmother's voice came from the other side of Rosalie's bedroom door.

Rosalie shot up out of bed and quieted her crying to listen. Who were they talking about? Was it her? She imagined they were probably embarrassed their own granddaughter had been passed over for some stranger in Dominic's eyes.

"I don't know, but she can't stay here," her grandfather replied.

Rosalie tiptoed to her door and rested her ear against the wood, listening while trying to control her fears.

Who can't stay here?

"I agree, it's far too dangerous. I'd rather her be safe in Dominic's care than remain here where she could be found."

Nothing her grandmother made any sense. Why would they care about Satcha's safety? They hadn't known her before; Rosalie was sure of it. She had no inkling in her mind that could recall anyone by that name.

"No, he can't be trusted with her. There's only one place to send her and that's Reeock. Hide her among the people."

"I feel like we are losing her all over again. Are you sure she can't stay?" Her grandmother stifled a sob that twisted Rosalie's heart. She wanted to open the door and console her.

"You know as well as I do that can't happen. I'll see to it tonight with the guards."

Footsteps faded away down the hall leaving Rosalie still listening by the door. When she was sure no one remained on the other side, she sat back on her bed and stared at the wall, trying to piece what she'd heard together.

She stared at herself in the mirror, her blue eyes surrounded by red and puffy cheeks and her long bushy hair, more disheveled than she'd seen it in a long time. Not since she'd lost track of time while walking through the forest taking in the beautiful nature and listening to the birds sing. It was a usual occurrence for her to get lost despite her years living in Rios, but she'd found herself walking straight into one of the defensive traps lining the border. She had tripped over a vine and suddenly was hanging by her right ankle, screaming while trying to keep herself covered when her dress fell over her face.

She didn't know how long she'd been hanging there when they finally found her. She'd cried all the tears her body had to offer and screamed until her throat was raw. She couldn't help but feel the same way now as she did then. Left alone crying and waiting for someone to come save her. It was a helpless-ness she'd grown used to.

She took a shaky breath as she tried to collect herself. She didn't *want* to be a damsel in distress waiting for someone to save her. She couldn't help but admire Satcha, a girl she barely knew. She didn't know why, but something about her screamed she was a survivor.

Rosalie didn't think she would ever be able to get the sight of Satcha's scars out of her mind. Never had she known such violence in her short, sheltered life, yet this girl—who seemed close in age to her—had endured so much. It made her fear the outside world. She'd overheard conversations between her grandfather and the village guards about the Enforcers from Neroso and their attacks on cities in both Austerland and Enross, but never did she imagine she'd ever witness what that damage was.

There was no way in her mind, a girl from Rios who picked flowers and nurtured her garden, would survive a journey to Reeock, like her grandparents planned for Satcha. How could they think it was right to send Satcha away to the same fate? She couldn't sit by and let this happen! She needed to act before a final decision was made—regardless of Satcha's connection with Dominic.

Rosalie straightened her dress and ran her fingers through her hair. She wiped any tear stains remaining on her pink cheeks and squared her shoulders. She needed to have a talk with her grandfather, and it wouldn't be one he'd ever expect to hear from her. With her mind set and no hesitation, she swung open the door and marched into the hallway.

CHAPTER 33

SATCHA

The orange sunset over the village reflected off the calm flowing river. Birds chirped and flew overhead while little firebugs glowed throughout the jungle. Satcha still found it difficult to understand why Dominic ever chose to leave this place, even if it was to protect it. It was beautiful, though she wasn't keen on the joyous villagers. Not that she wouldn't have loved to have her own house along the river's edge, but it made her uncomfortable how unaware and aloof they were to the dangers in the outside world.

"We should rest tonight. In the morning we can plan for our departure, once Lennox is well enough," Dominic said once they were in the house. He busied himself by laying out a blanket on the floor and setting a pillow next to the bed.

Satcha watched him hunker down on the floor in slight disbelief. Was he really planning on staying here with her? Again?

"I have something for you, by the way," Dominic said, pulling a small jar from his coat.

"What is it?" she asked, sitting up a little taller, curious.

He stepped toward her, his lips pressed tightly. She leaned forward, not able to help herself.

"I'm not sure if you would want this or not, but I thought I would at least give you the option. In this jar contains a special salve from the veneno flower—the white flower you found for Lennox. Helene has developed this salve with her... skills. It can remove any scar or blemish from one's skin," he explained. He opened the jar, holding it open for her to see a purple paste inside.

"I don't understand," she said softly, not able to take her eyes off the salve.

"It's a chance for a fresh start; you can get rid of your scars."

"That's impossible." She shook her head. Never had she considered she would have the opportunity to shed the marks on her skin. It was *impossible*.

"May I?" He held his hand out to her.

Satcha eyed him, searching for the joke but there was no mirth in his green eyes. She held out her hand; she had several scars on the back of her right hand, though she didn't remember where they'd come from.

Dominic scooped a pea sized dollop of the salve and massaged it onto her hand. The thick purple paste turned white as it soaked into her skin and a slight tingle spread across her hand where the salve touched her—not quite burning, but with a distinct heat to it.

"Look now," he said, releasing her hand.

Satcha gasped.

My scars are gone!

"How is such a thing possible?" she asked in amazement, tilting her hand side to side to catch the light.

Dominic smiled at her. "As I said, Helene has a unique gift for healing. This jar is for you. Wipe it all away if you want."

No one had ever given her such a gift before. Her eyes

couldn't help but linger on his smiling face as it was not often he smiled so widely. The long, thin scar on his face stood out more than she'd ever noticed before. She wondered why he'd never erased his own scar if he had access to this salve. From the moment she first met him, she wondered how he got it, but never got the courage to ask.

"I don't think I can accept such a gift," she said, dipping her head to stare at her unblemished hand once again.

"Why not? It's for you, I *want* you to have this, but I can understand if you don't want to use it."

"No, I do, and I appreciate it..." She hesitated. "But how can I accept this when you haven't removed your own scar?"

He said nothing. Guilt filled her belly and she ducked her head down, to not look at the jagged scar across his face.

"I'm sorry, I didn't mean to push you into anything. I—"

"No, no. It's fine," he said, breaking his silence. "I've just never considered it until today."

Satcha sighed in relief and gave him a small smile. He didn't return one, but he didn't look angry. He looked sad.

"I will accept this gift and use it if you will too," she said quickly. She was extending an olive branch to him, bridging a gap between them. She wanted so badly for him to take it, and that scared her.

Dominic inhaled deeply and kept it in his chest. He nodded in agreement.

Satcha dipped her finger in the jar, scooping a small amount of paste. She held her hand up to him, hesitating, giving him the chance to say no.

He didn't. He stared at her and gave a slight nod. He released his breath, closing his eyes for a second, before opening them. His beautiful green eyes met hers, and time suspended for a moment. Then he nodded.

She massaged the salve into his skin, ever so delicate. He

sat incredibly still, like he'd turned to stone. Within thirty seconds, the scar that once plagued his face had disappeared.

She shifted back, giving him space and heard him let out a soft sigh.

"It's your turn," he said. He jumped into action, rubbing salve on her left wrist where a scar from Enforcer bindings shone in the light. He meticulously went along her arms, erasing all the evidence of her scars. Every time his skin touched her, a shock rocketed down her spine.

"I think I'll need some help with my back too, if that's all right." She looked up at him, feeling more exposed than she'd ever felt before. A rush of heat filled her cheeks, embarrassed she'd asked, but he was the only one she trusted.

He nodded, swallowed thickly as he closed the space between them. Her mouth went dry as she turned from him, combing her hair over her shoulders, leaving them exposed thanks to the backless blue dress.

His hands rested on her shoulders, his thumbs rubbing against her skin, chasing away any fear inside her. He withdrew his hands and immediately she missed the heat and pressure of them against her.

Just as soon as his hands left her body, they were back on her massaging cold salve into her scars. She let out a sigh unsure if the tingling was the scars healing, or from his touch. Heat rippled along her skin, but not like before when her scars dissolved. This was new. She leaned back into his touch without realizing and rested her hand on his knee.

"I'm done. They're all gone," he whispered, his hands leaving her back.

Her breath was shallow as she turned to look at him. Neither moved. She fought the urge to reach for his hand and place it back on her shoulders, her neck, her side, *anywhere* just to have that feeling back. She couldn't help but think of him outside the Enforcer tower with his shirt off. His strong shoulders and chest...

A shiver rippled through her. Her surprise in feeling something she'd never felt before fell to the wayside as her thoughts provoked and stoked the fire more. She wanted to take that shirt off him and run her fingers along his muscles. Something she'd never imagined doing or thinking before. She was like a stranger in her own head.

She didn't know where to look. His eyes? His lips? She rubbed her wrist absentmindedly. Her heart beat so hard she was sure it would burst out of her chest at any moment.

A small smile appeared on his face, making her stomach do backflips. He wrapped his arm around her waist, resting his hand on her hip. The fire burning inside her heated at the touch of his hand and her stomach did backflips. Another shiver ran through her, and Dominic let out a quiet laugh, circling his thumb over her hip bone.

She gazed at him through her eyelashes wondering what it would feel like if he kissed her. As if reading her mind, he leaned down and after a brief moment where his lips hovered over hers, he kissed her. Electricity rushed through her veins, and she deepened the kiss greedily, as if she never would again. As if she would never taste his cool breath again or feel his tongue slip into her mouth ever so gently and meet hers.

She couldn't help but lean back against the pillow and let him follow her. Her hands glided along his back and pulled him close, tugging his shirt from his pants and finding his skin. Her awareness darted everywhere his hands touched, burning under his palms with her desire for more of him.

Her hands found his chest and fingered the buttons loose on his shirt. Without thinking, she reached out her hands and ran them across the smooth, hard muscles of his chest. A sigh escaped him, and his hands slid up the side of her hips, taking the hem of her dress along with them. An urgency took over, nothing else mattered but him. She ran her hands over his hard chest. His fingers touched the edges of her underwear and if the little hut burst into flames, she didn't care. All she wanted, all she craved, was him.

A loud knock banged against the door. Dominic groaned against her lips, his hands sliding down her legs. Satcha tried to catch her breath, fire still raging in her veins. There was a wild look in his eyes that told her he wanted this as much as she did. She didn't want to know who was at the door, she just wanted him.

"Ignore it," she choked out.

"Believe me, I want to." He sighed, and forcing himself from the bed, buttoned his shirt on the way to the door. Satcha lay on the bed, breathing heavily, annoyed at the interruption. What could someone possibly want?

It must've been someone with an update on Lennox. *He better be dead*, she thought savagely.

"I'll be right back." He doubled back to her, giving her a quick kiss on the lips before slipping out the door. It wasn't enough, she wanted more. She *needed* more!

She stared at the ceiling, her breathing slowing, but her desire didn't sober. It was an unwelcome distraction, one that left her with troubled thoughts. She'd let herself get carried away again with him. She needed to focus, not continue to attach herself to him.

Satcha strode to the sink and splashed water on her face. She couldn't hear Dominic outside. She was sure he wouldn't have left without letting her know. She peered out the window; the sun had set and the moonlight reflected off the river. Everything was quiet.

Too quiet. Her skin crawled in the eerie silence and knots formed in her stomach.

She wished she knew where her knife was; she had no means of protection. She crept toward the door on bare feet, listening for something. She wasn't sure what. Where had Dominic gone? She pushed the door open but before she could take a step, a hand reached out and grabbed her by the neck.

A figure with a black mask and a dark cloak held a hand over her mouth, quickly shoving a rag in it to keep her quiet. Before he could remove his hand, she bit down hard on his fingers and didn't stop until she tasted blood. The man screamed and ripped his hand from her jaw, but before she could move the man gripping her throat, the man hooked an elbow around her neck. She fought back wildly but couldn't break free from his strong grasp. If she had her knife, she would've had a fighting chance. She wasn't strong, but she was quick. And being quick made her deadly. But there was no getting out of this.

The two men restrained her hands, tying them behind her back. They adjusted the rag in her mouth and tied it behind her head. It tasted like sweat and dirt. She tried to spit it out, but it was tied too tight. Her eyes searched in the dark for Dominic, but she couldn't see anything except the cloaked men and the moon shining on the huts.

A loud noise interrupted the pounding of her heart. She turned, straining against her captors when she saw Dominic.

He fought against three more cloaked assailants, not thirty feet from her. One had tackled him to the ground, but he leapt up immediately, lunging forward, the others trying their best to grab hold of him. He held his own against them until a fourth man stalked up behind him and hit him over the head with a large piece of wood.

Dominic crumpled to the ground and didn't move.

She screamed for him, fighting through the gag, but it did no good. The cry ripped against her vocal cords, sending an invisible fire raging in her throat.

Her attackers carried her to a wagon, the tethered horses

shifting uneasily, and tossed her unceremoniously into a wooden box. The lid slammed shut. The loud click of the lock ricocheted through her bones. The box was solid oak and smelled like rotten fish, and had small holes on the side. She felt like an animal.

She tried to scream again, but only a whine came out. She kicked against the box as hard as she could, but the lid didn't budge. Her hands ached under her weight where they were tied behind her back.

Where are they taking me? Is Dominic okay? Who are they?

They couldn't be Enforcers; they weren't dressed like them, nor did she see any other part of the village under attack. If it were the Enforcers, there would have been steel vehicles rolling through the village, crushing everything in their path.

It had to be the villagers.

There was something weird about Aleksandr and the old woman. Why had they reacted to her name so strangely?

Satcha's throat could no longer take her muffled screams, dry and begging for a drink of cool water to quench the burning. She focused on the sound of hooves pounding against the ground. Every bump in the road made the box jump, sending her flying against the sides or hitting her head on the top. She prepared to be covered in bruises, not to mention splinters, once she escaped.

She was going to escape.

There was no chance to rest, only time for planning. The first snag in her plan was that she didn't know where they were taking her. Maybe the Free People of Rios had made a deal with the Enforcers? But that didn't seem likely; Enforcers didn't make deals. Maybe a deal with Austerland?

She kicked her feet in frustration. She wanted answers, but she wouldn't get them.

She let the rage and hate for her kidnappers build up inside her. She imagined her anger growing so deep, so consuming, that she'd burst into flames and burn the box open. She pictured slaughtering them one by one. She settled into her fantasy, conserving her energy, and started to plan her escape. They had to let her out of the box at some point; she'd get her revenge one way or another.

CHAPTER 34

ROSALIE

Rosalie looked through the whole house but neither her grandfather nor grandmother could be found. This only built up her rage as her feet raced from room to room with her fist clenched tight at her sides, feet stomping. Her nails dug into the palms of her hands, but she didn't loosen her grip, she wanted it to hurt. She wanted to know she could take the pain and live through it.

She made her way out of their living quarters and back to the dining hall. She would make a scene and didn't care who witnessed it; she needed them to know she was serious.

A scream tore through the air, breaking through the quiet night. Rosalie flinched and froze like a startled deer.

What was that? More importantly, *who* was that?

Rosalie lost all her nerve and unclenched her hands, red half-moon indentations in her skin. Footsteps rushed toward the door ahead of her, and Rosalie snapped into action, diving into the alcove and hoping whoever was coming wouldn't find her.

Has someone attacked the village? It's not possible...!

"How could you? A box? Surely, there were safer options

for her other than a box, Aleksandr!" Her grandmother's voice rang with anger.

Rosalie leaned back against the wall, reeling. She couldn't even begin to understand what had happened that day. Dominic returned to the village with a mysterious woman, Lennox was on the verge of losing his leg, and her grandparents had conspired to send the woman away to Reeock... Nothing made sense. Nothing.

"It's best not to think of it. I know it was harsh, but we can't have her coming back. She's much stronger than we expected, it was for her own safety as well as the driver's," Aleksandr replied. "The driver will sedate her and take her out once they get to Velha. We can't have her finding her way back here."

Rosalie peeked around the corner and watched as her grandmother fell apart in her grandfather's arms.

"They... wouldn't have... wanted this... We should be protecting her..." Helene sobbed.

"Helene, we are protecting her," Aleksandr said softly, wrapping his arms around her tightly.

"What's happened?" Rosalie's feet carried her out of the shadows to face her grandparents. All the rage left her body as she got a clear sight of her grandmother's distraught face, full of anguish and pain. She'd never known her grandmother not to smile and it hurt her to see her like that.

Her grandmother turned away and fled down the hall, leaving Rosalie and her grandfather staring at each other.

"Nothing is wrong, sweet Rose. You should head on to bed and get some rest." Her grandfather smiled, but it didn't reach his eyes. Something was wrong.

"Is Grandma all right?" She moved toward him but Aleksandr turned Rosalie by her shoulders back to her room.

"Your grandmother is having a bad night. The harvest feast was a special time for your mother and grandmother.

Every year she does her best to make it through without her, but there's a hole in her heart that will never be filled," he said without looking at her.

Rosalie had never seen her grandmother cry like that before, especially when it came to her mother. Her grandmother smiled sadly when she told her stories of her, but it was still a smile. This was something else. Rosalie remembered what sent her out of her room and stopped in her tracks.

"Why are you sending Satcha to Reeock?" She planted her feet firm, rooting herself like a tree.

"What?" Her grandfather's jaw dropped. "What would ever cause you to think such a thing?"

"I heard you and Grandma talking earlier. You said you were going to send Satcha away for her own good."

"By the Hawk! You've overhead something that does not concern you, my dear." He reached for her and hugged her close into his chest. "I'm not sure what you heard, but we have only done what's best for the girl and our village. Now, let's get you back to bed and I will find your grandmother. Perhaps in the morning you can pick her some flowers to raise her spirits."

Rosalie forced a smile for her grandfather, but something in her gut told her he was lying. More than that, he swept whatever was going on under the rug and suggested that poor, innocent, foolish Rosalie go pick some flowers like it would make everything all better.

"Goodnight, Grandpa," she said, kissing him on the cheek.

"Sleep well." He smiled at her before nudging her toward her room.

She took a deep breath and let herself thaw and forced her feet to take one step after the other back to her room.

She would let it go for tonight, but tomorrow, she had work to do. She needed to get to the bottom of this and wasn't going to let it go. For one reason or another, her grandparents didn't trust her. Maybe they thought she wasn't capable of becoming the next leader. If that was the case, it meant she'd failed them. She couldn't let that happen. When she awoke the next day, there would be no more tears, no more picking flowers and decorating tables. Instead, she would learn to be a leader. Someone her grandparents and her people could be proud of.

Chapter 35

Dominic

Dominic awoke with a pounding head. He sat with his ankles bound to the legs of a chair and hands tied behind his back. His head bobbed as he tried to stop the room from spinning. His vision blurred, and he squinted hard a few times under the harsh light of day streaming through the window. With each blink, the room slowly came into view. He was still in Rios from the look of the familiar building. It looked to be an old fishing shack, rough logs making up the walls with dried veneno ferns lining the ceiling.

What happened?

He searched through his mind to trace back.

Satcha... I was with Satcha... We'd just gotten back from the feast and...

He pictured his hands on her hips, grasping her tight as her hands ran through his hair. It was real and not just a dream. Images flashed in his mind of laying on top of Satcha, holding her in his arms, kissing her and sliding her dress up her legs... He felt himself twitch remembering the feeling of her soft skin and her lips on his, wanting more... the knock at the door.

Think... think... think...

He remembered walking outside as much as he wanted to stay in bed with Satcha and explore her body, but he left. He should've stayed. For the love of the Hawk, he should've stayed with her. When he opened the door there was no one. It should've been his first clue that something was wrong. It only lured him away from the small house and exposed for an attack.

The attack appeared in his head and played over and over. He'd let his guard down, assuming it was some kids playing a game but the village was quiet. Until someone hit him over the head. Everything was a blur from there. He swore he had seen Aleksandr standing next to the river, watching with a grim look on his face, making no move to help him—or Satcha.

Satcha!

Where was she? Why did they take her? He pulled hard against the bindings around his wrists, but they didn't budge. The rope dug into his raw skin. He was bound tight and there was no hope of pulling the ropes loose. He leaned forward, planting his feet flat against the ground, realizing the chair wasn't tied down. He only had a moment or so to break it before his captors heard the noise.

He braced himself before throwing himself backwards, landing on the floor with a loud thud as the chair broke under his weight, knocking the breath out of his chest. He rolled to his side, groaning in pain. He kicked his legs out, freeing them from the binding, but his hands were still bound behind his back.

Footsteps approached outside. He rolled to the wall next to the door. He used his feet to steady himself and push himself up the wall, ready to body slam whoever walked through the door. The door swung in, and a man stepped through holding a plate of food.

This was his chance. He threw himself at the man knocking him into the door, barely keeping himself steady. The man fell like a pile of bricks.

Dominic stepped over him and ran out of the house only to find Aleksandr and several of the Rios guards waiting for him.

"Calm yourself, Dominic. We mean you no harm." Aleksandr held his hands up in sign of peace.

"Then why did you attack me? Where the hell is Satcha?" he shouted.

"Satcha will be fine. She is safe and far away from here."

"I'll ask again and give you one last opportunity to tell me the truth," Dominic spat. "Where is she?" He'd never been so angry before. He'd been betrayed by his own village, his own people. How could they do this to him when he laid his own life on the line to protect them every day?

"I cannot tell you what you will not understand. Forget you ever heard the name Satcha and return to your army."

"And if I bring all the power of the Enross Army to your doorstep?" he asked, challenging the old man. His anger burned bright, a white fire inside him.

"Then the secret of her location will die with me. I suggest you focus your strategies on the war at hand. I am sure your General wouldn't be pleased with you."

Dominic seethed silently; he knew he couldn't use the army that way, he'd never get approval from the General to attack the village. The General had bigger fish to fry. Plus, as far as the rest of the country was aware, Rios didn't exist.

Dominic was trapped and he didn't like it. He'd grown so used to having control and power within the army. He forgot what it was like to be at the mercy of another.

"There, I think you've come to your senses." Aleksandr

motioned to the guard on his right. "You may take a horse and a few supplies to get back to your unit, but we will not be so kind if you should return."

The guard stepped behind Dominic and cut the ropes around his wrists. He flexed his fingers and rotated his wrists, considering. It would be stupid for him to attack now; he had no weapons and there were too many of them. He counted six, not including Aleksandr. Despite his age, Dominic knew Aleksandr was skilled in archery. He wouldn't make it far with his aim. He rolled his aching shoulders and massaged the raw skin around his wrists. It burned against his fingers, but he used the pain to ignite a fire within. He would find Satcha, and then make Aleksandr pay for what he'd done.

Helene appeared with a horse in tow. A saddle had been packed, ready for travel.

"Ah, thank you my darling," Aleksandr greeted his wife. She smiled at him with love in her eyes and touched his cheek. Dominic couldn't help but picture Satcha looking at him like that. Aleksandr turned to Dominic once again. "I trust you will understand why we wish you to take your leave immediately."

"What about Lennox?" Dominic asked. He couldn't leave him behind.

"When Lennox is well enough, we will give him a horse and supplies should he wish to return to the army. His aunt and uncle will care for him until then."

Dominic nodded and approached the horse with caution. He knew they wouldn't harm Lennox, he was one of their own, whereas he was just a drifter they'd taken in.

He took the reins from Helene, clicked his tongue to the horse and backed away from the guards before hopping into the saddle. He sent the beast straight into a full gallop away from the village. He turned his head back to see if anyone followed him, but they only watched him.

With no idea or trace of where Satcha had been taken, the only option he had was to return to his unit. He wished Lennox hadn't been injured, he could've used his help even if he would've made some crack about him caring for Satcha. Maybe he would've denied it previously, but it could no longer be ignored. He *did* care for her.

As strange as it was from the moment he saw her, near death in the middle of nowhere, he mourned her without knowing her. He didn't know or recognize her but had an urge to protect and help her. To keep her safe.

Satcha was strong. All those years never knowing who she was and being guided by Agatha had hardened her so she could protect herself, but that didn't stop him from wanting to be there for her. He thought back to when she'd saved him from the Night Raiders. So frail, so innocent, until she wielded that knife in her hand.

Her knife!

He'd kept it safe amongst his things in the village. He couldn't go back to get it now, but he planned on returning with her to claim it.

He forced the horse to charge through the jungle for a long time. The chestnut-colored stallion whinnied and fought back against the reins. If he didn't slow, the horse would collapse and be of no use to him. He relaxed his grip, allowing the horse to slow. The large animal huffed and walked to a slow pace.

There were too many unanswered questions for him to wrap his head around. For starters, what did Aleksandr have against Satcha? He was willing to help her before he knew her name. Why would her name change anything?

The bigger unanswered question was the fact he had no idea where to even begin looking for her. He tried to piece things together, but the only thing he was sure of was Aleksandr was not working with the Enforcers. He was against the

Enforcers and went to great lengths to keep the Free People of Rios safe—plus, Satcha would be of no importance to his uncle in Neroso. He wouldn't have known nor cared about her existence. No, this was Aleksandr's own vendetta.

After everything that happened, from the moment they'd left to infiltrate the Enforcer Headquarters, he was nowhere near the end of his mission. He still needed to find the damn Blood Scrolls, but now with Satcha being kidnapped, he found himself at a crossroads. Be loyal to his country and soldiers, or rescue Satcha. Satcha, a woman he'd just met... but there was something about her that drew him in. He'd die for her as he would lay down his life for one of his soldiers, but it was different with her. *He* was different with her.

There was only one thing to do.

He forced the horse into a gallop, riding hard back to the base. He needed supplies, and he needed a plan.

CHAPTER 36

ROSALIE

Rosalie lay awake in her room waiting for the sun to come up. She stared at her ceiling and practiced confronting her grandparents. She wasn't going to back down, nor would she cry. Not this time.

After leaving her grandparents the night before, she hadn't slept a moment, too bothered by their interest in Satcha. Not once had she ever met another who could turn her green with jealousy. How could she? She was Rosalie, Granddaughter of the leader of the Free People of Rios, beautiful beyond compare, and...

There was nothing to add.

Rosalie realized for the first time in her life she was nothing more than a woman born into a power she didn't earn and all she had to cling to beyond that was her beauty. Anyone could've been born in her position; her birth was luck of the draw, as was her beauty.

As much as she hated to admit it, Satcha was just as beautiful as she, if only a little rougher around the edges, but she could see why men would desire her.

Rosalie choked out a laugh.

"How could I be so shallow?" she whispered.

Who was Rosalie without her beauty and eventual title? She didn't know and nothing had even scared her more in all her life. Not the fear of losing Dominic, nor the unknown dangers outside of her small village. She was a stranger to herself.

The warm glow of the sun crept in through her bedroom window. Her grandparents would be up soon. She got out of bed and padded barefoot to her dresser. There was not a single garment of clothing inside meant for anything other than for beauty. To be looked at and admired. It made her skin crawl. If she'd been asked before today, she would've loved the attention of others, but now—she wished to hide herself away.

She dug through the neatly folded dresses until she found one that covered her skin more than any other. She never wore the pale blue dress. It covered her chest, fabric all the way to the base of her neck. There were no sleeves, but her legs were covered by the floor length skirt. It would have to do.

It seemed silly to try and make herself up for the meeting with her grandparents. Instead of combing her wavy hair and fighting the thick strands, she tied it away from her face, high in a ponytail.

Rosalie didn't linger in the mirror; she couldn't look at herself, too furious with her inner demons.

One task at a time, she told herself.

Her hand rested on the doorknob, trying to collect herself. She took a deep breath and squared her shoulders, preparing herself to stand tall and convey a new confidence that wouldn't be shrugged aside. She turned the knob and strode into the hallway.

The house was quiet, which was unusual. Her grandparents were early birds and usually fussed about in the kitchen with tea in hand. Rosalie could never understand how they could drink such a thing. As far as she was concerned, tea was dirty soil water.

But nobody stood cooking in the small kitchen nor sitting at the table by the window, overlooking the river. It hadn't even looked like her grandparents were up; there were no dirty dishes in the sink or tea kettle on the stove.

They can't still be in bed, she thought. There was only one place left that her grandfather, at least, would be this early. His study.

She stood outside the door to her grandfather's office and took a deep breath. She could hear muffled voices coming from inside the room, but that wasn't going to stop her. She swung open the door, not caring to knock.

Her grandfather sat hovering over papers at his desk, radio in hand.

"Rosalie! My dear, you startled me," he exclaimed.

"Why are you so interested in Satcha?" she asked. She stalked across the room and planted her feet firmly in front of the large desk.

"What do you know of her?" Her grandfather's eyes narrowed in the slightest before he regained his composure.

"I heard you and Grandma talking last night. Why would Satcha need to be sent to Reeock?"

"It's nothing to concern yourself with."

"I have had it with that answer!" she snapped. Aleksandr raised an eyebrow, and she almost lost her nerve, but plowed on. "You treat me as if I am a frail little girl; you always have, and I am tired of it! If I am to take your place one day, I must know."

"Rosalie, that girl is dangerous. You don't need to worry about her now that she is headed far away from here. As for your future role, I hadn't realized you had any interest in leading the People of Rios. I can't help but say I'm surprised, but also happy to hear it." He set the radio down and stood from his desk.

"You weren't planning on having me take your place?" she whispered, blinking back her tears.

"I didn't think it was something you wanted, but if it is, we can certainly discuss the possibility." He smiled and reached his arms out to embrace her, but she stepped back. He truly hadn't considered her. Her stomach twisted into knots and she fought back the tears welling her in hers. She'd cried enough all ready and wasn't going to be the frail little girl he expected.

"No! I don't want you to console me or offer me false hope. I can see exactly what you think of me and won't be a bother to your day." Rosalie stormed out of the room in a rage.

Her grandfather called after her, but someone on the radio cut in, taking his attention away from her. She didn't want him to follow her, all she wanted was to be alone with her thoughts and figure out what to do next.

CHAPTER 37

SATCHA

"Let me out!" Satcha shouted for what felt like the millionth time. Her voice sounded wild and hoarse. She had managed to push the gag out of her mouth with her tongue; it rested under her chin, tied around her neck. The inside of her mouth was uncomfortably dry with not even her own saliva to wet it, and she ached from the pulled muscles on the underside of her tongue.

Not once did her captors offer anything to eat or drink. They wouldn't break her; she wouldn't allow it. If they wanted her dead, they would've killed her already. They would have to let her out at some point, and she would be ready.

She didn't know how long they had traveled. It felt like a full day, but probably more. There were black spots in her memory, the passage of time hazy. The horses had stopped three times for a rest, but still, no one let her out of her cage. Trapped and angry. Despite her exhaustion, her rage fueled, stirring within her. Whoever captured her, they went after Dominic too, and she didn't know if he was dead or alive.

Like a dog beaten into a corner she laid and waited for the moment to take her revenge. She kicked against the lid, but it didn't move. She was sure something was piled on top, keeping her locked inside. The smell of salt and fish had filled her nose from the moment they sealed the cover over her. She wanted to puke, but she choked it down not wanting to lay in her own vomit.

How dare they do this!

She didn't know who they were, but she would find out. She would hunt them and make them pay. With the last breath in her lungs, she would inflict as much pain and suffering as she could before dealing the final blow.

She screamed once again as loud as she could.

She took a deep breath and centered herself. There was no point in wasting any more energy on an escape that wouldn't happen. She was at their mercy until they decided to let her out.

Sunlight flickered through the small holes on the sides of the box, shining into her eyes. She couldn't block it out with so little space, so she kept her eyes shut and listened to the trotting hooves. Night had just fallen when she'd been kidnapped. With the strength of the sun's rays, she was positive it was nearly noon the next day. Sweat pooled in the hollow of her neck and along her limbs. She needed water.

If they intended to kill her, they wouldn't do it by suffocating her in a wooden box. No. They wanted her somewhere else.

But where?

CHAPTER 38

DOMINIC

Dominic stared into the mirror on the wall of his small quarters. He watched the stone-cold face stare back at him. He still wasn't used to the missing scar. It took him by surprise; he'd nearly forgotten he'd used the veneno salve to get rid of it back in Rios. Now, though, there was a fresh, two-inch gash across his forehead taking its place given to him by Aleksandr's thugs. He couldn't look at himself any longer, disappointed in himself for being beaten. Disappointed about losing Satcha.

Dominic leaned his forehead against the wall and slapped his fist into the palm rock over and over as he scolded himself. He'd been stupid and careless. How could he, a captain of the Enross Army, be so foolish to fall for a trap set by villagers?

He tried his best to get some rest as per Ms. Alba's instructions, but his mind only wandered to dark places thinking about where Satcha could be. Contrary to belief, there were worse things than starving to death in the road. His mind could only conjure up the worst possible scenarios.

He hadn't expected the General to be back to the base so

soon, but he hadn't exactly kept track of the days either. He still wasn't sure how long it had been since they left the base originally.

The General wasn't in the war room, but in his lavish office. The rest of the officers kept minimalist spaces for the good of the army, but not the General. He preferred to surround himself with unnecessary items of luxury which left a sour taste in Dominic's mouth.

Dominic knocked on the mahogany door and waited for permission to enter.

"What?" Ballard yelled through the door.

Dominic bit the inside of his cheek before turning the gold-plated door handle. The door swung open, and he stepped inside to a whole different world as he crossed the threshold. There were no rock walls nor gravel floors like in the tunnels. The walls had been boarded up and papered in a rich red with dark wood paneling. Dominic's blood boiled over the wasted use of army resources. The floor was covered in a variety of animal furs. Bear, elk, moose, and others he couldn't tell. He tried not to draw his attention to one set of furs that too closely resembled the Sun Bears.

He held back the urge to vomit. He didn't know how the General would have acquired such a thing. The glow of the Sun Bear's life force no longer radiated from the pelt, leaving it a dull yellow. As much as he didn't agree with his uncle about sacrificing the people of the Free City for the great beasts, he couldn't deny a strong love for them.

He couldn't help but think of Koa, a young cub he'd looked after in the sanctuary. It was tradition that each Ursid, upon the age of sixteen, would take on their own Sun Bear as a companion. He tried for years not to think about Koa, his little warrior. The shame of leaving him behind was too painful to think about, but there was no way his uncle would've let him leave with the young bear.

"Oh, Lightwood, it's you. Come in, sit down." Ballard waved him inside, pulling him out of his thoughts.

General Ballard sat behind a large oak desk in the middle of the room. Golden light glowed from the oil lamps resting on both sides of his desk and hanging along the walls.

With his hands behind his back, Dominic pinched the raw skin on his wrist to hold back from looking at the pelt. After a moment, he sat in the plush chair across from Ballard and waited.

Ballard was already back with his nose buried in his paperwork. He didn't seem interested in starting any conversation with him. Dominic cleared his throat, but the General didn't look up. He tried again, a little louder.

Ballard glared over his reading glasses with annoyance. "Well? What is it?"

Dominic took a deep breath. He had been shocked to find the General would make a move on the tower and had been stewing over it since.

"Sir, I was hoping I could speak with you about the plans for the invasion of the Enforcer Headquarters. I believe there are underground tunnels beneath the tower with escape routes. If we attack, there's a chance they could slip through our forces and circle around us—"

"Enough! I wanted this handled months ago and you are nowhere closer to getting rid of the Enforcers than we were then. We'll blast them to pieces before they know what hit 'em."

"But sir, we should try to collect the Blood Scrolls. If we find the descendants, we can unite Enross and Austerland and have a fighting chance. We can't beat them on our own."

"I don't care about those damn bloody scrolls! I want the bastards dead and gone." Ballard threw his paperwork and his glasses on the desk before massaging his temples.

"That's the problem. So, we blow up the tower? Then

what? There are still more compounds around Enross *and* Austerland. More sail in every day from across the ocean!"

"Son, I suggest you keep your mouth shut or I will have you court martialed. I don't give a rat's ass what happens in Austerland. That's not my problem." Ballard slammed his fist on the table. "Now, get out of my office!"

"*Fuck*," Dominic swore under his breath only loud enough for his own ears. He forced himself from the chair and out the door without another word. He could've said so much more, and he wanted to. He couldn't believe his restraint.

He wanted to break something. Anything would do—but he couldn't let the soldiers see him lose control. He couldn't start a mutiny either. Morale was already so low within the army. Any further damage and all hell would break loose. If he couldn't stop Ballard from attacking, he would have to warn the soldiers somehow or at the very least prepare them for what was to come.

He headed back to his quarters but noticed Private Alderson standing guard along one of the escape routes. He was humming to himself, looking much too joyful for what lay ahead. The soldiers were not prepared for the battle that awaited them, which gave Dominic an idea.

"Private Alderson!"

The scrawny soldier bounded over to him with a wide smile, stopping abruptly with a salute. "Yes, sir, Captain?"

"Gather the infantry to the training grounds. I'm implementing a new training program, starting immediately. Have everyone ready in one hour."

"Yes, sir!" He saluted Dominic and lowered his voice trying to match Dominic's commanding tone, but his voice cracked.

Dominic shook his head as he watched the private run off to complete the task. If this was the one thing he could do for them, he'd make sure he did his job well and give them a fighting chance.

"I'm sorry, Satcha. You'll have to hang tight a little longer," he whispered.

CHAPTER 39

GENERAL BALLARD

A knock came at the door about an hour after Lightwood had left. Ballard groaned, not wanting to deal with any more lip about his plans.

"What is it?" Ballard sat back in his chair and covered the map with paperwork.

Ballard's new aide peeked his head around the door, only slightly ajar. "Captain Lightwood has left his quarters and has a group of soldiers working in the training grounds."

Ballard didn't bother learning the names of his aides, as he never had one longer than a month. Shortest tenure only lasted an afternoon. He couldn't take the constant pestering, asking what they could do to help. Ballard wanted his aides out of sight unless called upon.

"And?"

"Well, sir, you asked me to update you on the captain's whereabouts."

Ballard sighed. "Tell me when he does something out of his normal routine. It's his job to oversee the troops."

"Yes, sir."

The aide backed out of the office. Ballard felt his face grow red with anger. He fought the urge to throw something at the door. He'd need another aide—someone he could trust, since he was sure that idiot had gone around to others to keep a tab on Lightwood. A simple aide couldn't be trusted with such information. He needed someone with rank. He pressed the red call button on his desk.

"Yes, sir?"

"Have a meeting scheduled in the morning with Lieutenant Monroe."

"Right away, sir."

He'd trusted him before. With how Lightwood was acting, a captain's position could become available. Monroe would be eager to climb the chain of command.

He pulled a key out of his pocket and unlocked the drawer to his right. Inside the drawer, wrapped in a cloth, sat the communication pad. He unwrapped it and expected it to be blank as they hadn't sent him a message in months.

But green text glowed back at him.

We know what you plan to do. We will be waiting.

He dropped the pad and a chill ran up his spine. The impact sent a spiderweb crack across the glass. They knew his plan to deceive them somehow. How did they always seem to be two steps ahead of him? Maybe luck was on his side when Lightwood had returned. He would send him in first and let the Enforcers take care of the mess for him.

He looked at the broken pad, and despite the cracks, one final message flashed through the display, clear as all those before it.

Goodbye, General Ballard.

His breath caught. Not since he was a child had he been this afraid; not when he signed up for the army, not when he first stepped foot on a battlefield.

There was no time to wait.

He stood from his desk and walked to the bar housing several decanters full of gold liquid. He picked up a small crystal glass with shaking hands and poured the whiskey in much higher than appropriate. He usually tried to take his time and enjoy the luxurious scent and the tingling on his lips during the first sip, but he threw the entire glass back. He held his hand to his chest as if it would help fend off the burning in his throat.

He fought the urge to throw back his head and drink the whole bottle, and instead poured just one more glass. He took a small sip, letting it sit on his tongue. A fire burned in his mouth and saliva swarmed the foreign liquid forcing him to swallow. He did so with a gulp, the burning escaping his mouth and running down his throat and into his chest. His liquid courage.

He sat at his desk and repeated his small, tedious sips until the glass was empty and he had to fill it again. Before the first glass was poured, the bottle was full, but now the whiskey barely touched the bottom of the worn-out label on the front of the bottle, two inches above the bottom.

The room shifted back and forth as he struggled to put one foot in front of the other as he walked between his chair and the bar. He collapsed, narrowly missing his seat and winding up on the floor. He picked up the broken communication pad and threw it across the room so it slammed into the wooden door. It split into two pieces. He laughed to himself before reaching for his glass once again. He was glad to not receive any more messages from the Masked Man.

Ballard took one last drink, emptying his glass before he slumped forward on the desk. If anyone walked in, they knew not to wake him. His first aid had thought him dead and quickly learned the rules of working under the General. Ballard had grabbed his aide by the throat and threw him from his office, only to have soldiers strip him of his uniform and send him out into the forest for the night. He'd come back the next day and was given a new post; he didn't speak much after that, only enough to warn his successor. And since that first aide, no one dared wake General Ballard again.

Chapter 40

Lennox

Lennox needed to be out of bed, he couldn't sit around waiting for his mind to finish healing. He couldn't keep track of how much time had passed. He slept and woke at odd times of the day, only getting a few hours rest before falling back to sleep. His leg was still sore, more from his idle state than pain, but it was nothing compared to the restlessness of being confined to his bed.

The elders had woken him days ago to let him know Dominic had left and gone back to the base, but something seemed off. Dominic would never have left without speaking to him and giving him new orders. And they'd mentioned nothing of the nomad scum, Satcha. He didn't care that she'd helped Dominic get him to the healers in Rios. It all was a game to her; he was sure of it. She couldn't be trusted. Especially with Dominic.

He swung his legs over the side of the bed and tested his ankles, making sure there were no spasms nor resistance in his muscles. Everything seemed to work. He'd been lucky with his leg; the DEW blast had grazed him above the knee. Luck had visited him twice; being cured of the blood poison was close to a miracle. He owed the healers of Rios more than he could hope to pay back. All he could offer was his service in the army. A vow of protection for his home.

He didn't waste any time getting dressed. He pulled on a t-shirt, an old pair of pants, and his boots before he headed out. He needed to breathe fresh air. He needed to be outside of the four walls he'd been staring at for who knows how long. He could only remember opening his eyes for a few moments once or twice before succumbing to the heavy pull of drugged sleep.

He reached out to grasp the door handle only to have the door burst open, swinging toward him, narrowly missing his face.

"Oh, I'm so sorry, Lennox!" Rosalie clutched her hand to her chest. She looked as surprised to see him up as he was to see her. "I thought you'd still be in bed. I just came to check on you."

He rubbed his jaw, trying to hide his annoyance at her. So many people in the village loved Rosalie and doted over her constantly, but he could only manage to deal with her overly cheery presence in small doses.

"I'm fine. When did Dominic leave?"

"He left four days ago." Her usual bright-eyed and bushy-tailed demeanor was nowhere to be found. Her tone was flat, and she ducked her head, not letting her eyes meet Lennox's.

It was all very strange. Normally, Lennox would have to fight to not roll his eyes at her. Everyone knew of her infatuation with Dominic.

"Did he head back to base?"

"I don't know. I think so. All I know is he and Satcha are gone." She cleared her throat, her hands gripping the hem of her dress.

"You really need to get over your little crush on Dominic." The words slipped out before he realized, but he'd held his tongue long enough. Why was she free to share her feelings about Dominic, but he had to hide?

She tried to narrow her eyes at him and make herself look fierce, but she was as menacing as a kitten. "That's funny. I could say the same thing to you."

Anger filled him quickly and brutally. He couldn't help himself; he grabbed her neck and pushed her against the door frame roughly. Her eyes widened as she clawed at his hands, trying to peel them back to no avail.

"I don't care who your grandfather is. Say those words again and my face will be the last thing you see when you take your last breath." How dare she accuse him of such things! His face was burning, and he knew his cheeks were red. It all made him so angry. All this time, he'd hoped no one would know, but of course the one other person who spent their time yearning for Dominic would find him out.

"Hel—help!" Rosalie choked out.

"Lennox! Release her at once!" Aleksandr burst into the room. In one clean movement, he pulled his bow from his back, nocked an arrow, and pointed it at his chest.

Lennox gave Aleksandr a disgusted look before turning his eyes back to Rosalie. "This isn't over, little flower," he whispered, loud enough for her to hear before he pushed her away.

Rosalie fell to the floor and scampered backward to hide behind Aleksandr. The old man didn't lower his bow, keeping it pointed at Lennox, the threat of death in his eyes. Lennox knew Helene and Rosalie were all Aleksandr had left. Nothing would come between him and his family.

Lennox sighed and raised his hands above his head. "Relax, it was just a misunderstanding."

"I'm not sure what has come over you and Dominic Lightwood, but I swear the army has corrupted your minds and you've forgotten your allegiance to this village and its people." Aleksandr relaxed slightly but kept a firm grip on his bow. He turned to Rosalie and gave her a quick once over to see she was unharmed—she was fine, just crying a stream of tears that could rival the Rios River.

"Where did Dominic go?"

"Back to the army. I suggest you do the same." Aleksandr wrapped a protective arm around Rosalie, who leaned heavily against him.

Spoiled baby. He narrowed his eyes at her and wondered if it was all an act or if she really was as fragile as a rose petal.

"I'll need a horse."

"I'll need you to send two horses back to replace the loan we gave you and the one Dominic took."

He chewed his lip, trying to bring himself out of the rabbit hole of possibilities of why there was only one horse.

"And what of Satcha?"

"She travels alone without Dominic. Now, if you will excuse me, I need to tend to my granddaughter."

Lennox watched Aleksandr lead the crying Rosalie down the hallway. He had to leave as soon as he could. Dominic was free of the wretched Satcha and back at the base. Things could return to normal; they could get on with their task of stopping the Enforcers to keep the country and people of Enross safe. It wasn't Lennox's idea of a plan, but it was Dominic's, and Lennox would follow him into the fire.

Lennox didn't waste time gathering what things he had with him since it was just the clothes on his back, and he didn't even spare a second to say goodbye to Uncle Hamish and Aunt Gloria, the only blood family he had left. He needed to get to the base, to Dominic.

Aleksandr offered him no weapon, only the horse he promised with a few rations for the journey. It was all he really needed, anyway; he planned to get to the base as soon as possible. Back to *normal* as soon as possible.

Chapter 41

Dominic

Dominic spent four days watching the infantry soldiers train for battle, and with each passing day he grew more restless with uneasy guilt. Guilt for leaving Satcha to fend for herself and guilt for the lack of training his troops had to face off against the Enforcers. Regular rifles and shotguns were nothing in comparison to the armored tanks and uniforms of the soldiers, not to mention their hi-tech weaponry.

"What we lack in offense, we must make up for in defense," said Dominic.

Two hundred soldiers watched him as he walked down the middle of the training field. He would have liked more, but they didn't have the space in the training cavern. He scheduled the infantry in groups and put them on a training rotation. He led them every day through drills, only resting for three hours a night before he went back to work with the next group.

"The Enforcers have DEW technology. For those of you who do not know what that is, you will probably be the first to get shot, so listen up!" He motioned for Lieutenant Monroe to step in and take over. He'd explained it enough times in the past few days. The tall soldier replaced Dominic at the head of the room, while he slipped to the back to observe.

"Direct Energy Weapons. That's what will blast your ass to smithereens. Don't believe me? Ask Private Veron. Oh, that's right, you can't. He's dead." Lieutenant Monroe stalked up and down the line of soldiers, taking a different approach than Dominic would have. Monroe seemed to grow angrier as he barked out facts about DEW guns. A vein in Monroe's neck seemed ready to pop out of his tanned skin.

Dominic leaned back against the cavern wall, watching the soldiers flinch with every drop of spit that flew out of Monroe's mouth. He should've been angry just like Monroe, but he had too much anxiety to be angry. The General forced his hand getting these soldiers ready for battle—he knew they weren't ready for it. No number of stealth techniques could keep an entire army safe from what awaited them inside the Enforcer Headquarters. No doubt they would be waiting with a whole slew of new tech to test out on them.

He paced back and forth, working himself up; he couldn't waste another moment watching Monroe yell at the troops. He stalked out of the training grounds and didn't slow until he stood outside of the lab. The lab was the one place in the base other than the General's office that had been properly framed and the walls sealed. He rested his hands on the cold metal of the door for a moment, praying that when he walked through the doors, they'd give him good news.

Dominic forced the metal door to swing into the white walled room. Scientists wearing white lab coats stood around metal tables with microscopes, beakers, and metal parts of machines unknown to him. They didn't pay any attention to him when he walked through. They weren't soldiers, so they weren't required to stop what they were doing and salute him. He preferred it that way. They needed to focus; he didn't want them wasting time whenever an officer passed by.

At the back of the room, Dominic spotted Dr. Steltan. The man's elbow was propped on the desk, his hand bracing and holding his head up, as if he might collapse from exhaustion. Beneath Steltan's black rimmed glasses, bags hung under his eyes.

Shit.

Dominic knew he'd been pushing them hard to try and replicate the Enforcers' DEW tech, but he hadn't realized how grueling it must have been. He couldn't have them falling asleep or causing accidents trying to harness the energy. They'd already lost half of their team in the last explosion when they tried months ago.

Dominic had put a stop to all research after they cleaned up the wreckage. They built the new lab further away from the barracks this time, since they'd had minor cave-ins from the blast.

Dominic stood in front of Dr. Steltan's desk, but he didn't look up or acknowledge him. He kept flipping through his paperwork and scanning the sheets before him.

"I don't have any updates for you, Captain." Steltan gathered his papers and organized them together in a neat pile. He took off his glasses and rubbed his eyes.

"How much sleep have you had?" Dominic grabbed a chair from a nearby table and sat on it in front of Steltan's desk.

"What's today?"

Dominic sighed. They couldn't keep going like this, they'd burn themselves out. He looked around the room at the ten scientists. Bags lined their eyes the same as Steltan, some of them even a little further along in their exhaustion with their heads resting on the tables.

"Wrap it up for the day. Be back at 0800." He turned to leave but Steltan's voice stopped him.

"Captain, we can't replicate their blasters."

Dominic froze in place but didn't turn around. The rest of Steltan's team stared at him, waiting for him to blow up like General Ballard would have, but he kept his cool.

"Then make what you can," he said, keeping his voice level. He controlled his disappointment, holding it, and everything else, in.

His body, his mind, was filled with so many warring emotions. Disappointment, and yes, anger, about the failure of the lab team, but also—Lennox stuck in Rios, the General forcing the troops to march on the Enforcers, Satcha. And that was what he focused on the most, his anger at himself for leaving Satcha behind. He was torn between two worlds. His soldiers and country, and Satcha, who walked into his life only to steer him away from his loyalty. The more he thought about it, the more it became clear he couldn't have both.

He couldn't stay in the tunnels any longer. He stared down the long path feeling as if it might collapse in on him. He needed to breathe fresh air.

He kept his pace up, a brisk walk that deterred anyone from stopping him. Sweat collected at the base of his neck. He unbuttoned the top of his uniform.

Dominic pulled his radio from his belt loop. "Tower, come in."

"Tower here, over."

"Have a horse ready for me. I'm on the way, over."

"Yes, sir, Captain. Over and out."

He didn't clip the radio back to his uniform. He dropped it on the ground as he headed toward the exit. With his fists clenched at his sides, he stalked out of the tunnels and into the light of day. The sunlight's rays danced across his face; it had been days since he'd felt the heat of the sun on his skin. He inhaled deeply.

A soldier stood waiting for him with a black horse in tow.

He didn't have time to return the soldier's salute; he wasn't sure how long he had before the General found out he'd left.

Once out of sight from the base, he climbed on the horse and clicked his tongue. He raced through the trees, putting distance between him and the base. He'd only have a few hours before the sun would set and he could put his plan in motion. As much as he wanted to ride north and look for Satcha, he turned the horse south and headed for the Village of Carose.

He rode for hours, trying to keep off the main road, but when the trees grew thick, he couldn't avoid it any longer. The horse huffed and shook its head, refusing to go any farther. He hopped down and took the reins in his hand, walking alongside the horse. The sun would set in a half hour, giving him the cover of the dark, but also bringing new dangers of Night Raiders.

The horse pulled against the reins, leading Dominic to the side of the road. It reached its long neck up into a tree and pulled an apple from a branch.

"Fine, but only for a few minutes." He patted the horse on the shoulder and then after a moment of consideration, reached into the tree and plucked a bright red apple for himself.

He had a strong connection with animals, especially the horses he'd come to know at the base, but this was not one of them. He wondered if Baron, his usual chestnut-colored horse, had managed to find his way back to the base after their failed infiltration of the tower. He'd never checked the stables; there'd been so much on his mind. Another thing to feel guilty about.

Thoughts of Koa, his Sun Bear seeped into his mind again. The bear used to follow him everywhere, not like his uncle and his own giant beast, Rovoss. Gideon hadn't trained the bear well enough so guards and staff couldn't get near him, or else they'd be attacked. Though for whatever reason, they never attacked anyone of Ursid blood, as if the bears could sense their allegiance to the family.

He imagined Koa had grown to be as large as Rovoss, if not bigger, despite not being full grown when Dominic last saw him. Knowing the power Koa was capable of, he saw it best to have the bear trained under strict circumstances and thankfully, Koa had listened.

Dominic ran this hand along the neck of his horse, wishing he could see Koa again. He wondered if the bear would even remember him after all this time. It took everything in him to leave Koa behind and he fought hard every day not to think of him, but seeing the pelt had opened wounds that had never fully closed.

The clop of hooves sounded from behind him. An old man sitting upon a wooden wagon pulled by two white horses slowly walked toward them in the road. This man was of no threat to him; the scent of salt and fish tipped him off. The boxes must've been filled with catch from the sea village of Velha, east of Rios.

"Nice night." The old man in gray robes nodded to Dominic, stalling the horses ten feet away.

"Careful up ahead. Carose has been taken," Dominic said. He didn't want the man to head straight into danger. He probably had a family he worked hard to keep safe and fed.

"Thank you, kindly. I'm headed past there on the way to Reeock. I'll be sure to steer clear." He nodded once again to Dominic. "Keep care of yourself, soldier. May the Hawk watch over you."

"And you."

Dominic watched the wagon disappear down the road. Not many folk traveled to the old Kingdom of Reeock. It'd been ages since he'd been there with Lennox searching for the Blood Scrolls. It stood high on a hillside with tall stone walls. A fortress surrounded the large city nestled inside, but it had been a long time since the kingdom breathed life. Not since the ceasefire a hundred years ago. All that remained were caretakers and poor souls with nowhere else to go.

He had no desire to see it again, he wanted to keep the image in his mind of an old painting he once saw in Plumos. The canvas had been rough and old, and the colors were faded, barely holding an outline of the shape of the once great kingdom. He wished he could've seen its greatness for himself.

Two or three years back, in the City of Plumos, west of Carose, before Dominic was a Captain in the Enross Army, his platoon held a post for a few months tracking Enforcer movements. In his off-duty hours, he used to wander the streets instead of getting drunk in the pubs with his comrades. His captain at the time ordered him to keep away from the civilians, but he couldn't help but sneak food to the hungry children plaguing the streets. So many of them without families had to survive on their own.

It made him think of Satcha and wonder how long she'd been on her own after Agatha died. She never talked about it. Not like he'd asked her either... He almost didn't want to know the answer. When he first found her, she'd been covered in so many scars, he couldn't believe she'd even survived. He didn't regret his decision in offering her the veneno salve to remove her scars because she didn't need the added reminder of the abuse she'd endured and hoped it would bring her some solace. Removing his own scar hadn't helped him yet, but maybe with time. Selfishly, he also hoped if he could remove her emotional pain, maybe he could move past his own painful memories.

His fingers ran along his cheek where the scar once laid. In his darkest moments, he swore he could still feel the blade cutting through his skin. He'd been so damn close. So close to stopping his uncle, but fear had stayed his hand. He wasn't scared of the Masked Man, only afraid of taking his place if he killed him. His uncle was the only family he had left but despite the blood they shared, he didn't share his uncle's cruelty. Time and time again, he went against his uncle's orders to join rank with the Enforcers. He'd heard soldiers who'd returned from Vardya talk about the poor decaying land.

He begged his uncle not to harm them, but to make peace with them and provide help, but he was just a youth with no authority or life experience. He'd made a pact with himself that if he couldn't get his uncle to help, *he* would do something. He packed a bag and snuck out of the manor, only to find his uncle waiting for him.

Run from your blood.

The words had haunted his dreams every night for as long as he could remember. It wasn't until he met Satcha that the dream started to invade his sleep less often. It must've been nearly two weeks since he'd last dreamed of the night of his escape.

His horse nudged his side as if telling him it was time to move on. Dominic shook himself free of the memory. He mounted his horse and set off toward Carose with one mission running through his head: if Dr. Steltan and the rest of his team couldn't replicate the Enforcer weapons, then he would go and get the real thing himself.

CHAPTER 42

SATCHA

The smell of rotting fish combined with the heat of the box had finally gotten to Satcha. She tried in vain to aim, but there was so little room to move—bile spewed from her mouth, dribbling out onto her lips and chin.

How long have I been in here?

Where are they taking me?

Where's Dominic?

The same questions repeated in her head to the point where she could think of nothing else. Vomit clung to her, caking on to her skin and hardening into the fabric of the dress.

Muffled voices invaded her head. She wasn't sure what they said or if it was even real, but she strained her ears to listen. She kept getting distracted by the fish. The smell of it mixed with her vomit curdled acid in her belly, making her dry heave. Her insides ached and screamed with each lurch of her stomach muscles trying to pass whatever it could. Bile burned against her dry tongue. She couldn't take it anymore.

Satcha fought to cram her knees into her chest so she could plant her feet on the lid. With all her might and what was left of her energy, she pressed her feet against the lid and pushed. She groaned with effort, straining, but no matter how hard she pushed, the lid wouldn't budge. The wood creaked under the pressure of her feet but didn't have any give. One lone tear welled in her eye and ran hot across her cheek down into her ear.

She wouldn't die like this. She wouldn't, she couldn't, let it happen. Too much had changed in her poor, pitiful life— had it been before she met Dominic, she might've just given up and let herself rot there with the fish. But not now.

She braced her elbows against the sides of the box and kicked with all she had to give. She closed her eyes as she forced her feet upwards over and over. She wasn't just kicking at the lid, she kicked at everything that had ever beaten her down. Waking up on the shores of a river as a child with not a memory in her mind other than her name, Agatha teaching her the harsh realities of the world by trial and error, being captured by the Enforcers and tortured for stealing stale bread, starving often, learning to sleep through the cold bite of the night. She kicked for Dominic, for letting herself trust someone despite what happened in Rios. She kicked and kicked and kicked until something gave way.

The lid flew off and her legs kicked at nothing, pulling all the muscles in her lower back. The midday sun streamed onto her face, blinding her, while slimy decaying fish flooded into the box around her.

"By the Hawk!" an unfamiliar voice called from outside.

Satcha panted, fighting to catch her breath. She couldn't decide what part of her ached the most, but even slight movement left her joints screaming at her to stop. She forced her eyes open, black spots smearing across her vision as she tried to make sense of where she was, but she held strong. She would not be broken. Time and again, she survived, managing to push through her weakened state. She didn't know how or why she could, but she wouldn't question such gifts.

"Hey, Hugh! Get a load of what the old geezer was haulin'!" Hands reached around her, scooping out fish from the box.

"Well, that's a new way to get whores into Reeock. Hope they wash 'er up good first," a raspy voice said, laughing.

Whore? Who are they calling a whore?

She opened her eyes to see a shadowy figure hovering over her. She kicked out her legs again and connected with the first voice.

"Hey now! I ain't done nothin' to deserve that, little lady!"

She forced herself up right, heaving herself out of the box, but slipped over rotten fish. She fell back, sliding over a mound of fish on the horse-drawn cart, directly onto the hard ground.

"I am no whore," Satcha spat, pulling herself to her feet with deep heavy breaths, barely able to keep upright as her eyes played tricks on her. The world spun around her as she tried to make out who was before her.

"Well, if you ain't a whore, you must be a criminal. Bet there's quite a bounty on your head. If that old driver went through so much trouble to keep you hiding beneath all them fish guts," the raspy voiced man named Hugh said. He stood not ten feet from her, but she couldn't make out his face, only a blur of beige.

"I'm... no... criminal," she spluttered before she collapsed. From her hands and knees, she panted, trying to force herself to stay awake, but she was so tired. So thirsty. So sore.

"Hang on, little lady," the first voice said. A pair of feet landed next to her and blocked the sun from her face. "Take small sips."

Satcha felt something touch her dry, cracked lips. The cool wet touch of water trickled into her mouth and she choked on it as it filled her mouth, unable to make herself swallow.

"Errol, don't go wastin' our water on her," Hugh scolded.

"It's comin' from my can, mind yer own water," Errol shouted back. "Now little lady, take it nice and easy."

Satcha didn't care to listen to them bicker, instead she focused on trying to not drown herself. Water brought forth hope she could get past this. She needed to gather her strength and get back to Rios. She'd make Aleksandr pay for what he did.

"All right. That's enough!" Hugh yelled. The canteen's cool metal left her lips, taking the relief of water away too quickly. "We need some answers from ya."

Satcha caught her breath and realized she'd been closing her eyes. She sat back and rubbed her eyes, not caring about the fish slime still coating her hands. She squinted open her eyes and took stock of the men before her. They wore dirty, torn black clothes and were menacing looking.

Night Raiders!

She threw herself away, hitting her back on a tree. She set her jaw and braced herself for them to attack her.

"What do you want from me? I have no money."

"You don't think we know that?" Hugh sneered.

Satcha narrowed her eyes at him. He was the older of the two, likely in his late forties or early fifties by the scruffy gray beard and tangled hair on his head.

"Aw, Hugh, leave 'er alone. She's just as broke and scrawny as we are." Errol nudged Hugh's arm. He was younger than Hugh, perhaps in his late thirties without a hint of gray in his brown, oily mane.

"Now, don't try gettin' me to feel sorry for her. Y'all got me already in a heap of trouble lettin' you tail me around. We don't have time to waste, we gotta get off the road before someone comes."

"Let me go. Like your friend said, I have nothing," Satcha said, interrupting their bickering. She wished she had the energy to break into a run, but she could barely hold her own head up.

"How do I know there's not a bounty on your head? You could be lyin'—a criminal set for hangin'! I'm sure the guards of Reeock would know. We ain't too far from there."

"I'm sure the Reeock guards would not take kindly to two Night Raiders kidnapping a young woman, but by all means, let's go to Reeock and you can get your own hangman's noose. You don't look like a fisherman either. I'm sure the driver of the cart is a well-known trader. Or maybe you have another option"

Hugh stared at her angrily, but she wasn't going to give in. Neither he or Errol seemed anywhere as intelligent or swift as a typical Raider. These two were clumsy at best, judging from their thin, lanky limbs.

"What kinda offer are you making?" Hugh asked suspiciously.

"Get me to the Enross Army Base north of Carose and you will be fed and paid for your efforts."

"The Enross Army?" Errol's eyes went wide as he looked back and forth from Hugh to Satcha.

"Why would the Enross Army want anythin' to do with you, Fish Guts?" Hugh said, laughing cruelly.

"The captain is a friend who would be very grateful for my return." In truth, she had no idea how Dominic would react. She didn't even know if he was even alive!

He has to be, she thought to herself. *We didn't go through everything we did for him to just be dead. For it to end like this... No. He's alive.*

Satcha coughed hard, the air in her lung weighing heavy and dry against her throat. As much as she wanted to try and fight the two men off, she was in no shape to stand a fighting chance—but that wouldn't stop her from trying.

"Come on, Hugh, why can't we just give 'er a break and help 'er out?" Errol stepped in front of Hugh, his back facing her.

This was her moment. She could take a jagged rock from the ground and launch herself at him. She could see it in her mind, pressing the hard edge of the rock into the man's throat with what little strength she had left. He would flail but would be too shocked to put up any fight against her.

But she hesitated.

"If we had met a few weeks ago," she said slowly, "I would've slit both your throats without a second thought, but I am willing to make this offer to you in good faith. You don't know me, and I don't know the two of you, but we can help each other." She bit the inside of her cheek, hoping it would work. Dominic had rubbed off on her—she didn't want to kill these men. She'd had enough of killing.

"Hugh—" Errol said, wheedling. He was on her side, but she needed Hugh. Errol wasn't the decision maker of the two.

"Damn it, Errol! Shut up!" Hugh set his jaw and narrowed his eyes at Satcha.

Something told her that either Hugh wasn't used to having to make split decisions or he'd been calculating his own plan of attack. Either way, she was in control.

"Tick tock, Hugh. Who knows when someone might come along?"

"I'm thinkin' we are in a stalemate, as they say," Hugh said, smiling his cruel smile. "I know these roads like the back'a my hand, and I know the routine. Guards from Reeock will be travelin' through with supplies from Torta any minute now. We can stay here and wait for 'em if you'd like. Or you make us a more interestin' offer to take ya north."

She couldn't tell if it was a bluff or not, but she couldn't risk getting detained further. She racked her brain trying to run through options in her mind, but she didn't have anything of value to offer. She didn't own anything. She resisted the urge to fidget; she couldn't show any falter.

"I'm sure whatever the Reeock guards would offer, the Enross Army would happily reward you with my return." She had no reason to believe they could give them anything. She meant nothing to the Enross Army, but she had to risk it.

Hugh stifled a laugh. "Those idiots can barely support themselves!"

"Hugh, maybe she can help clear our names," Errol piped up.

Gotcha!

Satcha smiled; she could help with that for sure. With a little help from Dominic, she could try to wipe out whatever these two were wanted for.

"Done!" Satcha cut in before Hugh could speak.

"You think you can clear the name of two ex-Night Raiders?" Hugh didn't seem convinced.

"As long as you are ex-Night Raiders, my contact with the army should be able to help on my behalf. Agreed?"

"Come on, Hugh! Say yes!" Errol whined.

The clop of hooves sounded from down the trail within the trees. Satcha glanced up, but couldn't see anything through the thicket, but was sure the Reeock guards would soon appear as Hugh had warned.

"Fine." Hugh sighed.

"We gotta get out of here now," Errol said to her and held his dirty hand out to shake her hand.

"Later, we don't have time for that," Satcha said, her eyes scanning the tree line.

Errol nodded and ran off into the trees with Hugh not far behind him. Still running high on adrenaline, Satcha ignored the resistance in her muscles as she bounded through the woods, careful not to fall behind and lose the two men. She didn't know if she could trust Hugh and Errol, but she didn't have much choice. Hugh *had* told the truth about the Reeock guards passing through... She hoped he would continue his candor. Every step she took was one step closer north. One step closer to finding Dominic. One step closer to taking her revenge on Aleksandr.

CHAPTER 43

DOMINIC

Dominic stood on a cliff looking at what was left of the Village of Carose below. None of the original stone houses remained. Whatever rubble was left of the buildings had been hauled away, making room for green pop-up tents surrounding a newly constructed base. Another Nerosian tower. More and more Enforcers.

He clutched the reins of the black horse as if to steady himself from the sight, wishing he could bring the horse with him just to know that someone would have his back. He sighed. He'd have to let the giant beast go and hope it found its way back to the base. He searched through the saddle bags and kept what guns and bullets he could carry, careful not to weigh himself down. He opted for a 9mm pistol with a silencer. He couldn't risk the sound of a rifle giving away his position.

He clapped the horse on the backside, it whinnied and reared its legs up before taking off into the night, quickly fading into the cover of the trees. It was time for him to get ready for action. He backed away from the cliffside and made his way down the hill toward the village. They hadn't wasted any time constructing a replica of their headquarters. The new tower's rebar frame stood about twenty feet high. Under the moonlight, workers were harnessed and raised up over the sides of the tower welding new beams into place. Sparks flew down the side of the structure and reflected off the frame.

Once at the base of the hill, he could no longer see the tower nor the border of the village. He stayed low to the ground and crept through the trees, hearing the rev of engines ahead. He peered through the bushes to see tanks and armored trucks sitting single file in a long line toward the village.

"Shit." He hadn't expected the soldiers to have moved in so quickly. He scanned the tree line looking for the best way to sneak in and wondered how Satcha made it into these compounds. She only had her knife to protect her, yet she still went in knowing the dangers within. He wasn't sure if it was an act of bravery or desperation—likely both, knowing what little food she'd had.

Think like Satcha... Think like Satcha...

He thought back to when they met. Satcha didn't attack head on; she used her speed and the element of surprise to help her. He would have to do the same if he had any hope of entering undetected, not to mention getting out. He couldn't go in expecting, or starting, a gun fight.

No, he told himself. He would have to lay low and avoid any attention. He pulled out his pistol, holding it in his hands. For a moment, he considered stowing it somewhere so the temptation to use it wouldn't blow his cover, but he couldn't go in there unarmed. He put it back in his holster and hoped he wouldn't have to use it.

A light shone at the edge of the village. Two armed guards patrolling the perimeter walked past Dominic, not ten feet away from him. He stayed low and waited to see if they would turn around, but they kept walking along the border of the village. He checked over his shoulder to confirm there were no guards following. This was his chance.

He ran through the bushes after the two guards. He reached down, picked up a rock, and tossed it into a large tree set back into the woods. The rock caught in the leaves and bounced off multiple branches before falling to the ground.

The guards turned and aimed their DEW-powered rifles into the trees. He stayed back, not allowing himself to get too close until the most opportune moment. They walked into the bushes toward the tree, scanning, and the closer they got to the tree, the farther apart they spread themselves. Dominic crept forward, hunched over, waiting for the Enforcer on the far side to disappear behind the tree before he would attack the other.

He lowered himself to a crawl, holding his breath.

He was an arm's reach away from the closest Enforcer.

Three, two, one.

Dominic sprang up and tackled the Enforcer to the ground. He straddled the man and before the Enforcer could react, Dominic tore off his helmet, placed his hands on the side of the man's head and snapped his neck. He had only a moment to take out the other—if he didn't, he'd call for help and the alarms would go off. All would be lost.

Dominic rolled himself on the ground toward the tree. The second Enforcer rounded the great oak and scanned for his partner. Once again, Dominic lunged at the Enforcer from behind, but this time, he wasn't fast enough for complete surprise. He collided with the armored soldier as the man turned toward him and they fell to the ground in a heap.

The two rolled over each other, trying to pin the other to get the upper hand. The armor sank heavy into Dominic's chest, and he couldn't push the Enforcer off him. The Enforcer raised back a gloved fist and thrust it at Dominic, only catching him in the side of his face, but it still stung. The blow made him cry out and lose his focus for a fraction of a second.

"Stay down!" the Enforcer commanded, reaching for his radio. Dominic ignored him and curled up his knees between them, kicking out as hard as he could to throw the Enforcer off.

The soldier flew back and stumbled into the trunk of the tree, dazed. Dominic breathed heavily, scrambling off the ground toward the Enforcer. He tore off the Enforcer's helmet, pulled his gun from his holster, and fired between the soldier's eyes before he could retaliate.

The silencer had done its job. The Enforcer toppled over, crumpling to the ground. Dominic sat on the ground and stared at the sky, trying to catch his breath. It wasn't exactly how Satcha would've done things, but it got the job done all the same. It wouldn't be long before someone would call for an update. He forced himself up and pulled the body under the cover of some thick bushes.

He went back to find the other body, the one free of the smear of blood, and searched it for anything useful. He undressed the soldier from his armor and helmet—it worked well enough last time, and would give him enough protection to sneak in.

After putting the armor on, he finished off by placing the silver helmet on his head. He didn't like looking through the black visor; it reminded him too much of the training his uncle tried to put him through long ago. He checked himself over, making sure he didn't miss anything from the uniform. He was dressed the same as the other dead Enforcer laying on the ground, except for one small detail.

Dominic leaned down and looked at the belt around the Enforcer's waist. Shiny silver oval shapes were strapped to the belt. DEW explosives. *That could come in handy*, he thought. He carefully attached the belt around himself, picked up the dropped rifle of the Enforcer, and walked toward the village as if nothing was wrong.

Going against every instinct in his body, he stepped out from the cover of the forest and into the light shining along the perimeter of the village. Everything seemed fine. No one shouted or drew unwanted attention to him.

Two guards stepped out from behind one of the small, dilapidated buildings. He tried his best not to react, and kept walking, feigning a patrol.

"Where's your partner?" one of the guards called to him. As sweat dripped down the side of his face he was suddenly glad for the cover of the helmet. He swallowed his anxieties and readied himself for the worst.

"Went to take a piss." Dominic didn't stumble over his words and hoped they would buy into it.

"He couldn't wait five minutes for us to relieve you?" The other guard shook his head.

"You gotta go, you gotta go," Dominic said, and shrugged.

Both guards grunted and nodded. Dominic took a deep breath, trying to keep his cool.

"Well, I'm off-duty. Good luck to you." Dominic nodded and walked past them, holding his breath, and tried to not walk so stiff.

"Hey, wait!"

He froze before he turned around, expecting them to shoot him. He'd never been hit by a DEW weapon before, but he'd seen what they could do. He'd seen entire limbs vaporized, leaving only burned nubs of flesh behind. Lennox was lucky he'd only gotten clipped.

"Yeah?"

"Don't forget, you have to go help load up the supply trucks before you finish."

"Oh, right." Dominic turned back, heading right toward the newly constructed tower.

"Hey idiot!" the other guard called. "The loading bay is to the left."

"Right, thanks. Long night." He turned on his heels and started off again.

"Green horns," one of the men muttered behind him.

Dominic breathed a sigh of relief as the two Enforcers made their way to their patrol, leaving him to face his next obstacle. Up ahead, trucks lined up along a loading dock—and not a loading dock from a warehouse, but a dock on the river. A huge black ship rocked against its ties from the push and pull of the water.

Three Enforcers loaded large metal crates into the back of the trucks. So this was how they were getting their supplies to headquarters. They sailed from the Westim Ocean and up the River Sea. It's why they took control of Carose; they needed the port.

Sickness swirled in his stomach. He should've expected his uncle to take advantage of the Sea River. It cut off Enross and Austerland from sending aid to one another—that is, if they were even able to get along in the first place. Not to mention it allowed the Nerosians to attack both countries at their core.

They were in more danger than they knew. The only land connecting the two countries would be Novo to the south, but no one lived there. It was no man's land. Dominic looked over the wide river at Austerland far in the distance, just a line along the horizon. It only reminded him of the Blood Scrolls. More than ever, he needed them. He would reunite the forces of Enross and Austerland, then maybe they would have a chance against his uncle and the Enforcers.

He looked back and forth between the docking bay and the tower under construction. He couldn't risk losing this opportunity. His hands slipped to his side, making sure the

DEW explosives were still attached to his belt. He knew these could be timed—the original prototype had been in production when he was in Neroso—and while these were a little different from what he remembered, he was sure they were the same.

Dominic headed toward the tower, nodding to passing Enforcers. No one seemed to suspect him, but he couldn't take the risk of letting his guard down. He held his head high and his shoulders back, hoping no one would question him. He unclipped an explosive from his belt and let it roll down the side of his leg to the ground. Nudging it with his boot, he rolled it under a tarped-off area at the base of the tower. He did the same thing at each corner of the structure.

There was one final egg-shaped explosive on his belt. He looked around the compound but knew this wouldn't be where he would put the last one. It had to be somewhere it would hurt.

He would plant the remaining explosive on the docked ship.

He would have to act quickly, he only had about ten minutes before the bombs would start to blow.

He tried not to walk too fast to draw attention to himself, but it couldn't be helped. The longer he stayed there, the more likely he would get caught. He stepped up onto the platform attached to the ship. He didn't know how much damage the explosive would do against the metal, but he hoped it would be enough to delay them with repairs before it set sail again. Two Enforcers loaded the trucks along the docking bay while one stood back and supervised.

Dominic looked at the tall ship and didn't see any patrols on the upper deck. The anchor was drawn and hanging from its chains, offering the perfect five-foot opening to the hull of the ship. He glanced around quickly; no one watched him. Unclipping the explosive, he took a second to aim and hope for the best, before tossing it at the hole in the side of the ship. It landed with a clang.

"It's about time you got here!" one of the soldiers called to him, leaning against the wooden rail of the dock. "We're behind already." Dominic jumped, startled by the Enforcer. He had to play it off, hoping he hadn't been seen throwing the explosive.

"Sorry, relief was late for my patrol," he said, forcing a laugh.

"Typical. Can't count on anyone!" someone called from the second truck.

"Here's your keycard. Make sure you follow close and turn your tracker on when you engage the engine. Can't lose another one of these trucks." He handed over a silver keycard to Dominic.

The helmet hid Dominic's grin as a new plan came into mind. Whatever was in the back of these trucks would be a great asset in their attack on the headquarters. "It's my first run, I'll let you guys lead the way."

"Ugh, another green horn," the third Enforcer groaned.

The four made their way into the trucks. Dominic sat in the cab and tried to remember how to drive. It'd been nearly sixteen years since he'd been taught, but it couldn't have changed much. He put the keycard into the slot and flipped the switch on the dashboard. The engine roared to life as did the other three trucks. The dash panel was different than he remembered, with new tech added, but he was sure he could figure out most of the controls.

"Tracking on!" the Enforcer in the truck next to him called out the window.

Dominic gave him a thumbs up before finding the tracking switch on the dash. A red light lit up below, signaling it was on. One by one the trucks pulled out until it was Dominic's turn to follow. He watched the Enforcer in the truck next to him grip the steering gear sticking out of the dash. He looked down at his own feet and noticed no foot pedal, but a trigger on the steering gear. The driver in the truck next to him gripped the panel and pressed it forward, making the vehicle propel ahead. He pressed forward as gently as possible, not knowing how much pressure would move the vehicle. The truck crept forward. He pulled back on the panel to test the brakes, getting a feel for it, and sure enough the truck stopped.

The truck ahead of him honked and he pressed steering gear once again to follow them. They drove toward the gate on the edge of the village, armed guards standing at either side. They saluted the trucks as they drove by.

Dominic couldn't believe his luck. After everything he'd made it in *and* made it out. Satcha would no longer be able to brag about her ability to sneak in and out. He snuck into a tower compound! She hadn't even managed that. It was under construction, but she didn't need to know that. Now all he had to do was lose the other three and head back to his own base. He eyed the tracking switch on the dash. At the right moment, he'd have to remember to flip it off. All hell would break loose. But he'd be ready.

Dominic looked back at the ruined village and grasped the explosive control from his belt. If he didn't do it now, the controller would be too far to send the transmission. He pressed the button and kept his eyes on the truck ahead of him. Explosions went off one after another, five loud blasts ringing loudly through the night. Black smoke rose through the sky like a beacon of embarrassment for the Nerosians. The ground shook, he could feel it in the seat of the truck. Dominic looked back in the rearview mirror and couldn't see the tower frame anymore.

The two trucks ahead of him sped up, and voices poured

from the radio. "*Go, go, go! Get those supplies out of here! We are under attack!*"

Eager to slip away with the supplies, Dominic gladly pressed the steering gear harder, and followed the trucks with a small grin.

CHAPTER 44

DOMINIC

Half an hour after following the trucks along the rocky roads, Dominic hit his stride, falling in sync with the other drivers. He drove as if he'd done it a thousand times before. He didn't jerk to a stop when they slowed or rev the motor. Since he didn't know how to judge the timing of when to break off from the others, he kept extra distance between him and the truck ahead of him. They drove much faster than a horse could run. He tried his best to search the land for familiar signs of where they were, but nothing looked the same from inside the motorized vehicle. It didn't help that in all his time in this area, he'd always kept off the main road. The only ones who used it were the Enforcers.

Not once did he let his guard down—the impending fear of being found out kept him on his toes. The only thing keeping him sane was with each passing second, he drove closer to the base. Closer to safety and closer to getting whatever sat in the back of the truck to the base. He'd planned it all out in his head. When he got back to the base, he would drop off the supplies to Dr. Steltan and ensure the troops were ready to follow the General's orders. Then he would slip away when no one was watching to find Satcha.

The road grew narrow where the trees hugged along the edges, scraping along the sides of the trucks. Dominic released pressure from the steering gear and allowed the distance to grow between him and the truck ahead.

Twenty... Thirty... Forty... Fifty feet between him and the Enforcers. He couldn't keep it up much longer before they would notice how far behind he fell. Oak and birch trees gathered in a cluster, with barely any space between them; there wasn't anywhere to slip away to.

They drove for another thirty minutes. The wall-to-wall forest on either side of him started to thin and he was able to see fields of gold to his left. He guessed he was about halfway between Carose and the Enforcer Headquarters. By truck, he had to go about forty-five minutes north to reach the Enross Army tunnels. If he was going to do this, it had to be now.

He waited for a bend in the road and the trucks ahead of him to disappear. Instead of following, he swerved off between two large oaks on the side of the road. He flipped off the tracking switch, the red light disappearing.

He didn't drive straight out to the field, instead driving along the edges. He didn't want to drive too fast and stir up any dust or leave tracks.

"*Vehicle 407, can you please confirm your location? Is your tracker malfunctioning?*" a voice came over the radio.

"Shit!" Dominic kept one hand on the steering gear and with his other pulled out as many cords as he could until the lights on the radio dimmed. He had no idea if there were any other location or communication devices hidden in the vehicle, but he had to take the chance. He'd have to remember to get Dr. Steltan to do a bug sweep to make sure the vehicle was clean.

He took off his helmet as he weaved the truck through the

trees and ripped off the armor plating of the uniform from his chest. The closer he got to the Enross Base, the more he worried about friendly fire. There was no doubt they would be aware of his approach. They'd set up strong boundary lines in case of a surprise attack—a trap of his own creation from his time in Rios—and he feared he wouldn't even get to the gate before they fired on him. He would have to stop just before the boundary and show himself.

He expected he had another mile or so before they would attack, but he was wrong. A bullet exploded through the window, whistling past his ear. He yanked back the steering gear, abruptly halting the truck.

"Don't shoot!" He held his hands above his head as another bullet left a perfect circular hole in the windshield in front of him before burying itself in his shoulder. "Fuck!"

Blood poured out of the ripped flesh in his shoulder, but no more gunfire sounded. He whistled out his two-note code and thankfully, it was returned through the trees.

He swung the door open and dove to the ground.

Dominic tried to steady his breathing and ignore the burning radiating out of his right arm. With his left hand, he stood and closed the door to the truck slowly, trying not to make any sudden movements.

"Captain Lightwood?" Private Alderson bounded toward the truck in long strides. "I'm so sorry, Captain, I swear I didn't know it was you."

"Enough, Alderson." Dominic couldn't help but snap at the young private as he cradled his arm. His sleeve soaked through with a river of red. "Radio ahead for someone to come pick up the truck. I've got a gift for Dr. Steltan."

The private seemed like he wanted to apologize more, but Dominic's patience had worn thin from his mission. He needed Ms. Alba to patch him up quickly before the General called on him. He could only assume he would be stripped of his rank for acting without orders. Alderson radioed ahead and called for the medics. Dominic waved off the stretcher and walked to the hospital wing himself.

The marching of boots echoed through the tunnel and into the hospital wing. Dominic squinted his eyes open, bright lights blurring his vision. He wasn't sure how long he'd been out, but his shoulder didn't ache as much as it had before. His head swirled with a grogginess he couldn't shake, barely able to focus. He rubbed his eyes with his left hand, almost trying for his right, but it was strapped in a sling across his chest.

"Captain Lightwood. Wake up, sir." Lieutenant Monroe hovered over him. His vision steadied until he was able to see the dark angry face of Monroe. "The General is here to see you."

Dominic held back a curse. Of course, General Ballard wouldn't give him time to recover, he'd handle business first and kick him to the curb. He sat up, noticing an array of soldiers standing around, watching him.

An audience, great. Just what Ballard wants.

Dominic wondered if he would be used as a lesson to anyone else operating without his approval.

"Lightwood, glad to see you up, son," General Ballard said, appearing in the doorway. The soldiers moved aside for him to storm through, coming to a stop beside Dominic's bed. He snapped his fingers at a soldier without looking away from Dominic.

He glared at Ballard with his jaw set. He'd take whatever punishment came his way; he knew he did right by the troops. They needed to have a fighting chance when they stormed the Enforcer Headquarters. Now they had it.

But Ballard didn't yell or scold him. A young soldier

Dominic recognized as Ballard's assistant appeared at the General's side. He was a frail looking kid with sunken eyes and pale skin and holding a small, black box. Ballard took the box from him and turned to face Dominic with an odd grin.

"I've been waiting for this day. My protege to climb the ranks a little further!" Ballard clapped Dominic on his injured arm. He fought back a wince and held his breath, fighting off the shooting pains radiating through his arm. He hated Ballard calling him his protege, he'd earned his ranks by work ethic and service alone. "For your service to the Enross Army, you are hereby promoted to Major."

Ballard opened the box to reveal a gold major signet. He plucked it out and rested it on Dominic's gray t-shirt.

The soldiers around him cheered, but Dominic didn't know what to say. He watched Ballard slink to the back of the room with a dark, evil look on his face. Dominic didn't know why, but there was a feeling deep down in his gut telling him something was wrong. He almost preferred to be stripped of his captaincy and put back to first lieutenant.

He ignored all the congratulations and the many hands patting his good shoulder and watched the General leave the hospital wing. Ballard was up to something, and Dominic intended to get to the bottom of it.

CHAPTER 45

SATCHA

Errol whistled a joyful tune that put not only Satcha on edge, but Hugh as well. Errol seemed to be the only one interested in trying to talk and when neither Satcha nor Hugh responded, he didn't let it spoil his mood. As much as Satcha wanted to tell him to stop, she couldn't. It reminded her of Dominic and the whistled notes he and the Enross Army used to communicate.

She didn't know what to do when she got to the army base. Would Dominic be there? It was unlikely. Who knew what Aleksandr had done to him? She just hoped he was all right.

As much as she didn't like Hugh, Errol grew on her. She'd never imagined a Night Raider, or Ex-Night Raider as Hugh called them, could be kind. He shared his rations and water with her and when she didn't have the strength, he helped her along and kept pace with her despite Hugh's grumblings. She had a gut feeling Errol didn't like the business of raiding and perhaps was forced into it to survive. It made her feel sorry for him and give her a real reason to vouch for him to Dominic, but Hugh would be harder to make a case for—he didn't seem to respect anyone.

The one thing worrying her was who she would find at the Enross Base. Dominic and Lennox were the only commanding officers she'd met and neither of them were there. Maybe she could talk to Ms. Alba. She didn't seem to like Satcha much, but the soldiers listened to her, and even respected her.

Yes, Ms. Alba would know what to do. She'd find her and tell her what happened in Rios, and maybe she could persuade the officers to send a search party to look for Dominic. She didn't care about exposing the Free People of Rios after they'd kidnapped and boxed her up like produce for sale, not to mention hurting Dominic. Besides that, what made them so privileged to avoid the wrath of the Enforcers while the rest of Enross lived in fear and ruin?

Satcha followed Hugh and Errol along the trail through the woods and tried her best to ignore the angry growl coming from her stomach. But sinking her teeth into a nice and warm loaf of bread was all she could think about. She longed to smell the rising yeast in a baker's oven. So much saliva pooled in her mouth she was forced to swallow it, causing her stomach acid to rise up her throat. A sour taste lingered on her tongue making her wish she hadn't drained the jug of water she'd taken from Errol.

"How much farther until we reach the end of the Sea River?" Satcha couldn't take it much longer. Despite her racing mind full of determination, every cell in her body needed to stop and rest.

"Not far, maybe a half hour of walkin'," Hugh said through heavy breaths. He stopped and braced his hands against a tree with his head hanging low. Sweat dripped off his face and he panted hard as if the wind had been knocked out of him.

Errol wasn't fairing much better.

"I say we rest when we get to the river. Try'n get some fish and freshwater for the rest of the journey," Errol piped up. He wiped his forehead with the sleeve of his dirty tunic.

Hugh nodded, still trying to catch his breath. Satcha let out a low sigh, relieved she didn't have to speak up and be the one to ask for rest. It would also give her an opportunity to scrub off the dirt and vomit still caked on her skin.

She didn't want to show any weakness in front of the two men. The only thing keeping them on her side was her show of strength and her ability to take them by surprise. She didn't walk too closely, leaving enough distance between them to either attack or defend if need be. Hugh was a mystery to her. The only thing she could tell was he had been hardened by the life of a survivor. Night Raiding was a dangerous job and not one someone held for long. Kill or be killed was the life of the Night Raiders. Like Private Tom Alderson, far too soft for the army, she'd no doubt in her mind Errol stuck out like a sore thumb with the Raiders. She imagined that if the private had never found the Enross Army, he might've ended up like Errol. She guessed the only reason Errol had survived as long as he had was because of Hugh.

Despite her misgivings about Hugh, she envied their friendship. They had each other to rely on. It made her think of Agatha and how she'd guided her and taught her how to survive. It was different from what she'd felt with Dominic. Companionship without the difficulty of managing confusing romantic feelings of not only yourself, but the other person. She never had a friend before and the more she witnessed what she was missing, the more she wanted it. She found herself wanting someone to talk to—and not just Dominic. She wanted a friend to share experiences with, to ask questions to. To laugh with.

Satcha didn't know what to expect when she found Dominic. Would they go their separate ways? They both had their own paths, and she knew they didn't lead the same way. One of them would have to make a decision and she wasn't sure it could be her. The Free City still called to her; with the increasing threat of the Enforcers, Enross became more dangerous by the day, and she would need to leave soon. But not before she returned to Rios to settle things with Aleksandr.

Satcha watched Hugh from the corner of her eye and wasn't surprised to see him also watching her. He clapped Errol on the back and headed off through the woods, leading the way. They arrived at the Sea River well within the half hour he'd guessed and stood on the edge of the rocky shoreline with the smell of saltwater blowing in their faces. The great river separated Enross and Austerland, cutting Vardya almost in half, if it weren't for the deserted land to the south bridging the two countries together. As far as Satcha was aware, no one lived there.

The smell of salt in the air told Satcha one thing: they couldn't drink the water. Her mouth was so dry her tongue scraped across the roof of her mouth. Her lips had cracked down the middle and crusted over with dried blood. She tried her best not to lick them and make it worse, but she found herself unintentionally doing it every few minutes.

Not much farther.

"I need to wash up," she called.

She didn't wait for them to respond as she teetered across the rocky shore looking for a private place to bathe. She shrugged off her dirty dress; it couldn't be washed now since she had no clean clothes to change into. Stepping into the cold water, she hissed at the freezing chill on her skin, but relished it. Cold water meant clean skin.

She took a deep breath and lowered herself into the river, dunking her head in too. The cold chased away her tiredness as she fought against chattering teeth while she scrubbed her body and hair with urgency. She didn't waste time lingering; it was too cold. When she was satisfied with her job scrubbing the vomit from her skin, she scrambled out of the water.

Everything inside her told her not to put the dirty dress back on, but it was the only thing to cover herself and offer the slightest bit of resistance against the cold nip of the wind.

Satcha stumbled over to a large rock and sat, staring across the wide river in the dying sunlight. She could see Austerland off in the distance. She'd never been there before, but it looked the exact same as the Enross side. Far off, down the shore, the land jutted out and she could make out the curve of the docks in Carose.

"Miss, we can't stay here in the open." Errol lopped over to her and grabbed her arm. Satcha recoiled from his touch and jumped to her feet.

"We need to find water and some food," she said, rubbing her arm to remove the feeling of his touch.

"We have a safehouse with supplies in those trees," Hugh said grudgingly, "but we have to move. Neroso ships sail this river." Hugh stared out over the waters. Satcha couldn't see any ships, but she didn't doubt they were out there somewhere.

Satcha took one last look across the wide river. She tried to imagine standing on the Austerland shores looking out over the Westim Ocean in search of the island of the Free City. She didn't know how large the ocean was but seeing the great vastness of the Sea River told her paradise was much farther than she'd originally thought.

She followed Hugh and Errol from the shoreline into the woods. Errol didn't continue with his whistling, which made everything seem too quiet for her liking. No birds chirped as they had before, the only sound was a soft wind whistling through the air and rustling the branches of the tall trees. The men didn't seem to think anything of the quiet. They stomped through the woods, looking too eager to get to their safehouse. She stopped and rested her right hand against the rough tree bark of a great sycamore tree. She closed her eyes, letting her other senses heighten, especially her hearing.

Twigs snapped under heavy boots. There was a familiar gait to the steps, almost like a march.

Shit.

"Get down!" Satcha hissed at Hugh and Errol who'd kept on without her.

There was no time for either of them to react to her. Two Enforcers jumped out through the bushes with their blasters raised and pointed at them. Satcha dropped to the ground with only the slightest hope they hadn't seen her. She backed herself up against the sycamore tree and waited to be captured.

"Kneel and put your hands on your head!" one of the Enforcers barked.

Satcha froze, unsure if the command was for her. No one came. She tried to calm herself by controlling her breathing. She peeked around the tree. Both Errol and Hugh knelt with their hands on their heads, the Enforcers standing over them.

She hadn't been spotted. She returned to her hiding spot behind the tree and sighed in relief. She had two options. Try to rescue them or leave them. The old Satcha would've left them without a second thought, but this new person she found within herself, the person Dominic brought out in her, wanted to help them. *He* would've helped them.

Despite having no weapons, she hunched low to the ground and tried to circle around the bushes. A surprise attack was the only way she could rescue them. She crawled along the dirt, trying to use the lush bushes to conceal her. The Enforcers mumbled something to each other, too muffled for her to hear, but she was focusing on Hugh's stony face and Errol's quivering lip.

Satcha positioned herself behind the Enforcers, giving her

the short space of ten feet between them. She reached around on the ground trying to find anything she could use to attack with, but there was nothing. No rocks, no broken tree branches, no vines to wrap around an Enforcer's neck.

She locked eyes with Hugh who gave a slight nod to the Enforcer on her right, standing in front of Errol. She didn't need him to say the words; she knew what he was about to do. Hugh lunged at the Enforcer in front of Errol, taking both Errol and the Enforcers by surprise. Satcha leapt from her hiding place and threw herself at the other Enforcer, knocking him to the ground. The Enforcer's blaster tumbled out of his hands and fell in front of Errol.

Satcha did all she could to grip on to the back of the Enforcer's helmet and tear it off, but the Enforcer jabbed his elbow into her lower abdomen, sending her flying backwards. Satcha rolled to her side under the cover of bushes and tried to steady herself while Errol grasped the blaster. Suddenly there was a loud crack, someone firing a shot. It rang in Satcha's ears and echoed in the trees. She heard a body fall before another shot cracked, followed by a scream.

"Hugh! No!" Errol pointed the blaster at the Enforcer who'd been wrestling with Hugh. A bright light shot from the weapon and hit the Enforcer square in the chest, sending him flying backwards. Black smoke wisped up from the body as a horrible burnt smell invaded her nose.

Errol threw the blaster and rushed to Hugh, leaving Satcha alone to fight off the final Enforcer. The Enforcer grabbed her by the ankle and pulled her out from the bushes. She kicked at his grip to no avail. He yanked her so hard she thought her hip might come out of its joint. She rolled and sprung up to her feet to face him. The Enforcer grasped both sides of his helmet and pulled it off his head. A brown-eyed stranger stared back at her, his evil grin sending a shiver down her spine.

"You look familiar," he taunted as he stepped closer to her, trying to circle her. She wouldn't let him cage her like an animal—she followed his steps and soon they were circling each other.

"Strange, I've made a point of killing any Enforcers I meet," she spat, narrowing her eyes at him.

The Enforcer laughed, entertained by her. "No, I'm sure I've seen your face before. I never forget the face of anyone I give lashings to."

Satcha stiffened. He was the one who'd marked her. The one who'd beaten her near death. She remembered laying so still he thought she'd died. But it didn't stop him from lashing her two more times. Every nerve ending in her body told her to move and cry out, but she lay lifeless, waiting for it to stop. When he'd left her body in the middle of the street, she'd crawled away to nurse her wounds. Her scars had been removed, but she swore she could still feel them. She remembered the white hot fire as the whip tore through her skin and left it a bloody mess.

"Ah, so it is you. The one who got away. How about for old time's sake you turn around and show me my master-piece." He reached his hand to his belt and tugged off a white wand. He pressed a small red button on the side of the device —the top opened, a long whip snaking out. He looped it in the air before he swung his arm back and cracked it against the ground.

"Not a chance." Rage erupted in Satcha's veins, spreading through her like wildfire.

"Then why don't we make this a little more interesting? I have a new toy." He pressed another button and the whip hummed to life with electricity surging through the length of it.

Satcha didn't let it deter her. She'd only have one chance to attack before the whip tore into her like it had in the past. She wouldn't fare well with the new upgrade. He swung his arm back, the whip flying through the air behind him, but she was quicker than him. He beat people for a living, but she survived. She wouldn't let him take that from her.

She collided against the hard armor of his suit and knocked the air out of his lungs, forcing him to stumble back a step. The whip fell from his hand and lay crackling against the ground. She reached for the handle and searched for the button to turn off the electricity, but she had a better idea. She dragged the whip across the ground as she fumbled around to get in the right position. She hovered over the Enforcer ready to wrap the whip around his neck.

"No! Don't!" he screamed beneath her.

His body convulsed as the whip ran across his arm. A zap stung against her legs as she straddled him, but it was nowhere near as painful for her as him.

Good.

She pulled the whip closer, careful not to touch it and wrapped it around his head. It tightened around his neck and his screams became hoarse. She pulled tight on the whip, letting it cut off his airway. The shock of the electricity was an added bonus. Pay back for the damage he'd done to her. The shock burnt his face and smoke wafted up, filing her nose with the smell of death. Her stomach lurched and bile pooled in her mouth as she waited for him to stop moving and the life to fade out of him.

"You're right. This is more interesting." She stared into his wide eyes. His screams choked off and his face turned blue, his life slowly draining. He slumped limp against the ground, dead eyes staring into the sky.

Satcha switched off the electricity on the whip and scooted off the dead Enforcer. She wrapped her arms around herself, and a sob escaped her chest. How long had she wanted to get revenge on the Enforcer? She thought when she did, the memory of the pain would go away, but it didn't. It was still there, as powerful as ever.

"Satcha?" Errol sobbed.

Satcha rubbed her teary eyes and looked at Errol who stood next to her, pale as a ghost. He fell to his knees in front of her.

"He's gone."

"What?" Satcha cleared her throat and tried to collect herself.

"Hugh... They shot him," he choked out.

Sorrow filled her heart. Tears ran down Errol's cheeks, washing away the dirt and leaving streaks. Just over his shoulder, she could see Hugh's lifeless body. She knew what Errol felt, it was the same way she felt when she saw Agatha die at the hands of the Enforcers. If Dominic was dead, the hole in her chest would never be filled. She staggered to her feet and stood in front of Errol for a moment before kneeling in front of him. She wrapped her arms around his shoulders, but it only made him crumble more. She'd never consoled anyone before, or at least, she couldn't remember it, but she was sure this was the right thing to do. Errol wrapped his arms around her in return and held her tight.

Hugh knew he would die when he nodded to Satcha. He gave his life to protect his friend and in doing so, also saved Satcha. She was thankful for his sacrifice, and wouldn't let it go to waste. Too many civilians fell against the Enforcers, either dying or having to live by their rule, and she'd had enough. She would do what she could to help Errol after they found Dominic, and one day enact her revenge on all the Enforcers—starting with the Masked Man.

CHAPTER 46

DOMINIC

Dominic scolded himself as he watched over the troops training under Lieutenant Monroe. He hadn't found a single opportunity to slip away since he'd been released from Ms. Alba's care. Lieutenant Monroe kept an annoyingly close watch on him. The training with the DEW technology wasn't an easy transition for the soldiers either. Half of them were too afraid to go near them, while the other half recklessly wielded them with a lack of respect, putting not only themselves in danger, but their fellow comrades.

He tried often to slip away to spy on the General, and even once tried to get an audience with him, but Ballard had secluded himself in his office and seemed to be avoiding Dominic at all costs. On top of that, no matter where Dominic went within the base—or above ground to check in on those guarding the perimeter—he had a feeling someone watched his every move. He quickly grew suspicious the General was behind it. Lieutenant Monroe would take his eyes off the troops too often during training to find where

Dominic moved in the room. If only Lennox were here, he could've helped recon and buy him some time to slip away.

Dominic knew he had to test his theory out. He waited for Monroe to search the expansive training grounds for him again and headed for the exit. He hoped it was only nerves messing with Monroe's head, that he had been worried about trying to fill Lennox's shoes, but those shoes were too big for Monroe to fill. Lennox was as loyal as they came and would take a bullet for Dominic if need be. And he'd do the same for him—the brother he'd never had.

The heavy steel door swung slowly behind Dominic as he exited the training grounds. He hadn't even made it to the end of the tunnel before he heard someone catch the door before it shut. He almost smirked at the thought of being right; someone followed him, but it brought forth more questions than it answered.

Why are they watching me? Who gave the order?

There was no doubt in his mind it had been the General. He'd been blocking Dominic's search for the Blood Scrolls for so long, but now he wanted to march on the Enforcer Head-quarters without a proper plan? Why was he so interested in the tower? It didn't make sense. He didn't trust anyone but himself to investigate.

He needed to break into Ballard's office.

Dominic continued through the hallway, listening to the footsteps following him. He didn't look back, he wanted them to think they were being discreet in spying on him, though they were anything but. He thought the troops had been trained better, but this soldier was loud, followed too close, and stopped abruptly whenever he did. There was only one soldier that came to mind who could be so clumsy. Dominic stopped but didn't turn around.

"Private Alderson?"

"Yes, sir, Cap... I mean, Major, sir! Ugh—!"

Dominic turned to see Alderson laying face down on the ground, and assumed he'd been startled and tripped over his own feet. Dominic rolled his eyes and shook his head. He held out a hand to the young private who sheepishly accepted it. Alderson dusted himself off frantically before standing at attention and saluting Dominic.

"Sorry, sir."

"Private, why are you not in training?"

"Lieutenant Monroe assigned me to be your aide and suggested I stay close to your side in case you needed anything, sir." Alderson dipped his head and averted his eyes from Dominic's gaze. Alderson's lie shone clearly.

"Was there anything else the lieutenant ordered you to do?" Dominic couldn't help but press on as there was no doubt in his mind Alderson would break. He stood a little taller and squared his shoulders, making Alderson seem even smaller.

"Y-Yes, sir." Alderson lifted his head up, a new look on his face that surprised Dominic. Anger. Alderson set his jaw and clenched his fists at his side.

The anticipation gnawed at Dominic, and he fought the urge to grab the soldier's shoulders and shake the words out of him. He glanced around looking to see if anyone watched them, but there wasn't a soul in sight. He didn't trust that. He grabbed Alderson's arm and dragged him off to a small corridor.

"Alderson, what do you know?"

"I'm sorry, sir, they made me promise not to tell you, but they are watching you." The private spoke fast and paced back and forth in front of Dominic. "Lieutenant Monroe ordered Private Walton to follow you and report back your activities, but I knew something was up, so I volunteered instead."

"Why did you volunteer?" It struck Dominic as odd; he'd never known the soldier to volunteer for anything. Any orders he took on usually ended in a mess for someone else to clean up.

"I've had this sinking feeling, sir. Ever since you and Lieutenant Lennox left with Miss Satcha, things have been different around here. You've always been a strong and hard, but kind, leader... But those who've held your post while you were gone—Well, they've been handing out punishments I've never seen anyone in the army get before."

"What do you mean?"

"Well, sir, Private Haggard knocked over a supporting beam just outside of the mess hall. Lieutenant Monroe dragged him away with Corporal Maxwell. No one saw Haggard for a few hours. We'd assumed he'd been assigned cleaning duty in the toilets, but when he came back to the barracks..." Here, Alderson paused, taking a deep breath. "He came back naked, carrying his uniform piled up nice and neat, but he was dripping blood. Three lashes they gave him."

Dominic felt the color drain from his face. His stomach knotted, the urge to vomit swelling. How could they do such things? This was the very thing he'd wanted to protect people from—the evil doings of his uncle and his Enforcers. Yet here in his own unit, they were being beaten. Lashed. This was not the way of the Enross Army. Not *his* way.

"How come you've waited so long to tell me this? Did you report this to any other officers?"

"No, sir. We were told the new punishments came directly from General Ballard to incentivize the units to prepare for what was to come against the Enforcers." Alderson stopped pacing and leaned back against the wall of the tunnel. If Dominic wasn't watching him closely he would have missed it, but Alderson's pinched face gave it away.

"What's wrong with your back?"

"I... uh..."

"Spit it out!" Dominic's world crumbled around him.

He'd been the one in control, but Satcha had been kidnapped and his soldiers were being whipped under his watch. Any patience he'd had was long gone.

"I got five lashes the day you came back with the vehicle full of Enforcer tech for accidentally shooting you."

Dominic slid down to the ground and held his head. Pressure was building so quickly in his temples, he thought he might explode. He couldn't leave his men behind to face this on their own. They needed him.

I'm sorry, Tom," Dominic choked out. He did all he could to keep himself together. He couldn't bring himself to call the soldier by his rank or last name. It felt wrong, somehow. "Please know, had I known, I never would've allowed it."

"I know, Major. That's why I knew I had to volunteer—to find out what they were doing and why they wanted to keep an eye on you." Alderson held his hand out to Dominic, a mirror image from earlier.

Dominic took a deep breath, grasped Alderson's hand, and got to his feet. Alderson gave Dominic a sad smile. He grated on Dominic's nerves more often than not, but he was a good man.

"Thank you for telling me." He kept hold of Alderson's hand and shook it firmly.

"I've been feeding them garbage information, by the way. Reporting back bland information, nothing too exciting. Just that you go on your normal rounds and attend training. They don't seem to be happy with that. That's why the lieutenant sent me after you. He figured you were up to no good."

"All right, I need to make a plan. You need to keep feeding them the same information you've been giving. I think I have an idea to keep them off both our backs and give me time to get a distraction in place."

"A distraction, sir?"

"Yes, a big one. I need all eyes outside the tunnels. Including the General."

"We could stage a cave in."

Dominic stared in shock at Alderson who looked back at him with innocent, big blue eyes. He'd said the words so casually. Maybe he'd underestimated the private. Maybe there was more to him than the clumsy oof he'd always thought.

"That will work."

"I can get some of the others to help set things up. They've been talking. None of us are too happy with how things have been going, and we plan to form a union of sorts."

The more Alderson spoke, the more Dominic had to fight the urge to keep the storm in his stomach at bay. Sending Alderson to spy on him, punishments, and impending strikes within the army were not something he'd foreseen.

"As long as you can be discrete, do what you need to. Get back to me tomorrow after breakfast. I'll get a few things prepared for myself."

"Yes, sir!" The corner of Alderson's lips turned upwards into a big smile. He saluted Dominic before turning to leave but stopped abruptly. "Oh, sir. I meant to ask you. Where is Miss Satcha? She didn't come back with you. Is everything all right?"

"I'll explain later; let's get through this first and then we can worry about Satcha."

The private nodded and didn't argue, but he didn't seem too keen on the answer. Dominic knew that Alderson had taken a liking to Satcha when she was here—not in any way that made him concerned, but in a friendly way. He watched Alderson head back down to the main tunnel.

He was glad for some privacy; it was the first time he'd felt like he'd been truly alone since he'd returned to the base.

As much as he wanted to leave the base and search for Satcha, he couldn't leave the soldiers in this state. Not when they were being whipped and manipulated for the General's personal vendetta. He hoped she could forgive him because he wouldn't be able to forgive himself. But he'd made a promise to himself the moment he stepped foot in Vardya: he would do everything in his power to help protect people against his uncle and wouldn't let anything get in his way. He never expected to find Satcha though, and never imagined questioning his mission. *Was* he doing the right thing? Was leading the Enross Army the right move for him to protect people? He thought about everyone in Vardya suffering, not just in Enorss, but in Austerland too. He felt a twinge of guilt at the knowledge he'd done nothing to help those in Austerland since the ship sailed into port.

He tried not to scold himself for all the years he could've been doing more. He had managed to find out about the lost bloodline and the scrolls. He brought together troops for the army and saved many people from Enforcer attacks. But he wished he could've saved more, even if he did what he could with what he had. He'd done more than most. Maybe his reward after all this was over was to be with Satcha.

With a new mission cemented in his mind, Dominic found the determination he needed to pick himself up and get back to work. He rolled his shoulders and stretched. It was time to pay Dr. Steltan another visit.

Chapter 47

Dominic

Dominic kept to his usual daily routine by starting off the day doing a perimeter check with all the outposts. Nothing out of the norm, as expected. He made sure to make himself known to all he encountered. He couldn't risk anything out of the ordinary being reported back to the General of his movements.

Not today.

Today, Private Alderson and ten other soldiers he'd recruited would detonate a bomb in one of the tunnels. They had to be very strategic in which tunnel they would set off the bomb; it couldn't be a main access route, nor could it be anything to incapacitate any of the units, nor damage any supplies. He'd picked the corridor off the training grounds since it was close enough to force an evacuation as well as make it look like an accident from their new DEW tech.

He made his way toward the medical wing. He needed to be seen far enough away from the training grounds, yet close enough to the General's office so he could slip away and break in. It was the one thing that took him off his normal route, but he'd made himself an excuse.

He rolled up his sleeve, peeled back the bandages covering his gunshot wound, and took a deep breath. Taking the knife from his belt, he pointed the tip into his skin and ripped out the stitches. But that wasn't enough; he had to make a bigger mess, so he cut a jagged line, fully reopening the wound.

Thick, red blood rose to the surface of his skin and dripped down his arm. He wiped his knife off on his dark pants and pretended to stumble through the tunnel. Dominic landed with a thud and cried out for the added drama.

"Fuck!" he yelled. He needed witnesses so he didn't get off the ground, keeping his head low, waiting for the sound of running boots.

"Let me help you up, sir!" The private grasped Dominic's good arm and helped him to his feet.

"Thank you, Private." Dominic nodded to him and kept a loose hold on his arm, letting the blood soak through his sleeve.

"Major! Your arm!"

Dominic tried to hide his smile—the plan had started off brilliantly. He pretended to be in a haze and requested the soldier's help getting to the medical wing. He put on a good show as the private kept a grip on his arm and escorted him.

"Ms. Alba! Ms. Alba!" the young private called as they stepped through the door.

Ms. Alba sat at her desk with her glasses perched on the tip of her nose as she read through paperwork. Any other soldier, she would've sent a nurse to tend to him, but she stood and cleared her throat as she strode across the room. Her stern demeanor never wobbled in even the most critical situations. A young, red-headed nurse scurried over to examine his arm ahead of Ms. Alba.

"Shoo! Back to your chores," Ms. Alba scolded her.

"Yes, ma'am." The nurse ducked her head and busied herself with bed linens.

"Major, you must be more careful if you want this to heal." Ms. Alba peered at the open wound on his arm. "Luckily, it looks like a clean cut."

Dominic knew she could tell he'd done this to himself. She watched him closely, calculating whatever his motive might be. He'd been able to trust her, but he couldn't trust the others in the room. He looked around, counting the faces: the private who escorted him, a group of five nurses chatting by Ms. Alba's desk, and one sleeping soldier hooked up to an array of monitors.

"Why don't we give the major some privacy in the officer's exam room." She motioned for the private to escort Dominic to a door on the far right of the room.

"Yes, Ms. Alba."

Dominic nodded to Ms. Alba and headed to the exam room. The private held the door open for him. Like the General's office, this room was drywalled and painted in a pale blue. No mahogany wood furniture filled the room, but a stainless-steel table and a hospital bed that looked much comfier than that the soldiers used. It was the first time he'd been in the room because it was usually reserved for the General, in case of any medical emergencies.

"Thank you, Private. You may return to your post." Dominic watched him from the corner of his eye, but the young soldier didn't seem to notice anything out of the ordinary.

"Yes, sir, Major." The soldier saluted him and left.

Ms. Alba appeared with a tray of medical supplies, bustling in.

"An unfortunate accident, Major."

"Yes, it was. I tripped over my own two feet."

"Well, I hope next time you are more careful. We only have so many supplies to go around."

"True. I'll be sure to watch my step next time." He rolled his sleeve back and let her clean the wound.

"Lucky it's just a clean cut. You don't want to risk any infection." She glanced at him.

He knew they weren't talking about his gunshot wound. She saw right through him and his plans but knew not to ask any outright questions. He couldn't give her all the details either; putting her at risk of being part of his conspiracy was out of the question. "You're right. I think there's enough infected soldiers wandering around here."

"Should I have my nurses prepare for an outbreak?" She kept her eyes on her work, already moving over to stitching the wound back up.

"It's never a bad idea to be prepared and at the ready."

She stopped and looked at him, her eyes wider than normal. "It's been a while since my nurses have gone through an unplanned drill. Maybe it would be beneficial."

"There's no time like the present." He tried to keep his voice level but stared deep into her eyes. There were no other hints he could give her, he'd have to hope she understood.

She nodded to him and finished sewing the wound. She wrapped it in a clean bandage and washed her hands in the sink.

"You're all set, Major. I hope I don't see you back in here again."

"I hope you won't." Dominic stood from the bed and started for the door.

"Major?"

"Yes?"

"Do you think the General has been looking a bit under the weather lately?"

Dominic thought for a moment on how to answer the question. "You know, you might be right."

They stared at each other in silence; he could almost see

Ms. Alba's wheels turning. After a moment, she nodded and clapped her hands together. "Well, I must get back to work."

"Of course," he said. "Thank you for all your help."

The second Dominic's hand touched the doorknob a loud bloom erupted, echoing through the tunnel. The ground around them rumbled and Ms. Alba fell forward, but Dominic caught her before she could hit the ground. He steadied her back on her feet.

"Evacuate the medical wing. Sounds like we've had a cave in."

"Yes, sir," she said, exiting the room in a flurry, barking orders at her nurses to grab the emergency kits and stick to the evacuation plan.

Dominic ushered the nurses out, keeping to the back of the crowd as they entered the main tunnel. Soldiers lined up in a single file, making their way out. Lieutenant Monroe barked orders up ahead to let the General pass through. Dominic shook his head in disgust. Never would he rush himself to safety before making sure his troops were safe first.

He waited for the long line of soldiers to empty the main tunnel before heading toward the General's office. He needed to be quick, otherwise his absence would be noticed for roll call.

He burst through the door, going straight for the desk. The bottom drawer had been left open, which meant the desk was unlocked.

Good. A slip up by the General in not making sure his files were secure before evacuating.

Dominic flipped through the paperwork seeing nothing of any interest, it was only transfer paperwork for soldiers at different outposts and maps. Nothing he didn't already know. He was running out of time, so he moved to another drawer, just above it. He slid it open and froze in surprise. Sitting on top of some papers was something Dominic hadn't seen in a very long time. He couldn't help but let out a choked gasp and stumble back.

Sitting in the drawer was a black communication pad, or at least what was left of it. It laid in two pieces with cracks spidering across the screen.

Communication pads weren't part of the technology Enross had the capability of. There was only one army that had them: the Nerosians. He knew Ballard had been hiding something, but he never expected him to be working with Neroso. With the Enforcers. It changed everything. The odds were already against them with the planned attack on their enemy's headquarters, but this made it a suicide mission.

Chapter 48

General Ballard

"What the hell happened?" General Ballard slammed his fists on the table in the war room, causing all officers but Lightwood to flinch. He didn't like that. Lightwood should've been sitting there with his head sunk low instead of meeting his gaze. He wanted nothing more to reach over the table and make an example of him, but he'd held his restraint. Lightwood was too popular amongst the soldiers; he couldn't risk causing any further upset before they marched on the Enforcer tower.

"Sir, I think we should use this to our advantage." Lieutenant Monroe cleared his throat and stuck out his chest. He'd been extremely vocal and eager to please since he'd assigned him a special watch on Lightwood.

"Well spit it out. I don't have all damn day, Monroe."

"We've been training hard these past few weeks and with the cave in, the builders have restricted access to the training area until they can assess and repair the damage. Why don't we strike while the iron is hot and not let the soldiers grow lazy waiting?"

Wide eyes stared at him from around the room, Lightwood included. He smirked at the terrified look on the major's face. He'd gotten the reaction he wanted. Ballard looked past the officers at the map of Vardya on the wall. Soon, it would all be his. He only needed to take the tower. The rest would be easy. Although, it seemed such a waste to let the tower burn. He imagined himself sitting in an office, high up on the top floor. He'd look out his window and see as far as the eye could see. Not to mention, all those who lived beneath him. Far beneath him. He couldn't help the slow creep of a grin.

Emperor of Vardya.

All the officers waited for him to speak. Lightwood opened his mouth, but Ballard raised his hand to silence him. He couldn't risk Lightwood ruining his plans. Lightwood would also have to go—the impending battle was convenient for some friendly fire opportunities. Now that they had the DEW tech, who was to say what side the blast came from?

"All forces prepare for battle. Lieutenant Monroe, I think you've earned yourself a reward. I think the title *captain* is in order."

"Thank you very much, sir." Monroe's eyes beamed with pride. If it wasn't for Ballard's own mood uplifted at the thought of his own rank promotion, he would've scowled at the adoring gaze from Monroe. Although, Monroe had proved himself useful.

"Major Lightwood, you will lead the initial attack on the tower—"

"Sir—"

"I don't want another word out of you, Major. You have your orders."

Lightwood held his tongue. The fire in his eyes blazed, something the General was keen on extinguishing. If the major survived the first attack, he wouldn't last through the second wave.

"I want everyone gathering the troops and preparing. Go!

Now!" All the officers jumped to attention and saluted him before leaving the room. He called, "Captain Monroe! You stay here with me."

Lightwood left the room slower than any other and tried to catch his gaze, but Ballard wouldn't have it. There was nothing he had to say to him and there was nothing Lightwood could say to change his mind.

"Sir?" Monroe cleared his throat, almost begging for attention.

"I trust you to keep your discretion with this next mission I give you."

"Always, sir."

"Major Lightwood will lead the attack in the morning before dawn. He will fall to the Enforcer weaponry."

"Sir?"

Ballard groaned. He pinched the bridge of his nose and rubbed his eyes. How plainly did he have to spell it out?

"Major Dominic Lightwood will fall tomorrow at dawn by *use* of an Enforcer DEW blaster." He glared at the captain who gulped and shifted on his feet.

"Yes, sir."

"I know I can count on *you*."

"Yes, sir. You can."

"Good. See to it." Ballard turned his back on him and sat at the table, picking up his paperwork.

Captain Monroe stood for a moment as if waiting for further instructions, but Ballard had no interest in continuing any conversation with him. He'd said all he needed to and did not wish to be bothered any further. Footsteps headed for the door and soon it clicked shut, leaving the General alone with his thoughts.

"Emperor Ballard of Vardya," he said under his breath, testing out the feel of it rolling off his tongue.

He repeated it over and over, saying it a little louder each time. He couldn't help but scoff at the drab navy blue military uniform he wore for the Enross Army. Yes, he would need a new uniform. Something more regal. No more dark hues of blue and gray. He wanted bright red and gold everywhere. Red as pigmented as the color of the blood of those who stood against him. Perhaps a nice gold crown could be made in his honor.

He no longer wanted to sit upon an old throne like the ones in the Kingdoms of Reeock and Hortus. He wanted more. No wooden throne would do for him. He would have the titanium helmets of the fallen Enforcers melted down and have a throne made. He had no idea what secrets lay inside the Enforcer tower, but he was sure there had to be some sort of fancy room for the Masked Man. If not, he would have his soldiers expand the tower and add a grand throne room. From there he would direct his forces forward to Austerland and claim their resources for his own.

Emperor Ballard of Vardya.

CHAPTER 49

DOMINIC

The dark sky loomed, the blanket of stars twinkling merrily. Dominic missed the familiar clop of hooves as he and his troops made their way through the forest on foot. The only sound to be heard was the rustling of their heavy packs bouncing with each step.

It wasn't the first time Dominic had led troops into battle, but it struck him as odd, given his new rank, that he would be on the front lines. Though as much as it bothered him, it also gave him peace of mind. Private Alderson and the majority of those who worked with him on the cave were in his troop. At least he could keep an eye on them instead of sitting blind with the rest of the officers.

The troops stalking through the woods ahead of him were greater in number than the last time he'd come face to face with the Enforcer Headquarters. Ten soldiers had accompanied Lennox, Satcha, and him. Now, over seventy-five soldiers marched with him and were much more prepared. The vehicle he'd stolen had been loaded with enough DEW tech to arm one in five soldiers. He hoped it would be enough to take the Enforcers by surprise. Each soldier was trained in how to use the weapons, whether they carried the DEW tech or not. First opportunity they had, they needed to steal weapons from fallen Enforcers.

The tower glinted at them over the tops of the trees, growing taller as they got closer. The mirrored building sat silent. The calm before the storm. The troops lined the edge of the forest silently waiting on Dominic's orders. The Enforcers had widened the clearing around the tower, cutting down many of the trees. It left a lot of open space between the cover and the building—too long of a sprint to be safe. Two guards stood on either side of the main entrance, but Dominic couldn't see any others walking the perimeter.

Dominic radioed the two lieutenants he'd been assigned. "Team leaders, I need one team on the left and one team on the right. The rest will stay with me and face the doors head on. Over."

The sound of leaves crunching under boots and the soldiers breathing filled his ears. He hoped he'd been wrong about escape tunnels. There was only one other exit from the building and that was the docking bay in the back. Any return fire would come from the entrance.

He and the soldiers around him crawled forward until they were covered by thick green bushes and watched for movement.

"Sir, team two is in place, over," Lieutenant Baker reported.

"Team three also in place. We've got two guards patrolling from the rear and coming up to the front, over," Lieutenant Axely chimed in.

"Axely, take them out quietly. We need those radios intact. Over." Dominic raised his night vision binoculars and scanned the edges of the buildings. Nothing looked out of the ordinary from what he remembered of his time in the Free City, but that was a long time ago. There was no telling what new technology they'd developed.

"Sir?" Private Alderson crawled up next to Dominic, pale as a ghost. It was his first time out of training and on the front lines. His eyes were wide and his breathing heavy.

"Take it easy, Alderson."

"I don't know if I can do this, sir." He choked on his words. "I've... I've never killed anyone before."

"Corporal Downey, take the radio and wait for word from Lieutenant Axely." Dominic tossed his radio to the soldier to his left before turning to Alderson. "Alderson, we've all been where you are now—on the edge of battle. Not one person on our side or their side was born to be a killer. War is an unfortunate thing; it's either kill or be killed. These men around you, they're your brothers, and they need you just as much as you need them. Keep them safe and they will do the same for you. There isn't one soldier in this line up I wouldn't lay my life down for."

Alderson took a deep breath and nodded, holding back a quiver in his throat. "Yes, sir. Thank you, sir."

"You stay close to me, we will get out of this together."

Alderson relaxed his shoulders and smiled with a newfound confidence Dominic hoped would stay with him. He patted him on the back before turning back to the entrance of the tower with his binoculars.

"Sir, Lieutenant Axely has confirmed the two guards on the right side of the tower have been disarmed. He is in control of their radios, but they seem to be malfunctioning. A constant single is coming through. He reports it's the anthem of the Free City."

"Fuck!" Dominic pounded his fist on the ground. "They know we're here. We've lost the element of surprise."

As the words left Dominic's lips, a loud siren blared from the tower and spotlights lit up the sky, giving light to the open space below. The ground cracked, splitting into three different sections, mechanical doors revealing tunnels. Large armored vehicles roared to life and rose from the ground followed by a hundred soldiers on foot.

They'd known they were coming and were waiting for them.

Dominic reached for the radio from Corporal Downey and shouted into the device. "All units fire at will!"

The lieutenants didn't respond by radio, instead they started firing on the marching Enforcers. Bodies fell from the DEW blasts while the bullets of their rifles did little damage. Dominic knew that once ranks closed and both armies were upon each other, close combat would be what made the difference.

The titanium armored vehicles halted, and Dominic watched in growing horror as support legs mounted on the ground around all sides. The top of the vehicles opened, and turrets rose from within, manned by a heavily armored Enforcer.

"Take out those turrets now!" Dominic shouted over the sound of gunfire, pulling the trigger on his rifle at Enforcers running right at him. He aimed for the soft black neck guards. He could've taken a DEW gun, but he wanted his soldiers to have more protection. He had experience on his side.

Private Alderson hid behind a tree in the corner of Dominic's eye, clutching his DEW blaster. With every sound of a gun firing, Alderson flinched.

"Alderson! Start blasting!"

"Yes, sir, Major!"

Alderson aimed at an Enforcer running toward them. A bright light flew from the tip of the gun and hit the armored chest plate sending the Enforcer flying back, smoke rising from the wound.

Even with every Enforcer that fell, there were triple that,

running out from the tunnels below. They needed more men and more DEW guns. What they had wasn't enough. Bullets ricocheted off the armor and did little to stop the oncoming enemies. They needed backup. Fast.

"Corporal, radio back for more men!" Dominic called as he nicked the corner of an Enforcer's hip plate, throwing them off balance. The corporal didn't answer. He turned and searched for where he last saw him. The corporal lay ten feet back from his last position, and even from where Dominic stood, he could see the great hole in his chest and the melting flesh around it. "Fuck's sake!"

"I got it, Major!" Private Alderson fired off a few more rounds before running to the corporal's body. He scrambled around looking for the radio still clutched in the corporal's hand. "Base team, come in! Base team, come in! This is Private Alderson, we need back up, over!"

Dominic couldn't hear the reply, nor did he have time to wait for Alderson to report back: Enforcers had reached the tree line.

An Enforcer broke through his ranks and sat on top of one of the soldiers not ten feet from him, stabbing him with a knife. Dominic could see the Enforcer's hands wrapped around the soldier's neck, and it spurred him into movement. Dominic dove at him, knocking him off, and grasped a knife from the Enforcer's belt. He stabbed at his armpit quickly and methodically. The enemy soldier screamed in agony and rolled to his side, giving Dominic enough time to rip off the helmet and slash the knife along his throat, spraying blood into his own eyes. Dominic wiped his face with his sleeve before unclipping the Enforcer's weapon belt and securing it around his own waist.

"Major! Look out!" Private Alderson yelled and threw himself at Dominic. He landed on top of Dominic with more momentum than he would've expected. He waited for Alderson to roll off him, but he was dead weight.

"Alderson?"

The private coughed in Dominic's ear and a hot, wet liquid sprayed from his mouth. Dominic pushed and rolled the private to the side. Alderson's bright blue eyes blinked slowly at the red sky where the sun had started to rise over the top of the trees.

"Tom, answer me kid!" Dominic shook his shoulders but stopped when the smell of burnt flesh hit his nose. His jaw dropped and he rested the private back down, careful not to jostle him.

"No one was looking out for you sir," Alderson coughed out.

"Hang on, kid," Dominic said. He lifted his free hand and shot Alderson's rifle at an Enforcer. Chaos surged around him, a mix of Enforcers and his own soldiers battling.

"Gi—give... my best... to Miss... Satcha..." Tom coughed again and gasped for air.

Dominic grabbed his hand, not knowing what to say. He couldn't believe the fading soldier before his eyes was Tom Alderson. The clumsy private he'd scolded and complained internally about. Without Dominic's command, he had stepped into action and radioed for help—beyond that, he had saved Dominic's life.

"Thank you, Tom."

The corners of the young man's lips quivered for a moment before he sighed, body relaxing, his last breath escaping his lungs.

Private Tom Alderson's eyes glazed over, the red sky reflecting in them.

"Sir!" A soldier ran to Dominic and pulled him away from Alderson's body. "We have to fall back!"

Dominic shrugged the soldier off in a red rage and fingered

the stolen Enforcer belt for explosives. He mounted an egg-shaped bomb to the launcher on Alderson's DEW blaster and fired it through the line of soldiers right at the turret mounted vehicles.

"Get back!" Dominic shouted. As soon as they turned to run, the bomb went off, sending shrapnel flying into the marching Enforcers. The blast flattened any living being standing within fifty feet of the vehicle. Enross troops bounded toward them, finally arriving with reinforcements. If he'd only been a part of the General's planning, they would've been closer to provide relief.

Dominic fought in a frenzy, firing the fallen private's DEW blaster at any Enforcer within a twenty-foot radius. The blood of his fallen comrade coated his face. For the first time ever, he didn't know how he would get out of the situation. His men fell around him, dropping like flies, while somewhere out there in the world, Satcha knew nothing of his impending demise. His chest ached knowing he'd never see her again, but it didn't stop him from killing every Enforcer that stepped in his path. Every Enforcer he killed left Vardya a safer place for her. Wherever she was.

CHAPTER 50

LENNOX

L ennox saw the flash of the explosions in the sky long before he felt the ground shake. He hadn't wanted to travel near the Enforcer Headquarters, and hadn't realized how close he was, but now couldn't help but continue toward it to investigate. Gunfire and screaming soldiers rang out, echoing in the woods. There was only one army that could be facing off against the tower. The Enross Army. *His* army.

He forced his horse into a gallop; he couldn't let his brothers fight this war without him. He couldn't let Dominic fight without him, even if he had left him in Rios.

With no weapons at his disposal, he urged his horse on straight into the fray. Dominic would no doubt be smack dab in the middle of the fighting. He gave the tower a wide berth as he raced to the front entrance. Through the thicket of the trees Enross soldiers scrambled about, grabbing weapons, before storming the clearing of the oncoming Enforcer troops.

Lennox whistled out to the soldiers to let them know he was friendly. A faint whistle returned. He slowed the horse before hopping off and slapping its rear, sending it far away from battle. He jogged the rest of the short distance to a supply wagon loaded with weapons.

"Status report, private!" Lennox yelled at the young soldier standing guard over the wagon.

"Lieutenant Lennox?" The soldier looked as if he had just seen a ghost.

"Status report!" Lennox commanded again. He opened a wooden crate and dug through, attaching a utility belt around his waist, and securing a pistol in the holster.

"We're taking on heavy fire from some turrets they have mounted at the front, sir. They've got underground tunnels wide enough for vehicles to drive out, with more troops than we ever thought possible."

"Where is Captain Lightwood?" Lennox almost growled the words. He reached into the wagon to grab a rifle, but the private pulled back his arm.

"Major Lightwood is on the front lines, sir. And if you're thinking about going over there, don't take one of those. Take this." The soldier handed him a silver blaster that belonged to the Enforcers.

"How...? Never mind." Lennox gripped the blaster. He didn't need to know how they'd gotten them, but he assumed Dominic had something to do with it.

Lennox jogged through the trees keeping an eye out for any Enforcers. Other soldiers ran with him toward the fighting. Guns blazing, screams of fallen troops, smoke rising from explosions. This was war. But this was where he thrived. Like an animal trapped deep within him, he released it out of his soul and through his throat letting out an ungodly war cry. Around him Enross soldiers cried out their own raspy screams. There wasn't anything left for the Enforcers to take from them. They gave their lives to the cause, to protect Enross. He'd long awaited this chance to get out his demons.

He had almost reached the clearing when he saw Monroe hiding behind a tree like a scared little girl. His eyes were wide and he clutched his DEW blaster so hard the whites of his knuckles showed through his skin.

"Useless mongrel," Lennox cursed under his breath.

Lennox was about to yell at him when Monroe took a deep breath and aimed his weapon toward the clearing, but didn't fire. Out through the trees in the clearing, Dominic pushed the Enforcers back to their tunnels with Enross soldiers following him. He never could stay out of the action. He always had to put himself right in the middle of it. Lennox rolled his eyes and scoffed as he got closer, but Monroe still aimed his blaster, not pulling the trigger.

This struck Lennox as odd. He stopped and tried to line up what Monroe aimed at. It wasn't aimed at an Enforcer overcoming an Enross soldier, nor one running for the tree line, fighting to push the Enross troops back.

It was at Dominic.

Lennox nearly tripped over his own feet as he broke into a run, straight for Monroe who had finally placed his finger on the trigger. Lennox dove at him, hoping he'd made it in time, but the gun went off as they collided, but there was no time to check to see if Monroe's aim had shot true. Lennox rolled to his side and straddled Monroe.

"What the fuck are you doing?" Lennox threw back his arm, winding up to drive his fist into Monroe's face.

With as much force as he could muster, his knuckles collided with Monroe's nose. He felt the snap and pop of broken cartilage. Crimson gushed from Monroe's nose and mouth as he choked on the liquid.

"Just following orders, but I should've known the captain's little bitch would swoop in to save him," Monroe choked out. He reached out to grab Lennox's throat, but Lennox was too quick and hit him again.

"Whose fucking orders?"

Lennox couldn't understand it. Why would Monroe, as evil and demented as he was—or anyone in the Enross Army for that matter—want to kill Dominic? It didn't make sense. Monroe howled in pain and didn't answer. He gasped and choked on the air, splattering blood across Lennox's face. He didn't wipe off the spray of the hot liquid, instead grasping Monroe's throat and dragging him to the nearest tree. He pushed him against the trunk and tightened his grip.

"Who ordered you to kill Dominic Lightwood?" Lennox growled through his teeth.

Monroe spat more blood in Lennox's face and grinned. "I'm not telling you anything, boy lover."

Bastard!

There was no holding back the fire that raged within Lennox. He jerked Monroe forward and thrust him against the trunk of the tree headfirst and didn't stop until he could no longer hear the crunch of his skull. The back of Monroe's head broke apart and smeared over the tree. He let go of Monroe's neck and watched dispassionately as his body fell to the ground. Not even the healers of Rios would be able to bring him back. He panted hard, staring at the mess in front of him.

"Who's the little bitch now?" Lennox spat on Monroe's corpse.

Dominic. He had to find Dominic.

Lennox broke into a sprint. He'd never used a DEW blaster before but didn't let it stop him from firing at any Enforcer he saw. Ten bodies had dropped by the time he'd made it halfway between the cover of the woods and the entry to the tower.

Smoke rose from the Enforcer vehicles where the turrets had been mounted. The smell of burning fuel and melted flesh filled his nose. He wanted to unload his stomach, but there was nothing to heave up—it had been a day and a half since he'd left the village of Rios and hadn't eaten anything, only stopping to rest his leg. After seeing the smoking flesh of his fallen comrades, he was unsure if his appetite would ever come back.

All around him Enross soldiers faced off against the Enforcers with their titanium armor. An unfair advantage the enemy had over them, but that didn't stop the Enross Army. They'd long been trained for this. A death in battle for their country was an honorable one, an expected one. There was no fear on the faces of his comrades around him, only the determination to rid this world of the oppressive powers of the Enforcers and the Masked Man.

"Dominic?" Lennox called time and again, but there was no response. His throat tightened and he fought off the possibility he could be dead. He couldn't be dead. Dominic was skilled beyond any soldier he'd ever known. He racked his brains trying to think if he'd tackled Monroe before or after the gun had fired, but it was all a blur.

Lennox reached the trap door tunnels where only a few Enforcer troops remained. He couldn't believe their luck. He never would've thought it possible to hold off the Enforcers, let alone push them back into hiding in their tall tower of glass. The Enross troops cheered and whooped as the enemy retreated into the holes they had crawled out of. Bodies covered the clearing, both Enross and Enforcer troops alike.

"Cover me! We're taking the tower!" a voice yelled out.

A voice well-known to him. Lennox's heart hammered in his chest watching Dominic stand with fifteen soldiers around him, covered in blood and a rage he'd never seen before. A familiar fire blazed in his eyes.

The damn idiot is after the Blood Scrolls again.

The soldiers shouted and covered their commanding officer as they stormed the tower entrance. It left only one thing for Lennox to do: follow Dominic and keep him safe. There would be no talking him out of abandoning the scrolls, especially when he was so close to them. It was now or never.

CHAPTER 51

SATCHA

At the safehouse, Satcha was glad to shrug off the dirty dress and put on much more practical clothes. She took a pair of pants and a tunic, not happy with the fit, but relieved she could fight without exposing herself. They gathered as many supplies as they could carry from the safehouse before taking to the road again. They couldn't risk being caught by more Enforcers; the dead ones would be found soon enough, thanks to the tracking system in their suits. With no weapons to defend themselves, they didn't stand a chance against the soldiers a second time.

After an hour or so running in the dark, Satcha found a small alcove under a hill that was well-hidden behind some leafy bushes. They had to stop for rest, or they both would collapse. Errol forced her to eat a protein bar they'd found in the safehouse and took first watch. His eyes were still red from crying.

When he woke her up for her watch, she sat in the dark and thought about Dominic. It was all she could do. Anything more than that, like wondering why Aleksandr had them attacked and separated, was too much for her. She just needed to find Dominic and everything would be all right.

In the morning, she had to force Errol to run alongside her instead of walk. "Come on, Errol! We have to hurry!" The freshness of Hugh's death still seeped out of Errol's eyes. They'd left his body in a shallow grave near the river before heading to the safehouse. As much as Satcha had wanted to leave him and run, she knew Errol couldn't until Hugh had been given a proper burial. She knew it'd be cruel to force him —she wouldn't be able to leave if it had been Dominic.

"I'm tryin', Satcha." Errol hiccupped.

They gave Carose a wide berth and kept pushing the pace as much as possible. Satcha's legs wanted to give way, but she kept on forward, not willing to slow even for a second. Every second she wasted was another second away from finding Dominic. She couldn't remember how to get to the base, but she was sure they were heading in the right direction.

"We can't be much farther; this part of the forest looks familiar. The base has to be close."

"Why are we going so fast, Satcha? My legs hurt," Errol panted behind her.

"We need to find Dominic."

"Who?"

"Someone important to me." The words tumbled out of her. She bit her tongue in frustration; she didn't know what to call him, and she didn't have time to explain. There was no stopping until she found him alive and had him back in her arms. Thinking something like that was completely foreign to her, but she shrugged off her unease. The moment he had stepped into her life, everything had changed. And if he hadn't found her, she would've died in the middle of that road. Deep down, she knew she should be grateful, yet she still found herself slightly annoyed. He was a detour for her plans for the Free City. For paradise.

But she couldn't deny what she wanted. Dominic.

Errol breathed heavily but did his best to keep up the pace from behind her. Satcha tried her best to remember anything about the night Dominic brought her to the Enross Base. It all seemed so fuzzy in her mind. She tried to count the days in her head, but the time where she'd been captured was a blur. All she could remember from the night she'd arrived at the Enross Base was her blistered feet and tall oak trees.

"Satcha! Wait up!"

Satcha groaned yet slowed to a stop to wait for Errol. He half-limped over to her and bent over, resting his hands on his knees, breathing hard.

"I can't keep up with you."

"It can't be much farther. Just keep on moving." She hated trying to push him when it was clear he needed a break. She was tired too—her own heart thumped against her chest, as if it would burst out and bounce all the way onward to find Dominic.

"I don't think I can do it. I just don't have it in me." He lowered himself to the ground and leaned back against an oak for support. He tugged off his boots revealing his bloody feet. A feeling Satcha knew all too well.

"Maybe I should—" Satcha cut herself off and listened. Errol caught his breath and it steadied, but she heard something else. Something that sounded like galloping hooves pounding against the ground like thunder...

A lone horse without a rider ran past them, and on its back it carried brown saddle bags with woven baskets on either side. She'd recognize those baskets anywhere; the women in Rios made them. The horse had come from the village—but where was its rider?

"You don't see horses like that every day," Errol commented.

"Stay here and rest, I'm going to scout a bit further and see if the rider is somewhere near." Satcha didn't look at Errol, but at the trees where the horse came from. "I won't be long."

"All right—but be careful and take a weapon with you."

Satcha nodded and grabbed a knife from Errol's pack and left him the pistol, feeling more confident with a knife. With the knife tied around her ankle she unloaded some of the food and water from Hugh's pack which she now carried on her back. It weighed heavy on her, not like her own bag she'd left back at the army base.

She jogged through the woods to investigate. Despite the ache in her legs, she moved at a steady pace, stopping every twenty to thirty feet to stop and listen for any signs of life. The acrid smell of smoke tickled the inside of her nose, making her sneeze and her eyes water.

Poking out over the treetops, the Enforcer Headquarters glimmered in the daylight, with smoke billowing around it. She stopped dead in her tracks, not able to take her eyes off the gray and black smoke wafting up into the sky. Suddenly gunfire ripped through the quiet forest.

Dominic!

Without thinking about what danger awaited her, she ran toward the tower at full speed not caring for her own life, but for Dominic's. As much as she wanted to find him, she didn't want him to be *there* of all places.

Enross soldiers ran from the cover of the trees into the clearing where dead bodies from both sides lay scattered. Smoke plumed from scorches in burnt bushes and trees from blaster misfires. Even worse, smoke rose from bodies, sending a sickly smell into the air.

What had Dominic gotten himself into? She didn't know where to look, surrounded by death, it was all too overwhelming. Before she met Dominic, she would've run far from here, but now she ran into the fire searching for him.

She weaved through fighting soldiers, scanning the faces

for Dominic, but she couldn't find him. Dominic wasn't the type to sit back and watch his men fight for him, she knew he'd put himself right in the way of danger.

Damn it!

She gritted her teeth and fought off her survival instincts and ran toward the tower. At the very front, leading the soldiers into the building, was a face she'd recognize anywhere.

He's alive!

Happy tears streamed down her face, taking her by surprise. She wiped away the hot tears with the back of her sleeve.

Dominic pried open the heavy metal doors before slipping through. Two by two, soldiers followed him, while others ran around the sides of the building on a mission of their own.

"Damn it!" Satcha's chest heaved. Why did he have to go in? But she knew why—the Blood Scrolls.

As much as every cell in her body told her to stay away from the danger, she couldn't help but charge out of the woods and into the clearing, straight for the tower. She kept low to the ground to avoid being caught. Neither the Enforcers nor the Enross troops could get in the way of her. They were all too busy to notice in the first place. No one would stop her. A few stray Enforcers knelt with their hands crossed above their silver helmets, held at gunpoint by the Enross Army.

If Dominic needed to find the scrolls to be free of the Enross Army, so be it. She would help him and let his soul be at peace.

CHAPTER 52

DOMINIC

Dominic couldn't believe his eyes. They weren't losing and had a shot of winning. Even in all his hopes and dreams he'd almost given up on the idea of being able to take a stand against the Enforcers. Thanks to the stolen Enforcer weapons—possible with his own quick thinking and some dumb luck—they had been able to take out the turrets, and now stood at the door to the tall glass tower. Soldiers stood behind him, ready to storm their way in; they would take the tower while he searched for the Blood Scrolls.

How long had he dreamed of holding the Blood Scrolls and reveal the long lost line of Enross and Austerland? Too long. It'd been nearly fourteen years since he left the shores of the Free City on the Isle of Neroso, and he didn't regret it, but he'd give anything to see his uncle's face when he found out it was Dominic who'd ruined his plans.

"Get ready, we're going in!" Dominic stood with his back leaning against the door, ready to burst through and kill any Enforcer standing in his way.

"Wait!"

Dominic turned from the soldiers that lined up next to him and saw Lennox racing across the battlefield.

Thank the Hawk!

Dominic fought the urge to rub his eyes to make sure they weren't deceiving him. Lennox running on *two* legs. The healers in Rios had done their work well.

"About time you got here!" Dominic smiled and clapped his hand on Lennox's back.

"You want to tell me why Monroe just tried to take you out?"

"What?" But then he shook his head—he didn't have time to explain everything with the General. "Never mind, we'll sort it out later."

"I already did." Lennox turned from Dominic and looked to the group of soldiers behind him. "If any of you value your life and your dignity as a soldier in the Enross Army, you will think twice about turning on Major Lightwood. I will be first to drive a knife through your heart."

"We already know Captain Monroe is in General Ballard's pocket," said Private Watson, stepping forward. "Private Alderson gathered us in support of Major Lightwood. We stand with him, not the General. We stand for the people of Vardya."

The other soldiers nodded their heads in agreement. Dominic would have smiled at their loyalty but the image of Alderson lying dead next to him flashed through his mind. He would do this for him and make sure his name would be remembered for his bravery and loyalty to his country.

Clearing his throat and raising his voice for all his men to hear, he called, "I don't know what's waiting for us inside or what will happen if we make it out of here, but we accomplished something today. Now, the Nerosians know that we will *not* back down, and that we *will* take back our country!"

The soldiers roared to life and stormed through the

building with Dominic leading them, eliminating all who stood in their way.

CHAPTER 53

SATCHA

S atcha reached the far corner of the tower and was careful not to touch the glass. She still didn't know what would happen if she did, but she didn't want to find out. Enross troops sat on the ground not far from the door, laughing and nursing their wounds, celebrating a victory they hadn't yet won. She didn't recognize the faces of any of the soldiers from the tunnels as she crept along the side of the building toward the entrance.

The big doors to the building were shut, she grasped the steel handle and pulled as hard as she could.

"Hey, you! You shouldn't be near there!" a soldier called out.

She didn't look up, not able to risk the precious seconds. She slipped in through the door as soon as the space was wide enough for her body. She let go and the door snapped shut, just missing catching her ankle in its tight seal. A long, dark corridor faced her, and red lights flashed along the hallway in time with an alarm making her ears ring.

"*Code Red. All personnel report to your stations,*" a voice called out. Satcha froze, letting her eyes adjust to the flashing red. After a moment, the voice sounded again, and this time she realized it was a recording, the same message echoing throughout the hallway. She relaxed for a moment, racking her brain—she had no idea what she was doing. She had no plan other than to find Dominic and get out of the building.

Satcha ran through the hallway, not bothering to be quiet, as no one would hear her over the alarm sounding. There were no doors or passageways on either side of the long hall, and not until the very end did the corridor split off in two directions. Satcha glanced back and forth, unable to make out anything other than the shadows of bodies laying on the floor bathed in red light.

She didn't know which way to turn. Left or right? One could very well lead her to Dominic, while the other could lead her straight to an Enforcer.

She had to make a choice and fast. She sprinted down the right hallway and hoped she hadn't gone further into the maze of the tower. This corridor was the same as the other, no doorways but a lot of bodies.

The end of the hallway soon fell upon her again. She squinted in the dark, trying to see if the stairwell to her left was safe. She leaned back against the wall and pulled her knife from her ankle strap. She took a deep breath and then peeked around the corner to make sure the coast was clear. She darted to the empty stairs and slowly went halfway up, looking to see if there was anyone looking from above, but she couldn't see anything, just another flight of stairs to run up.

Three more flights of stairs later, she was panting hard when she came across a new hallway. This time she had three options: left, right, or straight. As she was deciding, she heard gunshots firing over the loud alarm from her left. She tore off to the right.

She was already at the very end of the hallway when she could finally make out the door in front of her. Its window was covered. She gripped the handle, but it was locked. She used the butt of her knife to smash the window, sending glass flying into the room. When she reached her arm through, her arm caught on a shard of glass and dug in, leaving a line of crimson. She gritted her teeth and unlocked the door, shouldering in and slamming it shut.

No red lights flashed in the room. The bright glow of a fluorescent light shone from the ceiling. She covered her face, shielding her eyes. Through the spaces between her fingers, she could make out a wall of electronic screens with two tall filing cabinets.

"What are you doing here?" An Enforcer stood behind a paper-covered desk.

Satcha gripped her knife and lunged forward, catching the Enforcer off his guard. She guessed this one wasn't a soldier as he recoiled from her with his arms flailing and a scream echoing in the room. She knocked him to the ground and the thin faced man in rectangle glasses whimpered, his wide eyes staring at her.

"Please, don't hurt me! I'm a clerical worker!"

"What's in these cabinets?" Satcha held her knife to the man's throat, but a shot fired from behind her and blasted into the man's face leaving nothing but a bloody mess of torn flesh. Satcha whipped around ready to face the new attacker.

Dominic and Lennox stood in the doorway with the red lights flashing from behind them.

"Satcha?"

Satcha's breath caught. Their short time together in Rios felt like a dream, something that was real but so quick it might've not even happened. But now, here he was, standing in front of her. She raced across the room toward him and he to her. She couldn't hold back her tears as she threw herself into his arms.

They collided, their arms wrapping around each other in a tight embrace before their lips met. She melted into him, slipping back into the memory of his last touch. Her desire for him was white hot once again, like it had been back in the tiny bed in Rios.

"Thank the Hawk you're all right!" Dominic pulled away from her and held her tight while he planted a kiss on her forehead. Her hands gripped his shoulders tight, not wanting to let him go again.

"Okay, that's enough! We have work to do," Lennox snapped. He pushed past them on his way to the cabinets.

"He's right, we can't waste any time. We have to find the—"

"The scrolls! Yes, Dominic, I think they are in here!"

His eyes lit up. "All right, we have to work fast; someone tripped an alarm, and this place is going to blow."

His words gave Satcha all the motivation she needed to tear herself away and start rummaging through the paperwork on the desk while he joined Lennox at the other cabinet.

She filtered through the paperwork, looking for anything that might look like a lineage tracker or family tree. But nothing on the desk was what they needed, just histories of different villages around Enross. *Reeock!* She looked for anything to do with the kingdom, but it was the same. Nothing to do with the Blood Scrolls, only maps and census reports. She kicked back the chair from the desk and tried pulling open the top drawer, but it was locked.

Satcha took out her knife again and stuck it between the crevice and pushed against the handle as hard as she could before the lock broke open and the drawer came flying out at her.

"You okay?" Dominic looked at her as if he might scoop her up and carry her away from this place.

"I'm fine! Just keep looking!"

"Lennox, get to the door and listen for how much time we have!" Dominic said.

Lennox ran across the room and propped open the door. The room filled with a red glare from the hallway.

"*All personnel evacuate. Six minutes and thirty seconds remaining,*" the robotic female voice announced. The voice began counting down from there as Lennox rushed back to his cabinet and began shoving papers into his bag.

Satcha dug through the drawer, finding a red folder with the seal of Vardya embedded on the front and remembered when Agatha taught her to read old war statues. She flipped it open and on the first page was a portrait of a couple embracing, a man dressed in a formal military uniform and a woman in a long gown. The face of the woman looked familiar to her, like she'd seen her before somewhere. The bottom of the portrait had an inscription.

The Reconciliation of Vardya. Prince Aleksandr, of Auster-land, and Princess Satcha, of Enross.

Satcha's heart stopped.

Princess Satcha?

She read the inscription again.

She stared at the face of the woman in the picture critically.

She recognized her own eyes.

No. It can't be.

She flipped to the next page and read through as quickly as she could. The pair planned to name their descendants after each other... Each male would take the name of the first Aleksandr of Vardya... And the female would take the name of the first Satcha of Vardya.

No! Satcha couldn't hold back her stomach. Vomit rose from her stomach and out onto the table in front of her.

"*Five minutes and twenty-three seconds.*"

"Satcha?" Dominic was staring at her, worried.

He can't know! It can't be me!

Whatever he expected from this long-lost heir, she couldn't give him it. She would not take up that banner. She had her own plans to deal with, she couldn't be the beacon of hope Dominic wanted.

She waved him off and flipped through the pages until she saw yet another familiar face. Aleksandr, the leader of the Free People of Rios, only much younger. Memories of her time in Rios swarmed back into her head. He'd lost his son, daughter-in-law, and granddaughter in the war, Rosalie's parents. That meant...

In a haze, a memory seeped through her brain she'd never remembered before.

Her as a young girl, blood dripping from her head on the side of a riverbank—she'd fallen and hit her head on a rock trying to escape. Her parents laying dead not fifteen feet from her with big, ugly wounds to their heads. The stomp of the soldiers' boots beat against the ground. Not knowing how she did it, but managing to throw herself into the river, letting the current take her away.

"Oh my Hawk!" Satcha ran her fingers through her hair, feeling the faint indent and scar on the right side of her head. It was true. The Blood Scrolls were real after all, and this red folder in her hands was the proof.

"*Four minutes and ten seconds.*"

"Satcha! We have to go, we have barely any time!" Dominic called from the doorway, Lennox already passed him, almost at the staircase.

Satcha had to think fast; Dominic could never know she was the one he searched for. She pulled off her pack and pulled out a fire starter and clicked it to life. She lit the folder on each corner, watching the flame lick across the papers and grow. She dropped it on the table and stared without blinking until the picture of the princess and prince disappeared into the flames.

"What did you do?" Dominic yelled at her. His eyes were wide as he watched the flames destroy the last piece of the red folder.

"'We have to get out of here now!" Satcha snapped back to life and tugged on Dominic's hand, pulling him out of the room. Lennox ran ahead of them clearing the way.

"*Two minutes and five seconds.*"

Satcha and Dominic raced down the stairs and through the long hallway back to the exit. The countdown continued to dwindle down. She didn't know what would happen at the end, but she knew they needed every second they had left to put as much space between them and the tower as possible.

"*One minute and ten seconds.*"

Dominic let go of Satcha's hand and slammed himself against the door, casting it wide open before taking her hand once again. She found it hard to keep up with his long strides as he ran and pulled them toward the trees. Soldiers of the Enross Army ran ahead of them, not slowing when they got to the tree line.

Behind them, she heard an explosion burst through the building, sending glass raining from the sky.

Dominic yanked Satcha forward and dove into the cover of the trees. A plume of smoke rose from the ground like a bubble surrounding the collapsed building. Satcha looked back through the smoke and the crash of the tower. If her fire hadn't destroyed the Blood Scrolls, the building collapsing did the trick. No one could ever find out what she knew.

"What have you done?" Dominic coughed. He lay on the ground next to her, all the color drained from his face.

"Nothing! It wasn't important, but we have to move. Who

knows how long it will take reinforcements to come from Carose." She struggled to get her legs underneath her, but she forced herself up and tried to help him, but he pulled away from her and stood. He was shaking.

"Were those the Blood Scrolls?" He grabbed her by her upper arms and held her against a tree.

"They're gone, it's over. Run away with me and we can go to the Free City—"

"There's no paradise in the Free City! Why do you think they are coming here? They are expanding for the sake of their own people!"

What? He promised to get me there!

Satcha stared open mouthed at him towering over her. "You're wrong!"

"Satcha, I'm not. I'm from the Isle of Neroso... I was born in the Free City. My uncle is the Lord of Neroso, Gideon Ursid. The Masked Man. I came here so I could stop him and help the Vardyians. My real name is Dominic Ursid."

Satcha's head felt like it was going to burst.

He lied to me?

A cry escaped her mouth as she yanked herself out of his hold. She grasped her knife and lunged at him, using the tree as a launch pad to knock him over. She straddled him, her knife at his neck, hot tears falling onto his face.

"Satcha, I'm sorry."

There was nothing he could say to her to make it better. He'd betrayed her. She had let him in, past all her walls and barriers. She'd trusted him and opened her heart.

He may as well have taken the knife from her hand and carved out her heart for all it was worth.

She choked out a sob and her hand shook as she hovered the blade over him. But she couldn't do it. She couldn't slash the blade across his neck. By the Hawk, she *wanted* to. She pulled back her knife and thrust it toward him. He didn't flinch as the blade dug into the ground an inch away from his ear. She climbed off him and ran off into the woods. She'd been so stupid.

Satcha ran off to the woods in search of Errol. She had to get out of there. With this newfound information, she would need his help yet again, but instead of going back to the Enross Base, they would head to Rios.

She needed to speak with Aleksandr.

CHAPTER 54

ROSALIE

Rosalie lay face down on her pillow, not wanting to leave her room. It'd been almost a week since Dominic and Satcha had disappeared without a word. No one gave her a reason other than it was time for them to move on.

She spent several days in a row avoiding her grandfather and thinking of sneaking out with a bow to practice archery, but she'd lost her nerve. She'd been hiding away, feeling sorry for herself ever since.

"Rosalie?" Helene called from the other side of her bedroom door. "Can I come in?"

Rosalie sighed and rolled onto her back. Her headache from staying cooped up in her room. She knew she needed to get out and get some fresh air, but she didn't have the motivation to do so.

"Yes."

Her grandmother opened the door and her upturned lips faded into a frown. Rosalie didn't like making her grandmother sad. She sat on the bed and tried to smile, but she was sure it was more of a grimace.

"Some things are just not meant to be." Helene sat next to Rosalie and wrapped her arm around Rosalie's shoulders. She squeezed her tight and rubbed her arm as if trying to massage life and happiness back into her.

Rosalie didn't want to hear that. She wanted her grandmother to be on her side, but she had a point. Dominic didn't love her, but she loved him. She needed to love him enough to let him go and love someone else, and if she couldn't do that, was it really love she felt for him? Or was it infatuation?

She sighed and shrugged her grandmother's arm from around her as she stood from the bed. She'd stayed in this little room for too long.

"I'm going for a walk." She leaned down, kissing Helene on the cheek. "I'll be back in a little while."

"Don't wander too far." Helene's frown turned into a small smile, but it still wasn't a happy smile. Rosalie could tell she was worried about her, but all she could do was let time heal her wounds.

The moment Rosalie set foot outside, the cool air filled her lungs and brought new life into her spirits. She felt her mood lift. The emptiness in her chest still lingered, but she couldn't sentence herself to her room anymore. She kicked off her shoes, letting her toes curl and dig into the cold ground. The sun glowed over the mountains, rising to bring in a new day.

Soon the rest of the village would wake and get started on their chores. She couldn't help but rush to the edge of the forest. She longed to be surrounded by trees. She loved lying beneath the tree branches and letting the sun filter through the leaves and tickle along her skin. She wished she had someone to share those moments with. Someone who could lay next to her and bask in the hot glow of the sun. She'd hoped it would've been Dominic but thinking about it now, she couldn't picture him lying in the woods just staring through the trees.

Dominic was too tense for frolicking through the forest with her. It made her question herself. Maybe she was too much of a free spirit. There were moments where she could have taken things more seriously, cared more about the outside world. Maybe there was something more she could do to help her people. She loved her people, there was no doubt of that. She knew one day her grandfather would not be able to lead the people any longer and someone would have to take his place. But could she do that if that day was today? She wasn't so sure she was up for the job. And as much as she was upset with his surprise at her wish to lead, she could understand his hesitation.

Her grandparents had kept her so sheltered from the outside world, how could she ever lead and protect her people if she couldn't even protect herself? She'd been so keen to tend to her garden and socialize that she'd never considered what might happen if the Enforcers ever found their hidden village. She'd never even seen an Enforcer before.

Rosalie leaned against a tree trunk and hung her head low. She couldn't help but let the tears fall from her eyes and stream down her cheeks.

Maybe that's what Dominic liked about Satcha. She seemed capable of taking care of herself and didn't need to rely on anyone. She'd never be a damsel in distress like Rosalie would be if captured. Her hand felt along the forest floor and gripped a jagged rock. She picked it up and threw it as hard as she could. It bounced off another tree right back at her, rolling next to her feet.

She sighed.

A thump hit the ground after the rock had stopped moving. She froze, wondering what could've made the sound.

The bushes to her right rustled. She stood slowly, not wanting to make any sudden movements.

Squawk!

Rosalie sighed. It was just a bird. How silly could she be? Scared of a bird. She relaxed against the tree and scolded herself. She needed to toughen up. Another squawk came from the bushes. There must've been a nest with babies inside the bush.

Rosalie stepped closer to the bushes, hoping that her suspicion was right and it was a baby bird. More tiny chirps sounded from the green bush. She pushed aside the top branches and looked inside to see a tiny bird that could fit in the palm of her hand covered in fluffy white feathers. It was stuck between branches and crying for help. She looked above her and saw a tattered nest hanging from a large branch. The rock she'd thrown must've shaken the tree just enough for the damaged nest to give way and the baby bird to fall. She reached through the leaves of the bush and carefully rescued the crying bird. It squealed louder as her hands neared.

"Shhh... It's okay. I've got you." She pulled the little bird out and let it rest in her cupped hands.

The bird's heart thumped through its chest against her hand, terrified. Rosalie looked around, there were no other birds in sight. Not even a chirp in the distance. She couldn't leave the little creature to fend for itself after she caused it to fall from the tree. It panted hard in her hands. Its tiny black eyes stared at her with its hooked beak open and reaching for her.

"Aw, you're hungry aren't you? I'll take you back to the village and find you some food. I'll dig up some nice worms and we'll get your belly nice and full."

The little bird squealed back at her as if to ask what took her so long. She cradled the bird against her dress with her hands cupped around it, careful not to let it squirm out of her hands.

A fire stirred within her that she'd never experienced before. Something about holding the baby bird appealed to her.

And she realized in that moment she wanted more than she'd ever imagined possible.

She wanted to protect the bird and give it a chance at life. She wanted to protect her people as her people had done for her. She wanted to be the one to keep her people safe.

She set her jaw and strode to the village with a new confidence. She wouldn't sit by and be the soft, flower-loving Rosalie.

She would be Rosalie, protector of Rios.

CHAPTER 55

GIDEON

S tanding in his office, Gideon looked out of the wall-sized window at his country. He clutched a glass of his favorite scotch and savored every sip, letting it linger on his tongue before swallowing. The sun reflected off the glass buildings in the city below, making it seem like it glowed. Blessed with the gift of light from the sun.

A knock at the door cut through the silence.

An Enforcer guard stepped through the door. "Sir, I have news from Enross."

A muscle in his jaw twitched and he bit back a curse. Couldn't he have one single moment to himself? He put the glass of scotch to his lips and took no time in savoring his drink this time. He chugged it and set the glass on his desk.

He sat in his high-backed black chair and sighed. "Get on with it."

"Well, uh, sir..."

"Oh, just tell me already!" He grabbed the bottle of scotch and filled his glass once again. He held it in his hand and watched the amber liquid sway side to side.

The guard gulped. "Tower One has been destroyed. The

Enross Army has taken out our forces there and we've retreated to Carose…which has also been attacked."

Gideon threw his glass at the wall. It shattered and sprayed the wall with his scotch. He slammed his fists on his mahogany table.

"Is there any good news?"

"We do know who the culprit is behind the attacks on Tower One—and Tower Two in Carose."

Gideon tapped his leather shoe against the tile flow, growing impatient. He leaned back in his chair and prepared for what was to come. He could only assume the bumbling oaf Ballard was behind the attack.

"Our intelligence has reported that they believe your nephew, Dominic, is behind the attacks."

"Get out! Now!"

The guard didn't hesitate and hurried out of the office. Gideon couldn't contain the rage building up inside him. He wanted to explode like a volcano and flood the land of Vardya with full force and destroy every last one of them—including his nephew. He knew Dominic had been alive this whole time, but never did he think he would cause him so much trouble. He'd let him play soldier in the pitiful Enross Army under that moron Ballard, but this changed things.

He picked up a black mask that laid next to his scotch bottle and strapped it around his head, covering his face. He rolled his neck. He was ready.

Gideon strolled back to his window, yet instead of looking at the city beneath him, he stared across the Westim Ocean toward Vardya. His reflection shone back at him, his scar reflecting in the light.

"It's been a long time, but I will be seeing you soon, dear nephew."

Return to the world of Vardya
in
Book Two

Did you enjoy the Rise of Vardya? Don't forget to leave a review on Amazon as well as GoodReads!

More books by E Whelly

My Beautiful Ghosts

The Mindless Ramblings of an 18 Year Old Girl : It's Just a Bunch of Sh!t Poetry

ACKNOWLEDGMENTS

Thank YOU for reading *The Rise of Vardya*! I appreciate every single one of you who have taken the time to read my words and continue to make this dream possible for me. I've wanted to be an author all my life and I have to pinch myself to remind myself that this is real. Thank you to everyone who came out to events to meet me and talk about my work. It's a surreal feeling I will never get used to.

Thank you to my husband, Dave, for always cheering me on and supporting me through the ups and downs of my emotional rollercoaster writing process. Thank you for being there to bring me back down as well as bring me up as I need it.

Thank you to my son, Grant. Nothing has made me happier than seeing you run around the room holding the very first copy of *My Beautiful Ghosts* yelling, "Mama wrote a book!" Thank you for also telling everyone we encountered for the month that followed, *Mama wrote a book*. It made for some awkward conversations at the grocery store that I was not prepared for but seeing you so proud of me has given me a sense of pride and happiness I never thought possible. I hope one day I can give you that feeling back, just so you know how special it is.

Thank you to the amazing team behind *The Rise of Vardya*. My editor, Kayla Ramoutar, you are an absolute angel with your patience! If it were not for your keen eye for characters, I fear Satcha, Dominic, and Rosalie would never have blossomed. My designer, Natasha Mackenzie, you did it again!

Once again, you have surpassed my expectations, designing an amazing cover for RoV. Your ability to take my imaginary world and turn it into something beautiful is second to none!

Thank you my mom and dad for being the supporting parents who tell everyone they meet that their daughter wrote a book. Even if it's in inappropriate situations... Mom... You did not need to get the car salesmen to buy my books just so you would buy a car from him.

Thank you to Memere for believing in me and always being ready to talk about books with me. I stand by my promise to you, if you want to pursue your dream to write a book, I will help you and stand by you every step of the way. You're never too old to follow your dreams.

Thank you to the rest of my family, Pepere, Aunt Darlene and Uncle Ricky, Jessica, Andrew, Ava, Mason, Ben and Shanice, Uncle Danny, Aunt Margo, Maddie, Brooke, and Frankie for showing up for me and being the best cheering squad I could have asked for.

Thank you to my bestie, Sam! You've been so supportive throughout this whole process of this book. I appreciate you taking time out of your day to come help me with my signings, taking pictures and being there for me.

Where would I be without Brandon J LeBlanc and Angela Van Leimpt? Not very far! Thank you so much to the both of you. Thank you for always pushing me through my Author Life Crisis, for seeing the light when I had my eyes shut, and keeping me grounded. We've been through so much in the last two years, writing our debut novels, learning the publishing world, TikTok, author events... I'm happy to have had the two of you to experience this with. Cheers to you both and Writer's Tears!

Thank you to Olivia Donovan... Nope, that's not right. Thank you to Mrs. Donovan, for being the spark that started the fire. Your high school writing class has forever changed my world and I will be forever grateful to your words of advice, teachings, and introducing me to amazing books.

Last but not least! Thank you to Ash Spanton, the stranger I met on Tiktok who has become a great friend. Thank you for cheering me up and reading the early drafts of *The Rise of Vardya*. If it were not for you, this book never would have evolved and taken on a whole new level. I will be forever grateful for all your advice.

About the Author

Emily Whelly was born in Saint John, New Brunswick. She's the author of the Amazon Bestseller, *My Beautiful Ghosts* and award winning novel, *The Rise of Vardya*.

She enjoys spending her time with her husband, David, their son, Grant, and their dog, Quinn, and three cats, Kili, Fili, and Merlin.

For more information, updates on new projects and how to connect, please check out www.ewhelly.com.

You can also find me on Social Media!

facebook.com/EWhelly

twitter.com/e_whelly

tiktok.com/@e_whelly